LIGHT

IN THE

SHADOWS

ALSO BY LINDA LAFFERTY

The Bloodletter's Daughter

The Drowning Guard

House of Bathory

The Shepherdess of Siena

The Girl Who Fought Napoleon

ALSO BY ANDY STONE

Aspen Drift

Song of the Kingdom

LIGHT
IN THE
SHADOWS

A Novel

LINDA LAFFERTY
and ANDY STONE

LAKE UNION
PUBLISHING

Published by Lake Union Publishing, Seattle

www.apub.com

Amazon, the Amazon logo, and Lake Union are trademarks of Amazon.com, Inc., or its affiliates.

ISBN-13: 9781542044080 (hardcover)
ISBN-10: 1542044081 (hardcover)
ISBN-13: 9781542044097 (paperback)
ISBN-10: 154204409X (paperback)

Cover design by David Drummond

Printed in the United States of America

First edition

Dedicated with love and respect to Stella Goldstein Daniels and Dorothy Ann Lafferty Lee, two wonderful, strong, elegant women who have been inspirations to both of us and our entire families

Authors' Note

This is a work of fiction. While it is based on historical events, liberties have been taken for creative license.

COMUNE DI PRIZZI, SICILY
2015

Weathered trees stand guard over the cemetery, their backs to the wind, their branches' sharp elbows raised against the harsh Sicilian sky. High on a hillside scorched in the summer, windblown in the winter, no one lies easy in these graves, but the living trudge up the steep path from the village below to bear witness to the perseverance of the honored dead. Almost every day of the year—saints' days, birthdays, anniversaries—summons men, women, families who know their presence is expected.

Today is a rare gentle moment for the quick and the dead. The heat of summer has faded and the first sharp edge of winter is yet to come.

Two men stand by the wrought iron fence of a family plot, watching while others tend the graves. One man lights a cigarette. He's wearing a suit, no tie, open collar, snap-brim fedora, black-and-white shoes. His suit jacket blows open for a moment in the breeze.

"She's here."

"Here?" The other man, older, keeps his jacket and collar buttoned.

"Up north. Chianti." An inquisitive shrug. "So? What do we . . ." His voice trails off.

"Watch her." The older man raises a finger to the side of his eye. "Only that."

A silence.

"But why should we—"

The older man cuts him off with a gesture, lifting his chin sharply. It is enough. "She is family. There is history. This much we owe her."

"Only to watch?"

The older man narrows his eyes, impatient at having to explain. "Watch and make sure nothing goes . . ." His hands, held in front of his chest, rise slightly, juggling possibilities.

"All right. I can go—"

The older man turns his head sharply to look at the other for perhaps the first time in this conversation. He flicks his fingers in impatient annoyance.

"Not you. Someone who can be . . . unseen. Why do I have to tell you this?"

Another silence. Finally, the younger man nods, finds the courage to speak.

"A friend might know someone. Family. I'll take care of it."

The day is ending. The wind picks up. The men trimming the hedges and the women cleaning the gravestones and tending the flowers hurry to finish.

The men in suits nod to the graves, cross themselves, and walk back down the hill.

Village of Caravaggio, Lombardia, 1577

A dark-haired boy sat on an overturned bucket, staring at the two dead men.

His grandfather had died during the night, his mouth open, gasping, choking on his hideously swollen tongue. Now the tongue had retreated back into his maw, hiding behind his brown, broken teeth like an eel.

The boy's father had lingered a bit longer, but his death had been just as painful.

In the dim light of the terra-cotta oil lamp, a flea skipped across his father's hairline and then disappeared into the folds of his wrinkled tunic, stained brown with sweat.

The two men had traveled back the forty kilometers from Milano just days before and had carried the plague with them to the hamlet of Caravaggio. Now they lay side by side in death.

The boy could not cry. He sat stunned, playing the scene of the dying men over in his young mind. He shut his eyes but still saw the mottled colors of their skin, their mouths twisted in agony, the silver translucence of their tears and sweat.

He saw dark browns and red, the palette of the night.

Michelangelo barely opened his eyes, his sight only a slit through his thick eyelashes. He studied the sunken lines of his father's face, his lifeless hand. Every minute detail of his father's corpse was branded in his memory with searing permanence.

His father had a raucous laugh and a swagger. He would throw his son in the air, making him laugh. He did the same with young Fabrizio, the marchese's son, only a few years older than Michelangelo.

Fermo Merisi. Bigger than life, a commoner who had charmed nobility.

Michelangelo opened his eyes once more to look at his father, at the hands and arms that had launched young Michele so gleefully in the air. They were as still as stone. And blackened—especially the fingertips. The forearms were puckered with purple welts.

The boy stuck his fist in his mouth, sinking his teeth into his first knuckle. Still, he did not cry, but stared hard at the dead men.

"You are the man of the family now," his mother had told him, grasping his shoulders minutes before. The raw crimson of her eyes had shocked him. They were the color of bloody meat.

The holy water that his mother had fetched from the town's spring, the fount where the apparition of Mary had appeared a hundred years ago, proved useless even after the priest's blessing. His mother laid her cheek against his father's chest after the death rattle. Then she fled sobbing to the Sforza palace to plead for succor from the widow Marchesa Costanza Colonna of the powerful Sforza family, rulers of Milano. Michele's older sister, Margherita, swept up his three younger siblings, taking them along with her as she fetched the gravedigger.

"Stay here, Michele," his mother had told her eldest son.

Michelangelo was alone in the room with the two dead men. The boy's mouth curled up in a snarl, his features pinched in rage. He hurled the flask of useless holy water, dashing it on the stone floor.

He watched the stone darken, the contrasting shadows etched at his feet. Then he looked up, staring at the corpses in the dark room.

Where is God? Where is Mary, mother of God?

He curled his small fists tightly, his dirty fingernails biting into his flesh. The hurt felt good, real. He could control the pain by releasing the pressure or make his flesh throb by contracting his fingers.

He wanted the hurt to match the pain in his heart. To match the black abyss of despair that seized him.

He stared down at his filthy nails and the little red gouges he had made in his tender palms. Faint traces of blood tinged his skin. A shiver rocked his body, and he realized how cold he was in the room with no fire. A darkness enveloped him, a curtain descending over his eyes.

He fought against the blinding rage. Inside his eyelids, he saw the image of the two dead men in sepia. Then, a splash of scarlet.

He felt warmth, a radiance. His eyes opened.

The slanting sunlight of October shone through the canvas-covered window. The light touched the face of his father, leaving his grandfather's open mouth in shadow.

He heard voices outside. The Marchesa Costanza Colonna had sent men to carry the bodies to the graves.

The little boy blinked in the sunlight at the warm glow that bathed him and his dead father.

There is God. The light.

Chapter 1

Roma
1600

A gust of wind whistled down through the ragged hole in the roof of the tiny apartment on Vicolo San Biagio, a few minutes' walk from Piazza Navona. Dry leaves skittered down a gap in the rafters, the wind teasing flames to leap in the lanterns hoisted above a boy sitting on the floor with a bedsheet twisted around his shoulders and stomach.

Twenty-nine-year-old Michelangelo Merisi da Caravaggio uncurled his finger from the paintbrush to rub soot from his eye. The blackened ceiling, thick with carbon from smoking oil lamps and torches, showered black flecks onto the artist and his subject.

"*Stai fermo*, Cecco," he said, raising a bushy eyebrow. *Hold still.*

"The wind," said Cecco, shivering in the makeshift white toga. "A rainstorm, Maestro."

The artist looked at the prickled skin of the thirteen-year-old, the fine hairs standing on end. Rain wept down through the hole in the roof, the droplets plastering the gauzy bedsheet against the boy's body.

"*Al diavolo!*" growled the artist, flinging his paintbrush across the room. *To the devil!* "I'm finished for the night."

The boy's eyes grew wide but he remained silent, scrambling to retrieve the paintbrush.

"Wash up the brushes and cover the paints. I'm going to the tavern," said the master, throwing a tattered velvet cape over his shoulders.

"*Sì*, Maestro," said the boy. The toga slipped from his body, and he set about his duties, still nude.

Caravaggio studied the boy's thigh where it met his buttocks, the indentation at his flank of muscle under the white skin.

God's perfection.

He felt himself stiffen under his coarse linen britches.

"Put on some clothes before you catch cold," he told the boy. "It won't do to have Bacchus with a red nose and phlegm, you shivering brat!"

He slammed the door, leaving Cecco alone in the drafty room.

∾

To hell with this. Caravaggio strode down the Via d'Agostino.

Cecco is no Bacchus! Bah, Mario Minniti with his ruddy complexion as a youth—there was beauty! How can I improve on that image? Yet the bedsheets become the boy. Who am I searching for?

A sword clinked at his side. He ran the risk of being arrested for carrying a weapon without a permit. He was no longer under the Cardinal del Monte's roof and had lost his protection—the local guards knew that. But he would not go out without his sword.

The Via della Scrofa—Street of the Sows—ran by several shops shut tight against the night's storm. The streetlight, an oil torch, cast a pocket of light on a stray dog licking at the bloody cobblestones where the butcher displayed his meats during the day. Above the dog, a skinned rabbit hung in the shop window, its pinkish-white flesh both innocent and lurid. The image caught the artist's eye—the naked meat exposed in the burning light.

John the Baptist!

He stopped in the pelting rain and laughed. The cur bolted away, tail between his legs.

Again? Why does the saint come to me over and over again? Does he have some prophecy to unveil?

His stomach growled, remembering the delicacies at the table of Cardinal del Monte, his early patron. Caravaggio had lived in his palazzo for four years. During that time, he and Cecco never worried about food or drink or punching holes in the roofs. At Del Monte's Palazzo Madama, he was a part of the pampered lifestyle of the cardinals, their vices beyond imagination to the simple poor of Roma.

"Who goes there?" said a voice in the night.

Michelangelo put his hand over the hilt of his sword. "A citizen of Roma!" he shouted. "What business is it of yours, *pezzo di merda?*" *Piece of shit.*

"Is it you, Michelangelo Merisi?" said a jovial voice. A pale face emerged in the light of the corner torch. The man's blond hair was plastered against his skull from the rain, a prominent blue vein pulsing on his forehead.

"Onorio!" said Caravaggio as the man embraced him. "Your swaggering would have invited a fight, *bastardo!*"

"As would yours. *Pezzo di merda* is your middle name!" said Onorio Longhi. "I'm dining at Osteria del Turchetto. Come along. Join me."

"*Con piacere, stronzo,*" said the artist. *A pleasure, you shit.*

As Caravaggio opened the tavern door, a hot blast of moist air enveloped him. The patrons' warm breath mixed with woodsmoke, roasted meat, and sour wine.

A few painters grunted greetings as Caravaggio and Longhi pushed their way into the crowd, securing the end of a plank table.

The owner of the tavern plunked down an earthen jug of wine and two clay cups.

"*Grazie. Cena per due,*" ordered Onorio. He turned to his companion. "I'm inviting you, Michelangelo."

"*Perché?*"

"Why? For not murdering me in the darkness!" said his friend, clapping the painter on his back. "Besides, everyone knows you have short arms when it comes to paying."

"Fuck you, Onorio."

"And because I have been offered a commission today to design a new building, one that will feed me for a year. We'll eat off it, brick by brick—"

"Michele, you dirty cur!" slurred a voice, clapping him on the back.

"And you, Longhi! The two most scurrilous villains of Roma!"

The pair turned to see a very drunk Giambattista Marino, the most celebrated poet in Italy, swaying above them with a loose-lipped smile.

"You, Marino—you accuse us of *mala fama?*" said Caravaggio. "You who fled Napoli after filling the mayor's daughter with child? I compete for space in Sant'Angelo cells with you, you butt-fucking scoundrel."

"It's a good thing you can paint," said Marino, "or I would have to kill you."

"As if you could!" scoffed Caravaggio. "In verse, perhaps."

"Ah, but your portrait of me," said Marino, wagging his finger, "forbids me to murder its creator."

"Write me a poem and eulogize me, cuckold-maker," said Caravaggio.

"*Comportati bene*, Michele. Behave! I think I have a new commission for you, you cock-lover."

Longhi laughed. Caravaggio shoved him with his elbow.

"Sit down, poet, before you fall down," said Caravaggio. "My ambition is to be as drunk as you are within the next hour."

Marino barely managed to swing his leg over the bench.

"Now tell me about this commission," said Caravaggio.

"The papal clerk—Melchiorre Crescenzi. I've recommended you to paint his portrait."

"Crescenzi!" said Longhi, rubbing his chin. "Now that's a rich bastard."

"And Virgilio Crescenzi's portrait too," said Marino. The poet squinted hard, trying to focus his eyes. "Is that a Knight of Malta sitting over there?"

Everyone at the table turned and stared at a bearded man in a black tunic, the eight-pointed Maltese cross emblazoned on his chest. He sat with two well-dressed nobles, guzzling wine.

"Slumming with the House of Farnese," said Onorio over the rim of his cup. "They must be out for a night of whoring."

One of the Farnese looked up. He tapped the knight on the back, saying something to him. The knight turned around, his mouth pulled in a sneer.

"Ugly face," said Caravaggio, staring back. "He's got eyes like a reptile."

The two men locked eyes. Caravaggio spat on the floor.

Marino pulled the artist's sleeve. "Don't get into a brawl with him, Michele. I know that one. He's a Roero and mean as a snake. The family shipped him off to Malta to get rid of him."

There was a sudden commotion and shouted obscenities as three women, lips and cheeks painted with red beetroot, pushed their way through the crowd of men.

"Ah, *ecco le puttane!*" growled one man. "The whores arrive!"

Caravaggio focused on one with long red hair. So did a drunken painter at the table next to him.

"Here's Anna!" roared the drunk. "And what a terrific arse she has! Who in this tavern hasn't had some of that?"

The red-haired girl turned on him amid the lewd laughter.

"Maybe you are the one with the terrific ass, Claudio. Not that it matters to me, but the pretty bugger boys certainly love it."

The drunken painter staggered to his feet and slapped the girl hard in the face.

Anna put her hand to her cheek.

"Serves you right!" said one of her female companions. She put her hand on her hip, turning toward the men. "These are our paying customers. Have some respect."

"Shut up, Doralice!" said Anna.

"You cost us money, you stupid *puttana*!" said the third woman, her painted lips pinched.

"Who are you calling whore, Livia?" screamed Anna. "*Troia!* You pig, you filthy slut!" She seized a handful of her companion's black hair in her fist.

Livia twisted, screaming. Her hand grabbed for Anna's necklace, breaking it. Ceramic beads bounced on the stone floor of the tavern.

"Dirty *figa*!" screamed Anna. "Cunt! My mother's beads!"

Doralice fumbled for a knife in her bodice.

"Break it up! Put down that knife, *ragazza*," growled the tavern owner. "Over here, *sbirri*! Arrest them!"

Two guards shoved through the crowd. One grabbed Doralice by her forearm, wresting the weapon from her hand.

"You three! Come with us," said the other, grabbing Anna Bianchini by her hair. Her long red locks shook free of their pins, spilling down across her shoulders and face. "You *puttane*! Whores should keep to the streets," said the guard, yanking the two apart.

Anna winced, her eyes cast down at the stone floor strewn with her mother's beads. A tear rolled down her left cheek.

Caravaggio was riveted, his cup of wine suspended before his lips. *That's it!*

"Get your hands off me!" screamed Doralice, struggling to wrench free of the policeman's arms. "You think I can't feel you grabbing my bosom? You pay before you touch me!"

"Desist, *ragazze*, or you'll spend your days in Sant'Angelo prison!"

Caravaggio set down his wine. He turned to his companions. "What's her full name—this Anna? Do you know her?"

"Anna Bianchini, one of Ranuccio Tomassoni's string of whores," said Onorio. "She and that Fillide Melandroni are from Siena, though Fillide is trading higher these days as a courtesan."

Longhi rubbed his thumb and middle finger together. *Money.*

"Anna beds down most of the regulars here," said Marino, gesturing with his cup. He laughed, tipping back the drink. He wiped his mouth on his sleeve. "Including me on occasion. She's a handful."

"I must have her," said Caravaggio.

As if he'd overheard the painter, the Maltese Knight stood. The *sbirri* backed away in deference as he approached Anna, his hand slipping down over her buttocks. He whispered in her ear and she nodded. They moved toward the door.

As Roero crossed the threshold, he turned and looked over his shoulder at Caravaggio. He made the sign of the *cornuto*, horns of a cuckold, and slapped Anna on the ass.

Cecco tied the waist string on his muslin trousers and put on a gray boiled-wool tunic, spotted stiff with paint. He still shivered as he went about his chores. He covered the mixed paints with moist rags and dipped the paintbrushes in a solution of turpentine in a wooden bucket. His fingers coaxed the paints from the hairs, careful not to dislodge any bristles.

Caravaggio always inspected his brushes carefully each morning. He had boxed the boy's ears before when he'd found a couple of bristles stuck to the edge of the bucket.

The apprentice allowed himself a few minutes for a brief repast. He took hard salami off the shelf and a loaf of stale bread. He poured himself some wine, sour and rough, to wash down his meal. Even though he knew Caravaggio had left, he looked over his shoulder. From the art supplies, he took the jug of walnut oil and poured a liberal splash on his bread. The oil spread its nutty flavor throughout his mouth, coating his tongue with its richness.

He closed his eyes and smiled.

As he ate, he stared at the twisted bedsheet that had served as his toga for the master's composition.

The cardinals would laugh at this painting of me. My body thin, my cheeks pale. What is my master thinking? I am no Bacchus!

Rag in hand, Cecco gave the greasy table a good scrub. The plank table was covered by an unfinished canvas Caravaggio had discarded. The grim face of a cardinal dressed in vermilion robes looked up at the boy. Cecco bent over his work, the painted double chin wobbling under the ministrations of the cleaning cloth. The portrait had long served as the dining surface for Caravaggio. Today's capon grease had left an oily smudge across the cardinal's face and left shoulder.

Cecco looked down at his dirty cloth and sighed. Precious bits of pigment—lead white, yellow ochre, and a pale blush of vermilion—stained his cloth. The forgotten cardinal—probably one who had fallen from favor and could not pay for his portrait—had been fading over the past months, disappearing day by day into the old rag.

After the master's supplies were put away, Cecco looked for his scrap of gesso-prepared canvas stretched on a frame of splintery oak. The boy's pigments were the cheapest form of color—charcoal dusts, ground-earth browns, and chalk white—but he focused as intently as if he were working with the most precious lapis lazuli, ultramarine, and gold.

His hands, still wet from washing up, cradled an earthen jug half full of wine. He set it next to some peaches, not yet ripe. Their first blush of color would contrast well with the terra-cotta pitcher.

Now I shan't draw a line but do as the master does. A few marks in the canvas—an abbozzo—*to set my composition, that is all.*

Vision! I must see the image.

Cecco closed his eyes, summoning up a mental picture. He set about his work, his tongue held between his teeth, working the thin wooden end of his brush partway through the gesso on the canvas, a series of indentations. He thought of his master's hands working and shivered.

Hands of a genius. Hands of a lover.

He was Caravaggio's boy. He shared the artist's bed, his thirteen-year-old body giving the twenty-nine-year-old pleasure when the master wasn't occupied with the whores of Roma.

But Cecco worried. He was growing older, an adolescent. Caravaggio reached for him less and less at night.

Perhaps it is his rage that interferes with his love for me.

Boys as sexual companions for older men—there were hundreds of people throughout Roma who thought it was a mortal sin, punishable by death. Cecco had the prestige of being the companion of Roma's most promising artist.

Sì. He gave his body to his master, a man with an insatiable appetite for life, art . . . and sex. He was Caravaggio's boy.

But Francesco Boneri—Cecco—was more than a model and a source of pleasure. He was also the maestro's apprentice.

Someday I will become a great artist too.

Chapter 2

Village of Monte Piccolo, Chianti

Her voice carried across the piazza, over the playful shrieks of the children and the murmuring of the nuns who stopped and turned when they heard her shouting.

Hands flying, black hair electric with outrage, she was berating the driver of a taxi stopped next to her. The nuns hurried across the tiny piazza, seeking safe distance from the erupting volcano of her temper. And standing across the piazza, pulling his scarf tighter against the winter wind, Professor A. R. Richman watched, thinking he was glad she was shouting at the taxi driver and not at him.

At seventy-five, Professor Richman was tall and thin, with unruly gray hair, worn a little long over his collar. He remembered all too well the last time a woman had yelled at him in public. It had been scarcely more than a year ago at the final departmental meeting before he'd retired after a career at Harvard focused on Akkadian and Eblaite cuneiform tablets—which he had to admit was not as glamorous as it might sound. The woman had been an associate professor who had disagreed with him, almost violently, over details of daily life during the reign of Sargon of Akkad. He had found leaving such disputes behind to be one of the great pleasures of retirement.

His retirement had so far been free of almost all disputes. It had been calm, placid—both delightfully and perhaps somewhat disappointingly.

His wife of almost fifty years had died within a month of his retirement, and suddenly adrift, missing her terribly, he had spent most of the year since then like a toddler at the beach, seeking the safety of shallow waters. Without any responsibilities and with—thanks to a solid pension and years of careful investments—the ability to pursue whatever course of action caught his fancy, he had nonetheless stayed perilously close to the life and the world he had known for so long.

He had focused his time and attention on a self-directed education in art history: reading deeply, auditing classes at the university, and spending his off-hours in the walnut-paneled confines of the faculty club, where he knew all the faces and felt no obligation to chat with any of them—which allowed him to neatly sidestep any concerns of whether they had any interest in chatting with him.

He might have daydreamed of retirement as an opportunity to break free of the routines of the past half century, to travel widely and maybe regain some of the recklessness of youth that had propelled him careening through Europe and much of the Middle East in pursuit of the archaeological mysteries that had captivated him in his college years. But those mysteries had, in the end, narrowed down to five-thousand-year-old fragments of clay tablets, and now, for all his new freedom, Professor Richman felt as if he was still deep in the ancient dust of Mesopotamia.

The sudden decision to attend a seminar in the tiny Chianti town of Monte Piccolo was his first determined attempt to shake off that dust and venture beyond the tidal pools where the toddlers played.

It was hardly a radical change from his old life. He was still an academic, still sheltered in the world of books and intellectual discourse. But he was living in a foreign land, trying to speak a foreign language, and—if this perhaps counted as adventure—sleeping on a hard, narrow bed in a cold, drafty room in a kind of dormitory with questionable lighting and highly inadequate hot water.

And now this.

"Vaffanculo! Testa di cazzo!"

The young woman's voice rose, strong in the cold air, with an edge both sharp and somehow cheerful. She was enjoying herself.

The professor didn't understand precisely what she was saying. Despite the hopes invested when his mother named him Aristotle Rafael Richman—an unlikely flight of fancy from a woman so serious—he was never gifted at languages, and years ago he'd given up trying. He could read and write ancient Sumerian, but modern languages were a challenge. Still, he could get by almost anywhere in the world on what he considered—not too immodestly, he hoped—his charm, bolstered by the assorted scraps of half a dozen different languages he'd picked up in spite of himself.

"Figlio di puttana! Pezzo di merda!"

In this case, he didn't need a mastery of Italian to get the message. The pitch and the tone of her voice made it clear. The expressions on the nuns' faces were only added confirmation.

"Pompinaro!"

The taxi driver threw up a hand in surrender and drove off. The black-haired volcano turned, laughing in triumph, and then, catching sight of Professor Richman, instantly changed—expression, stride, the tilt of her head—into a wholesome, all-American college student. Her wolfish grin of triumph was suddenly a sunny American smile. She acknowledged Richman with a wave of her hand as she strode toward him across the piazza. He returned her wave with a nod. No smile.

He wasn't looking forward to the day's expedition. He knew he had no one to blame except himself. And her: Lucy, as he still wanted to call her, even though she'd made it clear that her name was Lucia. Not Lucy. Definitely not Lucy. Fine. It was Lucia's fault. Lucia and the annoying seminar leader who'd paired them up for the semester's research project without any apparent thought beyond the fact that they'd both admitted they hadn't found partners on their own. Richman's excuse—though no one had asked—was that he was still feeling slightly awkward around the other students. Partly because he had just arrived in Monte Piccolo for the start of the January semester, while most of the others had been there since September, and mostly because the oldest of his classmates wasn't nearly half his age. And although she didn't offer any excuses, the young woman's reason for not having a partner was—Richman was certain, after a career of facing thousands of American college students—that she'd been too busy partying to even think about the classwork.

When the instructor had made the assignment official, Professor Richman, trying to make the best of their unexpected and unwelcome partnership, had offered an avuncular smile and said, "Well, Lucy—"

She had cut him off right there, correcting him sharply. "Lucia. My name is Lucia."

It caught him off-balance. He'd heard her talking and joking with the other students, and she was obviously American—he might not be a linguist, but Professor Richman knew a New York accent—so he'd assumed the familiarity of a standard nickname would be an easy opening.

He regrouped and tried again. "I'm sorry, my dear young lady, but—"

"I'm not your 'dear young lady' either."

Richman was baffled. His marriage had been childless, and his relations with younger women had been strictly professorial. He was used to more respect and a lot more leeway.

"Well, I suppose we—" he started again, but she cut him off.

"Never mind. We'll talk later."

She was looking over his shoulder, out the window into the piazza, where an absurdly handsome young man stood straddling a motor scooter, looking like a picture out of a fashion magazine in his black leather jacket and silk scarf. He cupped his hands around his mouth and shouted, "Lulu!"

She shouted back, "Moto! *Un attimo! Eccomi!*"

Her Italian was as natural as her English.

"Got to go," she said to Richman and ran past him out the door toward the young man on the Vespa.

That was two weeks ago. They had met twice since then to discuss their project—both meetings cut short when she had to rush off for another engagement. Probably with the young man and his Vespa. But they had agreed on a project. It was her idea, actually. Someone she knew—"Zio Te-Te," she called him, whatever that might mean—had a painting he thought was old. More than old, he was certain it was valuable. Examining it, tracing its provenance—its history—would be a perfect project, she insisted. And Richman had to agree. There was no question about her intelligence. She was smart, quick, incisive, and she knew her stuff. This seminar was the last credit she needed for her master's in art history—and she was planning on using her time here to get a start on her thesis.

That was all well and good, but now, standing in the piazza, Professor Richman was chilled and very certain that he would rather be in a warm café with a hot drink in front of him. She had told him her Zio Te-Te—by now he had worked out that "*zio*" meant "uncle" and "Te-Te" was some kind of nickname—lived a short drive from Monte Piccolo. Richman was wary.

Lucia's march across the piazza was interrupted when the same handsome young man on the Vespa—she'd called him "Moto," was that a real name?—skidded to a stop next to her, threw an arm around her, and gave her an exuberant kiss on each cheek. Richman speculated whether the assortment of buckles on his black leather jacket absorbed any sunlight to add warmth. For the boy's sake, the professor hoped so, since the scarf around his neck was more stylish than warm and he was apparently too fond of his hairstyle to crush it under a helmet—although Richman had to admit that if his own hair had been that thick and dark and looked that good tousled, he, too, would have gone hatless no matter the chill.

The young man leaned in and whispered something in Lucia's ear. She pushed him away and flashed a look as good as a slap, with a dismissive laugh that could safely be given only among the best of friends. He threw his hands in the air and laughed right back at her. He was slim without being scrawny, handsome without being cute, and in his tight black jeans and his leather jacket, buckles and all, he made his Vespa, his *moto*, look dashing without being ridiculous. He even got away with the silk scarf. And unless you looked very closely, you might not notice that his smile was perhaps a little too quick, too eager to please, and his eyes too liquid for the rest of his hard-edged outfit. But Professor Richman wasn't looking closely. And even if he had been, he might not have noticed. He specialized in objects—cuneiform tablets, works of art—not people.

Moto was part of Monte Piccolo's small, always shifting community of artists and art students and their friends and lovers, plus a steady trickle of college students drifting around Italy under the guise of a semester abroad. The art students accepted Moto as one of their own, even though no one knew what, if anything, he was studying. Or painting. Just as no one knew him by any other name than Moto. In the parties and the bars, people became friends too quickly to check names. No one ever asked. Not even his best friend, Lucia, who pushed him away now, threw back her tangle of black hair, and turned toward Professor Richman—becoming in that moment once again the perfect American grad student as her dashing young friend roared off across the piazza, scattering pigeons and nuns.

"Hey, Professor," she said, with another smile he didn't bother returning. "My car's a couple of blocks from here. Behind the church." And she marched off, leaving Richman to follow.

He did his best to keep up, cursing his damned knee, which still hadn't recovered from the twelve-hour trip from New York, even though it had been weeks ago. And he fought to keep from wheezing, his lungs, like his knee, still struggling with the change from New York to Chianti. Sea level to two thousand feet wasn't that much of a difference, but he was feeling it.

Lucia stopped and waited by a row of Vespas jammed helter-skelter against the curb—certainly she wasn't expecting him to ride on the back of one of those death machines. She'd said "car," and he was going to hold her to it. The moment she touched one of those contraptions, the whole trip was off. He slowed down to catch his breath.

She smiled again. It really was an engaging smile. "Cheer up, Professor. It's going to be fine. We'll drive over to Cortona, talk to Zio Te-Te, look at the painting, and come home. It's a great day for a drive, and we'll have the whole project under control. OK?"

He shrugged.

"Come on! Cheer up! It'll be easy. We'll be the stars of the seminar. You look like a perfect professor"—he didn't bother to point out that was because he actually was a professor—"and I'm the only one in the class who speaks Italian. We've got this. Let's do it."

He allowed himself a smile. Her enthusiasm was genuine and infectious. She took him by the arm and marched past the Vespas to a tiny beat-up Fiat jammed into the lineup. It wasn't much longer than the scooters, but it was a car.

She patted a dented front fender and said, "Professor, meet Otto." Richman thought for a moment.

"Otto? I've never named my cars, but I am under the impression that cars are always given women's names."

"Well"—for a moment she looked almost sad, then she shrugged—"this one's unreliable. It hates to work. And one of these days, it's going to leave me stranded in the middle of nowhere." She pulled open the driver's door. "Isn't that just like a man?"

And as she climbed in behind the wheel and slammed the door, she added, in a voice that seemed meant mostly for herself, "Bastard." Then she shook her head and laughed.

She started the engine, which sounded more like a lawn mower than a car, and Professor Richman wedged himself into the passenger's seat, deciding, what the hell, he'd consider this part of his Italian adventure. By the time he realized the trip was going to be hell on his knee, it was too late, the Fiat was on the move, swerving through the Vespas, rolling across the piazza—terrifying the nuns one last time—and heading out of town and into the hills of Chianti.

∞

"We have to go back."

They were sitting in the car on the outskirts of the tiny town—not Cortona, at all, as Lucia had promised, but an almost nonexistent speck of a village, far enough up into the Umbrian hills that the battered Fiat had barely managed the climb. They had already spent—"wasted," Professor Richman would have said—half a day at Father Antonio's chapel at the orphanage. Now, heading home, they'd driven less than a kilometer when Professor Richman had threatened to jump out of the car unless she stopped immediately and explained to him what she and Father Antonio—Zio Te-Te to her—had been talking about.

"It would have been hard enough for me if you'd been speaking Italian, but whatever language that was, I couldn't understand a word."

"It was Italian, Professor, the way we speak it in Sicily, where my family comes from—and Zio Te-Te's family too."

And then she told him about Zio Te-Te's plans: he was going to sell the painting and use the tens of millions of euros it was obviously worth to repair the orphanage, and buy books for the school and a new well for the village. That was when the professor cut her off.

"We have to go back. We have to tell him the truth. The obvious truth. He thinks he has a long-lost Caravaggio, and that painting is absolutely not a Caravaggio. He's delusional."

She reached down to release the hand brake and pull back onto the road, but with a sudden lunge and a twist of the wrist, he switched off the ignition and snatched the keys.

She laughed. "You're quick for an old man."

"And you're slow for a young woman. But we're still going back. We have to tell him."

"No! I can't break his heart like that." Lucia's voice was sharp.

Zio Te-Te had told her how he'd discovered the painting in a storage room at the orphanage, where it had been sitting for perhaps a century. He'd done what research he could, without a computer and without revealing his secret to anyone. And he was certain it was one of the paintings—four paintings, he explained, not three, the way everyone else mistakenly insisted—that Caravaggio had been carrying to Rome when he died. Now he was ready to announce his great discovery to the world. A new Caravaggio: *Il bacio di Giuda—The Judas Kiss*.

And Lucia wasn't going to let this foreigner, this American professor, destroy those dreams. Though she would have found it difficult, even impossible, to explain exactly why, she felt fiercely protective toward this much older man she barely remembered from her childhood in their small Sicilian village. Did he give her candy? Save her from bullies? Maybe. She really didn't remember anything from those days when she was so young. But she knew she felt that she had to shield this man who had been part of her distant past.

She glared, but Professor Aristotle Rafael Richman had faced off against more than a few angry young women in his career.

"If we don't break his heart today, think how he'll feel when he's a laughingstock on the front page of every newspaper in the country. Unveil a new Caravaggio, and everyone will be watching—and the moment that painting is shown in public, the experts are going to savage him. It will be a bloodbath gory enough for Caravaggio himself to paint. It'll make *Judith Beheading Holofernes* look like recess at play school."

"Don't make jokes!" She looked down, shook her head. "Te-Te . . ." Her voice trailed off. She didn't understand her feelings, but she had to accept them. Still, the professor was right. She glared at Richman and stuck out her hand. "Keys. We'll go back." He gave her the keys. She started the engine. "And don't be so pleased with your damn metaphor. *Judith Beheading Holofernes*!"

He said, "Don't you mean 'simile'?"

"You're getting your way. Don't be a sore winner."

And on the short drive back to the orphanage, he wondered exactly how the discussion was going to go. Father Antonio, Zio Te-Te—call him whatever you wanted—the priest wasn't going to roll over when they told him his painting was most certainly not a Caravaggio.

When Lucia had introduced them, the priest looked Richman up and down, gave a snort, and turned his full attention to the young woman he hadn't seen in more than twenty years. Lucia had explained it all to Richman on the long drive over the mountains. She knew him as "Zio," but Father Antonio wasn't anybody's uncle. And Te-Te stood for *"tipo tosto,"* a tough guy. He was Uncle Tough Guy, at least he had been all those years ago, before Lucia was sent to live with her grandparents in New York.

And the *tipo* from twenty years ago still looked *tosto*: a square head on a broad, stocky body and huge, rough hands—more like a hit man than a village priest who nurtured a school filled with orphans. Lucia was worried about broken hearts? Richman thought broken heads might be more his style.

But the painting wasn't a Caravaggio. Couldn't be. Yes, it looked old enough and dirty enough to have been kicking around since 1610—the year Caravaggio took the trip that ended with his much-disputed, still-mysterious death. But beneath that ancient dirt, the painting in the orphanage chapel revealed a hand other than that of the genius. It was the faces that gave it away.

Caravaggio painted real people, even in the most sacred of scenes. The faces of his saints were the faces of workmen and pimps and whores from the streets of Rome. Lesser painters relied on idealized images, distilled perfection: the Bible brought to life, rather than life itself made biblical. And the faces in this painting were exactly that. Too perfect to be real. Well executed, but not in any way the genius of Caravaggio.

Richman had seen that immediately, and he assumed Lucia had seen it too. To be polite, he'd studied the painting closely in the dim light of the sacristy and made noncommittal noises. He'd taken a few shots of it with his camera. Lucia had done pretty much the same, taking pictures with her cell phone—and mocking Richman for his "antique" camera, one that used film. "How are your pictures coming out?" she'd teased him, flaunting the digital images on her phone.

Then she and the priest had talked at length, intently, eagerly, in their incomprehensible dialect. Richman had stood, listening for a while, but eventually his knee began to hurt, so he'd found a chair and settled in, just watching from a distance, glancing from time to time at the painting: Judas embracing Christ, kissing him, while shadowy figures lurked in the background. It was hard to tell much through the grime of centuries.

One moment in the conversation between Lucia and her "*zio*" stood out. The priest had scars on his cheeks, both cheeks, running close to his eyes, as if he'd been clawed by a jungle cat. They were old scars, thick and white. Lucia had reached out tentatively, gently, and run her fingers across the scar tissue. She winced, as if the touch was painful to her. But the priest didn't react at all. He acted as if he hadn't even noticed she was touching his face. And then he bent forward and kissed her on the forehead.

Right after that, she and Professor Richman had left.

And now they were going back to do the right thing and shatter the polite fiction that the painting was a priceless masterpiece.

Lucia stopped the car, jumped out, and led the way around the back of the orphanage to the chapel. If Te-Te's heart had to be broken, then she had to be the one who did it.

She strode into the chapel and stopped short. Richman, hurrying into the dark room, stumbled and fell as he tried to avoid running into her. He banged his bad knee and yelped with pain when he hit the floor.

His hand skidded on something wet and sticky, and when he looked down, he saw it was blood.

Struggling to his feet, he could see in front of them a single outstretched hand highlighted by a shaft of sunlight slicing through the dark through a missing pane in the stained glass windows. His eye moved from the light into the shadow, and now he could see Te-Te—tough guy no longer—lying in a spreading pool of blood. His throat was slashed wide open and a bloody knife lay beside him.

Lucia raced toward the body, but she stopped at the sound of angry voices coming from the sacristy where the painting had been kept. Two men lurched out into the chapel, carrying the painting, their voices rising in a mixture of anger and panic.

"*Aspettare! No! Cazzo!*"

"*Idiota!*"

"*Stronzo!*"

Then they saw Lucia and Richman, and all four froze for an instant.

"*Cazzo!*"

One of the men suddenly had a gun in his hand.

He raced across the room, leaving the other man to struggle with the painting as best he could.

"*Fai il minimo rumore e vi faccio fuori tutti e due!*" *Make a sound and I'll kill you both!* His voice was a hoarse whisper.

The painting slipped from the second man's grasp and fell to the floor, cracking the gilt frame. He shouted and the man with the gun turned his head for an instant. Instinctively, Richman lunged for the gun, but he was far too slow, and the man stepped back and swung the pistol, slamming it against the professor's head.

Richman collapsed to the floor, twitched violently once, and then lay still, his face speckled with colors from the light shining through the stained glass windows, his fresh blood mingling with the congealing pool from the dead priest.

Chapter 3

Roma
1599

The young noblewoman Beatrice Cenci pressed her white-turbaned head against the bars of the cage as the wagon rocked over the cobblestones toward the scaffold. Strands of the young woman's hair, wet with perspiration, clung to her elegant neck. Her stepmother, Lucrezia Petroni, moaned in prayer on her knees next to her cage, her brocade gown torn and filthy.

Michelangelo Merisi da Caravaggio stared at the twenty-two-year-old Beatrice, committing her face to memory. He saw no fear in her eyes, only a dogged resignation.

"So innocent a face," said a bald-headed man to his wife. "A face that does not lie. I believe her. What father rapes his own daughter?"

"*Sì,*" said the woman. She dabbed at her eye with her fingertip. "I'd have killed the bastard myself."

"And bedding down the son too," said the husband, crossing his beefy arms over his chest. "May Francesco Cenci rot in hell! Serves him right they murdered the *stronzo*!"

All Roma knew that Beatrice and her older brother, Giacomo, had beaten their monstrous father to death with a hammer. Together the family had then pushed him from the ramparts of his castle to feign suicide.

Pope Clemente VIII showed no sympathy for the abused children and stepmother. Rebellion in the noble order—especially patricide—could not go unpunished. The pope condemned the entire family to death, except the youngest boy, twelve-year-old Bernardo. He was forced to watch the torture and death of his family. Pleas for mercy from the Roman people—both nobles and commoners—fell on deaf papal ears.

There was a scream like the shriek of a dying rabbit. Ahead, on the scaffold, Beatrice's brother Giacomo writhed in agony as he was tortured with red-hot pincers. The girl cocked her head, straining to hear the last syllables from her brother's mouth. Lines of anguish crumpled her brow. She extended her filthy arms through the bars toward the sound.

Caravaggio stood riveted.

Ah, Leonardo da Vinci! How cruel your advice to an artist to observe an execution.

"See the reactions of those condemned to death when they are led to their execution. Study those archings of the eyebrows, the spasms of muscles and the movements of the eyes. Examine their bodies after death to understand human anatomy."

Unlike Da Vinci, Caravaggio did not sketch the scene. Instead, he committed it to memory. His eyes homed in on the buckled muscle on the forehead of the anguished girl, her dirty hands and arms, the suffering that drew back the skin around her eyes in torment.

Thousands of Romans spilled out into the dusty streets, accompanying the carts along the Via di Monserrato, Via dei Banchi, and Via San Celso to the Ponte Sant'Angelo, to gape at the execution.

"I knew I'd see you here, Michele."

Caravaggio felt a hand clasp his shoulder and turned to see Orazio Gentileschi's hawkish face and spadelike beard. Beside him was a little girl, no more than seven, whose eyes were riveted on Beatrice Cenci.

"You brought Artemisia to witness this debacle?" said Caravaggio.

"She insisted." Orazio pulled out a small notebook and began sketching. "Look how the little brother suffers."

Standing horrified adjacent to the platform, young Bernardo was being forced to watch the execution of his mother, brother, and sister. When he fainted in the heat and horror, an attendant splashed a bucket of water on his face to revive him so he witnessed every minute of torment as Giacomo Cenci's living body was torn apart. Then his corpse was drawn and quartered.

But it was Beatrice's poise and grace as she walked to the scaffold that garnered the sympathy and pity of the Roman people.

"The father raped her when she was only a child, the *bastardo!*" whispered a grizzled man to his companion. He pinched savagely at a red wart on his face. "What justice is this?"

"What pope have we who condemns this poor girl to death?" said the younger man, crossing himself. "God would never mandate such suffering!"

"The pope wants the Cenci estate," muttered the wart-faced man. "After today he will have it."

Artemisia tugged on her father's tunic. "What is 'rape,' *babbo?*"

"I'm sketching, daughter," said Gentileschi gruffly. "I will explain later. Leave me in peace."

The girl nodded. She pushed Caravaggio aside with a gentle but firm hand so she could see better.

Caravaggio watched not only the faces of the condemned, but the outrage and compassion in the eyes of the Romans. He saw little Artemisia's face pull taut, a haunted look in her eyes.

"Is the girl all right?" Caravaggio asked her father. "Look at her, Orazio."

"She is a sensitive child," he said, still sketching. "With more heart and conscience than our pope and clergy, the disgusting swine."

"Perhaps you should take her home."

Gentileschi shrugged, exasperated. "Why? She is a painter too. She'll remember this day."

Caravaggio didn't answer. He thought of his father's and grandfather's deaths, the scene scorched into his mind forever. He nodded to the little girl, who did not reciprocate. Artemisia stared back at him, her eyes steady. She remained silent.

Something in her needs fixing. She may indeed be an artist.

The July sun baked the stones of the piazza, which reflected the merciless heat. The crowd pressed closer to the scaffold, sour body odors mingling. One by one people began to faint. Two were carried out dead of heatstroke.

No one could look away.

Two men dressed in formal cloaks of the papal justice stood to the right of the scaffold.

"Those two," said Gentileschi, looking up from his sketchbook. "They're the ones who asked the questions, watching the girl be tortured until she confessed. Ferrante Taverna, the inquisitor, and Mariano Pasqualone, the papal clerk."

"No remorse on their faces, the bastards," said Caravaggio, studying them. "No compassion, no empathy. They look bored. Especially that Pasqualone."

"They are bastard bureaucrats, heartless fucks," said Gentileschi. "They carry out the pope's dirty work."

Caravaggio glanced at Artemisia. She blinked, her eyes solemn. Then she turned back to watch Beatrice Cenci.

After watching the death of her brother, Beatrice betrayed no fear of her imminent execution. She walked like a martyr, dignity in her bearing. Without struggle, she knelt and bared her neck.

"Look at whom the Church condemns. Innocent souls!" wailed a woman.

Voices in the crowd shouted, *"Certo! Gli innocenti!"*

"Innocent lamb!" cried a fishmonger, stinking of his wares. "What justice is this?" He waved his arms wide, supplicating to the heavens.

"Shut up! You will be next, you fool," said the man's wife. "Stick to fish. What do you know of lambs?"

"Poor girl!" moaned a gray-haired woman in a ragged kerchief. "Spare that one, at least!"

The crowd hummed with dissention as the sun broiled overhead.

"Spare the girl! Spare the girl!" shouted voices in unison.

Beatrice Cenci lifted her head only enough to gaze out to her defenders, the mob who had gathered to witness her death.

The sword lifted.

The executioner's blade sliced through her neck as the Romans gasped. A spurt of blood stained the swordsman's tunic.

He looked down at his work and swore silently. Part of the noble-woman's neck remained intact, her head still attached. The executioner withdrew a dagger from a sheath behind his back.

Caravaggio's eyes were riveted on the executioner now, not the victim. The swordsman's face showed the concentration of a butcher as he bent to the practical task of severing bone and muscle from a piece of meat.

The girl's head rolled on the wooden scaffold and then came to an abrupt stop.

The people stood stunned. Even the *sbirri* with their swinging cudgels and curses could not disperse them.

As the sun sank mercifully into the west, its surrender flooded Roma in crimson light, coloring the ochre stucco a golden rose. Children brought crowns of flowers to adorn Beatrice's head, her bloody turban long discarded as the street sweepers rinsed clean the cobblestones. Mothers combed out the dead woman's hair using their bare fingers.

Mourners brought candles, costly to the poor, to line the biers of the dead, lit against the blackening night. Women, men, and children wept in the darkness.

33

Caravaggio saw the reflection of light dance in the still eyes of Artemisia Gentileschi.

Orazio Gentileschi put his arm around his daughter's shoulders and walked toward home. But Caravaggio, like so many others, stayed rooted in vigil, long into the night. The flickering candles lit the gash of Beatrice Cenci's severed head, replaced on her marble-white neck.

And for Caravaggio, a seed was planted for a masterpiece in his dark future.

Chapter 4

A Warehouse

Professor Richman woke once into a world of swirling shadows and lightning flashes and, later, woke again into a calmer darkness. A gentle hand stroked his forehead. His eyes weren't ready to focus. A face loomed over him. He twitched; the face became Lucia's. His head was cradled in her lap as she bent over him, her hand on his forehead. And beyond her was a room cluttered with broken furniture and piles of boxes. A faint blue-white light—moonlight?—seeped in through a window high above. How long had he been unconscious?—seeped in through a window high above. Where were they?

He tried to sit up, and her calm, cool hand clamped down over his mouth. She leaned even closer. "Not a sound." Her words were no more than breath in his ear. "Listen."

Beyond the pounding inside his head, he eventually could hear angry voices from the next room, muffled by thick walls and a heavy door. He couldn't understand a word, but she listened with fierce concentration. He let himself drift away again, but his mind filled with lightning flashes, disturbing images. The priest's body—yes, he had seen that. And the blood—yes, that was real too. And he remembered the painting and the shouting, and he veered away from the memory before it replayed the pistol slashing across his face.

It had gone quiet in the next room, a sullen silence. The professor struggled to sit up. Lucia steadied him and helped him rest his back against a wall. She leaned close again. "They're fucked. They have no idea what to do with the painting. Don't know where to go with it. Don't know what it's worth. No idea it was going to be so big. Idiots."

He didn't feel strong enough to point out who was in charge and who was captive.

"Where are we?" He tried to keep his voice as quiet as hers had been.

"No idea. It took hours to get here. Locked in the back of a truck. Didn't know if you were ever going to wake up."

The professor sat in silence for a while, trying to make sense of what had happened. He couldn't. He'd thought he wanted an adventurous new life—now he just wanted his old life back. As soon as possible.

With a sudden stabbing jolt of pain, his leg began to cramp. He lurched, trying to get to his feet, and in an instant she was up, steadying him in the near dark.

For a moment they stood, swaying, hugging each other for support. Then she gave a start, grabbed his shoulders, and slowly turned him—until, clutching each other in the darkened room, they were staring at the painting. The painting from Te-Te's chapel, with its cracked frame and too-perfect faces, leaning against a stack of cardboard boxes—but seeming to float in the dark, picked out of the shadows by the moonlight.

The professor closed his eyes. Someone had died for that painting. For that sad fraud of a painting.

But Lucia was transfixed. She settled Richman on a solid-enough box and walked a few steps to stand just outside the pool of moonlight and stare.

The moon was long gone, but Lucia was still standing in the dark watching the faintest gleam on the varnish of the painting when the shouting began again in the next room. Shouts of surprise, then anger, rage, and fear. A choking gasp. A struggle. A scream that was choked off. Silence.

Lucia whirled, grabbed the biggest box she could lift, and set it against the inside of the door. There were quick footsteps prowling the next room. The professor was on his feet, and together they staggered to the door with an even larger box. It hit the door with a thump and the footsteps stopped, then hurried across the room toward them.

The doorknob rattled. They abandoned stealth and raced to stack boxes against the door. The professor wobbling, doing his best.

There was pounding on the door, a fist. The pounding changed to thundering kicks. The boxes shook, but held. Lucia scanned the room for a way out, but everything was lost in shadows. The professor paused, swaying, one last box in his arms, when a gunshot sounded, muffled by the door and the boxes. The bullet didn't penetrate the boxes, but the professor sat down fast. There were two more shots.

Sitting on the floor, Richman reached out and slapped the side of one of the boxes. Lucia looked over at him.

"Books!" he said, managing a smile. There wasn't any point in keeping quiet now.

There was one more shot, and Richman scooted away from the pile. The saving power of literature only went so far.

The pounding began again. This time heavier. Sharp and heavy—an axe—and now there was a crashing and cracking. The door couldn't hold for long. Lucia grabbed Richman's hand and dragged him back toward the shadows. Another thundering blow. The sound of the door splintering.

And then, in an instant of silence between the blows, there were new voices on the other side of the door, clear and sharp. Lucia pulled the professor farther into the dark. A gunshot. A shout. A volley of shots. Lucia grabbed the professor, hugged him tight, and they turned to face the door, clinging to one another in a moment of simple survival.

And then the room exploded. Exploded out of the darkness behind them—not in front, where the noises and the danger seemed to be coming from. The force of the blast tossed them back against the boxes of books that had saved them from the gunfire.

Darkness closed in again.

A cell phone vibrated silently. The man pulled it out of his pocket, checked who the call was coming from, pushed the button to answer, but didn't say a word. After a moment of mutual silence, the caller mumbled, more than spoke, in Sicilian.

"*Fattu.*" Done.

"*Tutt'a ddui?*" Both?

"*Tutt'a ddui. È quacchi ccosa di cchiu. Quacchi ccosa di valuri ranni.*" Both. And something else. Something of great value.

The man didn't respond to that. He let the moment of silence stretch out. Then he hit the "End" button.

Chapter 5

Roma
1600

A chorus of cheers filled the grand dining hall at Palazzo Madama as Giambattista Marino finished reciting his poem in honor of Gran Duca Ferdinando de' Medici of Firenze. The *gran duca* nodded in acknowledgment, and Cardinal Maria del Monte rose to offer one more toast in honor of his esteemed guest as servants marched in bearing enormous platters of roast meats and fish for the assembled guests.

Far down the table from the host and his guest of honor, Caravaggio sat next to Galileo Galilei, who had traveled with the Florentine entourage of Gran Duca Ferdinando. It was not the first time the two had been seated together, and they took up an old conversation.

"Still lost in the heavens, Signor Galilei?" said Caravaggio, reaching for the pitcher of wine. "Deciphering divine movement of the stars for us ignorant souls?"

Galileo smiled, touching a blemish on his left cheek. "Indeed I am. And are you still painting prepubescent pretty boys?"

Caravaggio snapped his head around in anger.

Galileo rested his hand on the artist's forearm.

"Come now, Michele. I admire your work. I do believe you are a genius. But you must see how this"—he waved his hand vaguely to indicate everything surrounding them—"this decadence has corrupted your vision."

Caravaggio shook off Galileo's hand. "I don't know what you're talking about."

"Then you are blind, my friend," answered the astronomer, nodding toward his host at the end of the table. "You have mastered the perfection of nature in your art. You do not disguise God's beauty with unnecessary flourishes. I have never seen a better tribute to God's handiwork than your images. But you waste your time and cheapen your gift, painting luscious boys for lustful clergy."

Caravaggio's jaw tightened. The criticism blinded him to the praise. "And you stare into your telescope imagining heavens that don't exist."

"Quite the opposite. I imagine nothing. I trust only my senses, my eyes. I am not corrupted by theories or opinions."

Caravaggio hesitated.

I trust my senses, my eyes.

"But what of God?" said Caravaggio. He stared hard at Galileo's strikingly large forehead.

Galileo took a sip of *vino nobile*. "You have never struck me as a particularly God-fearing man, Maestro Merisi—"

"You are wrong. I believe fervently in God. But only God. God and Nature, nothing else!"

Galileo regarded him, his eyes focusing slowly. The time he spent studying the heavens had strained his sight for things close on Earth. "And truth?" he asked mildly.

"Truth above all, damn you! God and Nature are truth."

"So it would seem we agree," Galileo said, nodding, his voice still calm. "I cannot believe that the same God who has endowed us with senses to perceive his world and the intellect to understand it has intended us to forgo their use. I see God's world and accept the evidence of what I see."

He nodded to a servant, who filled his wineglass.

Caravaggio met the astronomer's eyes. "I trust Nature. That is all the God I need."

"Perhaps you are more of a scientist than you know, Maestro Merisi. Science illuminates the truth, like a shaft of light cuts through shadow."

Again Caravaggio hesitated.

Light and shadow.

"I'm no scientist," he insisted.

"Art and science are not enemies," Galileo countered. "Consider Da Vinci—"

"Forget Da Vinci! My art is unlike anyone before me."

Galileo laughed. "You are rather immodest, aren't you? Still, Da Vinci studied science and was not afraid to look beyond what pleased his patrons. He had vision and would not sacrifice that for all the gold in the world."

"What do you mean?" Caravaggio said, bristling.

Galileo shrugged. "These paintings of naked boys—those angels— are leading you away from your vision."

"I am paid well for them, I assure you."

"*Sì, sì.*" Galileo sighed. He sipped his wine. "I am sure you are handsomely compensated. But that is my concern. Your boys are amusing, but what do they have to say to humanity? 'Behold, I am beautiful.' And nothing more. Surely you have more to say, do you not?"

"I—"

Now Galileo's voice strengthened. He leaned toward the artist. "Beauty alone is not enough, Michele. It becomes boring in isolation. Like individual stars without a constellation. Not relevant to the greater heavens."

Caravaggio chewed viciously on his mustache. "And you, Signor Galilei. You say that our Earth is not the center of the universe . . . that our planet and the others revolve around the sun. That is blasphemy."

"I believe we revolve around the sun because I observe it. With my senses." He pointed to his face. "With my two eyes! You and I have this in common, Michelangelo Merisi." The astronomer served himself some small fish in oil from a platter offered by a servant. "We have the ability to perceive truth if we cast off the blindfold"—lowering his voice to a whisper, leaning closer yet—"the blindfold of the Church's overbearing doctrines. Otherwise we are forever handicapped, like hooded falcons. Unable to soar."

Galileo scooped up the fish and oil with a crust of bread, chewing thoughtfully. A small piece of parsley lodged in his teeth.

Caravaggio stared at the green splotch in the astronomer's teeth. He drew a deep breath, casting a glance around the room. Others were deeply engaged in conversations, boisterous and drunken talk. Giambattista Marino was moving around the room, receiving accolades for his poem.

A sudden commotion and a shriek of women's laughter sliced through the men's voices.

The courtesans had arrived at the farthest door, and all eyes were cast in their direction. Ranuccio Tomassoni entered the room, leading his flock, laughing at something the beautiful auburn-haired Fillide said.

Caravaggio twisted around in his chair. He locked eyes with Fillide. Ranuccio followed her glance to him, and his smile died on his lips.

"Ranuccio!" shouted a dark-bearded man from the middle of the room. His booming voice cut through the clanking of cutlery, chatter, and roar of drunken laughter. He was dressed in the black tunic of the Maltese Knights, the eight-pointed cross across his chest.

Caravaggio recognized those reptile eyes, slits of mossy green.

The knight crossed the room toward Ranuccio, clapping him on the back. Then he turned to Fillide, wrapping his arm around her waist. She pushed him away, laughing.

As the knight whispered in Fillide's ear, Ranuccio and Caravaggio exchanged a cold stare.

"Ah, the Knights of Malta grace Gran Duca Ferdinando's banquet," said Galileo.

"You know him?" said Caravaggio, regarding the knight with the same hostility as he did Ranuccio.

"Fra Giovanni Rodomonte Roero of Piemonte."

"Some knight! I've seen him before," said Caravaggio. "He keeps company with pimps."

Ranuccio hissed something to Roero. The knight's eyes shot to Caravaggio.

"You seem to have offended those gentlemen," observed Galileo. "Not wise having a Knight of Malta as an enemy, my friend."

Caravaggio turned away. He took a long draught of his wine. "Forget them!" he said. "I think you make enemies easily too, signore. The Church—a powerful adversary. Are you not afraid of the accusation of heresy, Galileo?"

"Are you?" said the scientist, his fingernail deftly dislodging the scrap of parsley.

The artist snorted his scorn for such fears. He gestured to a servant standing against the wall to refill his glass with wine.

When the attendant had retreated, Caravaggio said, "I have left Palazzo Madama."

"Ah," said Galileo. "Congratulations for escaping the holy orbit! Perhaps now you will have something more to say. You can listen to your senses without your patrons' chatter to divert you from the truth."

The artist stuffed a piece of crusty bread in his mouth and nodded, chewing vigorously. "I find my truth in the street. The beggars and whores. The fishwives and sausage makers, the swindlers and thieves."

The astronomer smiled. "Roma is your sun, Caravaggio. Find your heaven and fill it with stars."

Chapter 6

Roma
1600

Anna Bianchini lowered her hood as she walked into the drafty room and shivered. Her long red hair spilled down her shoulders.

"You are the one who sent for me?" she said, staring at the man in the black velvet tunic. The material was shiny, the matte worn thin.

I needn't have borrowed Fillide's good taffeta skirt. This is no nobleman!

"I have the money to pay you. I will want you for a few hours."

"A few hours?" she said, raising an eyebrow.

"Maybe longer. We'll see."

"Signore, I am good at what I do. A few hours—"

"Over here, *ragazza*."

"They call me Annunccia," she said. She cast a look around the room, inclining her head. "That big hole in the ceiling. You should fix that."

"Stand right there. Under it, where the light is the brightest." He moved her roughly as if she were a chair. "Now a little to the right. There!"

The morning light, fresh from the rainstorm, glanced off her cheekbone. He raised his hand, pressing his fingers to her cheek, tilting her head.

His touch sent a tremor through her body. She knew he felt it.

"Maestro," she murmured.

"Take off your cloak," he said. "Don't move from this spot."

"You want me here?" she said. "Do you not have a bed? A pallet perhaps?"

"Cecco," he called. "Take the signorina's cloak."

For the first time, Anna noticed an adolescent boy emerging from the shadows of the room.

"He's going to watch?" said Anna. "I don't do things in front of boys that age. It isn't right."

Caravaggio laughed. "It isn't right, you say? You are a whore."

"I've got my morals, Maestro Caravaggio," she snapped. "I'm a good girl in my way."

"Don't be angry," said the painter. "It stiffens your features." He laid his hands on either side of her shoulders, pressing her to her knees. "Think of your whorish ways," he said. "Remember them, Annunccia."

"You bastard," said Anna. Yet the power in this man's hands, pressing her to her knees, cast a spell. Her nose rubbed the velvet between his thighs. His scent was potent, like an animal's.

She fumbled for the strings on his trousers. She felt his arousal in the cup of her palm.

He closed his eyes, his hand resting in her hair. He drew a throaty breath. "Cecco! Bring a stool for the signorina. Now!"

Cecco ran toward Anna with a low stool.

Anna didn't notice. Her hands had slipped inside the artist's trousers, cradling him. A shudder rocked his body.

"Signorina. Not now," he said, drawing himself away from her. "Not now. Sit on the stool."

Anna's hand dropped at her side. "Not now?" she said. "But—have I done something wrong?"

Caravaggio helped her onto the low seat. "No. Now catch your dress hem in your hand like this," he said, showing her.

Anna lifted her taffeta dress into a bunch and settled onto the stool. As she sat, she reached out to smooth down her dress. "Fillide will pull my hair if I wrinkle—"

Caravaggio caught her hand.

"No," he said. "Leave it as it is. It is perfect."

She cocked her head at him. He drew her hand to her lap. "Lay your left hand in front of your wrist, like this," he said, moving her as if she were a doll.

"The box of jewels, Cecco. Fetch them. The flagon of white wine. Grasp it with a clean cloth. No fingerprints!"

"What are you doing, Maestro?"

"Now look down, Signorina Anna. Think of the shame you feel."

"Shame?"

"Look down, damn it! Think how it felt to be slapped in the osteria by a buggered painter in front of all the patrons. And publicly whipped in the Piazza Navona as a whore. I saw you—"

"Stop!" cried the girl. "You've got no right—"

"Ah! Think of the beads the other *puttana* broke. Strewn across the floor."

A wave of sorrow crossed the face of the prostitute, like a storm cloud racing across the sky.

"That's it! Hold that pose. Do not move a muscle and I will pay you well."

No sex! And paid all the same!

"Don't you dare smile!" snapped Caravaggio. "You are useless to me that way, you whore."

Anna looked down again, a hot rush of blood washing over her features.

She saw the boy Cecco's foot. A ringing shower of jewels—gold bracelets and necklaces, a strand of pearls—was scattered on the floor next to her.

"You are my penitent Mary Magdalene!" said Caravaggio. "You are magnificent, Anna Bianchini."

He drew his paint-encrusted fingertip across her jawline.

"I shall make you immortal."

Chapter 7

Monte Piccolo

Lucia woke, disoriented and thrashing. The phone! Her damn cell phone was ringing!

It wasn't on the bedside table. Where? There! The pile of clothes on the battered armchair across the room. She scrambled out of bed, dizzy. The room spun, she lost her balance, but managed to fall in the direction of the noise. She pawed at the clothes and the phone fell onto the floor.

"*Cosa?*" She was shocked at the sound of her own voice. Rough and raspy.

"Are you all right?"

It was Moto. Good. She didn't have the strength to be polite right now, and Moto wouldn't care. That's what best friends were for. He didn't wait for her to answer.

"I'll be there in ten minutes."

"Wait! What? The hell you will." She had to get a grip on things.

"We have to get to the hospital."

"Hospital? I don't need to go to the hospital. I'm fine." She wasn't sure she was fine, but she was certain she didn't need a hospital.

"Do you have any idea what's going on?" Moto sounded concerned, which was so unlike him that it forced her to stop for a moment. She realized she had no idea what was going on. Or what had gone on. How she'd wound up here, in her apartment in Monte Piccolo. In her own bed. More exactly, on the floor next to her bed.

"I just woke up. I'm a mess. I need an hour."

"Half an hour. I'll be there."

She shouted, "No!" but he'd already hung up.

She leaned back against the bed and ran her hands through her hair. They came away feeling filthy. She looked at them. White dust. Plaster.

So that had happened.

She remembered an explosion.

That really had happened.

No time to remember anything else right now. One of Moto's many faults was that he was always on time.

She hurried into the tiny kitchen, filled the moka with ground coffee and water, and put it on the stove to boil. Then she rushed into the bathroom for a shower. A glance in the mirror was horrifying. A glimpse of what she might look like if she lived to be a hundred. A hundred and crazy. Her hair was white with plaster dust, wild and tangled. Her face was white and splotchy with the dust and dirt. Her eyes were red-rimmed.

In the shower, she was reminded—as always—that the delights of living in a medieval building in a small Italian hill town did not include reliable hot water. She concentrated on doing the best she could with what was available, scrubbing her hair and face and body, watching the dirty water swirl down the drain and finding enough sore spots to make her think that maybe a visit to the hospital was a good idea. And all the while, she forced her mind away from wondering what had happened.

When she finished her shower, the moka was making its usual dangerous whistling—demanding attention and threatening an explosion if it was ignored. The whistle died—as always—as she hunted for clean clothes, and she poured a cup of the thick black coffee. She took a sip that burned her lips. The pain helped wake her up. Another sip, careful this time.

She looked at her clothes on the chair. Despite her digging through them for the cell phone, they still showed signs of having been folded neatly.

That wasn't her. Even at her best. Someone had undressed her and put her to bed.

Jesus!

She poked into her memory, and the images were terrifying: a bloody hand in sunlight, a knife, a gun, a blinding explosion. She didn't have the strength or the time for that right now.

She pulled on clean clothes. Jeans, T-shirt. Good enough. She glanced at the bed. The sheets and pillowcase were smeared with the dust and dirt from her body. She stripped the bed, pulled the coverlet up over the bare mattress, and threw the dirty linens in the closet.

She had a fleeting memory of stripping her bed in New York this same way in a clumsy attempt to hide a clumsy indiscretion, knowing she'd get caught, knowing she didn't care, knowing that son of a bitch deserved it. He'd started it with that . . . Stop! That was over. She was here.

Then Moto was banging on the door.

"It's open!" He knew that. She never locked the door when she was home.

He rattled the doorknob.

"It's locked!"

How? The old-fashioned lock on her door needed a key to lock and unlock from inside as well as out. She glanced around. Her keys had to be in the pocket of the filthy jeans lying folded on the chair. Yes. There. But how?

Either she had somehow gotten herself home, locked the door, folded her clothes, and crawled into bed while unconscious—or someone else had done all that for her. And then locked the door from the outside. With a key.

She couldn't think about it. She unlocked the door, and Moto was there, in his black leather jacket and silk scarf. His hair tousled as always by the wind. Such a pretty boy—but he was really worried.

He reached out and touched her cheek. She winced.

"Pretty good bruise," he said.

"It'll heal."

"You're all right then?"

"*Sì, idiota!* I'm fine." Even though they both knew she wasn't. "What do you know that I don't? I don't know anything. What happened?"

"You've been missing for three days."

"But I saw you in the piazza . . ." She wanted to say "yesterday." Right before she and the professor had left to visit Te-Te. But when was that?

Moto tossed three newspapers on the table.

The one on top of the pile screamed: *"Assassinio nella cappella!"* *Murder in the chapel.*

And below that, almost as loud: *"Morte nel nome dell'arte."* *Death in the name of art.*

She remembered Te-Te's face. His hand. The blood. She shivered.

The next day's paper was headlined: *"Assassini uccisi a Roma, ancora niente arte."* *Murderers killed in Rome, art still missing.*

Rome? That had all happened in Rome? Hours in the dark in that truck. They could have been driven that far.

And below that: *"L'eroismo dei carabinieri."* *The heroism of the police.*

So that was what she had heard through the door at the end. The shouting, the gunfire. That was the carabinieri. But something had happened before that. The screams. What was that? And who had been attacking the door with an axe? And at the end, the explosion? And . . .

This was completely out of control.

Then she looked at the third newspaper.

"Morto per un imbroglio." He died for a fraud.

The story called Te-Te a hero and made fun of him at the same time: a foolishly sincere old man of God, hero of the orphans, who had tricked himself into believing he had found a missing Caravaggio that no one else had recognized. And died for his mistake. The police had found a small photo of the painting that Te-Te had kept in his desk. Experts had taken one look at the photo and declared that the stolen painting was clearly not a Caravaggio. Couldn't be. No one with any knowledge of art could have looked at those too-perfect faces and made such a mistake.

The last line of the story was, *"Il peccato del prete era tracotanza."* The priest's sin was hubris.

Te-Te didn't deserve this. He didn't deserve to die. He didn't deserve to be mocked in death.

She wanted to hit someone—and Moto knew her well enough to back away, raise his hands.

She caught her breath. "Wait. What about Professor Richman? He was with me."

"That's why we're going to the hospital."

Nothing made sense, and asking more questions wasn't going to help. She'd have to figure it out as they went. She nodded. "Let's go."

As they walked down the stairs, she thought about having to ride behind Moto on the Vespa. Her car was still outside Te-Te's chapel, where they had parked it before the . . . Never mind. She was going to have to get back there somehow and then drive home. A full day.

But suddenly—right here, right in front of her building—there was her Fiat, with two wheels up on the curb, as always, right below a sign that said, *"Divieto di sosta."* No Parking.

Right where she always parked it.

But there wasn't a parking ticket on the windshield, which was some kind of miracle. She had been having a running battle with Vittore, the Monte Piccolo *poliziotto*, who apparently relied on parking fines for his income. She usually got at least one ticket a day—some days more. She would argue there was no reason for the "No Parking" sign, except so that he could write tickets. He would respond that reason played no part in this matter; it was a question of law, and if she didn't pay her fines, he would regretfully have to seize her car. She'd point at the car and scoff, "Who cares?"

He'd shrug. "So I'll throw you in jail."

And eventually she always paid the fines.

But today, there was a handwritten note under her windshield wiper. While Moto ran to get his Vespa, she read the note.

Addressed to *"mia signora"*—milady—it begged her pardon for ever having bothered her with those trivial parking tickets. He hoped she would forgive him for his unspeakable rudeness and she should rest assured that she would never be annoyed in that way again. He would protect her car with his life. And he signed it, *"il vostro umile servitore."* Your humble servant.

In a world that wasn't making any sense, she didn't trust herself to drive—maybe she had a concussion—so she climbed behind Moto, threw her arms around his waist, and held on tight as they raced thirty kilometers through the hills to the next town while Moto shouted at her over his shoulder. He had a cousin who worked in the hospital here, and he had told Moto about the American professor who had appeared that morning in what had been an empty bed the night before.

He said a lot more, but the wind blew his words away. Lucia tucked her chin and tried to let it blow everything else away too.

And when the memories came back anyway—the blood, the explosion, and, as she only now remembered, only barely remembered, the strong hands that grabbed her and pulled her out of the darkness and the dust—when all of that became too much, no matter how hard she tried to think of nothing but the wind and the clattering buzz of the Vespa, she swung her focus away from all of it and filled her mind with the image of the painting, as she had watched it through the night in that dark room, in the faint pool of smudged moonlight that traveled down and across the canvas, angled and shadowed onto the bodies, not the too-perfect, too-clean faces, but the battered hands and dirty feet of the carpenter and his betrayer.

And eventually the Vespa stopped and the wind died and they walked into the hospital, where the woman at the reception desk told them quite firmly that, no, there was no American professor there. No Aristotle Rafael Richman. Not now, not ever in the history of this small hospital. And she would certainly know.

Lucia turned to Moto.

"But your c—"

He cut her off by grabbing her arm and pulling her away from the desk.

Outside, before they got back on the Vespa, he said, "Someone wants it to be that way. They have their reasons. Don't worry. We'll find him."

And riding back to Monte Piccolo, while the Vespa buzzed and her wind-whipped hair lashed her cheeks, she had time to think that she had searched for Te-Te and found him—and that had ended so very badly. And now she was searching again. This time for Professor Richman. Despite Moto's empty reassurances—"Don't worry. We'll find him."—she couldn't escape the feeling that this search would end badly as well. Was that the fate of all her searches? Should she stop searching for things?

Those weren't questions she could answer—at least, not on the back of a Vespa, clinging to Moto as he careened through the Chianti hills.

The room looked like a scholar's office: dark wood and leather, subdued light, walls lined, floor to ceiling, with bookshelves crammed with leather-bound volumes. In one corner, atop a fluted walnut column, an ancient manuscript in Greek lay open under a protective glass cover. A small man sat in a large chair behind a massive wooden desk. A much larger man stood opposite him, in a pool of gentle light. Neither man spoke. A hush filled the room.

With no warning, the small man slammed the flat of his hand on the desk, and the room was filled with the unexpected thunder of the impact. His hand was outsized—sinewy and muscular all out of proportion to his frame.

But he was not in any way a man of reasonable proportions or well-fitted pieces. He seemed assembled instead from oddly chosen parts—not freakishly short, not quite, but seeming even shorter than he was because of his scrawny frame. He was dressed in a plain gray tunic, buttoned to the top, military in cut, but with no insignia, except for a small red cross embroidered on his chest.

His overlarge hands had still-larger thumbs, which, coupled with skinny arms and knobby elbows, could have once been the appendages of an awkward boy—now hardened into hickory as a man. His nose jutted surprisingly from his face, sharp, a dagger, the corvine beak of a raven, more threatening, if less impressive, than the hook of the eagle's beak. Beneath that nose, his lips were painfully thin and the pale-blue eyes above, magnified behind steel-rimmed glasses, could have seemed gentle, even kindly, but were glacial instead. He had small ears, tucked tight against his small skull, like a dog bred for fighting.

His voice was most often much deeper than seemed reasonable for his size, but right now it had risen in pitch, not to a squeak but to a knife edge.

"I *never* should have listened to you! *Never!*" He emphasized the word by slamming his hand on the desk again. "If we had acted immediately, the way I wanted to, we would have it right now and we could move on. But you urged caution, and now we've lost years of work. Years!"

The tall man across the desk stood at ramrod attention, not reacting by twitch or quiver to the noise or the accusations.

The thin lips beneath the dagger nose tightened again.

"So now we are distracted from our mission."

He leaned forward, steepled his fingers, closed his eyes, and made a conscious effort to relax his face. He nodded once, sharply, and broke the silence, his voice dropping back into its normal surprising register.

"Fra Filippo Lupo! Action report!"

The tall man somehow managed to draw himself up even more erect.

"*Sì*, Comandante Pantera! We lost two of our best men, both Knights of Justice, assassinated by the carabinieri. We will feel their loss most acutely. Before their deaths, they dealt properly with the two common thieves who brought this misfortune down upon our order and who paid the proper price for having allied themselves with the Turks by interfering with our sacred mission."

"And . . . ?"

"Sir?"

"And. What. Else. Do. We. Know." He bit off each word as it slipped past his tiny, sharp teeth and darted between those thin lips. Then he clamped his mouth shut, and the frigid blue eyes were hidden for a moment behind reflections off the lenses of his glasses.

"The painting was not in the room with the thieves, and our men were apparently trying to break down a locked door when the carabinieri arrived. One would assume they believed the painting was behind that door."

"And what else was behind that door?"

"We don't know, sir. There is reason to believe there were other people involved. Other people in the warehouse, at any rate."

"But the police report doesn't mention them, does it?"

"No sir."

"And the police were not the ones who blew out the back wall of the warehouse, were they?"

"No sir." The tall man began to shift uncomfortably, if imperceptibly.

"And the police do not have the painting, do they?" The improbably low voice was thundering.

"No sir."

"And we have no idea where it is, do we?" The thunder dropped to a whisper.

"No sir."

"Well, find out!" Thunder again. The little man was breathing harder now. "Or in the name of our Lord Jesus Christ I will have you disemboweled, Fra Filippo Lupo, before the assembled brotherhood of our blessed order. Do. You. Understand."

"Sir. Yes sir."

The small man's voice was suddenly calm, almost gentle. "I have taught you everything I can. You have been like a son to me. Use what you have learned and find what happened to the painting. And what happened behind that locked door."

Fra Lupo dropped to one knee and bowed his head.

"*Sì*, Gran Comandante Pantera. It shall be done as you have ordered."

The thin lips opened once more.

"Dismissed. Walk with the Lord."

Chapter 8

MONTE PICCOLO

They found Professor Richman at home in his own bed. Almost.

Professor Aristotle Rafael Richman was, in fact, in bed. But not quite his own bed. He was currently ensconced in newfound style in the owner's suite in the villa overlooking Monte Piccolo, where the art history seminar was being held. When he had first arrived, Professor Richman had been given what he considered a less-than-satisfactory room in the dorm-like annex where new students were housed. He had glumly accepted his assigned room, since he would only be there for a single semester. But he was certainly much more pleased with his current accommodations.

The *conte*—the count, who owned this villa and rented it out for art history seminars because he couldn't figure out any other way to pay for the upkeep of the vast, drafty building—had graciously moved to another room so the professor could recuperate in cordial surroundings. When the *conte* made the offer—expressing his deep embarrassment on behalf of his country that such a distinguished guest should have been subjected to such an unpleasant experience—Richman thought recuperation in comfort sounded like an excellent idea. He returned the *conte*'s gracious smile with one of his own and moved right in. His new life was on a more acceptable track.

When Lucia and Moto burst into the room that morning, the professor was sipping a deeply satisfying cappuccino. Lucia wanted to run and hug him out of sheer relief, but the cappuccino was in the way, and Professor Richman was not giving it up until he had finished the last drop.

Lucia's rush of affection stalled, and there was a brief awkward moment when the professor wiped a bit of foam off his lips, gestured toward Moto, and said, "I don't believe I have met your friend."

It took Lucia a moment to realize that they didn't know each other. Moto wasn't in the art history seminar, and Professor Richman wasn't in the bars at night. Two separate parts of her life in Monte Piccolo.

Lucia made a quick introduction.

The two men eyed each other. Moto reminded the professor of too many careless students who never finished their assignments and never seemed to care. Students who flaunted a youthful energy that they smugly knew the professor had left behind long ago.

Facing the professor's piercing look, Moto dropped his eyes, blushed, and stammered. Something in the appraising glance reminded Moto of his father, though no two men could possibly have been more different. He mumbled that he had to go and slipped out of the room.

Lucia and the professor were alone together again. Out of danger now, but bound by what they had been through when they hugged each other in the dark while a maniac with an axe tried to break through a door and get at them. They'd faced death together and survived. But now they were alive, life continued, and here in the elegant room and the dappled morning sun, they didn't quite know what to say next. Inextricably bound and at a loss for words.

The professor wriggled his shoulders and settled a little more deeply into the great mound of pillows on the enormous bed. The bandage on his head wasn't very large. The doctor had done a fine piece of work on the gash in his scalp, delicate needlework despite all the time lost while Professor Richman and Lucia were locked in the dark and then coated with dust.

"Breaded like a Kentucky Fried Professor," Richman tried to joke, to show how well he was doing, but Lucia wasn't laughing. She picked up a folded newspaper from the bed and waved it.

"It says we weren't there!"

"No," he said, trying to soothe her. "I read it very carefully myself. It doesn't say we weren't there. It just doesn't say that we *were* there. It neglects to mention us at all."

"It says Te-Te was alone all day in spiritual meditation. That he had given orders that he was not to be disturbed. No visitors."

"Exactly."

"And at the hospital they said you were never there."

"Also exactly the way I would want it to be. Embarrassing, really, as a visiting professor, to be pistol-whipped and rushed to the hospital. Makes me seem careless."

"But . . ."

"And besides the newspapers—which I'm certain had reasons of their own—there is apparently someone else who very much wants our presence to be turned into an absence. Literally. Someone represented, as you might recall, by a man with an axe. I don't know who and I don't know why and I don't want to find out. I am very glad to have that little adventure over and done with." He gestured at the room and the sunlight. "Certainly this is much nicer, isn't it?"

And when she didn't say anything, he went on, "Do you really want to rush off to your friendly local carabinieri and tell them that you—not 'we,' just you—were witness to a murder and you'd love nothing more than to be dragged into the maw of their investigation?"

And when she still didn't look convinced, he added, "We were innocent bystanders at someone else's accident."

And maybe because the bandage was a real one, even if it was small, and maybe because Lucia did instinctively hate the carabinieri, she let it drop. Besides, she was impressed by his spirit. He seemed to be handling the events—murder, kidnapping, explosion—better than she was. And he was nearly three times her age.

She pulled a chair close to the bed and sat down.

"I think it's real."

He raised an eyebrow. And winced. He was going to have to give up his quizzically raised eyebrow for a while. It pulled on the stitches.

"The painting," she continued. "I think it's real. A Cara—"

"Don't say that name." He cut her off. "That man was cursed. His name is cursed, and I don't want to be part of his story. Not even at this far remove."

She started again.

"I think the painting is . . . what Te-Te said it was."

"Don't be ridiculous. He was your *zio,* or whatever he was, but he's nothing more than an old—"

"Stop that!"

He could see she wanted to smack him, but the bandage and its magic seemed to hold for now. Her face relaxed and she lowered her voice.

"I'm serious."

So he was serious too.

"You saw those faces. There is no way that Michelangelo Mer—" He stopped himself. "Call him Michele. There is no way Michele ever painted those faces."

She nodded. "Maybe. But that night. That night in the dark. The way the moonlight fell, I couldn't see the faces. But there was something." She lifted her hands and twisted them gently as if she were trying to shape something out of the air. "I could feel those people in the painting." He was listening. "You don't have to see someone's face to know he's real. I couldn't see much in the moonlight, but I could see enough."

Professor Richman couldn't disagree with that. She'd seen what she'd seen.

And her certainty was a force.

"I could feel those people," she insisted. "They were real. Even in the dark."

"And the faces?"

"I don't know. Maybe someone painted over the originals. Cara—Michele's faces. I don't know why. I don't know who. All I know is what I saw. What I felt."

Professor Richman thought for a moment, then pointed across the room.

"Open the drawer. There. The desk. Manila envelope."

The desk—complete with painted cherubs and gold leaf—looked old enough for Caravaggio to have written letters there.

Lucia handed him the envelope and he opened it.

"This," he said, "must be for you." He handed her a folder labeled *"Bacio di Giuda." Judas Kiss.*

The folder held only a single sheet of paper, covered in scrawled handwriting.

Professor Richman shrugged. "I couldn't read a word of it."

Lucia translated as she went. It wasn't easy, but there wasn't much.

It was apparently written by Zio Te-Te—Father Antonio—who had traced the painting back to the family that had given it to his tiny church. Many generations back. Before there even was an orphanage. Back when the Catholic Church was much more powerful in this Catholic country and even such a tiny chapel had a strong congregation.

The name of the family was a blot. *Conte de . . .* something.

"How did you get this?"

"Curious, isn't it? Especially when you consider that we apparently weren't even there." He held up the large manila envelope. In sprawling, crude letters, it was addressed to *"Il professore americano, Monte Piccolo."*

There was a long silence. The professor waited with pedagogical patience. Lucia suddenly understood. "The children! The orphans!"

"Exactly. Remember all that whispering and scurrying when we got there and started looking for Zio Te-Te."

She gave him a tight smile. "If you want to broadcast something to the world, all you have to do is try to keep it secret from the children." She shook her head. "That must be how they knew."

"They?"

"The men who"—she raised her hands in a helpless gesture—"stole the painting, killed Te-Te. They . . ."

She stopped. Then started again.

"One of the children must have been bragging that the '*professore americano*' was coming to look at the painting. That's what brought those murdering thieves to the chapel. And now . . ."

She paused again and the professor finished the sentence.

"Now the children sent this to me because they want me—the famous *professore*—to prove your Te-Te was right, so they can be famous. Or rich."

"Or maybe they loved Te-Te." She gestured at the newspapers. "These guys are making him look pretty foolish right now."

She carried the single page with Te-Te's research over to the window and studied it in the sunlight.

"OK," she said at last. "After Conte Whatever, I think it says 'Villa Cesarina.' I'll look for that. That all happened"—she looked back at the scrawled document—"almost two hundred years ago. But families like that don't disappear. I'll find them."

"You mean, we'll find them. I'll be up and around in a day or two. We can do this together."

"I thought you were finished with this 'adventure.'"

He thought a moment.

"I'm finished with murder and pistol-whipping, thank you. But this is research. That is my specialty, you know."

She shook her head. "No. You'd just be in the way. I'll do the digging."

"Now really, my dear young lady—"

She held her hand up, with a smile that looked no less dangerous for being sincere. "Stop right there. If you call me 'my dear young lady' one more time, I will forget all about your heroic efforts that got you smacked in the head and I will give you a matching smack." She reached out and gently, but firmly, traced an *X* on the undamaged side of his forehead. "Right there."

Then she leaned over and kissed him lightly right where she had marked the *X*.

"I'll report back as soon as I find the *conte*."

She was halfway to the door when he said, "Wait!" She turned. "If I can't call you 'my dear,' I think I shall have to call you 'Lucy.'"

"That's what they called me in grade school," she said, "and I hated it. I'm Lucia now."

He made a sad face and she laughed.

"All right," he agreed. "I will call you Lucy only in private. Never in front of anyone else."

She took another step toward the door and then turned back. "And if you ever say 'I love Lucy' . . ." She drew an *X* on her own forehead and pointed to him. They were both smiling when she closed the door behind her.

Chapter 9

Monte Piccolo

"Did she really slam the door in your face? Literally? Precision in language is absolutely vital, my—" Professor Richman cut himself off.

Lucia raised an eyebrow and nodded. "OK, then. To be precise, she closed the door firmly. Very firmly. In my face."

"Tell me exactly."

Deep breath. "Te-Te's notes said the painting came from Villa Cesarina. Villa Cesarina was easy to find. And it has belonged to the same family—the Counts and Countesses dei Marsi—for just about forever. The current owner is the Contessa dei Marsi, an old biddy who had a nasty battle-axe—her maid or companion or whatever she is— guarding the front door. I gave her my nicest smile and said I needed to talk with the contessa, and she told me that the Contessa dei Marsi isn't receiving any visitors. I told her I had found the contessa's name in Father Antonio's papers, and that's when she got unpleasant. She said the contessa had never spoken to Father Antonio. They were very sorry about his unfortunate death—'unfortunate,' that's what she called it, the bitch."

"Now, Lucy—"

She held her hand up to stop him.

"She said none of it had anything to do with the contessa or her family and they refused to be dragged into that unpleasantness. And that's when she closed the door. Firmly. In my face. And locked it."

The professor sighed. "And then . . . ?"

"Then? Then I wanted to kick my way into the house and grab the contessa by her scrawny neck—don't bother to ask, I'm certain her neck is scrawny—and make her tell me where that painting came from."

"Lucy, my love. You would seem to be a woman of action."

"But I didn't."

"As evidenced by the fact that you're not in jail. One doesn't choke contessas. I'm not Italian, but I'm fairly certain that is a reasonable assumption."

There was a moment of silence. Professor Richman was out of bed today, sitting in a large armchair in a patch of sunlight that provided a little warmth in the wintry chill of the ancient stone building. Even the owner's suite didn't have very much in the way of modern improvements. Richman was wrapped in a robe with the family crest of the *conte*, who was apparently still happy—or at least willing—to give up his rooms to the convalescent.

"So," he said at last, "we don't seem to be getting anywhere."

"Just like the carabinieri." She handed him the day's paper. "There's a story on page twenty-something. Nothing new. Nothing at all, really. They're still 'investigating.' No new clues about the murders or what happened to the painting. Some worthless theories. And a couple of cheap shots about the 'fake.'"

He glanced at the paper and set it aside.

"No one's getting anywhere."

After a moment, she broke the silence. "I'm going to Rome. With Moto."

"Rome? Why Rome?"

"To actually look at Caravaggios. And, yes, I said his name. I'm not playing that 'Michele' game anymore. He was a genius, cursed or not, and I'll gladly be part of his story. And right now I need to stand in front of one of his paintings to be sure I'm right."

"I thought you were already sure."

"I'm sure what I felt when I was alone with that painting."

"Not alone. I was—"

"You weren't much company."

"Thank you for your kindness."

"As someone once said, precision is absolutely vital."

A moment of silence. Call it a draw. Lucia went on.

"I know what I felt that night, but now I need to spend time with a real Caravaggio and see if I feel the same thing."

"And if you do?"

"Then I'll be cheerfully willing to go back and choke some truth out of that contessa."

"Sounds like an excellent plan. But that car of yours won't make it to Rome."

There was no question about that, even though her car had, in fact, remained blessedly and amazingly free of parking tickets, just as Vittore—her *umile servitore*—had promised. Another mystery, but she was more than content to leave the depths of that one unplumbed.

She laughed. "We're taking the train."

Lucia hadn't told the professor the entire truth about why she wanted to go to Rome. She certainly did want to stand face-to-face with some of the city's Caravaggios. But she also wanted to see the warehouse where they had been held captive, where she had spent the night with the painting, where she had nearly died. She hadn't mentioned that to Professor Richman. He wouldn't have approved. Researching the painting was one thing. Chasing after the murder and mayhem that had swept them up was another.

Yet another one of Moto's seemingly endless supply of cousins was a Rome cop—*uno sbirro*—and had told him where the warehouse was. But when they got there, the entire block was closed off by police barricades. They were told by a guard that a building had been seriously damaged by an explosion as "part of a heroic police action." Lucia knew better. It wasn't the police who had blown out the wall of that warehouse and rescued her and the professor—and it certainly wasn't the police who had taken her home, put her to bed, folded her clothes neatly, and locked her safely in her apartment.

But that didn't matter. The area was closed—and even a call to Moto's helpful cousin couldn't get them past the barricades.

Things got worse yet that afternoon, when they finally stood in front of the three Caravaggio paintings in the church of San Luigi dei Francesi. They had walked past a row of side chapels that were dark, filled with paintings that were ignored, the same way Caravaggio's paintings had been ignored for centuries. But the Contarelli Chapel, where the Caravaggios hung, was flooded with light and mobbed with tourists. Even now in midwinter, Caravaggio was an irresistible draw. Guides lectured. Cameras clicked. The impatient elbowed their way to the front of the crowd, looked, shrugged, and moved on.

Lucia was crushed. It was hopeless. She dragged Moto out of the church into the cold. The stone buildings and cobblestone streets that reflected the heat and turned the city into an oven in the summer now hoarded the biting cold and damp. Lucia shivered and pulled her jacket tighter.

"I'm an idiot. I should have known it'd be mobbed." She stopped, looked around. "Let's go home." She'd had enough. "There's an afternoon train."

But Moto had a better idea.

"I can handle this," he said.

Lucia shifted uncomfortably on a cold marble bench in the Piazza Navona, home, even in winter, to a few desperate jugglers and clowns and artistic panhandlers. A freezing wind funneled through the narrow Via Agonale, and a would-be troubadour in a down jacket and knit cap gave up on his guitar, stuffed his cold hands in his pockets, and sang on, unaccompanied and off-key.

Moto had left her there with assurances he'd be right back. She'd tried warming herself with a bag of roasted chestnuts from a sidewalk vendor, but the warmth hadn't spread, and now the chestnuts lay in an uneasy lump in her stomach. As the last of the afternoon light drained out of the sky, Lucia surrendered to the cold and moved inside one of the cafés on the piazza whose winter prices still reflected their privileged summer position.

The chill and the dark and the overpriced espresso suited her mood. She idly considered taking a taxi to Fiumicino Airport and flying back to the States—or better yet, somewhere warm. She had her passport, her wallet, and clean underwear in her day pack. There was nothing in her apartment in Monte Piccolo that she cared much about. She could be gone. Just like that. She could escape the cold and the feeling of failure and the despair of seeing Te-Te lying dead in a spreading pool of blood. She thought about lying on a beach in the sun and just enjoying where she was. For once in her life. Instead of always searching for something or someone—or worse, drowning in the feeling that she ought to be searching, if only she knew what she was supposed to be searching for. She'd had enough boyfriends and lovers to know that neither love nor sex was the answer to that urge.

And that thought pulled her mind back to Te-Te and a question that continued to puzzle her. Why did she feel so deeply about a man she had barely known so many years ago? The horror of his death had been shattering. But even before that, in the short time they had spent at his chapel and orphanage, something deep had pulled her toward him, and she couldn't understand what it was. She remembered so little from those years. When she searched her mind for memories from that village in Sicily where she knew she'd been born, there was nothing but fog. She couldn't remember her mother or her father, no matter how hard she tried. And she did try. Desperately. But there was only the fog, and the harder she tried, the thicker it got. When she tried to focus on her parents' faces, the fog would close in completely, leaving her lost and alone. But if she looked sideways into her memory, occasional small details would come back to her. A sunny moment on a dirt street. A scrap of cloth. A laugh. And now Te-Te suddenly seemed to matter. But why? She pictured his face. Those scars. She had to—

"*Ciao, tesoro.*"

Moto was there beside her table, breaking in on her misery, smiling with pleasure.

"Everything's under control. Let's get out of this *trappola turistica* and find someplace decent for dinner. We have a few hours to kill and I want to stay warm."

Those few hours were more than a few.

They had a decent dinner and a cheap bottle of wine, then walked a block to a bar where they settled into a dark corner. Moto refused to offer even a hint of what he had planned, and Lucia found herself falling back into her fantasy of racing to the airport and flying someplace with palm trees and warm beaches.

Finally, long after midnight, he ordered *due caffè doppi*—two double espressos—one for each of them, and when they were finished, he led the way out into the dark, cold streets.

It was a short walk back to the Chiesa di San Luigi, but it was a very different world now with a few harsh lights and endless deep shadows.

A sullen priest was waiting outside and, without a word and certainly without a smile, he took them down a dark passageway beside the church, through a side door, and into a maze of corridors, and finally they were standing face-to-face with three of Caravaggio's early masterpieces: *The Calling of St. Matthew, The Inspiration of St. Matthew,* and

The Martyrdom of St. Matthew. Together they gave the arc of a religious life: from redeemed sinner to slaughtered saint. But it was the last of the three, the martyrdom—the murder of the saint—that held Lucia's attention.

They stood for a moment in silence. The church was as cold and dark as the expression on the face of the priest.

"No lights," he grumbled.

"I don't want light," Lucia whispered. The priest swiveled his head and looked at her, perhaps for the first time. "I can see the painting during the day. I need the quiet and the dark to feel the presence of the saint." That was true—she didn't add that she needed to feel the presence of the executioner as well as the saint, and all the figures screaming and fleeing in horror, including Caravaggio, who had painted himself into the crowd, fleeing with the rest, even as he looked back in pity and regret.

The priest nodded. His voice warmed, if only a little. "How long do you need?"

"Not very—" Moto started.

"At least an hour." Lucia was firm.

"I will return." And he was gone.

Lucia stood in the dark and felt the murder swirl around her. Even in the deep shadows, the muscular body of the executioner glowed with life and energy and sacred death—the same way the figure of Judas had boiled off the canvas during her long night in that storeroom. In both paintings, the light seemed to focus on the messengers of brutal death. Sacred and reviled.

Now, in the dark, the painting had clarity and focus that were missing during the day, when visitors were eager to feed coins into the meter that flooded the chapel with spotlights. It was meant to be seen in the dark, she thought. There were no floodlights in Caravaggio's day. His shadows blended with the shadows of the darkened chapel, and the scene of horror emerged from the dark.

Moto tried to talk to her several times, but she hushed him. She needed the silence as well as the dark, to feel the painting hum with life.

She lost track of time. The hour she had demanded might have passed, it might not, when the silence was shattered by a shout, footsteps sprinting in the dark, a crash, the sound of someone falling heavily. Then silence again, except for heavy breathing. There was a moment when she wasn't certain if the painting hadn't come to life, if those fleeing footsteps were the terror-stricken crowd racing away from the scene of the crime.

"Cazzo!" Fuck!

No, it was Moto.

She turned away from the martyrdom reluctantly. Moto was limping toward her in the darkness.

"What happened?"

"I don't know. I was back over there"—he waved a barely visible hand—"where it's really dark. And someone came bursting out—from behind a column, I guess. Almost knocked me over. I was chasing him, until I ran into that goddamn pew."

"Watch your language, boy." The priest materialized out of the darkness, as if he, too, had been watching them the entire time. "You will be leaving now. Both of you."

"What was he doing here?" Moto snapped at the priest.

"Who?" The priest sounded unperturbed.

"The son of a whore who was spying on us."

"Get out!"

The priest grabbed Lucia's arm, but she wrenched it away from him. Still, she followed as he marched them back through the maze of corridors and out a side door that slammed shut and locked behind them.

They stood alone in a dark space. A trap? Walls closed in around them, and far above, a slice of hazy sky reflected the lights of the city. But after the dark of the church, her eyes adjusted quickly, and she could make out a faint light in the surrounding darkness, which led her around a corner to a narrow alley running along the side of the church.

There was only one way out. To her left, the alley was blocked by a tall building. She grabbed Moto's arm, and they hurried the other way down the dank alley, stinking of ancient crimes. But who might be hiding there in the dark, before they reached the street? Who had been watching them in the church? Trying to pick her way across the greasy cobblestones, Lucia couldn't block the memory of the squeals of terror and death she had heard in the dark of the storeroom—or the sound of the axe splintering the wooden door. That had happened here. In Rome. Would it happen again? She fought to control her breathing and concentrated on keeping her footing. This was no time to slip and fall.

The other end of the alley was blocked by a wall. Lucia stopped, closed her eyes, even in the dark, to think. They had come in this way, following the sullen priest. There had been a small door set in this wall. Where was it? She ran her hands over the wood. Where was that door? Yes! Here! Her hands found the metal of a latch, and, forcing herself to slow down, she opened the door carefully.

Right outside, a patch of shadow resolved into a cowled figure, a monk. Next to her, Moto hiccupped in terror and she dug her fingers deep into his arm, half dragging him with her.

Deep breath. The monk took a step toward them, moving into a pool of light. She got a glimpse of his face as they hurried past—hard eyes above hollow cheeks deep within the cowl.

For an instant Lucia's mind was filled with a sense that there was something about that monk—not the menace in his eyes or the black of his robes. Something else. Something wrong. Something—

"Run!" Moto's hard whisper jerked her away from her thoughts, even as he yanked his arm free of her grip and started to sprint down the street. Caught by surprise, Lucia started to run too—and without knowing why they were running or where they were going, she raced after Moto into the night.

They turned a corner, then another. They dashed across a tiny piazza. She thought she heard footsteps behind them. Someone chasing them. Then she heard a rattle, a clatter, metal on metal, and the sound of breaking glass. A shout of pain. And then she could only hear her own ragged breath as she chased after Moto.

He ran for blocks, twisting and turning into one narrow alley, then another. Lucia lost all sense of direction, where they were or where they were heading, until finally Moto lurched into a doorway where they pressed themselves back into the darkness, gasping for breath.

She tried to speak, but he pressed a finger across her lips. After another few moments, he whispered into her ear, his breath still ragged.

"Gun! He had a gun."

"What?"

"A man in the piazza. Across from the church. Some kind of, I don't know, machine gun."

"The monk?" Now that they had stopped running, her mind went back to that dark monk, trying to untangle what she had sensed that was wrong about him.

"Not him. Across the street."

She tried to remember that instant when they'd stumbled out of the alley into the light of the piazza—dim light, but brighter than the alley—was there a man there? Across the street?

She burst out laughing.

Moto clapped a hand over her mouth, and she fought to control her laughter. Finally, with a deep breath, she calmed down, leaned her head next to Moto's, and whispered in his ear.

"That was a military guard. The Italian senate is in Palazzo Madama, right next to the church. We just ran away from the safest place in Rome."

"Sorry. Saw the gun and . . ." Moto shrugged in apology.

They stood quietly in the darkened doorway while their heartbeats slowed.

Then she realized what had been wrong about that monk. Such a small thing. But on his dark robes, there was a red cross—not a normal cross. Something different. Hard to get it clear in her memory, but it had been there. Blood-red on the black robes.

And now she peered out of the doorway into the darkened street. Looking to see if there was a dark-robed figure with a blood-red cross waiting for them.

No. She put that image away and stepped out into the narrow street.

"Where are we?" She refused to whisper.

Moto shrugged.

She looked up at the sign over the door where they had taken shelter and almost burst out laughing again.

"Al Duello."

"What?"

"Ristorante Al Duello. Caravaggio's duel. When he killed Ranuccio." That killing had sent Caravaggio running for his life, under sentence of death, fleeing Rome and beginning the years on the run that would end with his own death at just thirty-eight.

"*Basta!* No more talk of killing."

Lucia couldn't argue with that, and she peered carefully into the dark as they headed into the Roman night, watching to see if a blood-red cross would appear, floating against the black of a monk's habit—with hard eyes above, glittering in the dark of the cowl.

The rising sun, battered by the suburban clutter of buildings and power poles, bridges and tunnels, flickered at the edge of Lucia's vision as the train rattled north from Rome. She had tried to catch an hour's sleep on a hard bench at Termini station in Rome, but she kept waking in a panic as dark visions—hooded figures, glittering knives, blinding explosions—shattered her dreams.

Now, with a vile *caffè doppio* churning in her stomach and the sun in her eyes, sleep was out of the question, and she was trying to get Moto to explain exactly how he had arranged their late-night visit to San Luigi dei Francesi.

Moto, just as tired as she was, tried to rally and shrug off her questions with his cocky smile, a raised eyebrow, and a shrug. But—and maybe it was the wretched espresso—Lucia wasn't going to settle for that. She insisted and Moto's smile faltered. He looked down and hunched his shoulders.

"My father . . . Friends of my . . . my family. My f—" He looked down again. He was done. His too-eager smile was gone. His liquid eyes were moist.

Lucia let it go at that.

Family. That was going to be all the answer she got.

As the silence stretched out and the sun rose higher, she realized she knew nothing about his family.

And that was fair enough. He knew nothing about hers.

There was nothing secret about Lucia's family, nothing she couldn't talk about—but nothing she wanted to talk about either.

The first few years in Sicily were lost in the fog. The life she remembered started with her waking up one morning in America. In an American house. In a place called Long Island. Where nobody spoke her language. She had been sent there to be raised by her *nonna* and *nonno*—her grandmother and grandfather. She was never told why. She had asked over and over why she had been sent away, why she couldn't go home, where her *mamma* and *papà* were, but the faces of her grandparents had slammed shut. That would not be discussed. So she was left on her own to realize that her parents simply didn't want her.

She might have been five.

At first, her *nonna* and *nonno* were the only ones who spoke the same language she did. And they didn't have anything to say to her. The American house was their house, but America wasn't their country. They hated living in America. And she hated living in their American house.

Then her *nonno* died and she was raised by her *nonna*. And that was even worse. She had to be an American girl at school and a Sicilian granddaughter at home, in a house so filled with her *nonna*'s bitterness and rage that there was scarcely room to breathe. And certainly no room to talk, no room to ask why it had to be like this.

When she was still very young, she would wake up night after night screaming in terror from nightmares she could never remember. She would sit up in her bed, crying desperately. But no one would come to comfort her.

There was only Nonna. And there was no comfort there.

And why would she tell anyone about any of that?

It was over. Long past. Nothing to tell. Only things to forget.

She had gone to college close to the house on Long Island—there was no money to go anywhere else—in hopes of escaping, but by the time she graduated, her *nonna* was dying. The doctors called it cancer, but Lucia knew it was the rage that was killing her. So Lucia had to stay in that house and nurse the woman she hated through the final years of her terrible life. No matter how she felt about her *nonna*, Lucia was Sicilian enough to know that family is family and some obligations cannot be ignored. And she never let herself wonder if there was any family that would ever feel any obligation to her—or if obligations only ran one way.

And in the last year, the last months—maybe it was the drugs the hospice nurse gave her—Nonna had begun to talk. She would never answer questions. It was as if she didn't hear when Lucia asked about her mother and father. Her personal rules of *omertà*—the Sicilian code of silence—sealed her lips, even within her own family. Despite her insistence that family came first, before and beyond anything else.

But even though she didn't answer questions, she rambled, spinning out stories of a land torn by violence, where murder, if never casual, was ever-present, in senseless wars between Mafia families who fought for control of even the tiniest villages.

Kill when it is necessary. Don't question what you are told to do. That was the lesson Nonna offered her granddaughter.

And for Nonna, that was the way it was supposed to be. It wasn't a horror story of bloodshed, it was the way of life. You were loyal to your family above all. To your village and your neighbors, perhaps, because they were a kind of family, but higher loyalties took precedence. And sometimes neighbors must be killed if the family demanded it.

At times, in her rambling, it seemed as if Nonna was telling her own story, how she and her beloved husband, Salvatore, had been forced to flee their village, carried to this hateful America on a wave of blood.

And sometimes Lucia thought, *This is* my *story. My parents sent me here to protect me, to save me. But from what?*

Her questions were never answered. And in the end, Nonna's stubborn silence of *omertà* was replaced by the implacable silence of the grave.

And so silence was all Lucia was left with, where she should have had family. Silence and a fog that filled the place where her memories should have been—a fog that became deeper the harder she tried to see. A fog that shifted from gray to black. The blackness of the dreams that still wakened her from time to time, dreams of being helpless, of being dragged, jolting through the dark, the sound of breath rasping in someone's throat. Someone else's ragged breath, not hers.

Just that.

And why would any of that be something for Lucia to talk about to her friends?

After her *nonna's* eventual welcome death, Lucia had moved on to life in New York, jobs and boyfriends, more school.

And—at last—no family at all. No secrets to tell.

The train lurched. Moto, who had fallen asleep, slumped against her and sighed without waking. His mouth was open and he was drooling. Just a little.

She smiled. He was so handsome. She thought of the neighbors' dog on Long Island. A magnificent boxer, strong, almost heroically handsome, who constantly had long strands of drool hanging from his noble mouth. He was a dog, what did he care?

She wondered if that was the secret of Moto's family: he was part boxer.

She pictured the father he apparently couldn't speak of, sitting at the dinner table, burying his snout in a bowl of Kibbles 'n Bits, and she almost laughed out loud.

∾

Moto sat bolt upright, yanked out of an uneasy sleep by a vicious slap across the face.

His hand clutching his cheek, he looked around wildly for his attacker, but he already knew better. He knew that slap. So he wasn't surprised to find himself sitting alone in the train while everyone else in the car was doing what people do on trains—minding their own business.

He knew who had hit him. It was years ago, and the dream, more real than simple memory, was one he knew too well. And even now, awake, he was still haunted by the dream, and he could see his father's face, washed with fury and shame, blurred for an instant by his hand, lashing out, obliterating the room with that savage slap. And over his father's shoulder, through the pain, he could still see, always see, the slender figure of the man who had been sharing Moto's bed, grabbing his clothes and disappearing.

"You bring this trash into our house. Your mother's house."

"He isn't tr—" Where he had found the courage to even try to contradict his father was beyond Moto's comprehension. But he had loved that man who was now gone from his life forever.

Another slap, perhaps more savage than the first.

"Trash! I say trash. That's what he is."

His father's face had been red with rage, but now the color had faded to a harsh white. And Moto couldn't tell whether the emotion that tinged the anger was shame or sorrow. His father spoke, teeth clenched. His voice soft, pausing, not from emotion but as if to confirm to himself that this was what he was saying.

"I thought . . . I had . . . a son."

Asleep or awake, those words still echoed in Moto's mind every day.

Now, sitting alone in the train, he managed not to cry. He had learned long ago that tears didn't help. Nothing helped.

And as he stared at that bleak landscape, Lucia, filled with good cheer, collapsed dramatically into the seat next to him.

"If someone doesn't clean that toilet, I'm going to pull the emergency brake and—" She stopped when she saw his face. "What's wrong?"

He shook his head slightly. "Nothing." A shrug. "Just a bad dream."

Then, before she could ask anything else, Moto's phone rang.

"Cosa?" What?

He listened, his free hand gesturing to keep the conversation going.

"Sì . . . sì . . . sì . . . ma . . . Madonna! . . . Terrore!" Then he ended the call.

He thought for a moment, then turned to Lucia. His face was somber, but his first words didn't match the expression.

"We went to see the wrong Caravaggio."

"What?"

"My friend—*il poliziotto*—couldn't get us past the barricades to see that warehouse, but he just told me a few new details about what happened there."

"And . . . ?"

"We should have gone to see *The Crucifixion of St. Peter* in Santa Maria del Popolo."

"What is that supposed to mean?"

"When the police broke into the warehouse, they shot two armed men dressed as monks—"

"With a red cross on their robes?"

"He didn't mention that. He was busy telling me the rest of it."

"Which was . . . ?"

"The men they shot weren't the kidnappers. The ones who kidnapped you were already dead."

"From what we heard through the door, I figured that."

"One of them was crucified—"

"God!"

"—upside down."

"Like Peter."

"Exactly. And the other one . . ." He paused.

"Go on."

"Was beheaded."

"Shit."

Chapter 10

Roma
1602

Amor vincit omnia, a painting of Cecco as a joyous, beguiling cupid, was one of the prizes of Vincenzo Giustiniani's art collection. Giustiniani, a close friend of Cardinal del Monte and a patron of the arts, adored Caravaggio's work.

The naked prepubescent Cecco, flaunting brown-tinged wings and a playful smile, enchanted everyone who saw the painting.

Vincenzo Giustiniani's brother, Cardinal Benedetto Giustiniani, envied the magnificent work. He contracted Giovanni Baglione, one of Roma's most successful artists, to paint something similar.

For Caravaggio, this was a gross insult. He and Baglione were fierce rivals. No two artists hated each other more. But to the nobility, artists' spats were merely amusing anecdotes, not to be taken seriously.

"I will gladly take this commission," said Baglione, bowing to the cardinal. That bow concealed the sly smile on his face.

"I have a perfect image in mind," said the artist. "I'm sure Your Excellency will be most pleased."

When the canvas—titled *Love Conquers All*—was finished, Benedetto Giustiniani reacted with unbridled enthusiasm. He awarded Giovanni Baglione a solid gold chain as well as a generous commission.

The artists' world of Campo Marzio held its breath, waiting for Caravaggio's reaction.

Orazio Gentileschi stormed into Caravaggio's house without knocking. Caravaggio looked up from his makeshift table, where he was sucking on a chicken bone.

"Giovanni Baglione!" said Gentileschi. "*Cazzo!* The prick! First he copies my style, my angel Saint Michael . . . and now you! Have you seen his latest?"

"Don't speak to me about that cocksucker," said Caravaggio, wiping his greasy fingers on his tunic. "Half the painters in Roma imitate my work . . . you included."

"I do so in homage, *amico mio*. You are a genius," said Orazio. "Baglione is no friend. He steals every idea, every technique, makes a mess of it, gains commissions, and laughs behind his hand. The cardinals—even the pope!—love him."

"The pope doesn't know art from a wart on his ass," said Caravaggio. "As to copying my art . . . I forgive you, Orazio. I'd rather see you emulate me and improve your paintings than to propagate bad art."

Gentileschi grimaced. "Bad art. Like Baglione?"

"Like Baglione. *Certo.*"

Gentileschi chose to ignore the insult.

"You haven't seen his latest—Cardinal Benedetto commissioned a canvas to compete with your *Love Conquers All*."

"The cardinale has always coveted that piece," said Caravaggio. "I think he fell in love with Cecco's naked body. I know about the commission. I saw—"

"He has stuck his finger in your eye," said Orazio, gesticulating wildly. "You will be outraged!"

"I've seen it," said Caravaggio, shrugging. "It's a complete hash. With the devil turned away, only his badly painted back visible."

Orazio stopped and shook his head adamantly. "No, Michele. Not that one. He has painted a new version for Cardinal Giustiniani.

Only this time the devil *shows* his damned face . . . and it is *you*, Caravaggio."

"Me?"

"He has painted you, Michele, as the devil. You lying with a young boy."

"The bastard!" roared Caravaggio. "Take me to see it at once."

"It is at Cardinal Benedetto's home already. We'd have to be invited."

"I will visit his brother immediately and demand a viewing. There will be a price to pay for this!"

Vincenzo Giustiniani and his brother, Cardinal Benedetto, stared at Caravaggio as Caravaggio stared at the painting, his body trembling, his hands clenching and unclenching.

It was bad enough that the painting copied Gentileschi's angel Saint Michael in both technique and composition, as the angel rescued a young boy from Satan's lustful grasp. But worse—as Gentileschi had reported—Satan's red, leering face was a portrait of Caravaggio.

Ropy sinews tented Caravaggio's neck, and a blue vein throbbed in the center of his brow.

"You do not like it," said the cardinal. "*Ho capito.* I understand. But you must admire—"

"It is shit!" said Caravaggio. "Complete and utter *merda*!"

"Come, come, Maestro." The cardinal chuckled. "You and Baglione have your artistic differences, all Roma knows—"

"You call that *bastardo* an artist?" demanded Caravaggio. "Do you?"

The cardinal was taken aback, staring in amazement at the artist's fury. He was not accustomed to being spoken to in such a fashion—and certainly not by a man of such a low class.

"Come, Michele!" admonished Vincenzo Giustiniani, Caravaggio's patron. "Some tact, *per favore. Tu non hai peli sulla lingua.*" *You have a sharp tongue.*

"Baglione has no talent!" said Caravaggio. "You, Cardinal Giustiniani. You truly think he is admirable?"

"*Sì*, Maestro Caravaggio. And he is of a noble family. I'm quite pleased with this painting. I think I have quite a prize . . . plus a portrait of you in the bargain."

"And they say you gave this fraud—this imposter of an artist!—a gold chain," spat Caravaggio in reply. "You bought his abortion of a painting, depicting me as Satan? And rewarded him?"

The cardinal straightened his back in indignation.

"Michele, *amico mio*," said Vincenzo Giustiniani, taking the artist gently by the elbow. "May I remind you that my brother, the good cardinale—"

"To hell with him, Vincenzo!" said Caravaggio, shaking off Giustiniani's hand. "Look at that disaster! Are both of you blind?"

"I think you had better go now, Maestro Caravaggio," said the cardinal. "You are no longer welcomed as my guest until you can observe civility."

"Giovanni Baglione! This cunt of a—"

"Rafaello!" said Cardinal Giustiniani to his attendant. "Please see Maestro Caravaggio out. *Subito!*"

At once!

"What are we going to do?" ranted Orazio Gentileschi, talking above the roar of Osteria del Turchetto. "All Roma is talking about Baglione's painting. He as good as spat in your face. And that gold chain cost over two hundred scudi—"

"Don't remind me!" said Caravaggio, tossing down his wine. He thumped the earthen jug on the table for the waiter to bring more.

"Look how he flaunts his commissions. One after another," said Mario Minniti. "Aside from that flunkey Tommaso Salini, every artist in Roma loathes him."

"Shut up, all of you!" snapped Onorio Longhi, looking up from the rim of his wine cup. "I didn't come out tonight to listen to artists gripe. If you don't like what he's done—get even."

Caravaggio looked up, focusing his drunken eyes on his architect friend. "What do you mean?"

"Challenge him to a duel. You wear that sword on your side, Caravaggio. Use it!"

Mario snapped to attention, cuffing Onorio on the arm. "Onorio! Don't encourage him! You'll get him killed."

Caravaggio looked from Mario to Onorio. "By God, I will!" He tried to fill his cup. But the pitcher was empty. "Waiter, you cuckold," he said. "Bring more wine! *Subito!*"

The next day, an hour before sunset, Caravaggio waited on the Via del Corso, where he knew Giovanni Baglione would pass on his way home from his studio. Caravaggio stood for more than an hour in the fading light, his sword by his side.

"Go down the *via*, Cecco," he said. "He has to come soon."

"But Maestro," said the boy, "maybe he's stopped to take a drink in a tavern somewhere. Or he needs to discuss a commission—"

Caravaggio's hand tightened around the hilt of his sword. "Go! *Va' via!*"

Cecco scrambled away—this was not a moment to stay too close to his master. Or his sword. Along the Via del Corso, he wove around donkey carts piled high with casks of wine, the carriages of the Farnese and the Orsini, the waves of *contadini*, the farmers, making their way out of the city.

Finally, Cecco spied Giovanni Baglione striding along the street. He seemed in a sanguine mood, nodding to the noble passersby. His gold chain glittered in the fading sun.

The bastardo *wears his chain for all Roma to see. It would serve him right for some thief to snatch it from his neck. And strangle him in the process!*

The gleam of Baglione's sword winked from the edge of its sheath.

The apprentice turned and ran to inform his master.

"He's approaching, Maestro," gasped Cecco, out of breath.

"Is he wearing his sword?" asked Caravaggio, standing his ground.

"*Sì,*" Cecco panted.

"*Molto bene!*" Caravaggio stepped forward. "Stay out of the way, but bear witness."

Baglione came into view. He bowed to a cardinal and his entourage.

"Giovanni Baglione!" shouted Caravaggio, drawing his sword. "I challenge you!"

"Michele Merisi," said Baglione, stopping abruptly. The color drained from his face. "*Cosa?*" *What?*

"Are you hard of hearing or merely a coward? Draw your sword, man!"

Baglione looked from Caravaggio's sword to the crowd of onlookers forming. The Farnese carriage, emblazoned with a yellow shield and blue fleur-de-lis, stopped to allow its noble passengers to watch the encounter.

"You know that dueling is expressly forbidden in the city of Roma," said Baglione, his voice loud but shaky. He looked beseechingly at the Farnese carriage. No one came to his defense.

"I know Roma's laws. Now draw your sword," said Caravaggio.

"The penalty is *bando capitale.* Death, Merisi. Death!"

"I do not care," shouted Caravaggio. "Draw your sword, damn you. I have seen the painting in the salon of Cardinal Giustiniani . . . I have seen my face painted on your pathetic Satan. Now you shall pay for your insult."

Baglione felt the press of bystanders close in. He knew he could disappear into the crowd if Caravaggio approached. He caught a glimpse of the poet Giambattista Marino jostling to get a good vantage point.

If Marino sees me lose face, he will write verse and praise Caravaggio throughout Roma, thought Baglione. *I shall be the laughingstock of the city!*

Baglione swallowed. He gathered his wits and confidence, bolstered by the crowd in the Via del Corso. The color returned to his face.

"Quite the likeness, isn't it," said Baglione, raising his voice in a taunt. "You look the part with Satan's horns. Everyone knows you are a pederast!"

"Draw!" shouted Caravaggio.

"No," said Baglione. *"Sbirri!"*

"Make way for the papal guard!" shouted a voice down the *corso*.

The crowd hissed, disappointed that they'd be deprived of a duel.

"Codardo!" shouted voices. *Coward!*

"Where are your balls, man?"

"Defend your honor! Draw your sword!"

Baglione blew out a deep breath, his eyes seeking out Giambattista Marino.

I can't let that poet see me in this light! Mala fama . . .

Baglione swallowed hard. He fingered the gold chain around his neck, facing Caravaggio. "No! I shan't draw my sword, Merisi. I am a gentleman from a noble family. *Nobili*, do you hear me? I will not stoop to engage my sword with a petty commoner. And certainly not in the streets of Roma."

"Draw, you coward!" screamed Caravaggio, shaking with rage.

Caravaggio saw one of the papal guards running toward him.

"Drop your sword, Merisi!" shouted the guard.

Caravaggio shook his head adamantly.

"You might as well do as he says. I refuse to raise my sword against the likes of you," said Baglione. His fingers toyed furiously with his gold chain. "A pauper from the north, from peasant stock. You do not even have the right to carry a sword, you swine."

"Sheathe your sword this minute!" shouted another *sbirro*, approaching fast. "Before we drag you back to Sant'Angelo prison."

"You dirty bastard coward," shouted Caravaggio. "Baglione! You hear—"

"Leave this place, Merisi. Now!" Two more *sbirri* moved in behind him.

Red-faced and shaking, Caravaggio sheathed his sword and stalked away. He turned up a side street, disappearing into its shadow.

⌘

Caravaggio, Longhi, Gentileschi, and Minniti huddled over a parchment in Longhi's house. The bronze inkwell lay open on the table, two sharpened quills at the ready.

"You have the best handwriting, Longhi," said Caravaggio. "You and your poems. You write."

"I'm the creative genius at words here," said Longhi, tipping back a goblet of wine. "I'm no scribe. Besides, readers will recognize my handwriting." He gestured to Gentileschi. "You do it, Orazio."

Gentileschi grunted, picking up the quill. "I'll write, but don't flatter yourself, architect. Creative genius, my ass. You draw buildings and stick figures."

Longhi poured his guests more wine. "The hell with you. I paint as well as any of you lowlifes. And build the glorious buildings of Roma."

"And I have no literary ambition whatsoever," said Mario Minniti. "Drink up, my friends," he added, raising his goblet. "We've got to be good and drunk to reach down low enough for words to describe Giovanni Baglione. There is no painter in Roma as pompous."

"And as bad," said Caravaggio. *"O così cattivo!"*

"Do you think they will recognize my handwriting?" said Gentileschi.

"Disguise it. All anyone knows is your signature on your paintings," said Caravaggio.

"Then you should write it, Michele. You never sign your work."

"Shut up, Orazio. You've got the quill. Now use it."

"Quiet, all of you! I feel inspiration warming my heart, my throat," said Longhi, slamming down his goblet, wine slopping over the brim.

He stood and began to recite.

> *Gioan Bagaglia, tu non sa un ah*
> *Le tue pitture sono pituresse*
> *Volo vedere con esse*
> *Che non guardarnarai*
> *Mai una patacca.*

"Slow down," complained Gentileschi. "I can't write that fast."

"Drink more wine, Longhi," said Mario, brandishing the pitcher. "It will slow you down. And feed the muse."

Longhi took a long swig of wine, drops spilling down his chin.

"*Bene, bene*, Mario. You are a true Bacchus. Here come the next lines," said Longhi, wiping the wine from his lips.

> *Che di cotanto panno*
> *Di farti un paro di bragesse*
> *Che ad ognun monsterai*
> *Quel fa la cacca*

"*Eccellente!*" cried Caravaggio, clapping. His eyes shining, his teeth berry red with wine. "Let me have a go. I've got the muse singing in my throat. I'll set her free or she'll strangle me!"

"*Avanti,*" said Gentileschi, hunched over the parchment, quill at the ready.

> *Portala adunque*
> *Il tuoi disegni e cartone*

Che tu hai fatto a Andrea pizzicarolo
O veramente forbete ne il culo

"*Bravo*, Michele, *bravo*! Now let's write something that takes on his assistant, that go-between asshole, Mao," said Gentileschi.

"Tommaso Salini? I hate that fucker!" said Mario. "Shittiest painter in Roma."

"I've got it!" Caravaggio cleared his throat, thick with drink.

O alla moglie di Mao tu regali la potta
Che libelli con quell tu cazzon da mulo più non
la fotte
Perdonami dipintore se non ti adulo
Che della collana che tu porti indegno sei
E della pittura vituperio.

Longhi and Caravaggio sat back, satisfied smiles spreading across their drunken faces. Mario gave a low whistle of appreciation.

"Read it to us, Orazio. Let's see how it sounds," said Longhi.

"'Johnny Testicle, you haven't a clue that your paintings are woman's work,'" began Gentileschi. "Not insulting enough, Longhi! My little Artemisia could paint better at age six than Baglione can now."

"Continue," growled Caravaggio. "Leave Artemisia out of this."

"*Bene.* But she can, you know." He went on reading. "'I'd like to see you never earn a worthless penny with them—'"

"Too late for that," grumbled Mario. "Baglione's got the best commissions in Roma."

"'Because with as much canvas as it would take to make yourself a pair of baggy trousers, you'll show everyone what shit really is.'"

"A waste of canvas, indeed!" said Caravaggio. "Better used to wipe shit."

"I'll get to that. 'So take your drawings to Andrea the grocer so he can wrap his vegetables in them or plug up Mao's wife's cunt with them

because he doesn't fuck her anymore with that big mule's dick of his.'
Michele—that's tremendous!" said Gentileschi, roaring with laughter.
"It makes a cuckold out of Mao."

"Leave it. I like it," said Caravaggio.

"Let me write the second stanza," said Gentileschi. "He stole my
Saint Michael, for his fucking painting."

"Leave it to me," said Caravaggio. "I'm the one he painted as Satan."

The finished poem began to circulate throughout Roma. It was quoted
in Campo Marzio taverns by loud and raucous voices, fueled by drink
and grudges. Artists who hated Baglione recited the verses by heart,
even sang them at full lung in the streets after midnight. Mario Minniti
and other artist friends of Caravaggio's distributed copies of the poem
from studio to studio. All Roma's artists were eager to get a copy.

"Mao"—Tommaso Salini, who was slandered as the mule-dicked
cuckold—managed to get a copy of the poem from Filippo Trisegni, a
struggling artist, and with the verse in hand, he ran to Baglione.

Giovanni Baglione and Tommaso Salini filed a libel suit with the
governor of Roma, Ferrante Taverna, who had overseen the prosecution
of Beatrice Cenci.

Onorio Longhi left Roma abruptly, but both Caravaggio and
Gentileschi were arrested and imprisoned to face libel charges.

"Typical Longhi," growled Gentileschi. "He knows when to get
out of town."

"Longhi is of a noble house. They'd let him off anyway," said
Caravaggio. "And don't forget. I haven't seen you in a long, long time.
We're not friends, *capisci*? And I think your painting is shit."

Gentileschi frowned and then nodded.

"You're lying, right? To convince the judges?"

Caravaggio smirked. "Am I?"

The suspected authors of the verse were brought up to testify before the governor of Roma.

"You, Orazio Gentileschi, are accused of penning this verse," said the assistant magistrate.

"Impossible," said Gentileschi. "I know how to write but not very correctly."

"Tommaso Salini states that Filippo Trisegni was given the poem by an artist described as a *bardassa*. A catamite."

"I cannot comment on Trisegni's comments. But he has categorically denied Salini's testimony. Obviously Salini is inventing these accusations. I'm a painter, not a writer."

"Answer the question only, defendant," said the governor. "Next witness. Michele Merisi da Caravaggio."

Caravaggio took the stand, his posture stiff, his face composed with disdain for having to waste time away from painting to defend himself.

"State your profession," said the assistant magistrate.

"My profession is painting."

"What do you know of these verses, Maestro Merisi?" asked Alfonso Tomassino.

"I know nothing of them, Your Excellency. I have never heard of them before today."

"That seems quite unlikely," said the governor. "The verses are cited throughout Roma, I'm told."

"Forgive me, sir. I'm quite busy with my painting," said Caravaggio. "I do not have time to listen to gossip. I have many important commissions to execute." He darted a malicious look at Baglione, who was sitting on a bench.

"But you know many painters in Roma, do you not? The artist community is said to be quite close in Campo Marzio."

"I know many painters, some of them *valent'huomini*. I know Gioseffo, Carracci, Zuccaro, Pomarancio, Gentileschi, Prospero,

Giovanni Andrea, Giovanni Baglione, Gismondo and Giorgio Todesco, Tempesta . . . and others."

"These are your friends?"

"No, not all. And not all are good artists or *valent'huomini*."

"*Valent'huomini?* Worthy gentlemen? How do you define that?"

"*Valent'huomini* are those well versed in painting. Those who judge good and bad painters as I judge them. But those who are bad and ignorant painters will judge as 'good painters' those who are every bit as ignorant as they are," said Caravaggio, staring straight at Baglione. "It has nothing to do with social class or noble lineage."

"Surely there is more to a good painter than your definition? Can you elaborate?" asked the assistant magistrate.

"A good painter is one who knows how to paint well and to imitate natural objects well."

"That seems inadequate," said the governor. "I'm familiar with your canvases, Maestro Merisi, and while they are uncannily realistic, they are certainly much more than imitating nature."

Caravaggio shrugged.

"Are you good friends with Orazio Gentileschi?" asked the assistant magistrate.

"We do not speak. I have not spoken to him in perhaps three years. No, we are not friends."

There was a murmur in the courtroom.

"Caravaggio and Gentileschi are best friends," whispered an artist to another.

"Do you think Giovanni Baglione is a good painter?" asked the assistant magistrate.

"I do not know of any painter in Roma who thinks Giovanni Baglione is a good painter," said Caravaggio. "His *Resurrection of Christ*, for example, is a complete bungle."

Baglione's face colored red with indignation. Caravaggio stifled a smile.

"Do you write verse, Caravaggio? Did you write these verses in a vulgar tongue?" asked the governor.

"Your Excellency, no. I don't dabble in verse. My profession is painting, and I take it quite seriously."

"Do you know the whereabouts of Onorio Longhi?" asked the assistant magistrate.

"No," said Caravaggio. "I do not. But he is my friend."

A jangling of keys in the cell lock woke Caravaggio, who was lying on his flea-infested mattress. He crawled to his feet, blinking at the lantern in the guard's hand.

"You are free to go, Maestro," grunted the guard. "You have the right friends in high places. Cardinal del Monte and the Medici is the rumor."

Caravaggio shrugged. He picked a louse off his cuff and squeezed it between his thumb and fingernails.

"What's the chance, then, that the libel suit will be dropped?"

"Good," said the guard, gesturing Caravaggio to come out of the cell. "No one wants trouble with the Medici."

The libel suit was dropped after Caravaggio and Gentileschi both signed apologies to Giovanni Baglione and "Mao" and promised never to insult their honor again.

But what was done was done—and the popular verses about "Johnny Testicle" still resonated in the taverns of Roma, echoing through the dark alleyways and piazzas of Campo Marzio.

Chapter 11

Monte Piccolo

Professor Aristotle Rafael Richman sat in an overstuffed armchair, looking and feeling very pleased with himself. He was still enjoying the owner's suite at the villa and saw no reason why he might need to move back to the more primitive quarters he had been assigned when he arrived for the winter seminar.

"So, Lucy," he said, emphasizing the name for his own amusement, "you've decided to return to us. I was afraid you had disappeared forever into the backstreets of the Eternal City."

"Not this time, Ralphie."

"Excuse me?" Injured dignity. "What did you call me?"

"Oh, well, since you've decided to call me Lucy, I thought I ought to have my own special name for you. 'Professor Richman' is so formal. And 'Aristotle' and 'Rafael' are a bit stodgy. But I thought 'Ralph' was just about perfect. It's almost the same as 'Rafael.' And for friends as close as we are, 'Ralphie' is even better."

"Hoist with my own petard." He managed a smile. "You've been gone three days. I thought this was going to be a quick trip to look at a painting."

"We had a bit of a difficult night in Rome." She told him quickly about their visit to San Luigi dei Francesi, about Moto's unexplained magical ability to get them into the chapel in the middle of the night, about her feelings standing in front of the Caravaggio paintings in the dark, and about the mysterious man who Moto thought was spying on them. There was no mention of a monk with a blood-red cross on his black habit or of a panicked sprint through the dark streets. She still didn't want to tell the professor how deeply she was getting entangled in the events of the past weeks, rather than sticking to past centuries.

"And then," she finished, "we spent two days in Firenze on the way back."

"Looking at Caravaggios in the Uffizi?"

"Well, actually, yes. We went to look at *Medusa* and *The Sacrifice of Isaac*." She didn't mention the new details they'd learned about the deaths in the warehouse or that, having missed Peter's upside-down crucifixion, she thought she had to see the beheaded Medusa and Isaac's near miss, pinned on a rock with a knife at his throat.

She thought for a moment about the Medusa—the severed head, painted on a round shield that a warrior might carry into battle if he didn't mind sacrificing a priceless masterpiece for his personal protection. But the image, terrible to be sure, hadn't moved her. The horror was real enough, but the face was too alive—the mouth open as if to scream, the eyes staring in horror, the snakes writhing on her head, the blood spurting from the severed neck.

She had been more moved by the image of Isaac, pinned against a rock by his father, who held a knife at the boy's throat, ready to sacrifice his son at God's command. Isaac's bewildered terror was real and understandable. It bothered her that she was beginning to understand how he felt.

And then she pushed those thoughts out of her mind and told the professor, just because it was true, "Then we spent a day partying with friends of Moto's."

Professor Richman sniffed. "I hope you and your boyfriend had a good time."

"Boyfriend?"

"What else would you call him?"

"Friend."

"With benefits? Isn't that how you say it these days?"

"Oh dear. Ralphie, my sweet old fool. Moto is gay."

"Oh."

Lucia recognized his uncomfortable expression. Seventy-five-year-old professors might be perfectly willing to accept the idea that gays were an unembarrassed part of society now—but they didn't necessarily know how to react when they learned that someone they knew actually was gay.

Lucia had known Moto was gay almost from the moment she'd met him in a Monte Piccolo bar. Her first reaction had been that he was young, but he was almost absurdly handsome too—and the ugly breakup (*Jason, you son of a bitch,* she thought, automatically) that had been the most immediate reason for her decision to leave New York for an art history seminar abroad had left her open to an Italian affair, just for the hell of it.

And then, in the instant he smiled and said hello—with his too-eager smile and liquid eyes—she knew that friends were all they were ever going to be.

And when Moto turned out very quickly to be perhaps the best friend she had ever had—male or female—that was better than any quick affair. Better than any boyfriend, for that matter. *Especially you, Jason. You son of a bitch.*

But she wasn't going to tell Professor Richman any of that. So she shrugged.

"Don't worry. It's not always easy to tell."

And given Moto's stuttering when he tried to talk about his father on the train coming back from Rome, she thought that maybe he wasn't quite as totally unembarrassed about being gay as some young men might be. Families!

"Well, anyway," said the professor, picking up the thread, "while you were sightseeing and partying, some of us have been hard at work."

"And . . . ?"

"And, sweet Lucy, we will be having tea this week with the Contessa dei Marsi. She of the slammed door and the fortunately unwrung neck." He was clearly enjoying himself. "And we are going to discuss her family's gift of a painting to Father Antonio's church some two hundred years ago."

"Ralphie! How did you manage that?"

He smiled, his enjoyment impervious. "Old-fashioned charm. She's an old-fashioned woman and she appreciates being treated appropriately."

"With your Italian?"

"Charm is a universal language. You should try it sometime." He put his teacup down. "I'm sure you'd be good at it."

∞

The small man slammed his too-large hand onto the desk. The noise was explosive. The man standing across from him did not react at all.

Neither man had spoken a word since the tall man had entered the office. The man behind the desk often opened meetings this way. He nodded and let what could have been a smile stretch his thin lips. His pale-blue eyes refused to become kindly.

"Fra Filippo Lupo. What do you have to report?"

"*Si*, Gran Comandante Pantera! It was not easy, if I may say so, sir. Beyond what has already appeared in the newspapers, there are no additional details in any of the police reports. Even the most secret and closely held ones. Officers who have been useful to us in the past have nothing to add. I did find some who seemed to have additional information, but neither money nor fear could persuade them to reveal what they knew. I believe we are up against a force that inspires more fear than even we can summon."

The small man made an impatient gesture. "I am certain you have not come to report failure, Fra Lupo."

"No sir. I found a weak link. As you have taught me."

A raised eyebrow.

"The children, sir. The orphans. They were more easily . . . persuaded."

A definite smile from the thin lips. "I hope you didn't have to hurt anyone."

"Not badly, sir."

"Continue."

"There were two who visited the orphanage that day. An elderly professor from America and a young woman, *una ragazza italiana*, who seemed to know Father Antonio. They are both enrolled in some sort of seminar at Monte Piccolo. And there is a third person involved. A young man who was not there at the chapel, but who is clearly connected with the other two. But he is"—a dismissive shrug—*"un finocchio. Una checca."*

A stingy, thin-lipped smile from the small man. "A homosexual." He pronounced the word with a certain academic delight. "Another weak link to be sure. If we need one."

"Sir."

The hand slammed the desk again, and this time the tall man did flinch.

"But they are irrelevant! Fools caught up in something far beyond themselves. The painting is what matters. Where is the painting?"

"No one seems to know, sir."

The nostrils of the outsized corvine nose flared. "No one? No one? Someone must know. What you are telling me is that you have not found that person."

"Comandante. The police do not have the painting. I am certain of that. Our most powerful friends admitted it. They would not confess something so embarrassing if it were not true. And although they were not willing to confirm it, they quite certainly have no idea where the painting is or who has it."

There was a long silence. The small man had both hands resting on the desk, the fingers twitching idly, enormous carnivorous insects impatient for their prey.

"We need to know more about the two who were in the warehouse. And their *checca* friend."

"But they are irrelevant, sir. You said so yourself. A girl, a hapless old man, and *un finocchio*. They're no one. They're fools."

"Now you are the fool!"

"But sir, you said—"

And now the hand flashed down toward the desk but stopped at the last instant and rested soundlessly on the wood.

"Don't contradict me! Someone blew a hole in that building to seize the painting and that girl and the old man. If they were really 'no one,' their bodies would have been left in the rubble. Whoever took the painting took them as well."

"Sir."

"Find them. Learn what you can about them. Stay close to them."

"And the *finocchio*?"

"No one cares about *i froci*. He really is irrelevant—except that he is a friend of the other two. Keep a close watch on all of them. Find out who saved them. And why."

"Sir." Fra Filippo Lupo stood, straight and still.

"Our honor, the honor of our order, is at stake. Our sacred mission has endured for a millennium. We cannot be the ones who let it fail. The painting must not escape. The *terroristi musulmani*, the Muslim terrorists, must be defeated."

"And collateral damage?" There was an eagerness in his voice.

"I leave that to your judgment."

"Thank you, sir."

"Wait!" The small man paused and thought for a long minute. Finally, he said, "The girl. *La ragazza*." Another silence. "It must be her."

"Sir?"

"You said the professor is an American. It took us years to find that painting." A sudden deep breath. "Which we lost by waiting. Like fools! If I hadn't—" He stopped himself. "I cannot believe an American could have found that painting so easily or known what it was. And I cannot believe an American could have had friends who would act so swiftly and so efficiently to frustrate us. It cannot be the American. And"—he flicked his hand carelessly, as if he were brushing away flies—"it cannot be the *finocchio*. Watch them all. But the girl is the key."

"Sir."

As the tall man turned to go, the man at the desk called out to stop him.

"You're limping. What happened?"

"Nothing, sir. An accident. Running in the dark. Cobblestones."

"You tripped? Or you *were* tripped?"

The tall man drew himself up to ramrod attention. His dark eyes burned above hollow cheeks.

"It is nothing, sir. It will not happen again."

Lucia blinked and stopped, dazzled by the light. After hours underground in the contessa's archives—musty, wet, cold, she was certain, even in the heat of summer, and almost unbearably frigid now in winter—she had forgotten there was this much light in the world. And even dazzled, she immediately knew she didn't belong: dirty hands, dust in her hair, probably on her face too. Chilled and shivering.

The contessa broke off in midsentence and stared hard at Lucia, her glass of sherry suspended at the ready in case another quick sip was required in the face of this intrusion. From the moment she had greeted them—after the hard-eyed servant had let them into the villa—it was clear that the contessa was in fact far more formidable than Lucia had expected. And there was certainly nothing scrawny about her. She was taller than Lucia, and if she ran a bit to fat and wore too much makeup, she carried her decades well. She might not have been a real beauty, even in her youth, but she certainly still had an abundance of spirit and aristocratic bone structure that made mere prettiness irrelevant.

From time to time, a certain shadowed vagueness flitted through her eyes, as if she were—or wished she were—somewhere else. But she was far from the doddering biddy that Lucia had imagined in her fantasy of neck-wringing.

And right now, there was nothing vague in her gaze. Lucia was clearly intruding on a pleasantly civilized moment between the contessa and the professor.

The professor raised a quizzical eyebrow.

And—dusty, cold, likely smelling of the mildew from the archives, out of place and unwelcome—Lucia didn't care.

"Got it!" She was triumphant.

The professor's quizzical eyebrow turned into a smile, and the contessa downed the rest of her sherry, forced to fortify herself alone. Lucia had his full attention.

"What did you find?" There was eagerness in his voice.

"Judas"—they'd been referring to the painting that way among themselves, and for the moment, she forgot the contessa was even there—"came here in 1759 as part of the dowry for the fourth daughter of Cavaliere d'Estrato of Siena, given by her father when she married the third son of Ranieri dei Marsi."

She stopped to catch her breath and the contessa broke in.

"My many-times-great-uncle. Six generations back, to be exact. A young fool at the time. Famously foolish"—she shrugged—"in our family."

"Yes, well"—Lucia refused to be sidetracked by old family gossip—"the dowry. There's an inventory of the dowry. Not exactly a magnificent dowry, but I suppose fourth daughters had to go cheap."

"To third sons," added the contessa.

"Exactly." The professor wasn't going to be left out.

"It's still a pretty long list. And hard to read." She turned her gaze to the contessa. "You've had a few floods down there. Things are a bit moldy." Before the contessa could react, she pushed on—after a day down there, she needed to say it, but she wasn't going to dwell on it. "But the listing for the painting is clear enough once you find it. It's listed as 'Bacio di G.' Could be, has to be *'Bacio di Giuda'—'Judas Kiss.'* That has to be it. The listing's got the size about right. It even describes the frame pretty well. It's got to be our guy. Here"—she held out her phone—"I took a picture."

While the professor was angling the phone, squinting, trying to get a good look at the photo of blurred and blotched ink on faded parchment, Lucia added, "It gives a painter's name. It's hard to read. I think it's Fenelli. But lots of art got mislabeled back then."

"All nonsense!" The contessa waved her hand dismissively. "A complete fabrication. Not a word of truth."

"It's in *your* archive." Lucia was not about to give up her discovery. And if the old lady wanted to be difficult, Lucia had some leverage. She'd taken a detour through a series of letters from the late 1700s, filled with disturbing details of a virulent case of syphilis that ran wild for generations after it was introduced to the family by an old duke's young wife. She had pictures of those letters on her phone. Historical research.

"Do not presume to instruct me, young lady." The contessa couldn't suppress a delighted growl of a giggle, more dog than debutante. "It's a much better story than that." Leaning forward. "That young ruffian stole it. Antonio dei Marsi stole the painting from his father-in-law. His future father-in-law. He was hunting on the D'Estrato estates with some other young fools, and he saw the painting in a hunting lodge and he thought it would be fun to bring it home. So he did."

"And when the cavaliere found out?" As always, the professor wanted details.

The contessa smirked. "The cavaliere never even noticed. They were a particularly stupid family." She caught Lucia's eye. "That was centuries ago. We're well rid of the taint of that blood by now, my dear. Not a branch of the family that we're particularly proud of. Although they were for many generations quite tightly allied with the Knights of Malta. That is why they adopted the title of cavaliere. Valiant, I suppose, but stupid nonetheless. Yes, well, the young thief, Antonio, simply had the steward write the painting into the inventory. A meager dowry and a mean wife. My many-times-great-aunt was mean as a snake. Famously. In our family."

"So you knew all this," Lucia said. "About the painting. Why didn't you say something before I spent the whole day down there?"

Lucia was ready for her own glass of sherry, but no one was offering to pour one for her.

The contessa smiled and offered a vague shrug.

"I may have forgotten, I suppose. Sometimes everything is clear and sometimes it all just . . . disappears." Her hands were circling gently in the air. "Once there were so many . . . things, so many places. But that was all before our catastrophe. The war." Her gaze went soft. "If that beast Leopold hadn't provoked the Sardinian . . ." She shook her head. "So many things. Now all I have is . . . this." Her gesture swept wider to include the entire room, flooded with light that twisted and dappled through a long sweep of windows, glass slumped with the centuries. Lucia's research had revealed that the contessa owned, in addition to "this," a substantial villa in Rome and another in Fiesole, above Florence. And another somewhere in Piemonte. But this clearly wasn't the appropriate time to mention such details.

Lucia gave the contessa's story a moment of respect—but she still had her discovery. Then: "*Perfetto! Sì!* But it's still the same painting. And it came from the D'Estrato family in Siena. Stolen from the D'Estrato estate."

The professor was delighted. "It's a wonderful story." He poured the contessa another glass of sherry.

"The dowry inventory is all we need," said Lucia. "And I've got a picture of it. So, *grazie*. We're on our way."

The professor hesitated. Then he stood, bowed, and kissed the contessa's hand.

"My dear Agostina," he said as he straightened up. "This has been an unexpected pleasure. Perhaps we shall meet again."

She inclined her head, graciously, and he bowed again.

It seemed to Lucia that he was actually reluctant to leave.

You old goat, she thought, remembering a Watteau painting of a particularly lustful satyr ogling a beautiful nymph. Lucia hid her smile, thinking that the contessa was impressive enough, but even at her best, she was nothing like the Watteau beauty.

Walking to the car, the professor cleared his throat. "Many an important arrangement has been negotiated over sherry. And it got us a grand story, didn't it? Apparently this painting of ours has a long history of being stolen," he said, settling into the front seat. "I don't want you to think I've been wasting my time while you were hard at work. We all have our skills." She saw him glance at her grimy knuckles as she grabbed the steering wheel. "It's just that mine seem to keep my hands clean."

She was tempted to wipe her hands on his nice clean jacket.

"But"—he raised a finger for emphasis—"you made a great discovery."

His jacket was saved.

"And now, dear Lucy?"

"Siena."

Professor Richman smiled.

Chapter 12

Roma
1603

Caravaggio met his patron's gaze. "You wanted to see me?"

"I heard that Galileo gave you some advice a few years ago," said Cardinal del Monte.

"He suggested that I look beyond young boys for my subjects. And I am pursuing more complex compositions now."

"You are painting prostitutes into biblical scenes. Be careful. Your angels and little boys are titillating but innocuous. If you go against the Church—"

"I do not intend to spend the rest of my life painting fluttering angels or prepubescent boys playing the lute, or Cecco displaying his genitalia."

"Pity," said Cardinal del Monte, picking up an orange from a bowl in front of him and starting to peel it with a sharp knife. "You are so good at it. But beware. Popes are dangerous."

"I saw that firsthand with the execution of the Cenci family."

"And I witnessed the execution of Giordano Bruno, the heretic who believed that stars are distant suns," said Del Monte. "A horrifying sight."

"The poor bastard," said Caravaggio.

Del Monte cast a glance about the empty room before he spoke.

"A perfect example of what power the Church wields." He sighed. "I was an official witness as a cardinale. Bruno's only crime was lifting his eyes to the heavens and questioning Church doctrine. A man who believed not only that planets circle the sun, but in an infinite universe. Copernicus indirectly lit the fire of his execution."

"How different is this Dominican priest Bruno from your good friend Galileo Galilei? Will the Inquisition kill him too?"

"Watch what you say, Michele," said the cardinal, "lest you wind up at the stake. You are perceived as a provocateur."

Caravaggio shrugged. *"Nec spe. Nec metu."*

Without hope. Without fear.

Cardinal del Monte shook his head. "With that attitude, you'll meet the same fate as Bruno."

"The same? What have I done but participate in the occasional brawl?"

"Occasional?" Del Monte scoffed. "I seem forever to be intervening on your behalf. How many times have you been arrested now? Ten, twelve times?"

"I thank you for your interventions, Cardinal," said Caravaggio, bowing stiffly. He stared at the perfect spiral peel that descended from Del Monte's knife.

"It is tiring, I must confess," said the cardinal, frowning. "If you were not so talented, I shouldn't bother, Michele. It is your genius I am rescuing. But there will come a day where even I will not have the power to intervene."

"But even if I brawl, I am no heretic."

"The pope and the inquisitors are scrutinizing your paintings. Saints with dirty feet who look like day laborers—blasphemy! Prostitutes baring their cleavage posing as the Holy Mother. Oh, they have noticed, believe me. Why do you think your work has been rejected? The pope is wary—"

"And the pope's nephew Cardinal Scipione Borghese hounds me for more paintings. He eagerly buys any of my canvases that the Church condemns. I suspect him of fomenting dissention in order to purchase my rejected work at a discount."

Cardinal del Monte set down his fruit and held out his hand, his angular fingers spread in appeasement. "Watch what you say about Cardinal Borghese. He is the most powerful among us. One word from him and you'll be swinging by your neck at the Piazza Sant'Angelo."

"At least Scipione has excellent taste in art," said Caravaggio. "The scoundrel."

"Stay on his good side, Michelangelo," warned Del Monte. "He could either save your skin or prove a most dangerous foe. His uncle Pope Paul, like Clemente, has a taste for executing renegades."

Caravaggio said nothing. Del Monte could see a movement in his jaw as he chewed the side of his tongue.

"Is that all, Cardinal? Am I dismissed?" said the artist, his tone spiteful.

"No," said Del Monte, picking up the peeled orange and examining it. He nodded with approval at his own work. "One more thing. I have heard of your discord with Ranuccio Tomassoni. Some matter of a squabble over courtesans?"

"We've had some bad feelings over trivial matters. Bets on tennis matches. Tomassoni is a cheat. Everyone on the Via di Pallacorda knows that."

"I did not know you played tennis, Maestro."

Caravaggio worked his jaw in silence before responding. "I do, but I avoid playing with cheating pimps like Ranuccio Tomassoni."

"True, Ranuccio is a pimp—and he is a dangerous one," said Del Monte. "All the Tomassonis are vicious. And they have the backing of the House of Farnese. Watch out for him, Michele. He is a cutthroat, like his brothers."

"They are all sewer rats. I am not afraid of vermin."

Cardinal del Monte bit his lip, studying the artist.

"And I'm told you've had a run-in with a Knight of Malta. One of the Roeros from Piemonte."

"Who told you that?"

"It doesn't matter. The Knights of Malta are as dangerous as the Church. And more ruthless."

"I haven't seen Roero in months. I suppose he is on that rock of Malta where he belongs."

"Avoid him, Michele," said Del Monte. "Heed my advice."

Caravaggio bowed. "May I take my leave now, Cardinale? I have work in my studio to finish."

Del Monte sighed. He popped a segment of orange into his mouth, wiping his fingers with a napkin. "Go. Leave. My words are wasted on you, I can see that much."

Caravaggio bowed again and headed for the door.

"Create something miraculous, my friend. Some masterpiece that will remind me why I find you worth saving."

Caravaggio smiled. "*Arrivederci*, Cardinale."

Chapter 13

Roma
1604

Caravaggio's heart thumped steadily, reverberating against her cheekbone. Anna Bianchini lifted her head from the artist's chest.

Having worked as a prostitute since she arrived in Roma from Siena at age thirteen, she knew better than to make herself too comfortable on a man's body.

But she wanted this man. He had made her desirable. Rich men—even cardinals—sought her now, sending their lackeys to fetch her in the sordid streets of Roma. The Senese with the red hair, they said. The one Maestro Caravaggio painted: *The Penitent Magdalene.*

Anna felt warmth rush up her neck. Then her smile flickered as she thought of Fillide.

Anna's low upbringing and ordinary looks meant she never qualified as a courtesan the way her friend Fillide Melandroni had. Fillide had more ambition.

Fillide has no more culture than I have. Both our mothers worked as washerwomen, gathering piss from the stables to clean stains from dirty clothes. But Fillide has always had that self-confidence—she's a natural-born actress, that one!

Anna picked at her cuticles.

"Annunccia," said the painter, staring at her. He ran his index finger over the furrow between her eyebrows. "What are you thinking?"

"I should gather my clothes and go, Maestro Caravaggio."

"Call me Michele." He chuckled. "You've shared my bed and my canvases. We should dispense with the formalities, don't you think?"

"Were your patrons pleased with the paintings?"

"*Certo!* I've got patrons sniffing around for more work."

Anna's face brightened. "You will paint me again?"

Caravaggio drew in a breath, contemplating. He nodded, his beard scratching against the bedsheet. "Yes. Yes, I think I will use you," he said, looking across the room into the distance. "But I need another, another woman. One who has more of a biting edge."

Anna moved her mouth to Caravaggio's chest and bit his nipple.

"Ow!" he said, shoving her away roughly. "What the devil made you do that?"

"I know who you want, you bastard. You want Fillide."

❧

"He wants to paint me?" said Fillide Melandroni.

Anna Bianchini jutted out her chin. "He wants to paint us *both*, Fillide. He needs two models."

Fillide's mouth curved into more of a smirk than a smile. "Who shall I be?"

Anna narrowed her eyes. "He's my patron, Fillide. Don't you get ideas."

Fillide laughed, twirling a strand of hair around her finger. "He did ask for me, Anna. Business is business."

"He only questioned me about you. He hasn't actually asked you to sit yet."

"He will. I know it."

Annunccia narrowed her eyes. "Ranuccio better not find you hanging about Maestro Caravaggio. He'll beat you."

"Pff! As if he would! I'd be damaged goods. I bring him more money than all the rest of you girls put together. Besides, I have a great patron now with Vincenzo Giustiniani. Ranuccio wouldn't dare lay a hand on me."

Anna sucked in her breath through her teeth. "I'm only delivering the message because I told Maestro Caravaggio I would. But Ranuccio won't stand for—"

"Anna!" Fillide laughed, stroking her friend's wrist. "You worry too much. I have my own way of handling Ranuccio, you shall see."

Fillide toyed with a strand of hair grazing her neck. She wrapped it around and around her finger. "I think I will visit Vincenzo."

Vincenzo Giustiniani, one of the richest men in Roma, welcomed Michelangelo Merisi da Caravaggio into the Palazzo Giustiniani, a stone's throw from the Pantheon.

"*Siediti!*" said the nobleman, gesturing to a chair upholstered in earth-toned taffeta. "I want to talk business again with you."

Giustiniani poured his guest a glass of ruby wine from a carafe.

"I want you to meet someone," he said, handing the artist the glass. "I think you will be pleased to make her acquaintance. But then, any man would!"

"Who is that?"

"My mistress, the great courtesan Fillide Melandroni, the beauty of Roma. I want you to paint her for me."

Caravaggio smiled as he moved the rim of the glass to his lips.

Too much of a coincidence. This girl Fillide is shrewd. Sì! It will show on canvas.

"Antonio! Send in Signorina Melandroni, *per favore*."

"*Sì, signore.*"

"You will soon see why I want her painted. She is a beauty, though her lips are brutish, like a man's. Ah, but the kisses she bestows!"

"My lips—a man's?" said a low, melodious voice.

Caravaggio looked up to see a tall, strong woman, her forehead bunched up in consternation. He smiled. Despite the puckered brow, Fillide was ravishing.

"My petal! No one's mouth is like yours. Ah, see, Maestro Caravaggio, how her lips express themselves, mirroring the look in her eyes. Strength and character in every feature."

Fillide arched her right eyebrow, looking at the two men before her as if she were a bird of prey. "Ah, so this is the artist you will use." She looked Caravaggio up and down twice. "They say you paint well, signore."

"Have you seen my work, signorina?"

"I know your *Amor Vincit Omnia*, the little boy cupid, of course. *The Lute Player*—again a young boy."

Caravaggio nodded.

"Too boyish for me," the courtesan said, flicking her wrist dismissively. "Perhaps more to the tastes of the cardinals. I've seen the big one you did for the ceiling of Cardinal del Monte's—"

"Ah. *Jupiter, Neptune and Pluto*."

"Disgusting. With all the *palle* and penises dangling from the men's legs. I felt like Pluto was sitting on my face," she said, lifting her chin. "But I suppose the cardinals are particularly fond of it."

Giustiniani raised his hand in a vague attempt to stop his mistress's tongue from lashing the pope's chosen. He loved her dirty talk in bed, but never had he heard her speak like this in public.

Caravaggio parted his lips in a smile. *She has more spirit in her face than any courtesan in Roma. Ah, what I can do with this model!*

"I shall look forward to having my portrait painted by you, Maestro Caravaggio," she said. "I trust you will not make my lips look like a man's."

Fillide gave a smoldering, lascivious look to Giustiniani.

"I promise you no man could work the spell my lips cast." She curtsied to her patron, an insolent arch to her eyebrow. As she grasped her brocade skirt, Caravaggio recognized the fabric. He had painted Anna Bianchini in the same garment.

"May I be excused?" she asked her patron. "I have some business I must attend to."

"Certainly, signorina. I shall call for you later."

As she shut the door behind her, Vincenzo Giustiniani sighed in delight.

"Paint her well, my friend."

Caravaggio met his eye.

"Oh, I shall," he said. "You will see."

Chapter 14

Roma
1604

Ranuccio Tomassoni did not follow his brothers in the family tradition of soldiering. For generations, the Tomassonis had served in the armies of the Farnese family, fighting in Flanders, Hungary, and the fractured city-states of the Italian peninsula.

But the Farnese fortunes had faded and their personal armies disbanded. Now the Tomassoni family was destitute. Without war to occupy them, Ranuccio's brothers wreaked havoc in the streets along with other vagabond soldiers who had moved to Roma. They became the *bravi* of the Roman streets—thugs looking for a brawl or a prosperous shakedown.

The young Ranuccio—who had never served in the Farnese militia—gathered income from the streets off Piazza Navona, trading in whores to satisfy the appetites of rich clergy and aristocracy. The two girls from Siena, Anna Bianchini and Fillide Melandroni, provided a steady stream of scudi from the purses of randy men. Because Ranuccio's stable of girls was coveted, he was, like Caravaggio, often included in the debauchery of the Roman cardinals. Michelangelo Merisi provided the art, Ranuccio Tomassoni the women.

But when Tomassoni learned that Fillide was being painted by Caravaggio, his face twisted in anger. "He's up to no good, that bastard! If he touches my Fillide—"

"You mean if he touches her without paying, little brother," corrected his elder brother, Giovan. "If he paints the whore, she will be wanted by every nobleman and cardinale in Roma. Look at Anna's business now. No one can get enough of her *figa*."

"I don't trust him," spat Ranuccio. "I've seen how he looks at Fillide. And his arrogance! He swaggers about the streets with his sword as if he were a nobleman, spoiling for a fight."

"You do the same," snapped Giovan. "Both of you beg to be arrested."

Caravaggio finished the portrait of Fillide Melandroni in less than a month.

Vincenzo Giustiniani was pleased with the portrait. The artist's work sparked passion, and he sent more and more often for his mistress. His desire filled Fillide's purse, as well as Ranuccio's.

One morning, Fillide sat in front of a warped-looking glass as her maid, Matilde, brushed her long hair. The comb snagged in an unruly lock.

"Ow!" Fillide smacked Matilde's hand. "You are hurting me!"

"I beg your pardon, signorina."

"I do wish Signor Giustiniani wouldn't snarl my hair," said Fillide. "He is such an ardent lover. I have Caravaggio's portrait to thank for that. Perhaps he should take the canvas to his bed and not me?"

Matilde covered her mouth with her free hand. She locked eyes in the mirror with her mistress, and they both burst out laughing.

A rap on the door.

"May I enter, Signorina Fillide?" said a young voice.

"*Sì, avanti.*"

"A letter for you," said a servant boy, bowing. He offered a letter sealed with crimson wax. His hair brushed his eyes as he looked up to watch the lovely Fillide Melandroni open the parchment. She studied the scrawled signature of Michelangelo Merisi da Caravaggio at the bottom.

"Alvise!" she called to the boy as he walked toward the door. "Stay, *per favore*! Will you read this to me?"

Alvise Caretto nodded, taking the letter in his hand. He squinted hard, his lips moving slowly as the syllables stumbled out, one by one. "'Please—do me—the hon-or—'"

"Really, Alvise!" Fillide said, her eyes squinting with impatience. "You did go to school, didn't you?"

The boy blushed. "'—of—sit-ting for me—as a mod-el.'"

Alvise's face had colored deep scarlet. He looked down from the letter to the floor.

"*Grazie*, Alvise! You've made me a happy woman. Read on."

"'Please meet me tom-or-row evening at—Osteria della Lupa. Or any night this week. I will be there.'"

"Perfect," said Fillide, gazing back into her looking glass as her maid combed her hair. "Perhaps he will forget those little boys clad in bedsheets. This Caravaggio will make me known throughout Roma, and beyond!"

Fillide fingered the pearl drop earrings, her nail sliding across the black velvet nap of the pendants.

Were these the same earrings Annunccia wore in that first painting? She told me how strange he was, how he made her cry.

But I didn't expect this!

Fillide stared down at the freshly killed pig lying on Caravaggio's bed. Two fat flies crept about the animal's snout.

He is mad, this artist—

"Hold the sword here," said Caravaggio, taking her right hand away from her ear. His hands were firm against hers, making her grasp the brass hilt.

He positioned his model's arms and hands.

"And Abra, Judith's maid. That's you, Signora Rossi," he said to the old washerwoman standing next to Fillide. "You're looking on, eager to receive the severed head." He moved Signora Rossi a step to the left, his two hands adjusting her wrinkled face in profile.

He walked back to his blank canvas, consulting the marks he had made outlining his composition.

"*Che schifo!*" said Fillide, staring down at the bloody pig's head. *Disgusting.*

"*Brava! Sì, schifoso!* Focus on that disgust—and how will you sever the pig's head from its body?"

Fillide looked up, aghast. "I'm no butcher, Maestro Merisi!"

"That's the point, signorina. You are Judith hacking off Holofernes's head. You've never done this before—neither had she. You are saving the Jews from the Assyrian tyrant. I want you to figure out how it's done."

"Can I not have the male model here instead of a stinking pig?"

"No, Signorina Melandroni. There is no horror in a living model with no blood. Now sever the pig's head! Cut sinew from bone until it splits in two."

"*Bastardo!*" Fillide cursed.

"Do it!" said Caravaggio, his face darkening. "Now! Or leave my studio."

She looked down at the pig. She grabbed the pig's ear with her left hand, pulling the neck from the body, twisting its head to get a better purchase.

I wanted to be a Madonna! Not a butcher.

With the sword in her right hand, Fillide began to saw. Her face puckered in consternation, a vertical furrow erupting between her eyebrows.

"You are Judith, damn you!" shouted the artist. "Will you finish the deed or not? Or haven't you the courage, you who make a living on your back?"

Fillide threw the artist a dark look, enraged. She grasped the sword tighter, half inspired to take a swing at him. Instead, she took a step back from the pig's body to avoid the spilling blood. She stretched the sinews of the animal's neck, pulling the pig's ear, and began to cut.

Her forehead buckled in concentration.

"*Sì!*" hissed Caravaggio. "Hold it there. Don't move a muscle."

The old washerwoman stared over Fillide's shoulder. Fillide caught a whiff of her rotten teeth.

Why should this ugly old crone stand so close to me with her stinking breath?

"Signora Rossi," said the artist. "Stretch the cloth in your hands, as if you are preparing to wrap the pig's head in it. Keep your eyes on the sword."

Caravaggio stepped away from his canvas toward the tableau. He pried the pig's mouth open, exposing its teeth in pathetic horror. Then he smiled in satisfaction, nicking the canvas to mark where Holofernes's head would lie when he painted him the next day.

Chapter 15

PROVINCE OF SIENA

The Tuscan hills were a sea of sunflowers, the villa an island on the highest hilltop, looking out over once-vast estates. Those fields of sunflowers now belonged to a Dutch conglomerate that had bought them in the bankruptcy of a French corporation . . . and Lucia hadn't bothered to go any further into the past. After her day digging through the contessa's family archives, the official state property-tax records were almost too easy. She found that the villa itself, shorn of its fields—the villa where the D'Estrato family had retreated after one of their patriarchs was executed for treason against Siena in the late eighteenth century—was now owned by a man named Haziz Hafez al-Rachmaan. And about him, she cheerfully admitted to the professor, she knew only that he didn't sound likely to be the descendant of Italian nobility.

The professor had inclined his head in gracious acceptance of the limits of her research. He was less gracious when Lucia told him that Moto was coming with them to Siena.

"Why? He'll be worthless."

"He's my friend."

The professor had raised an eyebrow at that.

"You bring all your friends wherever you go?"

She gave that the response it deserved, a toss of her mop of black hair and a simple answer: "He's coming."

Richman tried a different tack.

"There won't be room for him in your wretched little car."

"First you insult my friend. Now you insult my car. If I'm next on your list, I suggest you stop right now."

The professor didn't say anything.

"Am I missing something here, Professor?"

He shrugged. "I thought we were doing this together. A research project. For the seminar. I wasn't expecting company."

She gave him a smile. "If I didn't know better, Ralphie, I'd say you were jealous." And before he could deny it, she added, "Maybe I'm being foolish, but things did get a little sketchy when we went to see Te-Te."

"Sketchy? We damn near got killed."

"That's why I thought it might be good to have someone else along. Just in case."

The professor shrugged, hardly mollified. "He doesn't particularly seem to be the bodyguard type."

Lucia laughed. "No. Moto's no *tipo tosto*. But he's good company, and as far as I'm concerned, he's family. He's coming."

She didn't mention that Moto's feelings would be hurt if they left him behind. Moto hated to be left out. He hated it when anyone suggested he wasn't up to a challenge, that he wasn't tough enough—even though "tough enough" was very definitely not his style.

"Fine," said the professor. "It's your car. But he's sitting in the back. I'm not going to cram myself in there."

"Of course not," said Lucia, and she couldn't resist giving him a kiss on the forehead. "It wouldn't be dignified."

The drive wasn't a long one, and Moto, if not much of a bodyguard, was certainly good company. Uncomplainingly ensconced in the back seat, he provided a steady stream of amusing chatter, keeping his Italian slow enough for the professor to understand what he was saying and mixing in his own broken English whenever possible.

By the time they crossed the sea of sunflowers and drove up the hill, the professor had joined in and all three of them were laughing as they parked in front of the villa.

And now, having introduced themselves—scholars on a research project, looking for D'Estrato family archives—and having apologized for arriving without an appointment, Lucia, Professor Richman, and Moto stood with Hafez al-Rachmaan in the rather grand entry hall. Al-Rachmaan's smile was welcoming, his tone was cordial—and he clearly considered them an annoyance. Even so, before he dismissed them, he was going to make certain they understood exactly how well he had done to wind up here.

"Archives? I'm afraid not. The failed aristocrats left us nothing but"—he gestured expansively—"these magnificent bones. Which we have been pleased to restore to life." His Italian was perfect. As was his English, which he switched to as soon as Professor Richman introduced himself—and which he continued to use, apparently just to annoy Moto, who was obviously having trouble following the discussion in a foreign language. The villa's proud new master had dismissed Moto with a glance. Motorcycle trash. So he tried to ally himself with the distinguished professor and went on in his smiling English about the art and the furniture they had gathered at great trouble and expense.

"*Ma nulla dal Cavaliere d'Estrato? Come può essere?*" Lucia had seen the look Hafez al-Rachmaan had given Moto, understood what he was doing, and wasn't going to let him get away with it. She was going to insist on speaking Italian. Even if it meant al-Rachmaan sent them away. But even as she insisted—in Italian—that there must be *something* from Cavaliere d'Estrato, she knew she shouldn't be surprised that they'd hit a dead end. The D'Estrato family hit a dead end of their own and vanished long ago—not all grand families have happy endings. There was no reason to expect there would be some kind of archive that could offer a trace of the painting as it passed through. One lucky break in the contessa's archives was no reason to expect another one at the next antiquity they visited.

"Well," al-Rachmaan admitted, "there are the books." And suddenly Lucia thought maybe she hadn't been so foolish after all. The owner spoke in even more firmly fixed English, his British accent softened by the indefinable trace of another language, an original tongue, worn smooth like river rock. He spoke the last word on a falling tone. Dismissive again.

"*Libri?*" Lucia was still insisting on Italian.

"From the seventeenth century. We found them buried in the rubble of the cellars. No wine down there, of course. Just the books. Mostly military history. Dreadfully dreary." Showing off his English. "Histories of the Knights of Malta. You know, D'Estrato was—"

"Yes, yes. I know," Lucia answered in English. If he really had something, he'd earned his choice of language.

"And a book of poetry, dreadful poetry by someone named Mario Fenelli."

"Fenelli?" Fenelli was the name listed with *Il bacio di Giuda* in the inventory of the dowry for the fourth daughter of Cavaliere d'Estrato of Siena when she married the third son of Ranieri dei Marsi. "Fenelli's not a poet. He's a painter." Lucia was staying with English. Moto was on his own.

Hafez al-Rachmaan raised an eyebrow. Still smiling. "Well, I do hope he was a better painter than poet. Dreadful poetry. Shockingly dreadful."

"Might we examine the document?" Professor Richman leaned into his formal professorial tone, but al-Rachmaan had apparently decided he'd been polite long enough.

"I'm afraid I really don't have the time for—"

"I have time, Father."

Lucia turned toward the unexpected voice behind her. A young woman in a black silk hijab, lightly embroidered with a red geometric pattern, her hair covered, a thin layer of material drawn across her face. "I think we should share what we have found. We must be hospitable. Perhaps their research will add to the luster of your art collection."

He nodded. Gracious if he must.

"Very well. Professor Richman, this is my daughter, Aysha. I hope you will pardon her interruption. I find that sometimes her education exceeds her manners. Aysha, if you wish to show the professor and his assistant the book, I will be in my office. I hope you will all excuse me."

"I'm not his—" Lucia caught herself.

"And when you are done, come see me."

"Yes, Father."

With a nod, Aysha led them out of the entryway and down a hallway, walls lined with paintings. As they walked, she reeled off artists and provenance, where and how each painting had entered her family's collection over the past decade.

"Your father seems very liberal to allow you to be alone with strangers."

"Yes. Perhaps." She answered Lucia with a smile that she expanded to include Moto. He smiled back.

When they reached the end of the hall, Professor Richman stopped.

"If I was listening properly to your fascinating tour, all your paintings are from at least a century after the D'Estratos lost control of the estate. Your father was talking about the historical accuracy of the renovation." Lucia was glad al-Rachmaan wasn't there to take offense.

"The paintings came first," Aysha admitted. "My father wanted a villa to match his collection, and this was the closest he could find."

Moto broke in. "You certainly seem to know the collection."

"I have a master's in art history from the University of Chicago."

"Really? Did you know—" the professor began, but Aysha was concentrating her smile and her attention on Moto.

"It was a very different world. In Chicago, my father was not there to supervise my life. I learned . . . a great deal."

She shook her head slightly, and the thin veil slipped down, revealing her full face, young, strong, beautiful. She gave Moto a smile that unmistakably meant he had blindly wandered into dangerous territory. He'd been flirting for fun. Suddenly, he was a nonswimmer thrown into the deep end of the pool. His eyes went sideways, looking for someplace to hide.

Lucia stepped in. "Can we see the book, Aysha? The poetry?"

Aysha laughed. She'd been flirting for fun too. She gave Moto another look, one that said she'd learned enough in Chicago to know exactly what Lucia had also known within moments of meeting Moto. She turned her smile to Lucia.

"I think my father's wrong about the poetry. It's much better than he wants to admit. But it embarrassed him to have me read it. Some of it is very . . . intense. Blunt." She shrugged. "And very crude."

"The penmanship or the content?" The professor demanded clarification.

"Yes, actually, both. Mostly it's fragments. Notes. A few lines of poetry. A lot of blots. You have to pick your way through it. My father doesn't have the patience. Or interest. And the parts that are more complete . . . that's what he can't allow me to read. Or stop me from reading." She couldn't resist teasing Moto with another smile. "Erotic poetry."

She opened a drawer and brought out a book—soft leather cover, stained and swollen, battered and bruised. She carefully turned a few of the parchment pages. They were filled as described: disconnected lines, sometimes paragraphs. Savage lines crossed out some sections. Scribbled notes at the edges of the pages. Smeared and smudged.

In all, incomprehensible.

"If we had it for a year, we might . . ." The professor let his voice trail off, sounding half wistful, half certain he didn't want the job.

"It cannot leave this building. I'm sure you understand." Aysha smiled. "In fact, I have read most of it and transcribed portions for my thesis. In Chicago."

She glanced at Moto again. Clearly just for amusement.

"Which was on . . . ?" Lucia kept the conversation going.

"How the love poetry of the seventeenth century reflected the devotional aspects of the art in the churches of the region."

"And does it?"

"No, sadly, not at all. I'll be discussing that issue with my advisor when the fall semester begins."

The professor seemed ready to ask who her advisor was, but Lucia kept on track.

"Could we see your transcriptions of the book? Or your thesis?"

"I'm afraid not. I can't share any of that until I publish. Certainly you understand that."

"Why not?"

Aysha ignored Lucia's question. "But I can tell you the best single passage." She turned to a page almost at the end of the book, looked down at what was written there, then recited in a soft voice, in a language neither Lucia nor Moto could understand any more easily than the scrawled handwriting.

"That's barely Italian," said Moto, thinking it was safe to reenter the conversation.

"It was the language of the taverns. Slang. Argot. Blunt and crude and sometimes overwhelmingly obscene. That was Fenelli's world and that was his language. He wasn't going to let anyone tell him how he should speak. Or write."

"Are you presuming to know what he was thinking?" The professor was in his oral exam interrogation mode.

"It's all footnoted in my thesis."

"Perhaps we could see the footnotes."

Aysha shrugged. "I'll translate that short passage. And then you'll go." Calm scholar's face. A slight clearing of her throat. "'And so I cross your borders, a gift of betrayal, the betrayal of a gift. My soul flies to you. I fall to my knees for you. Treasure knows its home.'"

In the frame of the hijab, her face glowed with emotion.

The professor jumped in. "But that's brilliant. Of course. Extraordinary. Tell me what you learned about him. About Fenelli."

Aysha beamed under the praise. "Just the end of his story. He was running from Naples. I think money was involved. Most likely a gambling debt. But it might have been a woman. I traced him as best as I could in the archives. In Naples. A dreadful place." She shuddered, still smiling with pride. She was having fun now. They were hanging on her words. "He sailed to Porto Ercole sometime in the summer of 1610. July, I believe."

Lucia broke in. "That was exactly—"

The professor cut her off. "Naples to Porto Ercole. That hardly gets him here, to Siena."

"And he went even farther north from Porto Ercole—a long way, in a big hurry. Into the mountains. Almost to the border with France."

Aysha paused.

"Why?" Lucia had no patience for cat and mouse.

"To visit his brother." Aysha paused again. "The painter."

To hug her or choke her. It was a close call, but Lucia calculated that not touching her at all was best. "His brother was the painter! Why didn't you tell us sooner?"

Aysha flicked the veil back across her face, then lowered it slowly. "A little mystery makes for a better story, doesn't it?"

Lucia reconsidered the option of choking her.

"Indeed," the professor agreed.

"And then?" Lucia was persistent.

"Mario Fenelli, the poet, spent almost a month with his brother, Federico Fenelli."

"The painter."

"Yes." Aysha nodded to the professor. "The painter. And monk. In a monastery outside Milano."

"Near Caravaggio?" Lucia could hardly stand it.

"What?" Aysha was puzzled.

"The town of Caravaggio. Outside Milano."

"Oh. No. Nowhere near there. At the edge of the Alps in the Aosta Valley, up past Piemonte. Mario spent at least a month there, in the monastery. And when he left, he had a painting. He brought it here. To Siena. I don't know why, but he came here to deliver that painting. And to die." She stopped for a moment. "The line I recited, 'A gift of betrayal.' That was almost the last he wrote. In most of the journal, his hand is strong. You can feel what a renegade he was. But at the very end, his writing is weak. As if he barely had the strength to hold the pen. And then he died." Touched by her own story. Pulling out of it. "I searched for his grave. In the Istrice contrada, in Siena. The Estratos had a palazzo there. That's where he brought the painting." Shrug. "But I never found anything."

Impulsively, Lucia hugged her, hard, like an old friend. "Thank you. That was amazing."

She got a shy smile in return. Maybe the first real smile they had seen.

The professor gave Aysha his hand. A formal thank-you.

Moto offered a last smile. Aysha grabbed him and hugged him, the way Lucia had hugged her. He blushed. She laughed.

And then, as they headed toward the door, the professor coughed, stopped, and clapped his hands to his face. Bright-red blood leaked through his fingers, down his chin.

Aysha gasped.

Lucia grabbed the professor's shoulders. "What's wrong?"

"No, no. Nothing really." His voice was muffled. He dug into his pockets for a handkerchief, more blood spilling down his face. "Just a bloody nose." He held the handkerchief to his face. "I've gotten them all my life. Give me a moment. I do believe we passed a bathroom back down the hall, didn't we?"

Still a little pale, Aysha nodded and waved her hand in the general direction, back down the hallway. "Around the corner."

"Yes. I thought so. Please wait and I'll get cleaned up. I'll be right back. The blood will stop soon. It always does."

Thirty-six hours later, by the light of dawn—their second dawn on the road, a grim industrial dawn on a highway west of Milan—the impulsive decision to drive straight through from Siena to the monastery where the two Fenelli brothers, poet and painter, had spent a month together was beginning to feel like a seriously defective idea. Moto's insistence that the drive would be five hours, six at most, had proven wildly wrong—although the fault lay with Lucia's Fiat more than Moto's knowledge of Italian roads. Optimism had disappeared with the first breakdown. Civility was gone by the third.

Now they were trying to recapture some sense of camaraderie with a quick breakfast at a small café, in hopes that caffeine, butter, and sugar would work their usual magic. They managed a groggy discussion comparing this glum landscape with the beauty of the sunrise on their first dawn of the trip, in the hills outside Parma, where the Fiat had sputtered to a halt, leaving them stranded for hours before a passing motorist had stopped to help. Eventually that discussion petered out and they sat in silence.

Staring down at her cell phone, Lucia gave a sudden strangled cry. The professor was sipping a caffè latte. Moto was brushing crumbs off his jacket. They both turned. She pointed at the phone and said, "Google News." Then she read: "'Fire destroys villa outside Siena. Two dead.'" Details were scant. The fire had started late at night. Two nights ago. Probably while they were stranded in that spot above Parma. Two bodies had been found. The ancient D'Estrato villa was completely destroyed. There was an investigation.

Moto said something about calling a friend, pulled out his cell, and walked out onto the terrace of the café.

"All right," said the professor. "I think that's enough."

"What?" But Lucia already knew what he was saying, and she wasn't surprised. The trip had been hard enough on her, and she wasn't half his age. So she didn't need to ask. But he answered anyway.

"We were just talking to those people. That beautiful young woman and her father. We talked to them and now they're dead. 'Two bodies.' I have no interest in being found as a body one morning in charred ruins or anywhere else."

She didn't have anything to say to that, so she let him go on.

"This is too ugly for me. There isn't anything in the world I want to know about badly enough to go any further."

She took a deep breath. He was right, but that didn't change how she felt. She thought about saying she was impressed he'd made it this far, then thought he might not take it as a compliment.

"I understand," she answered. "But I'm not ready to go home yet. I have to know what's going on. I don't like feeling I'm the fatal curse. Te-Te. The kidnappers—they deserved it, but still . . . And now Aysha. And her father—what was his name? Never mind. It doesn't matter now, does it? All of them. Gone. I have to know why. I have to know it wasn't me." In some remote corner of her mind, there had always been a feeling that death was shadowing her, waiting for a weak moment to reach out—not for her, but for anyone too close to her. As if she were death's messenger. It was a feeling so ridiculous that she had never confronted it. But it was too real to ignore. And choosing not to ignore it, she simply marched right over it and past it. That had always been her way. When nothing made sense, she didn't try to make sense out of it. She put her head down and kept going.

She shook her head. Time to keep going. "And the painting. *Bacio di Giuda*. There's something there." She half smiled. "I should be ashamed. People have been murdered, and I'm thinking about that painting. But . . ." She paused for a moment to figure out exactly what she wanted to say, and he cut in:

"But you can't stand it when anybody tries to push you around."

She managed a grim smile and a nod.

The professor answered with a nod of his own. "I'm sure there's a very fine bus back to Monte Piccolo. I'll go ask." And he was off.

Lucia finished her second *caffè doppio* and thought about that night alone in the dark of the warehouse with the painting. And she thought again about Te-Te, lying in a pool of his own blood. She had a few minutes to think, and then Moto and the professor rushed in from opposite directions.

"*Decapitati!*" Moto's voice was torn.

"Beheaded." The professor's was flat, stunned.

"What?" Lucia's head swiveled.

"Both of them! *Decapitati!*"

"What do you mean 'both'?" said the professor, almost sharply. "There was only one."

"No! Two!" Moto snapped. "*Decapitati.*"

"Wait!" She cut them off. "You're not making sense. Either of you. What are you talking about? Moto, what?" She held a hand up to hush the professor.

"Both of them. The old man and his daughter. Before the fire. They were tied, hand and foot, and beheaded. *Decapitati!* Both!" He glared at the professor, even as tears ran down his face.

"This is something different." The professor held up a small local newspaper. "The caretaker at the monastery—"

"Our monastery? Fenelli's monastery?"

"Except it's not a monastery anymore." He didn't wait for anyone to ask. "It's an Islamic study center. I mean, 'was.' It was an Islamic study center. Someone burned it down last night. After beheading the caretaker. They got here before us. Whoever they are."

No one said anything for what seemed a long time. Then Professor Richman said, "I'm going back to Monte Piccolo. I urge you to show the good sense to come with me."

Moto wasn't crying anymore. He met Lucia's gaze.

"I'm not giving up," she said, hoping to convince him she had a reason for what she was going to say next. "I spent a night staring at that painting, getting ready to die. I know what that painting feels like in the night. There's nothing for us here now. But I can't go home." A deep breath, then, "I have to go to Malta."

"Malta?" Moto's face was a mask of bewilderment.

"*The Beheading of St. John.* In the cathedral in Malta." She shrugged. "I know. Another beheading. I sound like a ghoul. But *The Beheading of St. John* might be Caravaggio's greatest painting. I have to know what it feels like, face-to-face. I can't explain it any better than that."

There was too much tangled up in her mind for her to even try to explain. Her fierce need to defend Te-Te—even though it made no sense to her—to save him from being savaged as an old fool who died for a fraud. Her haunted suspicion that death was waiting, peering over her shoulder, reaching out to touch anyone who got too close to her. Her feeling that if she just kept moving, she could leave that haunting behind. And the emotion that had filled her when she'd stood for hours in the near dark with *The Judas Kiss.*

She held Moto's gaze. "You don't have to come with me. You shouldn't come with me. But I have to go."

Moto looked back at her, then at the professor. He took a deep breath. "If you're going, I'm going." No tears. No smiles. Just a grim determination that seemed to match hers.

They stood in silence and then Professor Richman said, "You are as foolish—as recklessly stupid—as Caravaggio. Every time he had a chance to stay out of trouble, he made the worst possible decision. Why are you doing this?"

Lucia didn't have any answer except a tight-lipped shrug.

The professor reached out and put his hand on her shoulder.

"*Nec spe. Nec metu.*" He spoke the words as if they were a benediction.

Lucia frowned. "What's that?"

"*Without hope. Without fear.* It's Latin. They say it was Caravaggio's personal motto. And right now I suppose it ought to be yours." He shook his head. "But if you had any sense . . ." He trailed off into silence.

A moment later, determined to break the spell of that silence, Lucia grabbed the professor, kissed him on both cheeks, turned, gave Moto a hug, and declared, "*Nec spe. Nec metu* it is! Let's go!"

She told the professor to forget about taking the bus back to Monte Piccolo, and they drove him to the Milano Centrale train station, waited while he bought a ticket, and then walked him to the platform. Side by side, Lucia and Moto stood and watched as he headed toward the train. For a moment, he was lost in the surging crowd. Then he reappeared, standing alone. For a moment, Lucia thought how old and lonely he looked, then he turned, caught her eye, smiled, gave a jaunty wave, checked his ticket, and disappeared into the crowd again.

The room was filled with the musk of the thousands of old books that lined its walls. The small man breathed in the scent as if it were the aroma of a fine wine. After long minutes of silence, the tall man ventured to speak first.

"I have spoken to three of your old classmates, sir. Their admiration for you runs deep."

"Three? I gave you seven names."

"Yes sir. But my first contacts with the other four indicated that they might not support our cause, and I thought it best to go no further."

"Well done, Fra Lupo. Discretion is the better part of valor."

Lupo nodded. After all these years, he knew his commander's citations well.

But the small man raised a finger of warning and added, "Sometimes. Only sometimes."

Then he rose from behind the desk and walked to a corner of the room where two comfortable armchairs faced each other. He gestured to the tall man, who remained at attention in front of the now unoccupied desk.

"Come, join me. You have done well. I have said you are like a son to me. Let us sit and discuss these matters."

"Thank you, sir. I am honored."

The two sat, facing one another. The small man lounged back in the leather chair. The other sat straight at the edge of his seat.

"So! What have you found, Fra Filippo?"

"It was your friend in Milano, Professore—"

The small man raised an eyebrow. Fra Lupo nodded and did not say the name. He started again.

"Your friend in Milano put me in contact with a man in Palermo."

"Palermo?"

"Yes sir. He was very careful about what he told me, but he was certain that people behind the action, the explosion, at the warehouse were . . . well, all he would say was they were Sicilian."

"So, mafiosi."

"He was very discreet. He didn't use that word, but I am certain that is what he meant. It makes sense, sir. Who else could put that much fear into our usually helpful contacts?"

"I believe you are right." A moment of thought. "We must be careful."

"They are formidable opponents, sir."

"No, *figlio mio*, that is where we must be careful. The mafiosi are not our allies—sometimes I think the Sicilians are more like Turks than true Italians—but they are not our opponents. We must never forget who our real opponents are."

Comandante Pantera stood up and walked across the room to the book stand where the ancient manuscript lay open under its glass cover.

He looked down at it and read aloud—first in the original Greek and then in Italian—"'Show me just what Muhammad brought that was new, and there you will find things only evil and inhuman, most certainly his command to spread by the sword the faith he preached.'"

Lupo nodded. He could have recited the passage from memory. It had been the opening lines of the commander's thesis for his *Dottorato di ricerca in Storia*. The thesis, titled "Things Only Evil and Inhuman: A Scrupulous Examination of the Cult of Islam," had been savagely rejected in a clearly political act, which had ended Gran Comandante Militare Pantera's academic career.

The *comandante* brought his hand down gently, hovering over the glass protecting the manuscript, and said, "These are the words of Emperor Manuel II Palaeologus of Byzantium." He turned, took a step back toward Lupo, stopped, bowed his head, and said, "And may God bless His Holiness Pope Benedict XVI, our last true pope."

He raised his head and the two men shared a secret smile, for they alone knew—with doctrinal certainty—that it had been the *gran comandante*'s strong intellectual influence that had led Benedict to quote that exact paragraph in a speech at the University of Regensburg, a clear signal of his support for the *gran comandante*'s campaign to free the world from the danger of Islam.

Lupo clenched his fist and struck his chest over his heart. "I shall not fail our Holy Father, sir."

"And you shall not fail me either."

"Comandante."

"You have done well so far, but there is yet much further to go. The girl is the key to the painting. I am certain. Stay as close as you can. Do whatever you must. We shall know more. It is imperative. We may have to talk with her."

Chapter 16

MILAN

Moto chewed on a croissant and narrowed his eyes as he sipped a *caffè doppio* from a paper cup. He glanced left and right around the crowded Milan train station café. His eyes strayed up to the mirrored wall behind Lucia, where the café entrance and the busy hallway outside were reflected. He ducked his chin and spoke, so quietly that Lucia had to lean closer to hear him.

"Lulu—" he started, then stopped and twisted his face into a look of disgust as he held up the pastry and the coffee. "I don't know which of these is worse." He choked down the last bite of the croissant and followed it with the dregs of the coffee. Then he started again. "Lulu, we're going a long way out on a very thin branch, aren't we? No matter what we find, we're going to have a hard time convincing anyone else that we've got proof, any real link between the painting, between our painting, and . . . well, anything. I mean, Aysha had her research, her thesis, her footnotes. But she's . . . gone. And that book, the poetry, the notes, whatever was in it. It's gone too. There's nothing left."

"So?"

"So we don't have any proof. We don't have any evidence. Who's going to believe us if we decide it really is . . . you know, what we think it is?"

Lucia's dark eyebrows knitted, folding a deep crease between them. It was a scowl that usually preceded a storm. But the storm warning cleared, and she offered Moto an off-kilter grin.

"We can get there. But first I have to convince myself. I know what I saw, what I felt that night in the dark. And in Rome at San Luigi dei Francesi. But I need to see more."

Moto nodded. "As long as I don't have to drink any more of this motor oil." He gestured at the paper cup.

"Fair enough."

"What now?"

She dropped her voice. "I told you. The *Beheading.*"

"I hate that word. So . . . Malpensa?"

"It's too far to walk."

"And too wet to drive." He fell silent for a long minute. "Let me make a phone call first."

As they pulled into Malpensa Airport, Moto told Lucia to drop him at the terminal so he could go to Alitalia and buy their tickets while she parked the car.

With a prayer to the Saint of Lost Cars, Lucia left her battered Fiat in a vast airport parking structure, half expecting she'd never see the old wreck again—and as she walked to the terminal, she found herself compulsively glancing over her shoulder, checking to see if anyone was following her. She forced herself to stop looking. And then she forced herself to stop: *Stand still and think.* Crowds surged past her, racing to catch planes or meet family or heading to that concrete jungle she'd just left in hopes of finding their cars. Stepping close to a light pole, a rock in a strong current, she tried again to understand what she was doing. It didn't make any sense. This had all started with Te-Te, and Te-Te was nothing to her. A scrap of memory from a past that had never given her anything but pain. And the path she was following was obviously, ridiculously dangerous. So many people had died so fast. Why wasn't she running in the other direction? *Death-defying*, for her, had never meant anything more dangerous than jaywalking in midtown Manhattan.

Someone lurched into her, and she recoiled with a gasp—but it was just a clumsy tourist with too much luggage.

And that wasn't her either. Cowering in fear. She had to make up her mind right now. It was either go all in or go home. Turning around was tempting. Back to Monte Piccolo, finish the semester, then back to New York and back to her life.

That was a comforting thought, but part of her felt more alive right now than she ever had before. She liked that. No, she loved that. And she couldn't feel alive if she was constantly worrying about winding up dead.

So she had to keep going, and she had to stop worrying, and she had to stop looking over her shoulder.

Just then, the little man on the pedestrian crossing sign began to flash green.

Lucia laughed and stepped off the curb. *Nec spe. Nec metu!* She was all in.

She had no trouble finding the Alitalia counter—or Moto. He was screaming at the ticket agent, his voice at a pitch that cut through the normal hum of airport noise. She heard the voice. She could see it was Moto. But it didn't sound like him at all.

"You son of a bitch! That's it! Fuck you!" That couldn't be Moto. But it was. "We'll fly on Meridiana. They'll get us to Naples!"

The clerk offered an official airline smirk. "Not from Malpensa, they won't."

"I don't care! Fuck you!"

He spun away from the counter and grabbed Lucia's arm as the agent shrugged and called, "Next!"

"Come on! Let's get the car. We'll fly out of Linate."

She started to object. None of this made any sense. But Moto was marching away too quickly for her to do anything but hurry after him, wondering what had just happened.

When they got to the parking garage, she tried to tell him the car was on Level 3, but he wasn't paying any attention. He strode into the crowded elevator, then stepped back out, pulling her with him as the doors closed. He jogged up the stairs instead, with her following, deeply confused. On the next level, the doors of another elevator were opening, and as the only passenger stepped off, Moto rushed into the empty car and pushed the button for the top level.

Lucia didn't bother to say anything. She wondered if the bad coffee had blown some kind of circuit in his finely balanced Italian mind.

When the elevator doors opened, they were blocked by a Biancheria Biancaneve—Snow White Linen—delivery van, backed up so close to the elevator doors there was barely room to squeeze by. But Moto didn't squeeze by. Instead, without hesitating, he opened the rear door as far as he could in the tight space between the van and the elevator and climbed inside, pulling Lucia in after him.

Almost the instant he closed the door, the engine roared and the van pulled away.

"Moto! What the—"

He put a finger to his lips and gestured for silence as the van rumbled and bumped down the twisting ramps of the parking garage and onto the highway.

Lucia let the silence stretch out in the thick air and windowless dark as the tires hummed down the autostrada and the van swerved through traffic. Little by little, her eyes adjusted to the faint light that seeped in through the gap in the ill-fitting rear door. The van gave a violent lurch and her stomach lurched in sympathy. She considered whether to throw up on the clean linen—the snow-white linen—that surrounded them or, perhaps more appropriately, on Moto.

She wrestled her stomach under control and finally broke the silence.

"Moto"—she kept her voice low—*"che diavolo stiamo facendo?"* *What the hell are we doing?*

Even in the dim light, his smile was nearly dazzling—broad and gleaming white. That, at least, was the Moto she knew.

"*Cara mia*, if someone is following us, there's no reason why we should make it easy for them."

She considered that—but not for very long. "So why were you shouting where we were going for everyone in the damn airport to hear?"

The smile didn't waver. "I said Naples, didn't I?"

"Yes. But you also shouted we were going to Linate. Don't you think they can figure out where we're going once they catch us there?"

"But we won't be there, will we?"

"Damn it, Moto! Don't play any more games with me."

"This luxury limousine is on its way directly to Aeroporto Il Caravaggio. Not Linate." And before she could say anything, he added, "Don't you think that's appropriate? Given our mission? Really, Lulu, don't we have to remain faithful to our hero, Michelangelo Merisi da Caravaggio?"

Lucia refused to be amused. "And what's going to happen when we get there and the driver finds us in the back of his van?"

"He won't."

"How can he—"

"Don't worry. He won't see us."

She puzzled over that for a long minute. Then, finally: "Who are you? And what have you done with Moto? He was my best friend. I loved him."

The dazzling smile. "And he loves you. But he thinks you shouldn't ask any more questions right now."

They sat in silence for a while, and then Lucia started talking, her voice subdued, almost as if she were talking to herself.

"We need to find our way. From Caravaggio to the painting. From the painting to Caravaggio. Meet in the middle. Once we know for sure, we can fill in the missing pieces. Look"—her voice got stronger—"we have the painting at the orphanage. We have that. It's a fact. And we know the orphanage got it from the contessa's family. And we know they had it because some thieving Dei Marsi ancestor stole it from that idiot in Siena, Cavaliere d'Estrato. That's all solid. We've got the evidence, the dowry inventory. That's clear too. So we have both of those. The painting. The trail to Siena. That's solid. And Aysha had her research. It's all gone. But she had it. She was certain of it. And that takes the painting all the way back to Porto Ercole. From the orphanage"—she wanted to say "from Te-Te," but she didn't—"to the contessa. From the contessa to D'Estrato. From D'Estrato to Fenelli and back to Porto Ercole. In the summer of 1610—the last time and place that anyone saw Caravaggio. Even if the evidence is gone, we know that happened."

The van rocked on its tired springs, lurched, and slammed into a pothole.

"I know. There are gaps. Big gaps. And we'll never fill them because it's all gone. Lost in the fire. But we know—*we* know—and we can keep following the story. If we're right, we'll find the trail again."

Professor Richman settled into the first-class compartment with a smile. The Santa Maria Novella station in Florence was much smaller and simpler than Milano Centrale, and he'd had no trouble finding the train to Siena—which was not the train back to Monte Piccolo, where Lucia and Moto thought he was headed. He'd been perfectly sincere when he said that he was disinclined to risk death by fire or beheading. But now that the two reckless young fools were charging off on their own, he felt reasonably safe returning to Siena to do his own research. He didn't need anyone holding his hand. He was going to enjoy working on his own.

If there was any substance to the story that poor young woman had spun for them, then there ought to be some hard evidence remaining in Siena. The fact that the girl hadn't been able to find her poet's burial site seemed more likely to reflect shortcomings in her research skills than the actual absence of a grave. If Mario Fenelli had existed, if he had died in Siena, if he had been buried there—then Professor Aristotle Rafael Richman was certain he could find some evidence. And even if he didn't find anything, well, a few days on his own would be a pleasure. Keeping up with Lucia and Moto was exhausting.

The laundry van jolted. A sharp turn. Then another. Lucia was thrown forward as the brakes slammed on, then again as the van lurched backward in reverse. She heard a muffled curse, and in the near dark, she could see that Moto had been buried in an avalanche of snow-white linen. He cursed and thrashed and fought to free himself. In other circumstances, Lucia might have laughed. Now she wondered if Moto's dirty footprints on the linen would be the final mistake that got them killed.

They sat silently in the dark, breathing heavily. She heard the driver's door open and slam shut, footsteps circling to the back of the van. As the latch clicked and the rear door opened, Lucia braced herself for whatever might come next—discovery, arrest, desperate explanations. Moto had refused to offer any guidance. The door opened and her eyes were dazzled by the light, but not for long. They were parked inside some kind of building, and her eyes adjusted quickly. The light was dim, bright only by contrast with their hours in the dark.

The driver was standing outside the open door, a clipboard in his hand. He stared right at them and looked right through them, as if they weren't there. As if the pile of disordered linen didn't exist. He seemed to be counting bundles on the shelves, and then he turned away. The van was backed up to an elevator, and the driver pushed the call button. Lucia could hear the elevator creaking down the shaft. It stopped, and as the doors opened, the driver bent down to tie his shoelace. Moto grabbed Lucia's hand and pulled her out of the van and onto the elevator behind him. The doors closed and the elevator lurched upward.

Moto had a brief moment to offer his usual cheerful smile.

"See? Under control."

The elevator stopped. The doors opened. Four men in military uniforms were standing immediately outside. Two rushed into the elevator. One grabbed Moto, one Lucia. A third, carrying an assault rifle, stood guard. The fourth, with a hand on a holstered pistol at his hip, said only, "Come!" And they were hurried—half dragged—down a long, dark hallway.

Lucia started to object, but the man with the pistol hissed, *"Silenzio!"* And the man who held her arm in a fierce grip spun her halfway around and gave her a look that convinced her that *silenzio* was indeed a good idea.

Minutes later, they were led into a room flooded with fluorescent lights that flickered and pulsed and filled the air with the buzz of a swarm of industrial hornets. The walls were bare, the floor concrete, everything tinged a faint green by the flickering light. After depositing Lucia and Moto, firmly and silently, in a pair of unpadded metal chairs, on opposite sides of the room, three of the uniformed men left. The fourth, the one with the assault rifle, stood by the closed door, silent, impassive, his face, like the walls, tinged green. There was no insignia of any kind on his uniform. Moto wasn't smiling now; he sat, as silent and impassive as the man with the gun. Lucia tried to ask what was happening, but the man by the door took a threatening step in her direction, and she fell silent again. Time passed. Occasionally the room vibrated with the roar of a jet taking off.

After what felt like an hour but could have been half that—or twice that—the lock clicked, the door opened, and the three men returned.

They led Lucia and Moto—firmly, but perhaps more gently—down the long hallway. Lucia fought to calm herself. Whatever lay ahead, panic wouldn't help. Maybe, she thought, that was why Moto seemed so calm. He was making certain he was ready when action was called for.

They went through a doorway, then down another hall and through another door. Lucia tried to keep track of the twists and turns, but it was hopeless. There was no way she could find her way back if they somehow broke loose. At one final doorway, the man with the pistol entered a series of numbers on a keypad, then held a plastic card against the pad and the door clicked open. On the other side was what looked like a standard airport security system: a walk-through metal detector and a conveyor belt for luggage, leading to an X-ray machine. The man gestured for them to take off their shoes, empty their pockets. Suddenly, it was shockingly normal. Just another visit to the standard hell of airport security. She slipped out of her shoes, took off her belt, dug her cell phone out of her pocket, and put her shoulder bag—somehow still miraculously with her—on the belt. As she walked through the metal detector, it occurred to Lucia—fleetingly, pointlessly—that their luggage, the two small suitcases they had taken for their trip to the villa in Tuscany what seemed like many weeks ago, had been left behind somewhere along the way. In the van? In the elevator? In the parking garage at the airport in Milan? She couldn't remember, and it really didn't matter, did it? Clean underwear was the least of her worries right now.

Behind her, she heard Moto cursing. "My cell phone!" He slapped his pockets in the standard hopeless search for something too bulky to

be misplaced in his tight jeans. "Fuck! It must have fallen out in the—"
He turned to go back the way they had come, but the man with the pistol grabbed his arm and wrenched him back toward the metal detector.

"No! I have to—"

The man pulled Moto closer and gave him a shove that sent him stumbling through the metal detector, into Lucia, almost knocking her off her feet. She grabbed him to steady them both, and she could feel he was trembling as energy surged through him. She didn't know what was going on, but she knew there was nowhere to go. No turning back. The man with the pistol entered numbers on another keypad. The door swung open to fierce daylight and the smell of jet fuel. They stepped outside onto airport tarmac. The roar and rumble of a jumbo jet taking off shook the air. A few yards away, dozens of passengers were boarding a bus that would take them to their plane. Lucia thought about screaming for help, thought about breaking loose and running. They wouldn't shoot her here, in front of so many people. She was glad she'd calmed herself to be ready for this moment. Her muscles tensed. It would be desperate, but—

The man holding her released her arm and stepped back. The man with the pistol handed Moto some papers and said, "Your boarding passes."

Moto nodded. He took Lucia's arm, gently guiding her onto the bus. Nothing to it.

Wedged in the crowd on the bus, she leaned against Moto, her cheek pressed to his, like a pair of lovers, and whispered, fighting to control her emotions, "What's happening?"

He pulled his head back slightly. He was in control of himself again, and his smile was as wide and innocent as sunrise on the Mediterranean. "We're going to Malta. Wasn't that the plan?"

She didn't know whether to hit him. Or hug him. Or kill him. Or cry. She settled for none of the above.

But she was tempted to reconsider the second of those three options an hour later when the plane landed. In Naples, not Malta.

∞

If keeping up with Lucia and Moto was exhausting, hunting for a four-hundred-year-old grave in Siena on a cold, rainy winter evening was much worse. On the long walk back to his hotel, through twisting, dark streets, Professor Richman kept himself moving with the thought that it would be too ironic to die alone in the cold after lecturing his young accomplices about the foolish danger of their plans. Death by murderous thugs was terrifying, death by irony was humiliating—and he'd be dead in either case.

Hours later, wrapped in a thick hotel robe, he emerged from a long, hot bath and, wreathed in steam, stepped into the bedroom of his hotel suite. He relaxed with a sigh of pleasure into the thick, soft leather of an armchair, picked up the house phone, and ordered an extravagant room-service dinner. He knew he deserved it.

To pass the time while he waited for his dinner, the professor went to the small safe in the room's walk-in closet, punched in the combination—the number of the apartment where he and his wife had lived as newlywed graduate students in Boston—and pulled out a small book, its soft leather cover stained and swollen, battered and bruised. The journal of Mario Fenelli, poet, adventurer, thief.

He held the book a long time, his face blank. Then his lips tightened and his shoulders raised slightly, almost a shrug. The murders of the young woman and her father were certainly tragic. But now the fact that he had borrowed the book—definitely borrowed, he had absolutely intended to return it—had proven providential. The book was irreplaceable. Invaluable. And now saved. It had been worth the bloody nose, a maneuver he had been able to call on almost at will throughout his life, but one which he thought he had left behind long ago as he reached the tranquility of what were supposed to be peaceful twilight years.

He paged through the book gently. He was going to need a lot of help interpreting the scrawled words. He closed the book and considered names, scholars he could rely on, colleagues he could trust. There were more than a few—and certainly some of them would still be alive.

His thoughts were interrupted by a knock at the door. An impressively fast performance by room service. He hurried to the closet and locked the book in the safe again, as the knocking repeated, more firmly this time. Professor Richman pulled his bathrobe tight and went to the door, calling, *"Sì, sì, arrivo!"*

He flung the door open and was stunned for an instant. A heavy-set man in an overcoat stood in the hall. Definitely not room service. He started to explain that the man had the wrong room, but before he could find words, a meaty hand shoved him hard and he stumbled backward into the room. The door slammed shut.

"Dov'è lei? Dove sono loro?"

"What?"

Thrown off-balance by the stranger's presence and his thick, guttural accent, the professor couldn't understand anything the man said. The intruder took a menacing step forward, and the professor replayed the questions in his mind. *Where is she? Where are they?*

"Who?"

The man spoke more slowly, clearly.

"Non sprecare il mio tempo." Don't waste my time. He held his big hands up, about a foot apart, as if he were going to reach out and crush the professor's skull. "Lucia and the *ragazzo*. Where are they?"

"I don't know."

The man stepped even closer. He reached out and patted the professor's cheek. It didn't feel like a playful gesture.

"Don't lie to me. Not ever. *Capisci?* Where are they?"

To his surprise, the professor found the courage to lie one more time. One last time, he hoped.

"I told them they were crazy. It was getting too dangerous." That much was certainly true. "I didn't want to know what they were doing or where they were going."

The man's eyes narrowed. "Dangerous? You don't know what is dangerous. Listen to me. You went to the villa outside Siena. All three of you. Then you went north. Then you stopped. Turned around. Went back to Milano. You hear what I'm saying? *Capisci?* They left you at Milano Centrale. They went to Malpensa. Then to Aeroporto Il Caravaggio. Then they disappeared. Now tell me. Where were they going?"

Aeroporto Il Caravaggio? This thug already knew more than the professor did. He looked to heaven, but there was no rescue there. He was going to lie again.

He raised his hands. His best Italian shrug of bewilderment.

"I don't know. I don't know. I don't—"

The man put his hand in the middle of the professor's chest and pushed him. He stumbled backward, tripped over an ottoman, and wound up sprawled in a chair.

The man pointed a warning finger at him, reached in his pocket, and pulled out a cell phone. He punched in a number and held the phone to his ear. While he apparently waited for an answer, phone in his left hand, pressed to his ear, he reached under his overcoat with his right hand and pulled out a pistol. He held it up to make sure the professor saw it. Then he started talking into the phone, rapidly. The professor couldn't understand a single word. He kept his eye on the gun, now waving in the air as the man gestured while he spoke into the phone.

Though he couldn't understand what the man was saying, the professor thought it sounded as if he was having an argument. His voice got louder, the tone took on a hard edge. His gestures with the pistol were more violent. After a long silence, he nodded sharply, spat out a final phrase, and snapped the phone shut.

He brought the pistol to bear on the professor and cocked the hammer.

The professor had escaped a kidnapping, fled from beheadings, fought through the cold Siena drizzle, and now he was going to die in his hotel room. In his bathrobe. This was beyond irony.

He grabbed the arms of the chair and levered himself forward, saying, even as he struggled upright, "I will die on my feet, you bastard."

There was a long moment. The gun pointing at the professor's chest never wavered.

"If you shoot me, everyone will hear. You'll never get away."

The thug smiled and nodded judiciously, as if acknowledging that the professor had a good point. He switched the gun to his left hand and dug his right hand into his overcoat pocket. A moment later, there was a metallic click and a long knife gleamed in the thug's thick hand. Lowering the gun, he raised the blade and took a step closer.

In a moment of determination that, if he was going to die, he should die well—and even finding an instant to think, *Nec spe. Nec metu*—Professor Rafael Aristotle Richman took a sharp breath and spat into the man's face. His mouth was dry and all he managed was a fine spray of spittle, but some of it splattered on the weathered, dark-browed face that was going to be the last thing he saw on earth.

Chapter 17

Roma
1605

Cecco had acquired the skill to discern the quality of pigments and haggle for the best price for his master. Now, Caravaggio trusted him to procure most of the raw colors for his paints. The most costly ones the artist bought himself while still instructing the boy how to determine quality and value.

"Look at the consistency of color in this lapis lazuli," Caravaggio said, poking an irregular stone in his palm.

"Handle it carefully, Maestro," said the merchant. "If the color rubs off on your hand, you'll be required to pay for my loss!"

"I'll pay when I'm satisfied with its value, signore!" said Caravaggio, turning away from the merchant. "As if the color can rub off a hard stone!

"See how this piece compares with the last?" he said to Cecco.

"I see the color is true throughout," said Cecco quietly. He studied the precious nugget carefully. "And there are no clumps of intensity or texture."

"And the vibrant color," said Caravaggio in a whisper. He nodded to his student.

"Are you buying or not?" said the merchant, his breath hot on Caravaggio's shoulder.

"I don't use lapis lazuli much," said the artist, setting down the stone. "Blue is not my color. It rarely visits my palette." He turned away. "Come on, Cecco. Let's go. I want to take a look at the yellow ochre at Rafaello's shop."

As they turned to leave, the merchant plucked at Caravaggio's sleeve.

"*Aspettate*, Maestro! Wait, *per favore*. I'll make you a special price."

Caravaggio nodded, darting a look at his pupil.

One day, as Cecco wound his way through the streets of Roma toward the pigment merchants, he chanced to see the three Tomassoni brothers. Behind them walked two of the Giugoli brothers, Ignazio and Federigo, walking with their sister, Lavinia, Ranuccio's wife.

Cecco crossed the little *vicolo* to avoid confronting them.

Ranuccio laughed loudly.

"Where are you going, little catamite?" he scoffed. The Giugoli brothers guffawed at the insult.

"*Bar-das-sa!*" sang Ranuccio in a taunt. *Fuck boy.*

"Leave him alone, Ranuccio," said Giovan, the eldest Tomassoni.

Ranuccio made a sour face, unleashing another volley.

"See how you walk, you *finocchio*! Caravaggio knows not how to fuck or paint!"

Giovan grabbed his brother by the neck of his tunic, jerking him around to face him.

"I told you to leave him alone, Ranuccio. Leave him in peace."

"Why should I?" snarled Ranuccio. "He is an abomination, as is his master."

"He's a boy, you idiot. I want no quarrels with Caravaggio," said Giovan. He pushed his brother hard, making him stumble and fall to his knees. "You'll end up skewered through the liver, you stupid fool."

Cecco hurried ahead, almost running toward the pigment merchants on the banks of the Tiber.

Later, Cecco walked home along Via di Ripetta. In a bag by his side, wrapped in a moist linen rag, he had the *terra di Umbria*, Umbrian earth, a moist clay. He knew it would make a perfect burnt umber with careful heating, a rich dark hue that would enchant his master. He also carried a stoppered glass bottle of fluffy crimson powder—madder root from Smyrna, more precious than even the Dutch root. And there was a good nugget of—

Cecco halted in midstep. Across Via di Ripetta, he spied Lavinia Giugoli Tomassoni walking alongside her younger brother. She whispered something in his ear and he nodded. He scowled at the apprentice like a mad wolf.

Lavinia approached Cecco. He tried to hurry by, but she stopped him, putting her moist hand on his bare arm. He pulled back at her touch.

"*Aspetta!* Wait," she said. "I want to apologize for my husband insulting you."

Cecco bowed his head, unable to speak. He felt the heat rise from his neck.

Lavinia's voice was high-pitched like a little girl's.

A most unusual octave for a grown woman.

"Truly, I apologize," she said. "It was cruel of him. It has nothing to do with you, *ragazzo*."

Cecco looked into her eyes. She was quite pretty in a fair-haired, blue-eyed way. But the impression she gave Cecco was that she was a weak imitation of beauty, faded like colored linen left in the sun. She did not have the color and passion of a Caravaggio model. And her voice irritated him.

Why is this woman speaking to me? Could she not leave me alone?

"My husband is a very jealous man," she said. "And a dangerous one. Please forgive him."

"*È niente,*" Cecco mumbled. *It's nothing.*

Please let me go before Ranuccio comes and sees me talking with you!

"I make you uncomfortable, I see," she said, scanning his face. "I'll leave you in peace." Before she left him, she squeezed his arm, leaning close. He smelled a unique scent of jasmine on her skin.

"Give my salutations to your master," she said. She left, the cloying perfume still lingering in the air.

Chapter 18

Valletta, Malta
1605

The wind raced wet and cold off the sea, rattling the windows of St. John's Cathedral. Winter storms often battered the remote outpost of Malta, a rocky speck in the Mediterranean, south of Sicily.

Alof de Wignacourt, grand master of the Knights of Malta, shivered under his wool tunic, boots, and leggings. A nagging cough rattled the eight-pointed cross hanging on his chest. The tomblike air trapped in the limestone church made his aging bones ache. He thought of his home in Provence, with its aroma of lavender and linden trees, abuzz with honeybees.

Wignacourt lifted his head from prayer, looking up past the simple altar at the stone block wall.

Les pierres, calcaires.

Limestone. The bones of this rocky island. How humble a tribute to our Saint John. A pauper's offering. No glory here!

The Knights of Malta have aided and defended Christians since the medieval ages, in Jerusalem and beyond. Should not the oratory of our glorious Saint John be properly adorned with his image, rather than this barren face of rock?

Wignacourt shifted his weight on his knees. He suffered from old wounds from the Great Siege of 1565, when he was but seventeen years old. The grand master winced, then cursed at his body, shutting his eyes tight.

"*Tais-toi!*" he mumbled aloud.

Shut up! This is a moment with God, you fool. Not a time to console the flesh.

Dear God. Bless our Maltese order, our eight houses of nations, les huit langues. *Together we from so many countries pray with one heart, our devotion to you dictates our lives.*

Help us to heal the sick in our infirmaries and give them comfort. May we defeat the barbarian Turks who thirst to murder us and grab our fortress outpost of rock. May these islands stand as a bastion between the infidel barbarians and Christendom of Europe.

He opened his eyes again to see the candlelit crucifix on the altar. He gazed beyond the altar at the empty expanse of limestone blocks.

How the stone begs to be adorned with the grace of God. A painting depicting our great saint and his martyrdom—

He felt a presence hovering by his right shoulder. The aging knight swiveled his head to see nothing but unadorned stone.

Chapter 19

Roma
1605

Mario Minniti lit a candle and lumbered up the stairs of 19 Vicolo dei Santi Cecilia e Biagio. Despite the fact that Mario had known Caravaggio since the first year he had come to Roma, he had never visited his bottega in this house. He saw the gaping hole in the roof and stopped to stare up at the bright stars glittering above his head.

"Idiot," he mumbled. "Incorrigible arrogance."

Minniti knew Caravaggio as well as anyone alive.

Of course he would need a source of light. Certo *he would not worry what the landlady had to say about the damage.*

He spied Cecco asleep in a cot alongside Caravaggio's bed, snoring softly.

The boy has grown—he is no longer the cherub Michele painted in Love Conquers All.

Minniti grimaced. *Like me, he will have outgrown his usefulness as a lover.*

Minniti remembered drunken nights when he and Caravaggio, young apprentices at Cavaliere d'Arpino's studio, had found pleasure in each other's bodies. They had no money for food, let alone whores, so they had made do. But in Roma, while a young boy was not uncommon in a man's bed, a boy beyond puberty was considered disgusting.

Mario walked closer to the sleeping boy.

See the pimples on his face, the stray dark facial hairs of a man. I'm sure he cannot appeal any longer to Michele. Cecco is purely an apprentice now. So Michele seeks out whores.

As Mario watched, the sleeping boy's eyelashes fluttered. He stared up into Mario Minniti's face. Startled, he sprang to his feet.

"It's all right, Cecco," whispered Mario. "*Calmati!* Relax. Your master told me to wait here for him. He wanted me to see a new canvas."

Cecco stood naked. Minniti saw the curly mat of pubic hair and dangling penis as the adolescent pulled on his leggings.

"I'm sorry I startled you," said Minniti. "Michelangelo gave me the key when I wouldn't wait any longer."

"It's all right, Maestro," said Cecco, his voice still hoarse with sleep. "*Va bene.*"

His voice has changed, thought Minniti. *He is indeed a boy no longer.*

"Where is my master now?" asked Cecco, fumbling with the waist tie of his leggings.

"In Piazza Navona arguing with a tavern owner about being cheated. Overcharged for his wine and supper, he claimed. I had enough of it and told him I'd meet him here."

Cecco rubbed his eyes. "Did he have his sword?"

"Yes," said Mario, shrugging. "And his dagger too. He will probably be arrested again. His shouts attracted the *sbirri* and he insulted them as well. I'm tired of defending him. He drags every one of us into his Greek drama."

Cecco laughed softly. "You know as well as anyone."

"*Sì,*" said Mario, shrugging his shoulders. Then he looked the boy square in the eyes. "The two of us know him too well. How is he treating you, Cecco?"

Cecco blushed hot red and looked away. "I'm learning a lot. I think my own art is improving."

"So he tells me. Might I see some of your work?"

The boy swallowed hard. Minniti could see his Adam's apple bob.

"I would be honored to show you, Maestro Minniti," said Cecco, nodding. "But I beg you not to judge me too harshly. I'm only begin—"

"Let me see it, Cecco. I'm not such a cruel master as our friend. He showers me with insults about my own paintings—and always has!"

Cecco's mouth twisted in a shy grin.

He walked to the far corner of the room, where he stored his canvas and colors. As he unrolled a painting, Minniti could see it was prepared in black gesso, imitating Caravaggio's style.

The canvas spread open, spilling luscious images of apples, pears, and grapes in a bowl, two amber-burnished lutes, and a scattering of leaves on the sunlit floor.

Minniti stared at the brushstrokes, the shadow and light that imitated Caravaggio himself. Yet there was a spark of Cecco's own vision.

He has a gift.

"They are good, Cecco. You have a knack for the shadow. And perspective. Really quite remarkable, Signor Boneri!"

He clapped the teenager on the back. His fingertips met bone, and he flinched.

Skinny bugger.

Cecco did not notice. He ducked his head in humility, absorbing the compliment.

Mario smiled at the boy. *What a hard life he must have, enduring the wild tempers of Michelangelo.*

"Have you given much thought to your future?"

"I hope to find a patron one day, like Maestro Caravaggio has done. But I wish to remain by his side forever. I am devoted to him and his art. He is a genius."

Mario could not hide the sadness in his eyes. Cecco saw it there.

"Have I said something wrong, Master Minniti?"

"No, no. Of course not. Well . . ."

"What is it?"

"Caravaggio is a difficult man to . . . remain friends with. I am as close a friend as he has ever had, I believe. But it becomes a nightmare. His rages."

Cecco nodded, his face betraying fear. "I worry about him. He and Signor Tomassoni—"

"It's more than just Ranuccio. Michele has a fight to pick with the whole world. See how he has not returned even yet? I will wager he has been arrested again."

Cecco's face tightened with worry. "I should go, then—"

"And do what? Don't you know that you could bring him more trouble?"

"What do you mean?"

"At your age. You living here with him."

"I am his apprentice," said Cecco, swallowing hard. "I—"

"And you have shared his bed. There are laws, Cecco. He could be put to death. As you grow older, the clergy will no longer look the other way."

All color drained from the boy's face. Minniti felt a rush of compassion and grasped the boy by the shoulders, squeezing him gently.

"You must understand that. The same could have happened to—well, I have been in your situation. I loved Caravaggio, but then we both grew up. It's only now that I realize—"

"I—I should go," the boy stuttered. "I must look for my master."

"And if he is in prison?"

"I will tell Cardinal del Monte. And the Marchesa Colonna."

Mario expelled his breath in a deep sigh. "His guardian angels. Always to the rescue. And you. Looking out for him like a faithful dog."

"He is my master!" said Cecco, his eyes flashing. "I—"

The door downstairs banged open.

"Mario!" shouted a drunken voice. "Mario, you Sicilian *bastardo*! You cowardly scoundrel. Where were you when I had to defend my honor from these Roman nincompoops?"

Mario shook his head. The faithful Cecco's face shone with relief and the faintest hint of pride.

Cecco never grew accustomed to the women in his master's bed. Night after night, Caravaggio would stumble in drunk with whores or loose women, and occasionally young boys. As his fame grew, sometimes he would return with more than one lover at a time.

The whores offered their bodies for free. They clung to the artist, charmed by his reputation, rough demeanor, and bravado. The women of the night hoped for a chance to model for a masterpiece. But it wasn't only the prostitutes who found their way into his bed . . . there were clandestine trysts, even with married women who wanted Caravaggio.

In the cramped apartment at 19 Vicolo dei Santi Cecilia e Biagio, the upstairs room was used as a studio, and one room was used as a kitchen and shop, leaving only one small bedroom for both artist and apprentice. Cecco's pallet was set in a corner, across from Caravaggio's bed.

The boy had been with Caravaggio since he was very young. He learned the sounds of sex as a young child before they held any significance. Long before Caravaggio ever reached for him as a lover, the boy had been exposed to the sounds, smells, and sight of lovemaking.

Lusty laughs and obscenities drifted across the room where the apprentice lay, trying to sleep. The musky smells, acrid and potent, wafted from the sheets. The sounds of sucking, slapping flesh, creaking boards, and animallike screams of pleasure and pain penetrated the boy's ears, even as he plugged them with paint-stained fingers.

There was plenty of sex. It mattered not if it was with male or female. Caravaggio's appetites were insatiable. He wasn't bisexual but omnisexual. His lovemaking was rough and selfish, though his partners begged for more, trying to worm their way back into his embrace even when he spurned them.

One night, Cecco was fast asleep, dreaming of a seashore next to shallow turquoise waters glistening with silver fish. Caravaggio stumbled in drunk with a woman every bit as intoxicated as he was. Raucous and more belligerent than usual, the artist began tearing off his lover's clothes. She shrieked with joy.

Cecco turned over under his blanket, facing the wall.

Ah, but tonight's lover was a squealer! For every kiss, lick, and poke, she screamed like a stuck guinea pig.

Cecco pulled his pillow over his ears, fighting to fall back asleep. But something about this woman haunted him. From her clothes and the scent of her perfume, Cecco knew this was no whore.

What does it matter? I want to return to the seaside. To the blue waters and teeming fish. The sand warm under my feet.

"Ah! Ah! Ah!" panted the woman under the artist. "Take me, Michelangelo. Take m-m-me!"

Cecco's eyes flew open. He knew that shrill voice.

No, Maestro! No!

Cecco sat up in the moonlight, staring over at the bed.

"You are an animal in bed, Lavinia," growled Caravaggio, pumping hard, his knees bent, hovering over the women's body.

"What's the matter?" gasped Caravaggio, going at her faster. "Doesn't Ranuccio ever give it to you?"

Cecco stopped breathing.

The woman shrieked in orgasm, her scream piercing the night.

Chapter 20

SIENA

For a room-service meal, the dinner really was extraordinarily good. And having finished every last bite despite a bad sore throat, Professor Richman treated himself to a ridiculously expensive miniature bottle of excellent single-malt whiskey from the minibar. The price was absurd—perhaps to be expected at the best hotel in Siena—but a man certainly deserved some kind of celebration after escaping certain death.

Extending that celebration to a second tiny bottle—which he sipped much more slowly than the first—the professor let his mind wander back to the moment when the thug, a knife in his hand and spittle on his face, had lunged forward and grabbed the professor's throat in a grip that seemed likely to kill him in seconds without need for the knife. Surprised at his own calm, the professor had waited for death, staring into his assailant's eyes—and realized he was watching a struggle for self-control. He saw self-control win out. The grip on his throat relaxed, and the professor gasped for air. The man shoved him back into his chair, snarled an incomprehensible obscenity, and slipped—silently for someone of his size—out of the room.

Professor Richman had still been recovering his breath when his dinner arrived. And hungry though he was, he took his time answering, peering carefully through the peephole before he opened the door.

❧

"Why don't you use my cell phone?"

It was the third time Lucia had asked, and now that they were sitting in a cheap Naples hotel room, Moto finally had a chance to answer. The first time she had asked was in the airport after he had explained that, yes, they were in Naples, not Malta, and it was all according to plan, but now everything was a mess because he'd lost his cell phone and he couldn't call the people he needed to talk to for the next leg of the trip. And now they needed to find a taxi.

The second time she'd asked had been in the taxi on the way into town—rocking over huge, uneven paving stones that looked to have been there since Roman times, threading their way through an impossible throng of people and motorbikes and enormous buses that crowded the narrow street beyond all reasonable belief and filled the air with a thick mix of exhaust fumes and blaring horns—and he'd simply gestured at the madness surrounding them. But now he had to answer.

"I can't use your phone because they won't answer."

"Why not?"

"They won't answer unless they know the number the call's coming from. They know my number. They don't know yours. They won't answer."

Lucia's eyebrows knit. The deep crease appeared. "Who are these people, Moto?"

"Just . . . people. Friends."

"Moto . . ." There was a warning in her voice.

"Lulu, don't ask. I trust them with my life. With your life. Our lives. I can't tell you any more than that."

"That's not good enough."

"I can't."

"I don't want their names. But I need to know more than I do. You want me to trust them because you trust them. But right now I'm not sure I know who you are."

"You know me."

"No, I don't. I mean, yes, I do. But I'm finding out there's a lot about you that I don't know—and it's been smacking me right in the face all day. You going crazy at the Alitalia counter. The laundry van. The driver who looked right through us. The men with guns. The boarding passes. And now your mystery cell phone. Moto! Who the hell are you?"

The room was silent for a long time—silent except for the endless din of traffic and the buzzing of the hotel's neon sign that was right outside their window.

Finally, Moto said, "My father is a businessman. A successful businessman. He has a lot of connections. He has interests in a lot of companies. OK?"

"And . . . ?"

"One of those companies is Biancheria Biancaneve. They go everywhere. Everyone needs clean linen. Even airports. So . . . there are"—his hands waved vaguely—"people, people who work for my father. And I can ask for a favor. They want to make my father happy. They want to make me happy."

"Even airport security?"

"Everyone needs clean linen."

Lucia fell back onto the bed. The springs creaked. She stared up at the water-stained ceiling and shivered in the damp chill.

"Trust me," Moto said.

Lucia closed her eyes.

"So if that settles your question"—he sounded a little annoyed—"I've got a question of my own."

Lucia nodded.

"Why are we making ourselves crazy—why are we risking our lives—chasing after that worthless bastard?"

"Caravaggio?"

"You know any other worthless bastards?"

"You want a list?"

"Never mind. Yes. Caravaggio. I never knew much about him. Only the name. So I've been reading about him, and—"

"I thought you hated to read."

"Don't make fun of me." But he was smiling. "You dragged me into this mess."

"That's what friends are for."

"Thank you?" A moment to share a smile. Then: "I wanted to know what I'm risking my life for. And Caravaggio was a worthless, mean bastard. He betrayed everybody who got anywhere near him, anyone who did him a favor. And those little boys! That painting of Cecco as Cupid? How old was he? Twelve? Fourteen? And you look at that painting, and you know Caravaggio was—"

"OK. I get it. You're right. So . . . ?"

"So why are we chasing after that miserable bastard? That's what I asked in the first place."

And Lucia wasn't certain she had the real answer. But she did have an easy answer, so she gave it. "We aren't chasing the miserable bastard. We're chasing the genius. The genius that's in his paintings. Sometimes we have to put up with bastards—if they're geniuses."

And Moto seemed to accept that. It was a perfectly good answer. They were chasing the genius, not the bastard.

But Lucia wasn't sure it was the truth.

Because still she wasn't certain why she cared. Why she was chasing anything. Man or genius. Why she didn't just let it go.

But Moto was satisfied, so she gratefully let it drop.

And again, for a long time, there was only the sound of traffic and the buzzing of the neon. Then Lucia sat up and her face was alive again.

She hugged Moto hard.

"OK. I'm still not sure I know who you are, but I can't stop trusting you now," she said. "So what do we do?"

"A good night's sleep," he said. "Some decent coffee in the morning. And then—we're in Naples, there must be a few Caravaggios in this town. Right?"

The coffee was strong. The pastries sweet and buttery. Moto glanced at the morning paper while Lucia finished her research on the cell phone Moto refused to use.

She put down the phone. "OK. Three Caravaggios here. *Seven Acts of Mercy. Flagellation of Christ. Martyrdom of Santa Ursula.*"

Moto raised his eyebrows. "So? Which do we see?"

"Right now, I don't care about mercy. And I'm not in the mood for another dead saint."

Moto pursed his lips in a soundless whistle.

"Tough talk."

"You asked."

"So . . . a little flagellation to start the day?"

Lucia nodded. "They say the painting's a 'sadistic ballet.' That feels like the story we're in, right?"

"Suits me." Moto's cheerfulness was unabashed.

"And your friends? The ones who don't answer the phone."

"Nothing to do but wait and see."

Lucia stood and stared at Christ's writhing body and the dark faces grinning in the shadows behind him. The museum was quiet in the winter. They were almost alone in the gallery. The guards were bored. Lucia stared.

At one point, her cell phone rang and she hurried out into the hall to answer it.

"Thank you for calling me back. I know how busy you must be, but as I said in my message, I'm working on my thesis on the spiritual impacts of lost art, and I would love to be able to include the insights of a man as distinguished as you."

She paused a minute, listening, then said, "Well, of course I can. I understand how busy you are. OK, Via del Cerriglio. We'll be there." A short pause. "My associate and myself."

Then she went back into the gallery.

An hour later, she went back out into the hall. Moto was there. He'd given the *Flagellation* a good long look and had been wandering through the museum ever since.

"There are a couple of Titians here you really need to see."

"I'm sure I do, but we don't have time, because we have an appointment to meet with Umberto Bruno, professor emeritus of the Università degli Studi di Napoli, who has dedicated his career to the details of Caravaggio's time in Naples."

"How did you manage that?"

"I called him. He called me back." She held up her cell phone. "These are really handy. You ought to get one."

Moto's hand automatically went to check his pocket for the phone that wasn't there. "Where are we meeting him?"

"Locanda del Cerriglio."

A moment of silence, then she giggled.

"How cool is that?"

"Are you crazy?"

"I know."

"That's where Caravaggio was almost killed."

"I know."

"And what about the guys that want to kill us?" Moto gestured helplessly. "Lulu . . . you're . . ."

"I know."

✷

Early winter dark had fallen by the time they had walked the hour and a half—including time for getting lost—it took them to get to the Locanda del Cerriglio. Four hundred years after Caravaggio's time in Naples, the neighborhood had almost certainly improved. There was a nice-enough hotel down the block and a few high-class stores around the corner. But Naples was a city of chiaroscuro, where there were always shadows within the light, and the corner where the Locanda del Cerriglio was tucked was more than dark enough.

And after they stood waiting for nearly an hour, more than cold enough.

Moto shivered and stamped his feet. "Apparently, *professori emeriti* don't have to be on time."

Lucia checked the time on her cell phone again. Despite the long walk, they'd been there early. The professor was more than half an hour late. As she stared at it, the phone buzzed in her hand.

Her side of the conversation was short.

"Yes . . . I . . . but . . . OK. Well, can we—"

She stared at the phone for a moment, then put it back in her pocket and turned to Moto.

"That was strange. The professor. He was so friendly this afternoon. Now he just said he wouldn't be here. That was it. Not sorry. No offer of another time. Fast and cold and then he hung up on me."

"Great. Now what?"

Lucia shivered and glanced around, peering into the dark. "I don't know. Maybe we could have dinner at Locanda del Cerriglio."

Moto started to answer, but a metal garage door right behind them rattled open, and a man in a black monk's robe lunged out, clapped a hand over Lucia's mouth, and dragged her back inside. Moto leapt to grab her, but a second man in black robes jumped out of the dark building, knocked him flat, kicked him in the head, and then ran to help the first man wrestle Lucia into the dark of the garage.

Moto struggled back to his feet and started after them, but a third man, in a leather jacket with a fedora jammed down on his head, rushed past him, knocking him sprawling again, and raced into the darkness where Lucia had disappeared. From inside the garage, there were shouts, the sounds of a struggle, a scream—was it Lucia? Moto tried to get up again, but his head was spinning and he had to fight to keep his balance.

Suddenly, Lucia emerged from the dark, half running, half dragged by the man in the leather jacket, who spun around, grabbed the metal door, and yanked it down, slamming it shut. He stood, breathing heavily, blood running down his face from a gash—a knife wound—across his cheek. It hadn't been an easy rescue. He'd lost his fedora somewhere in the struggle.

"*Idioti!*" he spat. He grabbed Moto by both shoulders, stared him in the eye, looked as if he was about to say something, and then slapped him hard across the face.

A car roared up, and the man shoved Moto and Lucia into the back seat and clambered in after them, pressing a handkerchief against his bloody cheek as the car raced into the night.

Moto started to say something, but the man gave a wordless growl that left no room for anything else as the car surged through the streets, the impenetrable traffic of Naples somehow parting magically before them.

The car finally stopped in a narrow alley, just around the corner from the sputtering neon sign in front of the cheap hotel where the day had begun. The driver climbed out and pulled Lucia and Moto roughly into the street, leaving the other man in the back seat, blood soaking through the handkerchief and running down his jaw.

The driver raised his hand, and for a moment, he looked ready to slap Moto, the way the first man had. But then he turned his attention to Lucia.

"Get out of here." His voice was a low growl. His accent guttural. "Go back to your fucking books. There's nothing for you here. You're in over your head. You'll drown. And next time we won't be here to save you."

He glanced back at Moto again and took a step closer. He raised a finger in warning. Moto's face was set in a scowl, trying to match the man who moved even closer and rested that single finger against Moto's chest.

"Do you understand? We're done. No more. You're on your own."

The other man was out of the car now. He had taken the blood-soaked cloth off his face, and the wound gaped, blood crusting and still trickling down his jaw and onto his neck. He leaned close, dabbed a finger into his bloody wound, reached out, and drew a line in blood down Moto's cheek.

"Next time," he hissed, "your blood. Not mine."

He turned his head and spat.

Chapter 21

Roma
1605

Onorio Longhi turned down the tiny street in Campo Marzio at three o'clock in the afternoon. The cold wind whistled around the corner, biting his face. He crossed his arms against his chest, ducking his bearded chin against the gust. His stomach growled as he thought of lunch.

Artichokes. Swimming in garlic oil. Ho fame. I'm hungry, damn it!

He could already taste their clean flavor and tenderness in his mouth. No restaurant prepared *carciofi* better than Il Moro on Via della Maddalena.

As Longhi rapped on the door of 19 Vicolo dei Santi Cecilia e Biagio and entered, he immediately felt the draft of the frigid air pouring in through the roof.

He gazed up at the coating of black smoke coloring the walls. His eyes followed the light to the gaping hole and the charred bits of rafter.

"Why must everyone gawk up at the ceiling like a lost goose?" said Caravaggio, buckling his sword around his waist. "I can't paint without light, damn it!"

The architect stared up and whistled. "Does your landlady know?"

"It's none of her damned business. She let this house to me, the sour old bitch."

Longhi shook his head.

"Enough! Let's go. I'm hungry enough to eat my canvas."

Longhi pointed to Caravaggio's sword. He shook his head. "*Cazzo!* You know the guards will arrest you again if you carry that weapon. Leave it here. You don't need it. I've got mine."

"The guards can take it up the ass," said the artist. "I'll tell them I'm still in Cardinal del Monte's household—"

"Bah! You haven't been with him for a year now! Michele, you are no nobleman, they—"

"Shut your mouth, you swine."

"No!" said Longhi, standing with his hands on his hips. "They'll throw you in prison again, you hardheaded idiot!"

Caravaggio waved away his friend's words. "I can talk my way out of trouble."

"Don't be a fool, Michele. Leave the sword. I can defend both of us with—"

"Shut up, Onorio, or I'll cut your tongue out. And if we are to eat on Via della Maddalena, they'd better prepare my artichokes properly. Last time I was at Il Moro, they tried to serve them to me swimming in oil."

"So what? Alla Romana, in oil," said Longhi, shrugging.

"The oil way is *merda*," Caravaggio said, tightening the buckle another notch on his waist. He opened the door for his friend, and they descended into the narrow backstreet off the Piazza Navona.

Longhi shrugged. "Alla Romana with oil isn't bad. I've had them both ways there."

"Some Milanese you are! The way to ruin an artichoke is to cook it in oil."

"*Cazzo*, Michele. I say they are good both ways. What is your problem with a little olive oil?"

"*Schifoso!* To take such a delicacy and smear it in greasy olive oil. Disgusting. Rancid, I bet. Sweet butter—but these *porci romani* don't understand good cookery."

"Basta!" said Longhi. "What the hell do I care about you and your fucking artichokes? Tell me something interesting. What about that Fillide—now she's a *figa* I'd like to peel."

Caravaggio shrugged. "I paint her. That's all."

"Of course you haven't had her in bed. She'd make you pay dearly to touch her sweet ass. Or Ranuccio would. Pay through the nose."

They turned down the street to Piazza Navona.

"She's an honest whore," said Caravaggio. "Giustiniani has her in his bed and she doesn't mess with anyone else."

"Pff!" Longhi laughed, throwing back his head. "An honest whore, indeed! She's always ready for a roll with Ranuccio."

Caravaggio's eyes narrowed. "You don't know what you're talking about."

"The hell I don't! That whore has a soft spot for her pimp. And I hear she's raging jealous. A regular hellcat."

"Che cosa?" said Caravaggio, stopping. *What?*

"Here we are."

Longhi grabbed Caravaggio by the arm and headed through a doorway crowded with men, cups of wine in their hands.

"And look who's here!" shouted Longhi when they were inside the tavern. "Mario Minniti! My friend Bacchus." Longhi waved wide at the Sicilian painter, and Minniti waved back from a corner of the tavern. He was wedged in between two other men who talked over his head. "We'll have to squeeze in."

"Aspetta! Wait! What about Fillide? Finish what you were saying, Onorio."

"I'll tell you everything. But let's get a place at a table first or we'll never eat."

Longhi and Caravaggio plunged into the noisy crowd.

"Over there," said Longhi, pointing to two customers pulling coins from their purses at the end of the table down from Minniti. "Grab a place, quick."

"Amici!" said Minniti. He turned to the men sitting between him and his newly arrived friends. "Signori! Would you mind moving together here so I can join my friends? I see you have finished your meal."

The two men grumbled, waving them away.

Longhi put his hand on the hilt of his sword, standing his ground. "Don't make me repeat my friend's polite request," he growled.

The diners grumbled again but slid across the rickety bench groaning with the shift of weight.

The two artists and the architect squeezed together. Harried waiters rushed through the crowd, carrying enormous trays of pasta, salami, pig's trotters, and roasted meats. The air was filled with the smell of woodsmoke and garlic-laced olive oil. Caravaggio spotted a terra-cotta bowl brimming with artichokes that glistened in oil.

A waiter plunked down a jug of red wine and wiped the sweat from his brow. "Signori. What do you desire? The Siciliano here has already ordered."

Minniti grunted. "This Sicilian hasn't been served yet. Do your job!"

"The stew," said Longhi. "The one you served to the man with the plumed hat over there."

The waiter looked over his shoulder. "Pig's tripe. Spicy."

"Sì," said Longhi. "With bread. Lots of it."

"Same," said Caravaggio. "But first artichokes. Make them with butter, no oil."

The waiter lifted his chin, then spat on the floor. Caravaggio's back stiffened as he glared from the waiter to the glistening spittle.

"Your accent, signore. You are from the north?"

"Milano," said Longhi. "Both of us. But we're Romans now, aren't we, Caravaggio?"

"Prepare the *carciofi* in butter, *cameriere!*" said Caravaggio. "The way they should be."

"You make mine with oil," said Minniti. "I've had them here. Not as good as in Sicilia, but they are good. *Molto buoni*—"

"You damned southerners and your fucking olive oil," said Caravaggio. "In butter, damn it! Make them proper or I'll leave without paying."

"The cook will make them proper," said the waiter. He rubbed his thumb hard against his mustache. "And you'll pay or I'll call the guards on you."

"I'll show the *sbirri* what I think of them. Go ahead!" Caravaggio touched the hilt of his sword. "Call them!"

"Waiter—give us more wine," shouted a drunken man down the table. The waiter strode off, cursing.

"Michele!" said Longhi. "You are a colossal ass! You know he'll spit in our food now."

"Never mind the fucking waiter," said Caravaggio. "Tell me about Fillide. What did you mean about Ranuccio Tomassoni?"

"What about Ranuccio?" said Minniti. "He's trouble, that one. Always ready to draw his sword."

Longhi took a long draught of wine. "I shouldn't have told you, Michele. You take all *a cuore*, to heart. You start to pout . . . and the next minute you explode in a rage."

"Tell me, damn you!" said Caravaggio, clenching his fist.

"Let me get drunk first," said Longhi.

"Here," said Minniti, lifting the jug of wine and pouring Longhi another cup. "*Salute!*"

"Tell me!" said Caravaggio.

"All right, all right," said Longhi, draining his cup. "Day before yesterday, Fillide found another whore in Tomassoni's bed. Prudenza Zacchia, the one with breasts the size of August melons. Who knows where his wife was, the slattern! That one might as well be a whore—"

"Damn you! Tell me about Fillide!"

"Don't be impatient, *amico*," said Longhi. "Anyway . . . Fillide pulled the whore out of bed by her hair and then cut her with a knife. She tried for a *sfregio*—a slash of revenge—across the face, but Prudenza put up her hands, warding her off."

Longhi poured himself another cup of wine and crumpled up laughing.

"What happened?" demanded Caravaggio. "What's so funny?"

"Prudenza ran screaming to the guards. They arrested Fillide. But when they let her go, she went straight to Prudenza's house and tried to cut her again! She was screeching, 'I'll get you next time and cut you right! You'll never work again.'"

Minniti roared with laughter. "That sounds like Fillide! What a wench—there could be no better match for Ranuccio, the son of a bitch."

Caravaggio threw a smoldering look at his artist friend. He saw the color blooming on the Sicilian's cheeks from the wine, reminiscent of his painting of Bacchus that so enchanted the cardinals.

"Tell us more, Longhi!" said Minniti.

Longhi wiped the wine from his mouth. "Prudenza's mother made a complaint to the authorities, but Fillide kept it up. 'I'll get you proper next time, you dirty whore! Stay out of Ranuccio's bed, *puttana*!'"

Minniti sputtered wine across the table. "She's got spirit, that whore!"

Caravaggio stared fixedly across the smoky room. His vision blurred, and from the corners of his eyes, he saw blackness descend like a curtain.

He knew it far too well. He closed his eyes, shaking his head.

Longhi stopped laughing, noticing the change in his friend.

"What's the matter, *amico*?" said Longhi, wiping his mouth. "Come on. Fillide is just a whore like all the rest. But Tomassoni has his hooks in her heart. And his *pene* in her—"

"Shut up!" said Caravaggio savagely. "Don't you know when to shut your mouth, you dirty pig?"

"Who are you calling a pig?" snarled Longhi. "Just because I call a whore a whore?"

"It's true, Michele," said Minniti. "You know none of them are Madonnas, no matter how well you paint them. Any more than I am Bacchus! Let it go."

The waiter returned with two servings of artichokes, four in each clay bowl.

The artist stared down at the food. His mouth hardened. The corner of his left cheek twitched. "Which are the ones in butter?" demanded Caravaggio.

The waiter shrugged. A couple of customers called for wine. Another called to pay for his meal, banging his cup on the table.

He shook his head in exasperation. "Smell them, Milanese!" snapped the waiter. He turned to clear the plates of the men next to them.

"What do you mean, smell them!" roared Caravaggio.

"Michelangelo, *tranquillo*!" said Minniti. "Settle down, he—"

Caravaggio seized one of the bowls and dumped the artichokes on the table. "Insolent bastard!" he shouted at the waiter, leaping to his feet. "You think you are serving some damned bum! I'll show you who I am, you cuckold!"

The men next to them jumped from the bench, their plates and cups clattering.

"What in the name of God is wrong with you, Michele?" said Longhi. "I'm hungry. Let's look for a fight after we eat!"

The artist hurled the wine pitcher at the waiter, hitting him squarely on the cheek.

"*Merda!*" said Minniti. "There goes lunch."

The waiter pressed a hand to his face, his fingertips coming away bloody.

Caravaggio reached for his sword.

"You are crazy!" said Longhi, grabbing him by his elbow.

The waiter ran from the restaurant, lumbering down Via della Maddalena toward the police station, his food-stained apron flapping.

With one hand on his sword, Minniti grabbed an oily artichoke from the broken crockery, tore away the leaves to the heart, and stuffed it in his mouth. "Let's go," he said through a mouthful. "That waiter will be back with the *sbirri*, you fucking idiot!"

"Come on!" said Longhi, grasping his friend by the back of his tunic and yanking him away. "They'll throw you in prison for this one."

Chapter 22

Roma
1606

Fillide shifted her weight on her knees. She smiled, reflecting.

A whore knows this position too well! But with Caravaggio, I am dressed in silks, with gold and silver threads—and I am a saint on a red damask cushion.

Her right shoulder leaned against a broken wheel. She glanced nervously at the spike level with her neck.

"Don't shift your gaze," said Caravaggio from behind his easel.

Fillide slid her right finger along the flat of the dagger blade.

"I like that," said the artist. "Keep that pose."

Fillide toyed with the dagger in minute movements.

Of course he'd like that. He lives his life on a sharp blade.

She listened to his brushstrokes.

He used to talk more, didn't he?

"Do you think God's thunderbolt really broke the wheel for Saint Catherine?"

"Don't talk. I'm painting your face."

Fillide fell silent. There was a change in Caravaggio. He used to be more at ease with her, if not while he was painting, then afterward. He would tell her about the lives of the saints, something she knew little about. It excited her to know that she represented such brilliant, brave lives: Judith, who killed the horrible Holofernes, or the holy Madonna, or now Saint Catherine. These women—so remarkable.

She recognized herself from the cuticles of her nails to the damaged finger of her left hand to the oily sheen on her eyelids. She had counted the lines in her forehead in the painting of Judith and Holofernes.

So powerful the way he portrayed them in paint—and how he could betray them in flesh and blood.

After the foreplay of bloody slaughter, he'd pulled her toward him, cupping the small of her back, sliding his hands down to her buttocks. Taking her.

Of course she had lain with him. Any man who could know a woman's body and portray even its imperfections with such beauty—what woman would not want to make love to such an artist? Their lovemaking was secret, of course—Ranuccio was a dangerous man. He despised Michelangelo Merisi.

No good would come of that.

But for the last two sittings, Michelangelo had not pulled her to his bed. He painted silently as always but did not speak after their sessions. He seemed to want her to leave when the work was done.

"Fillide. Do you remember the reception and banquet for Gran Duca Ferdinando de' Medici at Palazzo Madama?"

"Sì. Of course. Why?"

"There was a Knight of Malta there that night, an acquaintance of Ranuccio's."

"Fra Giovanni Roero?"

"An ugly sot. He was whispering in your ear."

A smile crossed Fillide's mouth. "Don't tell me you are jealous, Michele!"

"Did you lie with him?"

"Of course," she said, toying with her earring. "He pays well. Whenever he is in the city, he asks for me."

"I thought he was confined to Malta."

"Pff!" said Fillide. "The knights head for the mainland every chance they can. Malta is a rock surrounded by sea."

Caravaggio frowned. "When that bastard was buzzing in your ear, he looked over at me. Did he say something about me?"

Fillide cocked her head, thinking.

"Oh, *sì!*" She laughed. "He said you looked like a dirty Turk. That your head would look better stuck on a pike in front of St. Peter's Basilica."

"A Turk?" Caravaggio said.

"The Maltese knights hate the Turks," she said, shrugging, "especially their religion. He wants to put all the heathens' heads on pikes. Don't be cross, Michele."

"Why shouldn't I be?" said Caravaggio, shaking with rage.

Fillide moved toward him, combing her fingers through his thick mat of dark hair. "All swarthy and hairy, my love," she cooed. "You do look like a Turk!"

Caravaggio pulled away from her. "I'm finished for today . . . that may be all," he said, stepping back from his canvas to regard it. He picked up a towel and wiped his brush.

"May I see it?" asked Fillide.

The artist chewed at the corner of his mustache. "*Sì.* Why not?"

Fillide gathered up her skirts and walked to his side.

"Oh!" she gasped.

Fillide stared at the richness of the fabric, the red highlights in the midnight-purple brocade.

But it was her own image that made her gasp in delight.

"It is astonishing. How did you—oh, Michelangelo! Look at my face, my hands. What a gift you have—"

"Not your face or your hands, Fillide," he said, inspecting the bristles of his brush. "They are Saint Catherine's."

Fillide straightened her back. "*Certo*. Of course I know that. But it is my likeness," she said. She put her hand over Caravaggio's.

This hand has made me a saint.

She caressed the rough skin and kissed the cuticles that smelled of paint and walnut oil.

And turpentine.

Caravaggio pulled his hand away. He continued cleaning his brushes.

"I suppose I should go," said Fillide, coloring with anger.

The artist shrugged. "Before you leave . . . I saw a woman in your company last night," said Caravaggio. He put down his rag and looked at her. "A most beautiful woman. Dark hair, luminous eyes. She was kissing a young child in an older woman's arms."

"Maddalena—Lena. Lena Antognetti."

"Lena. She is the most exquisite creature. Her eyes are so innocent. Luminous with purity—"

"For a whore." Fillide's face hardened.

"A *puttana*?"

"She stands in the Piazza Navona. That is her territory."

"And the child she kissed?"

"The child is hers. A bastard. Lena should give him up to the milk nurse, but she won't. The little boy is bad for business."

"Does she—have a steady patron?" asked Caravaggio.

"Why this sudden interest in another whore?"

"Don't be ugly, Fillide. Business is business. Tell me about her."

"She lives off and on with Gaspare Albertini, but their relationship is unsteady. She used to have highborn patrons, but now she stands in Piazza Navona. Since the baby's birth, the cardinals don't want her."

"Because of a child?"

"Pff! Of course! The holy servants of Christ want to forget that sex begets children. A baby is too sharp a reminder for a *cardinale*."

A smile broke over the artist's face. She saw his white teeth gleam under the shaggy ends of his mustache.

Enough about Lena Antognetti! Speak to me of more saints.

Fillide gazed at her likeness still wet with oil. Saint Catherine.

I am astonishing. All Roma shall admire me.

A slow smile of pride bloomed on her face. Her place was secure. "Would you like to meet her, Michelangelo? Lena?"

Caravaggio nodded. He put his brush down and caressed Fillide's cheek. She dipped her chin into the palm of his hand like a house cat.

"Very much," he said. "Do you think she would pose for me?"

Fillide sighed, her breasts rising and falling above her cream-colored bodice.

What a strange man. He has no idea what he means to me.

Ah, but what matter?

She looked back at the painting and lifted her chin with pride.

"Ah, Michelangelo, you fool! What woman wouldn't?"

Chapter 23

*Roma
1606*

The wind blew a gust through the side street leading to Piazza Navona. Fillide covered her face, waiting for the whirlwind to subside before introducing her friend to Caravaggio. "I'd like to present Maestro Michelangelo Merisi da Caravaggio," said Fillide to the raven-haired woman holding a toddler. "This is Maddalena Antognetti and her son, Antonio."

Caravaggio swept off his cap, bowing low to the fair-skinned beauty and her squirming son.

Fillide made a face, her hand on her hip. *This is the way he greets a whore!*

"*Piacere*, Maestro," said Lena, extending her hand awkwardly from underneath the plump baby's leg.

"Lena, he would like you to model for a painting," said Fillide.

The baby grasped his mother's chin.

Lena swiveled her head away from the baby's sticky fingers. "Me, signore?"

Fillide lifted her chin imperiously. "Just as I have posed for him."

"Would you come to my studio, signorina?" said Caravaggio. "I live off the piazza, on Vicolo dei Santi Cecilia e Biagio. Number 19."

"Mamma!" cried the little boy. "*Giú, giú!* Down!"

"It would be my pleasure," said Lena, setting the boy on the ground to walk.

"Tomorrow?"

"Yes, but . . . I care for my baby."

"*Sì, sì.* Bring the child. He, too, can model," said Caravaggio, tousling the baby boy's hair.

"Ow!" said the toddler. He looked at the artist solemnly.

Fillide arched her brow. "Two for one. You are a sly dog."

∽

"Look downward at the spot I've marked on the floor. Pretend you see someone—no, two people—kneeling at your feet. Poor, supplicating pilgrims, weary from their long journey. Drinking in your blessing."

Lena inclined her left shoulder, her chin dipping toward her shoulder blade.

"Like this?"

"Look a little more to your left. I want to see your right profile. Your long neck," said Caravaggio, tilting Lena's chin toward her left shoulder. "Do you feel the light on your throat?"

His fingers lingered on her skin.

"Yes," she whispered. "The warmth."

"That's perfect," he said, stepping back. "Don't move." He began painting with feverish strokes.

The baby, Antonio, began to whimper. He stretched his arms up toward his mother, who was gazing down at the floor.

"I'm sorry, Maestro Merisi," she said. "The baby—"

"Pick him up," said Caravaggio, his brush still moving.

"But—"

"Pick the child up. Go back to your spot. Hold him as you would naturally."

Lena smiled quickly at the child and took him in her arms. She hitched him up on her right hip, her right hand spread around his back, her left hand stretched over his knee and cradling his bottom for support.

"Cecco!" said Caravaggio. "Bring the white cloth. Place it under the signorina's arms so its folds drape over her right wrist."

Cecco picked up the prop reluctantly. Caravaggio noticed his sullen look and hunched shoulders.

"Hurry! The light is fading," said Caravaggio.

The boy tucked the linen into Lena's hand, fanning the fold. He gave one loose twist and threaded the end of the cloth across her right hand, leaving the end draped toward the floor.

"Damnation, see how her eye wanders?" said Caravaggio. "Her boredom shows! It's all wrong. Kneel, Cecco. Give the signorina a focal point."

"Me? Kneel?"

"Now, damn it! What's wrong with you?"

Cecco's face seized in despair. He fell to his knees, and a splinter pierced his skin. He winced.

"What are you doing with your face? Stop it!" said Caravaggio. He stepped back behind the easel.

"Pray to her," said Caravaggio, his face obscured by the canvas.

"Come?" What?

"Damn you, do as you are told! Fold your hands in prayer. Look up to her, beseeching. Beg for her blessing."

Cecco bit the inside of his mouth. He felt the bits of sand from the dirty floor bite into the skin of his knees, the splinter stinging.

Pray to her? How dare you ask me this! Your new lover, this whore!

"Soften your face, your eyes, Cecco! You are adoring her, not haggling for fish at the market. Let her see your eyes so that she will feel your need and bless you."

Need? I need nothing but your love, Maestro. Why can you not understand this? You torture me with your whores—

Cecco lifted his eyes, flashing with anger at the prostitute who would usurp his place in his master's bed.

I hate you! I—

He blinked. He looked again at Lena. Instead of a rival, he saw a mother's kindness in her eyes, a loving look of compassion.

Cecco thought of his home in Caravaggio, the little village in the north where he and his widowed mother had lived in a wooden hut, destitute. He remembered the tender hands of his young mother, hands that smelled of warm bread.

"Go with Signor Merisi," she said. "Learn everything he teaches you. Someday perhaps you will become a great artist. Make me proud, *figlio mio*."

My son.

He blinked again, surprised as a tear rolled down his cheek.

"Lena," whispered Caravaggio, his breath filling her nostrils. His fingers were entwined in her black hair, caressing her throat. He extended her long white neck, moving his lips over her skin. "My Madonna."

She smiled, her lashes flickering. He moved his lips to her breast, lingering there, his tongue caressing her nipple. She arched her back in ecstasy. The moonlight glanced off her white bosom and throat, casting her face in half light, half shadow.

"*Sì,*" said Caravaggio, watching her mouth open into a perfect O. He drew up on his elbows, staring at his lover's body. "I shall remember you exactly so. Forever."

Baby Antonio murmured in his sleep from the pallet next to the bed.

Cecco, unable to sleep, watched the two lovers from the corner of the room. He knew his master had stopped his lovemaking because he saw a painting. *A very good painting.* Caravaggio was composing the outline and brushstrokes as he hovered over the rapturous Lena.

He is a thief. He steals the very likeness of a human being, from the dirty cracks in their heels to the spittle on their lips. But he is not content with that now. Not with her. His greed is godlike. He must possess her soul, thief that he is.

Cecco knew he would see her again in paint. Again and again.

The boy bit his lip to keep from crying. The metallic taste of blood filled his mouth and he thought of metal coins.

Mariano Pasqualone, the same heartless papal attorney of the Cenci executions, walked along the Tiber River bordering the Ortaccio di Ripetta—the "evil garden" where the prostitutes of Roma made their homes. It had rained hard the day before, through the night, and into this morning. The river was swollen and had seeped over the banks, as it often did in this poor neighborhood. The water trickled down the stones of the road, meandering capriciously.

Pasqualone sat on a grassy knoll at Emperor Augustine's mausoleum. The loamy soil had reclaimed the ancient stone tomb, and the poorer prostitutes plied their trade in the verdant hideaways. He heard the satisfied grunts and moan of a mercenary soldier as the client bent a young girl over a moss-covered rock, sliding himself between her buttocks.

How I hate this place.

Mariano Pasqualone was far from his home near his workplace in Pope Paul's legal offices in the Quirinale. But the red-light district of the Ortaccio di Ripetta drew him more nights of the week than not. For on the Via dei Greci lived the only woman to possess his heart: Lena Antognetti.

For her, I'd give my life. Her black hair, creamy white bosom. And those flashing eyes, fierce yet doelike with innocence, not like any streetwalker.

He had fallen madly in love with Lena. He begged her mother to grant him her daughter's hand in marriage.

Maria Antognetti's reply was a flat no. Pasqualone was a lawyer, a lawyer for the pope, but a lawyer nevertheless. Maria was certain that he, like all lawyers, would go straight to hell.

"But how can you refuse me, a gentleman with a good profession?" argued Pasqualone. "Lena stands in the Piazza Navona, selling her body to strangers! I want to marry her and give her a good, secure life as my wife—"

"Go away, signore! I want my daughter to enter heaven . . . How could she if she were to marry someone in your cursed profession?"

"I work for His Holiness, the pope!"

"It makes no matter to God who you work for," said Maria, making the sign of the cross. "You are a lawyer. You shall be damned." And she slammed the door in his face.

Pasqualone could not get over his devotion to Lena. He was condemned to walk the Piazza Navona looking for her, and if she were not to be found, he haunted the Ortaccio di Ripetta, dodging the solicitations of dozens of other prostitutes along the Via di Ripetta.

When the enthusiastic noises of the soldier and whore became unbearable, Pasqualone stood up and brushed the damp leaves and grass from his pants. He walked toward Via dei Greci, but before he had reached the Antognetti house, he saw Lena walking swiftly in the direction of the Piazza Navona. In her arms she carried her baby, Antonio.

She could not ply her trade with a baby, could she?

I will follow her to her spot. I will pay her for the entire evening. I shall convince her to marry me!

He walked about thirty strides behind her, but close enough that he imagined he smelled the rose water on her warm skin. He was surprised by how quickly she covered ground, even carrying a child. He had to run a few steps to try to catch up with her.

She entered the Piazza Navona and darted through the noisy crowd—the jugglers, the horsemen, the chestnut vendors, the gypsies, soldiers, and noblemen. She sought out two prostitutes, a redhead and an olive-skinned brunette. She talked to them briefly, then continued on her way, emerging out the other end of the piazza onto Via della Scrofa, walking toward Palazzo Madama.

Pasqualone frowned. He panted hard as he hurried after her.

Surely she isn't entertaining the cardinals, not with a baby in tow!

When she turned into the tiny street of Vicolo dei Santi Cecilia e Biagio, blood rushed to Pasqualone's head, which throbbed in fury.

"Damn him!" said Pasqualone aloud. He recognized the house of Michelangelo Merisi da Caravaggio.

He bit his fist with rage until his knuckles bled. He turned back toward the Ortaccio di Ripetta.

Mariano Pasqualone knocked on the door. Maria Antognetti drew back the bolt.

"*Buonasera*, Signor Pasqualone," she said, crossing her arms and frowning.

"You, Maria Antognetti, refuse to give me your daughter's hand in marriage! An admirable offer, a secure and honorable position as my wife."

"*Sì*. That is because, you, signore, are going to hell."

"Hell? *I'm* going to hell? Do you know what your daughter is doing now?"

"She is posing as a model for the famous Maestro Caravaggio," said Maria. "He has paid us in advance. He shall make my daughter famous."

"Posing! Do you know what a scoundrel he is? He keeps company with the lowest life of Roma. He brawls in the streets and taverns and knows the inside of Sant'Angelo prison like his own wretched apartment! He will corrupt your 'sweet' daughter—never mind that she stands nightly at the Piazza Navona!—and drag her into the flaming inferno that Dante D'Algieri so vividly described. She shall be seated at the right hand of Satan, as Caravaggio will be the devil's guest of honor."

Maria covered her mouth. "No!"

"*Sì!* You can keep your precious daughter. If she is so vile as to pose—and you must know what that means!—for Caravaggio, I want never to look upon her again!"

With that Pasqualone turned on his heel and marched off into the night.

Maria Antognetti pounded on the door of 19 Vicolo dei Santi Cecilia e Biagio, splinters tearing at her laundry-raw skin.

Cecco opened the door. "Signora? Are you lost?"

"Lost!" she wailed. "All is lost. My daughter will go to hell. This is a den of iniquity!"

Caravaggio came running down the stairs, wiping his hands on a rag.

"Signora Antognetti! Please come in. It is very late for you to be out in the streets of Roma."

"I've had the most dreadful conversation with Mariano Pasqualone—"

"Mamma! Is that you?" said a voice. Lena descended the stairs dressed in a wine-colored velvet blouse and a long black skirt. In her arms she carried little Antonio swathed in white linen. "Why are you here?" asked Lena. "What on earth has happened?"

"That lawyer, your suitor—Signor Pasqualone—came to our house."

"Mamma," said Lena, glancing quickly at Caravaggio. "He is not my suitor—"

"He said awful things happen under this roof," wailed the distraught mother. "And that I'm a bad mother for letting you keep company with Maestro Caravaggio."

Cecco saw his master's eyes burn with rage, his mouth puckering up as if he had tasted something bitter and foul.

He's going to explode . . .

But instead, Caravaggio took a deep breath. Slowly, he composed his face, although Cecco could still see a spasm pulse in his left cheek.

"Signora Antognetti," said Caravaggio, bowing deeply. "Perhaps you would like to come upstairs and see what transpires in our studio. I'm putting the finishing touches on the painting tonight. I'd be honored if you would be the first to lay eyes on it."

"I don't know," mumbled Maria, crossing her arms tight. *"Non lo so . . ."*

"Come, Mamma," said Lena, stroking her cheek. "You have nothing to fear."

Maria nodded weakly and allowed Caravaggio to take her arm.

"Lena, please go ahead and take your pose," said the artist. "Your *mamma* and I will follow."

Lena nodded. She hitched baby Antonio up on her hip and climbed the stairs.

"Now, Signora Antognetti, if you will allow me to escort you up the stairs, I shall show you our studio. Cecco, fetch the signora a glass of wine."

"Subito!" said Cecco. *Right away.*

"Now watch the stairs, signora. There are a few that are a bit rickety."

Maria darted a look at him.

"Here we are," said Caravaggio, releasing her arm at the top of the steps. "My studio."

The woman gasped as she walked into the room. Blazing lanterns were pulled up by ropes and gathered into groups of two or three, illuminating Lena as she stood by a door that led into another room. Her head bowed, she looked at an invisible spot on the floor where Cecco had once knelt.

Maria shivered as she felt a cold draft. She looked up and saw the bright stars twinkling through the hole in the roof.

Cecco returned with a glass of red wine and a stool for the signora.

"Grazie, ragazzo," said Maria, taking a seat. She sipped the wine tentatively and looked at the scene before her. A pool of flickering light glanced off Lena's cheek and hands, her other features obscured in shadow.

Cecco took his place on the floor again, engaging Lena's gaze as she wrestled with the squirming baby on her hip.

Maria's tense face released in a faint smile. The baby, Antonio, reached his chubby hand out to her.

"Nonna!" he said. *Grandmother!*

"Oh! *Nipote mio!*" she said, her hands extending toward her grandson.

"Signora Antognetti," said Caravaggio. "Would you be so kind as to come behind my easel and see the painting?"

"*Sì*, Maestro," said Maria, ducking her chin humbly. She walked to the easel. She kept her eyes lowered, looking at the artist's boots.

"Behold, your daughter, Maddalena. The Virgin of Loreto!"

The woman raised her eyes to the painting. She put her hand to her mouth and gasped. *"Dio mio!"* she said. *My God.*

Lena was the Virgin incarnate, a gold halo floating above her head. She held the baby on her hip—the baby who was clearly our Lord Savior—as she blessed two weary pilgrims. The travelers had cast their staffs aside and clasped their hands in prayer, their bare feet thrust behind them, lined with dirt.

They are praying to my Lena. And my grandson.

"Are you satisfied now that your daughter is honored?" said Caravaggio softly. "All Roma shall kneel before her. She is the Madonna."

Cecco pricked up his ears. It was rare to hear words of comfort from his master's lips. He turned to watch this singular occasion.

What rare kindness my master shows this old woman! The mother of a whore.

"I suppose the lawyer was madly jealous," said Maria. "He said such hateful things about my daughter . . . and about you."

Caravaggio scowled, looking away from the woman and into the darkness.

Maria Antognetti clasped her hands together. "You will see that no harm comes to her, won't you, Maestro Caravaggio?"

"Signora Antognetti. She is my most perfect model . . . and muse. I will protect her, I promise."

Cecco winced. He only wished these words were true.

Chapter 24

Roma
1606

By midday, the Piazza Navona was packed. People gathered around the pens of animals—horses, pigs, sheep, and goats. Cages of cackling geese and squawking hens lined one corner of the market. Dozens and dozens of tents shaded bright vegetables fresh from the countryside. Even in the shade, melons warmed, giving off a perfume of ripe fruit, competing with the sharp animal smell of the fresh cheeses.

Most of Roma packed into the piazza ringed by the horse-racing track of tufa soil, an ancient traditional sport that still continued. By the late afternoon, most of the Romans were drunk on cheap wine brought from the countryside vineyards. Voices rose and men swaggered, boasting with a rush of wine-fueled courage. Hands lingered on the hilts of swords and daggers as both laughter and insults grew louder among the crowd.

As dusk approached, the *contadini* began taking down their tents and packing up their wares, preparing to leave for the countryside. Children were gathered up, and the peasants, like geese protecting their goslings, kept a wary eye on the drunken citizens.

Mariano Pasqualone walked alongside his friend Galeazzo Roccasecca, a colleague from the Quirinale, responsible for penning correspondence for the pope. They were passing the church of San Giacomo degli Spagnoli, in front of the Triton Fountain.

"I told her to keep her whore of a daughter!" said a drunken Pasqualone, his voice rising against the plashing waters. "I wash my hands of the sordid slut."

"Perhaps you were a bit rash, Mariano," said Roccasecca. "I know how you adore that girl. After all, Lena has a baby to feed! If Caravaggio is paying her to model, isn't that better than—"

Out of the corner of his eye, Roccasecca saw a swift movement. A figure bounded between them, a black cape swung around one shoulder. The man pulled a small sword from under the cape and clubbed Pasqualone viciously on the head with the hilt. The lawyer fell to the ground, unconscious, blood gushing from his head.

The caped man sprinted away into the crowd.

"Cazzo!" Roccasecca said, kneeling beside his friend. He slapped Pasqualone's face. "Mariano! Mariano! Can you hear me?"

Pasqualone groaned, clutching his bloody head. *"Assassinio!"* Murder!

"I think you are still very much alive," said Roccasecca. "But you have been wounded. Quite seriously."

A pool of sticky blood puddled on the stones of the piazza.

"I'm done for!" moaned Pasqualone.

"Who was that man?" asked Roccasecca, opening his friend's collar. "Who would want to harm you?"

"It had to be Michelangelo. Michelangelo Merisi da Caravaggio! Assassin!" Pasqualone struggled to rise and then collapsed with a groan.

Roccasecca looked around frantically for help.

"That Caravaggio is a madman!"

Chapter 25

NAPLES

"Lulu? Didn't you hear what he said?"

"I heard him."

They were back in their depressing hotel room. Moto had scrubbed his face, washing every speck of blood off his cheek, but he still raised his hand to touch where it had been smeared—with the threat that next time it would be his blood.

"Moto, did you know those guys?"

"What?"

"They acted like they knew you."

"I don't have a lot of friends who are thugs in Naples. Trust me on that."

"They acted like—"

"Lulu. My friends don't smack me across the face. Anyway, he was right. We're over our heads. We should go back to what we know."

"What's that? Vespas?"

Moto snapped, "What's wrong with Ves—" He caught himself. "Nice try, Lulu. You know what I'm saying. We're not detectives. We do better in the library, the archives. Well, you do better. You're a scholar."

"Oh, so now I'm a scholar. Just because you want to go home."

"That's not fair. I'm not afraid." Now there was real heat in his voice.

"I don't care about fair." She answered with heat of her own. "I know that painting's a Caravaggio and I'm going to prove it. Do I have to do it alone?"

They were both breathing hard. The unspoken question hung in the air: Why did she care so much? People were dying all around them. They could be next. Why was Lucia so desperately determined to keep pushing? If Moto demanded an answer, Lucia knew she wouldn't have one. There had to be something, something lost in the fog of her memory. But what could—

Moto broke into her thoughts.

"No. You don't have to do it alone. You don't have to do it at all. We could stop all this craziness and go home. I think—"

"Don't think! I'll do the thinking. I'm the scholar."

"Fuck you, Lulu."

An instant of heated silence and then they both laughed.

After a moment, he asked, "So how do we get to Malta?"

"What happened to your friends?"

"My friends?"

"Moto! Your friends. They got us here. They were supposed to get us the rest of the way to Malta, but you lost your cell phone. Moto?"

He raised his hands. Pure Moto, a helpless gesture.

"Forget them. No more help there. We're on our own." Suddenly, he looked serious. No more helpless gestures. "If we need to do this, we can do it. I don't need anyone's help." He jerked his thumb toward the window. "Especially those creeps."

"Moto! Wow! Where did that come from?"

"I'm tired of getting pushed around. Tired of people laughing. I'm tired of those thugs."

Out of nowhere, a new Moto. Lucia didn't know what to say.

So she said exactly what she was feeling.

"I don't understand what's going on here. Who are these people?"

"Which people?"

"All of them." She started a list, ticking items off on her fingers. "The two guys who murdered Te-Te, stole the painting, kidnapped me and the professor. Then whoever killed them and started smashing the door to get to us. The carabinieri killed them, but then there's whoever killed Aysha and her father at the villa. And the caretaker at the monastery. The beheading. The crucifixion. That sounds like the same gang." She shivered. "Jesus, Moto." She went back to the list. "And whoever blew a hole in that warehouse, grabbed me and the professor, and got us out of there. Who was that? Are they the same people who saved me last night?"

Moto shrugged.

Lucia wasn't done.

"And who has the painting? Where is it? I don't understand any of it."

Moto offered a grim smile. Something the new Moto could do. "You don't understand anything. But you're still certain we have to go to Malta."

"Exactly."

"Right now?"

She managed a smile of her own. "If we don't know what we're doing, we'd better get started or we'll never get anything done at all."

"I'm not seeing a lot of choices for Malta." Lucia had been frowning at the screen on her phone for a long time. "We could fly there easily enough."

"No way. The airport's too exposed. Too many people watching for us—and we don't know who they are."

"The only other way's by ferry," she said.

"OK."

"No, it's not. All the ferries stop in Sicily."

"So what?"

"I'm not going there." Her voice was flat. A simple statement.

"But maybe we need to go there. Caravaggio was there."

"I know. But I'm not setting foot on that island. Not ever."

Moto raised his eyebrows and gestured: *Why not?*

"It's complicated."

He kept staring, waiting for more.

"My family's from there," she admitted.

"So is mine."

"My family's complicated."

Another silent gesture: *Whose isn't?*

Lucia thought about her *nonna*, about the burning rage she had brought from Sicily into her bitter exile in America. Lucia had grown up scorched by the flames, and she was not going to set foot on that island of contagion ever again in her life.

She thought about explaining all that to Moto. He was her best friend, why not let him into that part of her life? But she found herself close to tears just thinking about it, and she set it aside. Not now. Maybe not ever.

Before she could think of what she wanted to say, Moto held his hands up, palms toward her, bringing that topic to a close. "It doesn't matter. I'm not setting foot on that cursed island either."

Now it was her turn to demand more information, and Moto—the new Moto?—was willing to give it. He laid out his own story: knowing who he was—who he was attracted to—from a very early age and knowing he couldn't tell anyone. Even though everyone seemed to know it anyway. Never having friends in school and, worse, always knowing that his entire family—his father above all—was so deeply disappointed. Ashamed. And telling him, showing him, in so many ways, so many times, that even though they loved him, he could never be a real part of the family. He was not a real man.

He started strong, as if he'd been waiting a long time to tell her this, but he didn't get far before his voice faltered and faded.

And now they were both near tears.

With nothing left to say or ask, Lucia rolled herself, fully dressed, in the coverlet on the bed and took refuge in sleep.

Moto sat by the window with the neon light flashing on his face in the dark.

"Lulu! Wake up!" Moto was shaking her. "We have to go."

Groggy, disoriented, wrapped in a filthy coverlet on a thin mattress in a cheap hotel, Lucia struggled out of ugly dreams into ugly reality. The flickering neon of the hotel sign still filtered through the threadbare drapes.

"What time is it?"

"Three o'clock."

"Morning or . . . ?"

"Morning."

She shook her head to clear it. Moto was insistent.

"Come on! We have to go. Now!"

"Where are we going?"

For a moment, Moto's smile lit up the room.

"We're going fishing."

When Professor Richman woke up, his sore throat was worse. And when he looked in the mirror, the bruises on his neck were frightening. But he decided to wear his wounds proudly. He'd come by them honorably. He'd faced that thug down. And an extravagant room-service breakfast helped to ease the pain. And now he smiled as he examined the photographs that had been delivered to his room by the bellhop as he was finishing breakfast. The concierge had done an impressive job, getting the roll of film developed and printed in less than an hour. The professor wasn't even slightly embarrassed by insisting that it was urgent, even though the film had been sitting in his camera for weeks. After all, he'd been recuperating from the unfortunate events at Te-Te's chapel, and after that, he'd been rather busy.

The prints weren't very large, but after a career deciphering cuneiform tablets, the professor never traveled without a high-power magnifying glass—and now he reveled in the fine details that his "antique" camera had captured on film. He made a mental note to point out to Lucy that her cell phone camera instantly produced digital blurs that were as worthless as they were immediate.

He bent to his task and, as his eyes focused on the pictures he'd taken that afternoon at the orphanage, his mind was flooded with a series of images: the first time he had seen the painting in the dark of the sacristy and known in an instant that it could not possibly be a Caravaggio; the second time he had seen it, as the two thugs dragged it into the chapel, with the dead body of Lucia's *"zio"* lying on the floor in a pool of blood; and the last time he had seen it, in the half-light of the warehouse, as some maniac tried to smash through the door with an axe.

Professor Richman was not by nature given to deep reflection. He took life as it came—often enough for better, but occasionally most certainly for worse. His academic career had been satisfying, if not dramatic. His marriage had been much the same. And since both had ended—one very much as expected, one very much by surprise—within weeks of each other, he had been dealing with this new life of his.

Now he stopped to consider how it had become clear that "wake me when it's over" was not a good approach to life.

He found himself thinking through the stunning disruptions of the past weeks that had brought adventure, violence, injury, moments of terror, and moments when he surprised himself with courage he didn't know he possessed. It made him wonder what his life might have been if he'd made different choices much earlier, if he'd sought adventure instead of comfort and certainty. He might have been a hero. He might have been dead. It made him smile.

But now he was here. He was alive and, as he sat up and stretched his back, he was comfortable.

Congratulations were in order.

He accepted them graciously.

And enough of that.

He bent back over the photographs.

Chapter 26

Roma
1606

The Marchesa Costanza Colonna received Cardinals del Monte and Benedetto Giustiniani at her brother's Asciano residence, Palazzo Colonna on Via della Pilotta. Not far from the Quirinale, the palazzo was one of the finest in all of Roma.

"So once again we must save our wayward friend," said the Marchesa Colonna once the cardinals had taken their seats across from her.

Del Monte glanced at the frescoed ceiling above them.

"I have sent word to my niece, the Princess Doria in Genoa," continued the marchesa. "She said that her husband, Giovanni Andrea Doria, has offered refuge."

"The Dorias? They are relatives of Ottavio Costa as well, are they not?" said Del Monte, turning to his cardinal companion.

"Is not all Roma related?" said the marchesa. "*Sì*, Giovanni is Costa's nephew."

"Bless the prince and your loving niece. Your intervention on Merisi's behalf is generous," said Cardinal Giustiniani. "Michele is a difficult man. I've had my own run-ins with him—if not for my brother, Vincenzo, I might not intervene."

"We all intervene when it comes to genius, my good friend," said Del Monte.

"Michele will, of course, be expected to paint something in return for their hospitality," said the marchesa. "But we think he will be much safer in Genoa."

"This is marvelous news, my dear marchesa," said Cardinal del Monte.

"Attacking the pope's legal scribe was rash," said Cardinal Giustiniani. "We will have to work with the pope's nephew Cardinal Borghese to allow Caravaggio back into Roma."

Cardinal del Monte pressed his lips tight together, bleeding them of color. "Yes. Only Scipione Borghese can arrange that solution."

"Cardinal del Monte, you may tell Michele that all is arranged. I trust he will travel in your carriage?"

"He should travel in mine," said Cardinal Giustiniani. "I know my brother would want that. Cardinal del Monte has no business to conduct in Genoa, while we often do with family matters. Roma already suspects Del Monte of harboring Michelangelo."

"It's true," said Del Monte. "Too many times he has fled there after a crime. He returns like a dog running with his tail between his legs."

"Then it is settled. I'll send a coach this evening to Palazzo Madama," said Cardinal Giustiniani.

"I greatly appreciate your efforts," said the marchesa, rising. "I thank you, good cardinals, for your act of compassion in protecting our mutual—and immoral and totally incorrigible!—friend. He shall live in Genoa until this situation settles."

The marchesa folded her hands together and drew a deep breath.

"I pray to God Almighty this papal notary does not die from his injury."

Chapter 27

Roma
1606

Cecco spotted Lena in the Piazza Navona. She was back to her usual spot near the church of San Giacomo degli Spagnoli. Her head drooped like a wilting flower.

Cecco bit his lip watching her. Two signori passed by him close enough to hear.

"*Guarda!*" said a man in a crimson velvet jacket. *Look!* "That's the one Caravaggio made into a Madonna. The Church rejected the painting."

"Why?" asked his mustached companion, running his eyes over Lena's body.

"Too lascivious. Her breasts falling out of her bodice. But Cardinal Borghese hangs it now in his palazzo."

"I would like to have laid my eyes on that one before Borghese snatched it," said the man, toying with the ends of his mustache. "*Che bella!*"

"Fancy her in your bed tonight? She's fallen on hard times, this Madonna. I hear she's cheap nowadays."

"I wouldn't mind her blessing my *picio*."

They both laughed and walked on. Lena looked down at the gray stones of the Piazza Navona.

"Lena," Cecco called to her from the shadows. He walked to her side. "I have word from my master!"

"Oh, Cecco!" she said, her eyes lighting up.

"He is returning from Genoa. Signor Pasqualone has recovered," he said.

Lena's body unfurled like a fern tendril in a shaft of light. "Cecco!" Before he knew it, he was enclosed in her embrace.

She's so warm . . . like a mother. She smells of toasted bread.

"I'm unable to eat or sleep, worrying about him," said Lena. "He will be the death of me, I swear it!"

A hand reached out for Cecco's shoulder, shoving him away.

"Get out of the way, boy," growled a voice.

Cecco looked up to see a Knight of Malta approaching Lena.

"How much?" he said to her, eyeing her bosom.

"It depends on what you want," she said, lowering her eyes to the paving stones.

"I want everything. I'm as fierce as a rutting ram, whore."

Lena colored. "Come with me to my pallet," she said, not daring to look at Cecco.

"Up the ass," said Roero, looking squarely at Cecco. "I want that too, *puttana!*"

Lena shuddered, looking beseechingly at Caravaggio's boy. "I do this to feed my son," she said. "God forgive me!"

"Come on, whore," said the knight, pushing her on. "I don't have all day—I'm in port for only three days. Your artist friend might return before I sample your wares."

He turned toward Cecco.

"Tell your master what I'm going to do to his girlfriend."

He cupped his groin and roared with laughter.

It was an ugly sound.

Two days later, Caravaggio invited Lena to dine with him at a little tavern on the Campo de' Fiori.

They sat across from each other at a tiny table.

"Ah!" he said. "To be back in Roma. You cannot imagine how I lusted for this city."

He drew in her scent, his nostrils flaring.

"I want to paint you again," he said.

"Michele!" she said, her throat flushing in delight.

"Dead," he said. He bit into his pasta, a devilish smile on his lips.

"Dead?" Lena stopped eating her plate of lentils and set down her spoon.

What homecoming is this? Lena thought.

"An attorney for the pope has commissioned it," said Caravaggio through a mouthful of food. "He wants it to hang in his chapel in the Carmelite church over in Trastevere, Santa Maria della Scala."

Lena pushed her lentils around the earthenware plate. "A Carmelite church?" she said. "No order is stricter."

A gleam came to his eyes. "*Sì*, damn them. High morals and pigheaded."

Lena thought of the latest rejection. "But Michele, how will you depict me?"

"Not you, the Madonna," he said, his smile fading. "Dead, of course. Very dead."

"But surely the Church wants the ascension of the Virgin, entering heaven, angels—"

"What do I care? They are foolish sots. Mary died—her body was left behind, like all the rest of us will be!"

Lena took a deep breath, her white bosom rising in her low-cut bodice. Two men eating next to them stopped talking to admire her.

"Eat your food," snarled Caravaggio. "She is not here for your entertainment!"

The customers hunched over their plates, grumbling.

"Will you pose for me, Lena?"

"Of course, Michele," she said. "But . . ."

"But?"

"Could you . . . would you consider their wishes? Letting Mary ascend to the heavens in—"

"Lena! *Basta!*" said Caravaggio. The men next to them stopped chewing, hearing the anger in his voice. Lena recoiled, snapping her mouth shut.

"How I execute the painting has nothing to do with you! Or anyone else!" Caravaggio said. "I paint according to my heart. What I see before me. I already have the vision!"

"Oh, but Michele!" said Lena, tears springing to her eyes. "What of the rejection of the last one?"

"What of it? Politics!" said Caravaggio, growling. "Hypocrisy. I blame it on that Baglione—a jealous artist, spreading rumors, inciting fear. He wants all the commissions."

"Do you think . . . my breasts—"

"Your breasts are beautiful. Exquisite! Does the Church really think the Madonna had no breasts? The clergy officially declares a healthy bosom unholy. They say that to depict Jesus Christ naked with a *picio* dangling is blasphemy. Made in the image of God, says the Bible. Does a naked child not have a penis?"

Lena's face crumpled. "Antonio is such a darling baby. How could they not love him?"

"Two days it lasted in that damned chapel. A mule cart carried it away to whom? The pope's nephew Borghese again!" said Caravaggio sourly. "He bought it for a hundred scudi. He was waiting like a vulture. Borghese knows good art—it doesn't bother him to see a beautifully bosomed woman. He coveted the painting!"

"But I can never see it again?"

"No. You can't. And the *popolani*, the common people I painted it for. They will never see it again. Not in my lifetime."

Lena said softly, "I'm sorry, Michele."

"There are some *brutti* bastards in Roma," he said, taking a deep draught of wine. He looked away bitterly.

Lena reached across the table and took his hand. "And what of the painting for Sant'Agostino?" she whispered, squeezing his fingers gently.

His scowl faded. "Ah, you humor me, my Lena. You know as well as I. Lines out the door from both directions, Piazza Navona and Via della Scrofa. Poor bastards broiling under the hot sun, waiting to get in. I've seen pilgrims praying to the painting itself. They see themselves in it, the way I intended. The *popolani*."

A rosy glow colored Lena's throat and face.

"That's right, *bella*. They come to see you."

Caravaggio touched her cheek with his hand, his fingertip stroking her skin.

"Come on. Let's get out of here," he said, his voice thick. "I want to hold the Madonna in my arms, under the bedsheets where no one else can see her. Tonight I don't want to share you with anybody, *bella mia*."

Chapter 28

Roma
1606

Cecco looked at the finished canvas. Lena was painted in a red dress, sprawled across a bed.

Her mourners stood stricken with grief, the woman attendant next to her sobbing. Caravaggio had added a few touches to Lena's face to make her almost unrecognizable, especially in death.

But Cecco knew.

"What do you think, Cecco?"

"Well . . . she is certainly dead."

"Certo!" said Caravaggio, raising his arms overhead to stretch. "Mary is a real woman. Not a being spiraled up to heaven with a flock of angels, not a cloud of mist disappearing into the sky. She is dead. Gone."

Cecco's eyes scanned the canvas. Dark. Even darker than usual, much of the canvas in organic carbon black tinged in copper resinate for sepia tones.

Then there was the silvery white, an ominous light on the dead Virgin. Cecco picked at his fingernails, remembering the buttery yolk for the egg tempera that his master mixed with his oils to render flesh tones.

The flesh tones of the living. Dead Mary had no egg yolk, no warmth.

The red drapery Cecco had arranged—under his master's supervision—as a canopy over the deathbed was filled with menacing shadow. It hovered like a bloody storm cloud, billowing and diving over the Madonna. He noted the light reflecting off the neck and back of a young Mary Magdalene bent over in a chair, sobbing. The clarity of the Magdalene's exposed skin and spine conveyed vulnerability, a pathos that struck the boy's heart.

Mary's face and lifeless hand over her swollen belly were also awash in light, as were the bald pates of the mourning apostles. There was a rumor that his master had watched the fishermen drag a woman's dead body out of the Tiber, studying her swollen features.

I hate seeing Lena dead. Cecco fought a shiver. He realized his cheek was wet. *But he's right. It is a masterpiece. I want to fall to my knees and sob.*

"Do you think they will like it, Maestro?" said Cecco, his eyes still engaged on the painting. "Your patrons, the Carmelites?"

"Bugger them if they don't," said Caravaggio, wiping his hands on a rag.

"It's good. Very good," said Cecco.

"It's better than that," snorted Caravaggio.

The Carmelites did not like the painting. It was removed within days, and another artist, Carlos Saraceni, was contracted to paint a more suitable image.

"To hell with these pricks!" said Caravaggio, drinking his second pitcher of cheap wine in a cramped osteria off Via della Scrofa on Vicolo della Vaccarella. "I waste my paint and talent on the fucking bastards."

"The painting is magnificent," mumbled Mario Minniti, keeping pace with his friend's alcohol consumption. "Fucking morons. Philistines!"

Onorio Longhi squinted at his two artist companions. He was so drunk he could barely keep himself upright on the bench; twice, Mario had had to grab his shoulder to keep him from toppling over backward. "It was the dead part," Longhi said. "They didn't like seeing the Madonna dead."

"Instead of spiraling up to heaven?" said Caravaggio. "Like some sort of homing pigeon?"

"They didn't like seeing her dead," repeated Longhi. "And they certainly didn't like knowing she was your whore."

"Shut the fuck up, Onorio!" said Caravaggio, half rising. The cords in his neck jutted.

"*Tranquillo,*" said Longhi, waving his hand. "Lena is beautiful. The painting is magnificent. But you didn't do a good enough job disguising her. Romans recognize her features, Michele."

"She doesn't look like—"

"You need to use a different model," said Longhi, sloshing more wine in his cup. "One who not all Roma knows so . . . intimately."

Caravaggio grasped his temples in both hands, propping his head up. "Two rejections within months. Damn them!"

Mario lifted his eyes from the rim of his cup, trying to focus on Caravaggio.

This rejection could be the tipping point.

Mario tried to form words of comfort, but his lips and brain were numb from drink. "Where is it going?" he asked. "Did Borghese get his hooks in this one too?"

"No. Rubens has bought it for Duke Gonzaga. It will be going to Mantua."

"Mantua!" said Mario. "At least that Rubens knows good art when he sees it."

"For a Flemish Protestant," grumbled Onorio.

"Bad luck, Merisi," called a voice from the next table. Mario recognized Captain Petronio, a guard from Castel Sant'Angelo, where Caravaggio had been imprisoned on numerous occasions. "I saw the Dead Mary as she was being hung in Santa Maria della Scala," he said. "She brought me to tears."

"You are a good man," said Longhi, staggering over and clapping the captain on the back. "*Cameriere!* Bring this good signore from Bologna more wine. Charge it to me!"

"I've got to take a piss," said Caravaggio, hauling himself to his feet. "Cecco, watch my sword."

"*Sì*, Maestro."

Caravaggio lurched toward the door.

"*Vaffanculo!* Carrying that sword again," said Mario. "He's going to be arrested."

"He's used to it by now. They should reserve his cell at night at Sant'Angelo. He knows all the guards by name. Right, Captain Petronio?" said Longhi, gesturing broadly to the guard.

Petronio raised his cup to Longhi, smiling. "He's a regular, all right."

Mario focused unsteadily on both Cecco and Longhi. "I'm worried about him. That's two rejections in a row. It's a spear through his heart."

"He's brewing up some madness," said Longhi, sucking on his thumb where a splinter had lodged from the plank table. "I—"

The door of the tavern banged open.

"Oh, *cazzo*!" said Cecco, under his breath.

"*Cosa?* What?" said Mario.

"Look who just walked in."

Ranuccio Tomassoni stood right inside the doorway. Behind him were his older brothers, Alessandro and Giovan Francesco, and Ranuccio's brothers-in-law, Ignazio and Federigo Giugoli.

A man with a black tunic pushed his way past the Giugoli brothers, keeping step with Ranuccio. When he turned, Cecco saw the white cross of Malta stretching from his breastbone to his groin.

He remembered the man's hands on Lena's bosom and shoulders that day in Piazza Navona.

"*Portaci vino!* Bring wine, you cuckold! *Cornuto!*" shouted Giovan as the Farnese alliance commandeered a table from two scraggly *contadini*. The peasants scattered like pigeons.

"They must not have encountered Michele outside or he would have pissed on their legs," said Mario, snapping to his senses. "Let's get out of here before trouble starts—"

"Let it brew," said Longhi. "We can handle these bastards."

Ranuccio caught sight of Longhi.

"Longhi! Where is your failed artist friend? He owes me money."

"I don't have any failed artist friends, Tomassoni," said Longhi, sobering on the spot. "Only geniuses. With sharp swords and big balls."

"Where is he? He's been keeping my whores as models. He owes me whether he can sell those pieces-of-shit canvases or not."

Caravaggio staggered in, still fumbling a knot in his trouser tie. "You're the *pezzo di merda*, Ranuccio. You piece of shit, I don't owe you anything."

The waiter scurried to the Tomassoni table with two pitchers of wine.

"You paint my whores. Mine, do you hear?" said Ranuccio. "Annunccia, Fillide, and now Lena."

"Lena's not yours. I pay her. That's between her and me."

"She's a fine piece of ass," said Roero.

Caravaggio focused his bleary eyes on Roero. "How would you know, *bastardo*?" He turned back to Ranuccio. "Does your friend with the monstrous cross pay? Or do you let him dabble for free?"

Roero stood. Ranuccio motioned to him to sit.

Ranuccio picked up his cup of wine and drained it. "Leave Fra Roero out of this. You owe, Caravaggio. You owe me!"

Caravaggio clenched his teeth, looking like a mad dog pulling at the end of his chain. "Go ahead! Try to get a scudo from me, you dirty pimp! Next time, I'll use a Roman whore everyone knows even better," said Caravaggio. "Your wife, you *becco fottuto*!" *Cuckold!*

"She's a tasty bite," said Caravaggio. "But oh, what a squealer!"

Mario watched as the Tomassonis and Giugolis reached for their swords. Roero had already drawn his, which gleamed silver in the lantern light.

"Outside! You *fallito*—failure—of an artist!" said Ranuccio, spittle glistening on his lips. "Or are you too busy wasting paint for your next disaster to be rejected by all of Roma?"

"I'll second you!" shouted Longhi. "As will Mario."

Mario mumbled, *"Merda!"* Then in a loud voice that cracked: "I will! *Sì!*"

"Count me in too!" roared Captain Petronio. "I'm sick of you Tomassonis and your arrogance!"

"This quarrel doesn't involve you, Bolognese!" said Giovan Francesco.

"It does now," said Petronio, rising. "I second Caravaggio."

Caravaggio grabbed his sword from Cecco.

The three Tomassonis, two Giugolis, and Roero stormed out the door. Onorio Longhi, Mario Minniti, Captain Petronio, and Caravaggio followed them out, and the ring of metal sliced the night as they unsheathed their weapons in the Via della Scrofa.

"Put your sword away!" shouted Giovan Francesco to Roero. "You'll be banned from the order. The Farnese will blame us for dragging a Maltese Knight into a brawl."

"As will the pope," said Federigo Giugoli.

"The bastard insulted me!" said Roero. "I shall have revenge—"

"Put it away, I say!" commanded the elder Tomassoni, shoving the knight out of the fray.

Caravaggio lunged at Ranuccio, who took two steps back, nearly toppling one of his brothers.

"Fermi! Indietro!" yelled Onorio Longhi. *Stop! Get back!*

"Come on, you coward!" shouted Caravaggio, waving his sword. "Lay on!"

Ranuccio took a step forward, engaging Caravaggio's sword at midlength. Caravaggio's jaw was clenched, and he pushed Ranuccio farther up the street. The clashing blades sent passersby scattering while attracting a crowd of ruffians who roared bets above the clanging metal.

The fight advanced up the street farther toward the Via di Pallacorda and the tennis courts.

"What set it off?" said an old soldier to another mercenary in the jostling crowd.

"Tomassoni and Merisi have been trading insults for months."

"It is a tennis bet," said a young noble dressed in velvet.

"A woman, more likely," said the old soldier. "It usually is."

A Roman artist from Campo Marzio recognized Caravaggio. He shouted in a drunken voice his encouragement. "*In culo alla balena*, Caravaggio! Good luck! In the ass of a whale, God's protection of Jonas himself!"

Ranuccio sweat long shadows into his tunic, the stink of garlic, wine, and nervous body odor wafting from under his arms with every attack as Caravaggio forced him back farther and farther up the Via della Scrofa.

Mario watched his friend under the flickering light of the street torches. Except for the intensity of his jaw, Caravaggio showed no fear—only a pulsating rage glimmering in his eyes.

How did I get dragged into this? Dueling is illegal in Roma. The whole bunch of us will be imprisoned. And if anyone is killed—

Caravaggio feinted and Ranuccio threw up his blade in a parry. Caravaggio circled under the blade in a deception, striking Ranuccio.

Ranuccio stumbled back, falling at Roero's feet. The knight jumped back as Caravaggio closed in on his fallen opponent.

"Give him mercy, Caravaggio!" shouted Roero. "He's on the ground. Be a Christian! Damn you!"

"You insult my woman," snarled Caravaggio, showing his teeth. "I insult your manhood!"

Caravaggio pointed the tip of his blade at Ranuccio's groin and aimed at his *palle*. As he thrust forward, Ranuccio twisted and the sword missed its mark, tearing into Tomassoni's thigh.

Ranuccio screamed. Blood sprayed from his femoral artery, freckling the cobblestones. Caravaggio stood over him, panting. He saw a pair of boots just beyond the victim's writhing body. His eyes climbed higher, seeing a tall figure looming in the shadow, an enormous white cross hovering over the dying man.

"You dirty murderer!" snarled Roero, his face twisted with hate. "You struck a man while he was down! Coward!" He drew his sword.

"You dog, slinking in the shadows," said Caravaggio. "Come out and fight!"

Roero lunged. Caravaggio held his sword vertical, parrying Roero's thrust, a bright clang echoing in the darkness.

Giovan Francesco leapt in, his sword engaging Caravaggio's.

"I'll kill you myself!" said the elder Tomassoni as his blade clanged against Caravaggio's. "Stay out of this, Roero!"

"You scoundrel!" cried Onorio Longhi, drawing his sword. Within seconds, all parties on both sides, except Roero, were engaged in the fight. Ranuccio's blood pulsed a sticky pool around him, soaking his leggings.

Captain Petronio jumped into the fight, drawing Giovan Francesco away from Caravaggio. The older Tomassoni brother was the most experienced from battles and an even match for the Bolognese. The Giugoli brothers struck metal with Mario and Onorio.

Federigo Giugoli's sword glanced off the side of Caravaggio's head.

"I'm dying, brothers!" wailed Ranuccio. Roero backed away from his dying friend, fading farther into the shadows. Already a small crowd had gathered.

Giovan Francesco clubbed Captain Petronio's sword out of his hand and struck savagely at the soldier's left arm, then hacked at his leg, slicing to the bone again and again.

"God curse you!" screamed the captain. Blood pulsed from his wounds, soaking his tunic.

"I told you to stay out of this!" shouted Giovan Francesco, watching his opponent crumple clutching his wounds. "I'm coming, Ranuccio!"

The Giugoli brothers locked arms to carry Ranuccio to a barber-surgeon. Giovan Francesco ran ahead, clearing the crowd as they rushed toward Piazza Navona.

"Cecco!" gasped Caravaggio, holding a blood-soaked hand to his temple.

"Maestro!" Cecco answered, his voice cracking.

"We've got to get Michele and Petronio to a barber-surgeon," said Longhi. "Can you walk, Michele? Mario and I will carry the Bolognese."

"Where?" said Caravaggio.

"Pompeo Navagna's shop," said Mario. "Cecco, run alert him!"

The boy ran, pushing the crowd out of his way.

The four men made their way down Via della Scrofa.

"Keep watch for the police, Michele" said Longhi, ducking under the threshold of the barbershop. He and Mario maneuvered Captain Petronio through the doorway.

"A bloody mess you bring me," said Pompeo Navagna. The barber sponged the blood from Caravaggio's wounds. He packed gray-green moss into the gaping skin.

"Face wounds," said the barber-surgeon, turning away to attend the Bolognese. "A glancing blow. You'll bleed but survive. Your friend here, on the other hand—" The barber inspected the captain's left arm and leg and whistled through his loose teeth. "Now here's a different story," he said, shaking his head. "This signore is mincemeat!"

The barber dug at Petronio's arm wound with long pincers, extracting a piece of bone, then another and another.

"Your bone is shattered, Capitano," said the barber.

Petronio bared his teeth against the pain as another fragment of bone was extracted from his arm.

Then the surgeon moved on to his leg.

"Eight stab wounds in this left thigh alone. Let me—"

Cecco burst into the room from the Via della Scrofa, where he had been standing guard.

"The *sbirri* are coming! They are following the trail of blood."

"The papal guard will not be far behind," said Longhi. He pulled Caravaggio up by the back of his tunic, twisting it in his fist. "*Bastardo!* We're done for! Run for it! You too, Mario."

"But I didn't—" said Mario.

Longhi grabbed him roughly by shoulder. "Listen to me! Ranuccio will surely die. We'll all be executed for participating in a duel."

"But my business. My art, my wife—"

"Run, Minniti!" shouted Longhi. "Run!"

The men tumbled out of the barbershop into the road, leaving Petronio to the surgeon's care.

Caravaggio grabbed Cecco by the shoulders, looking him in the eye. "Take care of the canvases. Promise me."

"*Sì!*" shouted Cecco, looking over his shoulder at the approaching crowd. "*Va' via*, Maestro!" *Go!*

"Take the paintings to Palazzo Madama and Cardinal del Monte. I'll send word there—"

"They're coming, Michele. Run!" shouted Longhi.

Flaming torches lit the far end of the street. Shouts, curses, and the sound of boot heels on stone became louder as the *sbirri* approached.

Caravaggio ran, his hand pressed to his temple. His wound began to bleed again, spotting the cobblestones with blood.

Cecco stood like a statue in the road. He watched his master disappear into the dark streets off Via della Scrofa.

Chapter 29

MARSAXLOKK, MALTA

"I think I hate you."

"I think I hate myself." A long silence, and then he said, for what seemed like the hundredth time, "I didn't know you got seasick."

And Lucia, again for what seemed the hundredth time, answered, "Neither did I—until I got trapped in that garbage scow for two days." And then, quickly, heading off another hundredth repetition, "I know. Fishing boat. Not garbage scow. But Jesus, Moto . . ."

And then she let it drop, because he'd been every bit as sick as she had—maybe even worse—and they now were, after all, in Malta, still queasy and trapped on a bus that spewed diesel fumes as it chugged through narrow streets on the hilly island, but otherwise in good shape. Alive, anyway.

When Moto's cousin's rusted fishing trawler had slipped into port at dawn after two days on a rough winter sea, Lucia and Moto had staggered ashore, reeling from nausea and ignoring the smirks of the crew.

"Let's find the nearest hotel."

"No." Even seasick, the new Moto was taking charge. "We have to keep moving."

"Right now, this damn street is moving. I swear, Moto, I'm going to throw up again."

"No, you're not. We have to get away from the coast. If they found us in Naples, they can follow us here. They'll check the ports."

"You're getting paranoid. No one followed us onto that damned boat. We must have lost them. We're in the middle of nowhere."

Moto raised a warning finger. "The Malta Tourist Bureau won't appreciate that remark."

With that, he half dragged her onto a bus that took them to another bus and then a third bus. Malta was warmer than Rome, but as if to make up for that, it was raining steadily, and after long waits at bus stops, they were both soaking wet by the time they got on the last bus. Still fighting the nausea, Lucia stared out the window at the passing fields of dark green speckled, even in midwinter, with bright-yellow flowers—so cheerful it made her want to punch someone in the face.

Finally, after more than an hour, they staggered off the bus in Rabat, a city right outside the walls of Malta's old capital of Mdina, where they found, yet again, a cheap hotel room and, yet again, passed out fully dressed—wet clothes and all—on the bed.

Lucia was not going to cry. She would not let herself. She might have dedicated her life to studying art, but she had always felt that people who wept openly in the presence of great art were just showing off. But now, staring at *The Beheading of St. John the Baptist*, she felt tears flooding her eyes. She blinked hard, unwilling to let the tears fall or to wipe them away.

Not that anyone was paying attention to her. The brightly lit room in the Valletta cathedral was much larger than the dark chapel in the church of San Luigi dei Francesi in Rome, but even on this midwinter morning, it was filled with a bustling crowd. There were a hundred people talking, pointing, corralling children, answering cell phones, and taking pictures despite the prominent signs declaring that photography was absolutely prohibited. From time to time, a guard hushed the mob with a sharp, "Shhhh!" And then, little by little, the murmur rose again.

But none of it mattered to Lucia. The enormous painting's focus, power, and clarity swept everything away. The crowd and the noise that had indeed distressed her when she first walked into the room faded quickly. For a long moment, she forgot to breathe, and then, when breath returned, her eyes filled with tears.

She blinked again and focused on the painting. The central drama was intense, a tight cluster of figures: the saint lying dead—no, she decided, not dead, dying, his blood still spurting—after the savage slash of the executioner's sword, that sword now dropped clattering on the stones of the courtyard; the executioner, one hand reaching down to grab the saint's hair, his extended arm an arrow, like the neon sign outside the Naples hotel, pointing to the moment of death, while his other hand reached behind him for his knife to finishing severing the head; the young woman—was she Salome, who had demanded the saint's head? No, certainly a serving girl, this was servant's work—holding out a platter to receive the severed head; an old woman, clutching her own head in horror; a prison guard, pointing sternly, trying to take control of the moment.

It was a frozen instant of horror and death. But it wasn't the death that brought those tears to her eyes and held her attention.

It was the life.

Life pulsed from those figures, from those bodies. Even from the dying saint. From the half-naked executioner, master of death. From the servant girl, the guard, the old woman staring in horror. And from the two other prisoners, figures Lucia had overlooked at first, but who now riveted her attention, peering through the bars of a shadowed window at the fate they might soon enough share.

The genius of Caravaggio was the life force that surged off the canvas.

And now, as that force vibrated within her, Lucia was sure: the same force had surrounded her and held her in the dark of the warehouse as she waited and wondered, like those two prisoners witnessing the beheading, whether her life would be sacrificed next.

She didn't know how long she stood there, caught in the spell of that moment—a living moment painted four hundred years ago, a sacred moment from two thousand years ago—but she hardly moved until the spell was broken.

Broken by the shard of memory of other beheadings that had happened only days ago.

And suddenly she felt lost and alone in the busy room and she spun around, looking for Moto. But he wasn't there and a sense of menace closed in around her. Someone was hunting her, someone wanted to kill her, and she was all alone in the crowd.

She fought down the panic. Murder in the cathedral? No, certainly she was safe here at least.

But she had already seen murder in a church, seen the real blood on the floor, Te-Te's blood.

Stop it! She'd told Moto she was sure they were safe here, that they'd gotten away from whoever was chasing them. She'd meant it then and she'd have to keep believing it. If she didn't, she'd fall apart. She reminded herself of the vow she'd taken outside the airport, however long ago that was: she was all in. No hesitation. No falling apart. No hope, no fear.

She turned back for one last look at the *Beheading*. Yes. She had seen what she needed to see. The painting—"their painting"—was a Caravaggio. It had to be. She turned and slipped silently from the room.

Moto was standing right outside, waiting patiently, watching the crowds that surged into the room.

∞

"When do we get out of here?"

After another long bus ride in the rain, from Valletta to Rabat, they were back in the hotel.

Lucia answered Moto's question with one of her own.

"How do we get out of here?"

"No boats?"

"No boats. No ferries." And just to be clear: "No Sicily."

"It's too far to swim." No answer to that, so he went on. "That means we have to fly."

"And no help from your friends?"

"None. We have to go like ordinary people. Go to the airport, buy a ticket to Rome, and hold our breath until we're somewhere safe."

"OK. So . . . when's the next plane?"

"Look it up. You're the one with the phone."

After a long silence, broken only by an occasional muttered curse, Lucia tossed her phone on the bed. "Tomorrow morning."

"All right! A big night on the town in Rabat. I always wanted to party in Malta."

"I thought we were keeping out of sight."

"I'm guessing the January bar scene in Rabat is pretty much the same as keeping out of sight."

"It's only three o'clock."

"Nap time!"

Moto stretched out on the bed, and Lucia sat in the room's only chair and idly browsed through websites on her cell phone. For a long time there was silence.

Then Lucia stood up and announced, "I'm going to see the grotto."

"What?"

"The Grotto of Saint Paul. He was shipwrecked on Malta—it's in the Bible—and he lived in a cave in Rabat. It's a ten-minute walk from here."

"When did you suddenly get religious? Did you make some kind of bargain with God if he'd get you off my cousin's boat?"

"If I'd made a bargain with God, it would have been to send a wave to wash you overboard—and a whale to swallow you—for dragging me onto that scow."

"Hey!"

"I know, I know, it's a noble fishing vessel. Anyway, no religion involved. I was reading on the web that Caravaggio visited the grotto, that he got some inspiration for the *Beheading* there. As long as we're stuck here, might as well go. You coming?"

"It's a grotto, right? So it's underground?"

"Sure. Want to see a picture?" She held up the phone.

"No, thanks. Not me. I figure I'll spend enough time underground when I'm dead. Until then, I'm staying up here in the fresh air."

"Seriously?"

"Seriously. Underground scares me. You go ahead. I'll stay here."

"I guess I can't tempt you with a side trip to the catacombs. They're connected to the grotto." Moto shuddered dramatically. "Thought not. OK. I'll be back soon."

"Tell Paul I said hello. Put in a good word for me."

Lucia closed the door behind her, took a deep breath, and headed down the stairs. There was nothing to be afraid of. She'd made up her mind about that.

After she was gone, Moto sat alone in the room for a while. Then he shook his head, shouted, "No!" to the empty room, grabbed his jacket, and ran out, stopping at the front desk to ask directions.

As he walked across the small town, he muttered, "No, I'm not." And then: "I can do this."

❧

Lucia's breath rasped in her throat. She wasn't certain where she was or how she'd gotten here, but there wasn't time to think. Only time to run.

The grotto had been dark, cold, and empty. The woman at the ticket window had barely glanced at her, just taken her money and waved her through. Down a hallway, down a steep curving stairway, and into the dark. There was a dimly lit room with two small chapels and then, around a corner, the grotto itself, low and dark, cut into the rock, a statue of the saint in the middle of the small space. The article she'd read had talked about Caravaggio and the power of the shadows, but she wasn't seeing it, wasn't feeling it. All she felt was alone. She understood why Moto hated the idea of being underground.

She turned to leave, but as she was about to start up the curving stairs, she heard footsteps above coming down. She heard the rustle of heavy fabric and remembered the monk in Rome in the robes with the blood-red cross, the strange cross—and suddenly she realized that she'd been seeing that cross all day. It was a Maltese cross, each of the four arms flaring from the center to the end, each with a notch in the end. An eight-pointed cross. The symbol of the Knights of Malta, the Knights of St. John. Briefly Caravaggio's saviors, his path to a pardon. And then his sworn enemies. Perhaps his murderers.

And now perhaps hers.

There was nowhere to go, only the single flight of stairs leading up and out.

Without time to think—or to remember her vow that there was nothing to be afraid of—she darted into one of the two tiny side chapels and squeezed down behind the altar. As she crouched there, holding her breath, she had a moment to think, *Great, I'm desecrating one of the holy places of Christendom. Now I've got God pissed off at me too.*

Then she heard the footsteps reach the bottom of the stairs and go around the corner to the grotto. Now! She leapt out of the chapel and sprinted up the stairs.

She ran. Not knowing where she was going, she ran. And she heard the footsteps hurrying after her.

A corner of her mind wondered how fast they could run in those robes.

A sign to an exit. A staircase leading up into the light. She could see the ticket window where she had entered, but before she could race up and out, she glimpsed a dark-robed figure standing by the door. No!

She turned and barged through a set of glass doors and down another steep staircase, back into the dark.

And here the darkness was deeper than it had been in the grotto, the ceiling lower, the passageway narrower, the floor uneven, dim lights at intervals along the walls. She stumbled and almost fell.

She was in the catacombs, ancient burial chambers the Romans had carved into the soft rock of the island. Passages branched off left and right, a bewildering maze honeycombed with rooms cut into the rock, tombs large and small.

She was surrounded by ancient death, and behind her she could hear the footsteps of very modern death hard on her heels. No way of telling where the passages went or why. No time to stop and consider. Only time to run.

Her strength was fading fast. After two days seasick on the boat and no more than a few hours' sleep, she didn't have anything left. She could feel her legs giving way beneath her.

With a last burst of strength, she dived into a low chamber in the wall to her right and crawled as far back as she could go. The chamber narrowed, the ceiling just a foot or two above her head. She fell into a hole—an empty grave carved in the rock floor.

Lucia flattened herself against the bottom of the shallow grave and fought to quiet her breath. The footsteps were still coming, not running now, marching with the certainty of a predator that knows its prey is trapped. Her muscles tensed. Dead tired, near collapse, she wasn't going down without a fight. She remembered a self-defense class in college. Groin and eyes. She pictured her knee exploding up, her hooked fingers clawing. Someone was going to get hurt.

The footsteps passed the alcove where she was hiding, and for a moment she allowed herself to hope. Then they returned, more slowly, pausing often. She heard voices muttering, indistinct, incomprehensible.

A moment of silence.

Then someone grabbed her leg, fierce fingers digging into her flesh. She kicked out wildly and felt her foot connect with something solid. There was a curse, but the grip on her leg didn't loosen, and she was yanked brutally over the rough stone of the chamber and out into the passageway.

Hauled onto her feet, she desperately tried to jam her knee into the attacker's groin, but his long robes entangled her leg. She tried to claw his eyes, but the cowl protected his face and he crushed her against him in a bear hug that immobilized her. Someone else grabbed her legs, and together they carried her down the tunnel. She tried to scream, but her face was pressed against his chest, and the cloth of his robe muffled her.

She was writhing and fighting for any leverage she could find, but the men who held her were too strong. She tried to wrench her head back from the robe that gagged her, and for an instant, as they passed one of the lights set into the walls of the tunnel, she could see that her face was crushed against the blood-red Maltese cross on his chest. In that brief instant, there was something else . . . but she didn't have time to think what it was. She was fighting for her life.

And losing.

Crushed against the man's chest, she struggled to breathe. She felt consciousness slipping away. Darkness fluttered at the edge of her vision. A corner of her mind warned that if she passed out now she would never wake again. She tried one last frantic explosion. She got one leg free, kicked again, and connected again.

But it was hopeless.

She was finished.

And suddenly the air was pierced with the shriek of a siren. A moment of silence. Then the siren again.

Then an amplified voice echoed through the tunnels.

"*Attenzione! Attenzione!* Everyone must leave the catacombs immediately! *Attenzione!* Guards will guide you to the nearest exit. Leave immediately! *Attenzione!*"

And then the siren again.

The siren continued to wail and the announcement repeated.

Then she heard voices calling.

"Police! This way! Everyone! Now!"

The men carrying her exchanged a few quick words in an incomprehensible language—Arabic?—and dropped her on the stone floor. She fell heavily. One of the men kicked her hard in the ribs, and then their footsteps raced off. Her mind registered the sound: one of them was limping.

Lucia lay on the floor, gasping for breath, wondering if her ribs were broken.

Then she heard heavier footsteps approaching. The guards were coming. She couldn't let them find her like this. She scrambled to her feet and tried to brush some of the dirt and dust off her clothes. She fought to get her breathing under control—although a little panic might not be out of place, given the sirens and the warnings and the guards.

And then a policeman clad in heavy riot gear marched down the tunnel. He didn't care how she looked. He harshly ordered her to keep moving through the nearly empty passages of the catacombs and out into the last fading light of the day.

She stood, drinking in the cool, fresh air and trying to understand what had happened. She wanted to close her eyes to concentrate, but when she did, she felt fear boiling up inside her. She turned, trying to look calm, and scanned the area for anyone in a monk's robe, but the street was filled with ordinary people in ordinary clothing hurrying on about their ordinary lives.

Lucia wasn't certain what to do, where to go. She wanted to run back to the hotel, but she didn't know who might be hiding, waiting, along the way. She was too tired to think where to go, but she couldn't stay where she was.

A hand grabbed her arm, and she spun around, ready to punch, kick, claw for freedom.

"Lucia!"

It was Moto.

"Moto! How did you . . . ? Never mind! Get me off this damned rock!" And she hugged him so hard he squeaked.

Chapter 30

Roma
1606

Cecco pounded the brass knocker on the Palazzo Colonna door. A guard opened the door and grabbed the boy by the scruff of his neck.

"What business do you have disturbing the peace at this hour?"

"I must speak to the marchesa! Let go of me, I beg you! I come in the name of Michelangelo Merisi da Caravaggio."

"That ruffian! You—"

"The marchesa needs to hear my news! It is most urgent!"

The guard let go of the boy. Cecco straightened his blood-splattered tunic, smoothing down the cloth with his shaking hands.

"State your business," said the guard.

"With your permission, I cannot. It is only for the marchesa's ears."

The guard wiped his mouth with the back of his hand. "Damn you. I cannot disturb the marchesa."

"You must!" pleaded Cecco.

The guard blinked, focusing on the panic shining in the boy's eyes. "I will send a servant to wake her son, the grand admiral. Wait here."

The door clanged shut, the sound reverberating in the night air. Cecco drew back into the shadows, away from the flaming torches of the palace.

❦

"What? He murdered a man?" Costanza Colonna's hand flew to her mouth. The motion was reflected many times in the gilded mirrors of Palazzo Colonna.

"Not just any man, Mamma," said her son Fabrizio, grand admiral of the Maltese Fleets. "One of the Tomassoni brothers. They may kill him before the Roman guards can catch him."

"Madonna!" she said. Fabrizio watched his mother's hand quiver. When she lowered her hand, he saw the sorrow ravage her face.

Michele, you dog! Look how she suffers for you, thought Fabrizio.

"You see his predicament," said Fabrizio. "He will either rot in a cell in Sant'Angelo or be run through with a Tomassoni sword. He must flee Roma. Cardinal del Monte houses him but only temporarily. The pope will demand his arrest. Dueling—a murder!—is punishable by death."

Costanza Colonna's gray eyes shimmered. "What more can I do for this Michelangelo Merisi?" she said, throwing her hands in the air. Again, the gesture was reflected in the wide mirrors. The first faint shards of sunlight announced the dawn, a rosy glow coloring the marchesa's reflection.

"He cannot stay away from trouble. Pff! Any more than you, Fabrizio!" said the marchesa. She ran her hand through her silver hair, deranging the coiffure her handmaiden had so hastily fashioned. "You both must have drunk from the same malevolent fountain in the village of Caravaggio, cursed be the two of you!"

Fabrizio made a sound of disgust. "Do not compare me with Michelangelo, Mamma! You still think of us both as little boys."

"You were both up to trouble even when you were toddling. But the grief you both bring me has grown bigger than both of you. Murder?"

"I have washed my slate clean with the Order of Malta."

The marchesa drew in a deep breath, expelling it in a sigh. She touched the cross that hung on a golden chain around her neck. "Thank

God for that! If only Caravaggio could do the same. Grand Master Wignacourt and the knights' vows of chastity and obedience would cure the ruffian of his ill nature soon enough."

"Michelangelo—a knight!" scoffed Fabrizio. "He'd probably find every prostitute in Valletta, bed them down, and then insist on making them all Madonnas."

A wan smile crept across the marchesa's face. "Incorrigible, our Michele—but he is a genius. He brings fame to Caravaggio, your birthplace and our lineage. He will be remembered long after we Colonnas are dead."

She stopped to look out the window at the Piazza Venezia—at the early-morning commotion with carriages and wagons as Roma started the day. Beyond, she saw the green of the overgrown fields and the crumbling stones of the Roman Forum. A shepherd stood with staff in hand, watching his flock and the sunrise.

"Why should he not become a knight?" she said, still watching the shepherd. "We know many types of men who wear the Maltese cross—some are louts, brawl like *bravi*, and frequent brothels, yet they are in good standing."

"But Mamma! Michelangelo has no noble blood. It is impossible."

"There must be a way—"

"Only the pope could make an exception. And Roma has decreed Caravaggio's death."

"Michelangelo's father was such a good, simple man," said the marchesa, shaking her head. "A worthy servant and friend to your father . . . and to me."

Fabrizio waved away his mother's words. "Mamma, you have told me many times."

He raised his hands, palms turned upward in supplication. He had known Michelangelo as a childhood friend, one of the servants' boys who was standoffish and shy, unlike his father. But as young children, they had played together—building forts, whittling swords from branches.

Fabrizio looked out the palazzo window at a bird lighting in the branches of a cypress tree. The clanging of the bells of the Santi Apostoli next to the palazzo frightened the bird away, a flapping of black wings gleaming in the early-dawn light.

"I've heard rumors that the grand master is seeking a painter," he said at last.

The marchesa's eyes opened wide. "An artist for the Order of Malta?"

"To commemorate the knights."

"Oh! Fabrizio! Michelangelo would be perfect! You could talk to the grand master and—"

Fabrizio held up his hand. "Patience, Mamma. This is a delicate matter. It would be best if handled indirectly. I shall speak to Ottavio Costa, who owns several of Michele's paintings. Costa is a relative of Cavaliere Malaspina. If he suggests Caravaggio to Malaspina, and Malaspina talks to the grand master, there is a good chance of success."

"Oh, dear boy. You must speak with Costa immediately. Shall I invite him to dine?"

"No. I will pay him a visit. The sooner, the better. These things take time."

"In the meantime, where shall Michele flee?"

Fabrizio rubbed his beard with a thumbnail. "Temporarily, he could take shelter in our estate in Zagarolo."

"But that's too close to Roma! A half-day ride and the papal guards will seize him."

"They'll have to learn his whereabouts. And I don't think Pope Paul V—or any pope—would want to anger the Colonnas," he said, setting his mouth hard.

"Still. Zagarolo is too close. Unless we can arrange a pardon . . ."

"This is no tavern brawl, Mamma. It's murder!"

"Michele could go to Napoli," said the marchesa, clenching and unclenching her fingers. "He would be protected there under Spanish law. The pope could not interfere with a sovereign state."

Fabrizio shook his head ruefully. "He might be safe . . . until the Tomassoni brothers hunt him down. Those brothers will not forget Ranuccio's murder."

The marchesa patted her son's hand. She felt how his skin was weathered from days at sea.

Admiral! How the Maltese Knights have changed my son's fortunes.

"Let's let this play out," said Fabrizio. "Malaspina may save Michele's miserable skin, the idiot!"

"You are right, my son," said the marchesa. "*Va bene*, I will send him to Zagarolo—close enough to Roma should he receive a pardon."

"Mamma!" said Fabrizio, throwing his hands in the air. "Michele will never receive a pardon from the pope!"

"At least the Alban Hills will be a stepping-stone. I know Michele," she said, knitting her fingers together. "He would rather die than be banished from Roma."

"He should have thought about that before he started killing Romans, especially those associated with the noble houses."

"Zagarolo first, while I make arrangements. Then Napoli. But hidden away."

"All right," said Fabrizio. "Napoli should suit him. The dark alleyways, cutthroats, and thieves will give him a deserving welcome."

Chapter 31

Alban Hills, Lazio
1606

By the rocking and jolting of the carriage, Cecco knew they were climbing a hill. His fingers sought the crimson velvet, drawing back the curtain just enough to peek out at the Alban Hills.

As the coach emerged from a dark forest, Cecco saw the Colonnas' feudal town of Zagarolo perched on the rocky hillside. The stuccoed ochre buildings stood on a rising line of stone, cut with steep ravines.

It looks like the spiny back of a dragon, hunching over the forest.

The secluded outpost was perfectly suited for hiding a man condemned to death under a *bando capitale*.

The coach jolted toward the ancient Roman gate, replete with a seated Jupiter and an eagle. Thunderbolts were carved into the marble.

"Look, Maestro," said Cecco softly, pulling back the curtain.

"Cover the window, damn you!" moaned Caravaggio, holding his bandaged head. "The sun hurts my eyes!"

Cecco let the heavy cloth fall back into place.

"Did you pack up all the pigments? My brushes, my—"

"Maestro. Everything of value I have packed. I had so little time."

Caravaggio groaned. "Give me a drink of water."

Cecco passed a flask to his master.

The coach lurched over the rough stones, the water spilling over Caravaggio's threadbare tunic.

"Al diavolo!" he shouted. *To the devil!* He pounded the front board of the carriage to signal the driver.

Cecco looked at his master's bloody bandages, which were turning brown with the heat.

"How are we so fortunate to receive such succor from the Colonnas, Maestro?" he said. "She must love you as a son—"

"Ha!" said Caravaggio, taking a sip of water. "I believe she is as superstitious as a gypsy. I am the blessed boy born on Saint Michael's day, the date of her father's victory at Lepanto. She has always doted on me like a favorite son."

Cecco said nothing. His head rocked with the motion of the coach.

"Did you tell Lena what happened?" asked Caravaggio.

Cecco shook his head. "Maestro, forgive me. I had no time."

"I shall send word," said Caravaggio, picking scabbed blood from his bandages. Cecco watched the artist examine the color, turning his fingertip in the dim light, then pulling the edge of the window curtain back to shed sunlight on the bloody scab.

Cecco smiled wearily.

His mind is muddling over the pigment and how to create the perfect paint to capture that color. Dried blood.

The coach stopped, punctuated by the snorts of the horses.

"Maestro Caravaggio," said a voice at the carriage door. *"Benvenuti a Zagarolo.* You remain under the protection of Duke Marzio Colonna."

Caravaggio pulled back the curtain. A bearded man in a brown velvet suit stood on moss-covered stones. Behind him rose a twelfth-century palazzo of limestone and marble facing.

"My name is Rafael di Cortello. I am the steward of the palazzo in the service of Duke Colonna," said the bearded man, opening the carriage door. "If you will follow me, Maestro Caravaggio, I shall show you to your rooms in the—"

"Where will I paint?" said Caravaggio, clutching his bandaged head. "Is there sufficient light?"

Di Cortello drew a quick breath, taken aback. "Of course, Maestro Merisi. The marchesa has arranged everything to meet your demands. I know of your fame as an artist."

Cecco watched silently.

And as a murderer?

∞

Cecco had barely finished his dinner of roast partridge and artichokes before his master set him to work.

"Unpack the pigments and begin grinding both burnt and raw umber. And red ochre . . . plenty of it. Set up the easel facing Roma. North by northwest."

"But the light at this time of the—"

"Do as I say," snapped Caravaggio. "I do not need the light now."

Cecco bowed, excusing himself from the table.

∞

Caravaggio arranged for a pallet to be brought in for the boy, despite the fact that Cecco had been given his own room.

"My hours are erratic," said the artist to Di Cortello. "I must have the boy at my beck and call."

"As you wish, Maestro," replied the steward.

Since the night of Ranuccio's death, Cecco had slept little. As he lay down, he noticed that the pallet smelled of fresh lavender and sunlight, the bed linens dried in the breezes of the Alban Hills. And then, in a moment, he was profoundly asleep.

In the deepest hour of the night, as the moon spilled its milky light across the room, the boy awoke. Caravaggio stood by the window, looking toward Roma.

Cecco watched his master's hand rise and fall, silhouetted in the moonlight, orchestrating the night. Rubbing his eyes, Cecco realized the artist was not conducting but sketching. Drawing an image from memory.

Cecco watched the movement of the imaginary brush held delicately between Caravaggio's index finger and thumb. Following the motion, Cecco could see the outline. A drawing of a reclining figure— a woman?—her throat bent back, her mouth dropped open.

Early the next morning, the sunrise only a smudge of crimson on the horizon, Cecco opened his eyes. His master stood before the easel, wiping his paintbrush. He looked over to the waking boy.

"Buongiorno, ragazzo!" he said, stretching his arms over his head.

"Buongiorno," said Cecco, trying to catch a glimpse of the canvas.

Caravaggio covered the painting, something he never had done before.

"Do not look at this," he said to Cecco. "This is private, for my own pleasure. Do you understand?"

"Sì, Maestro," said the boy. *"Ho capito."*

"Now. I'm eager to start a new canvas this morning. Get up and grind some *verdaccio.* I need a blue green for Jesus's robe."

"Jesus?" said Cecco, pulling on his pants.

Caravaggio nodded. *"The Supper at Emmaus."* The artist took on a distracted look. "Send word for the cook to prepare lamb. A rack, the bones exposed—a cheap cut. The scrawniest, most gristly piece the butcher can provide. I must have it for this afternoon's session."

He stopped for a moment and closed his eyes. Then he turned slowly back toward the window.

"And Cecco," he said, staring into the distance. "Do you remember the old woman who posed for me with Lena? For the Madonna of the Palafrenieri?"

"The signora from Via della Scrofa?"

"The same. Describe her," said Caravaggio. "Draw her in words for me, every detail you remember."

Cecco touched his fingertips together in a temple, pressing them against his forehead. He closed his eyes, remembering. "Her face was a map of wrinkles . . ." he started.

"*Sì.* Go on. Where were the wrinkles set . . . what angles?"

Cecco opened his eyes, looking out the window to the steep ravines gouging the rocky hill below. He turned back to face his master. "Deep canyons rutting her skin from cheek to mouth. Her eyes were sunken caves in her skull."

"*Sì,*" said Caravaggio. "*Bene!*"

"Her skin drew tight around her cheekbones." Cecco made a slash with his pointer fingers, making a V. "This angle. Like a clenched fist across knuckles, all sinews tying in a knot at her pointed chin."

"That's it. Yes, now I remember."

"But . . . you softened that in the shadows of the painting. She looked benevolent."

"She had to be. She was Saint Anne. But I remember the sharp chin. The angled face."

"Ah!" said Cecco, snapping his fingers. "She had a goiter—not large like the woman in *Judith Beheading Holofernes*, but easy enough to see—right under her neck, on her right collarbone."

"Excellent!" said Caravaggio. He reached for his paintbrush and, taking the blunt handle, began to press into the prepared black gesso. "Go on, Cecco. Go on."

"The part in her hair. A white line in coarse dark hair. Dirty, ill-kempt. I remember she smelled of rancid oil, a greasy smell."

Caravaggio made another depression in the gesso. He stood back, looking at his mark. He made a few slight lines with lead white, blocking out a position. Then he used his brush to make a quick sketch in dark paint, a figure, faint as a ghost. Cecco saw the outline of the woman emerging in the corner of the painting.

Like the mysterious painting in the moonlight, the old woman was drawn from memory, something his master had never done before.

❧

Ottavio Costa quizzed his personal secretary, who stood before him with a large, carefully wrapped package.

"You say this arrived in a Colonna coach?"

"*Sì, signore,*" said the secretary, bowing his head.

"And there was no letter?"

"No, signore. The driver said only that it was a painting, to be delivered exclusively to your hand here in Roma. And that you should judge its value. The coach will pass by again tomorrow to receive either the money or the painting to be returned."

"It can only be . . ." said Ottavio Costa, his eyes wide in anticipation. "Open it, *subito!*"

"*Sì, signore.*"

Costa watched his secretary struggle with the twine. "Cut it," he said. "But be careful! You must take care, Sebastiano!"

The secretary at last freed the package of the final strand of twine. He pulled back the vellum, exposing the painting.

"*Dio mio!*" gasped Costa. "It is magnificent!"

When the secretary said nothing, Costa explained, "It is our Lord at the Supper of Emmaus."

The secretary leaned the painting against the wall and retreated a few steps. He studied the painting, twisting his lips.

Look how haggard is our Lord Christ! The wispy red beard of a beggar. And what a piece of gristle and bone that old woman serves him. Does she not realize who he is? God on Earth!

"I shall have it!" said Costa. "Open the coffer and take out five hundred—no!—six hundred scudi. Have it ready for the driver. My God, what a treasure I have procured."

The secretary nodded, then furrowed his brow beyond his master's sight.

Now we support a murderer!

❦

The Colonna steward, Di Cortello, knocked on the door of Caravaggio's room. The tang of turpentine stung his nostrils.

"Why do you interrupt me?" said Caravaggio, dabbing at his painting. He turned gruffly to address the intruder, paintbrush still in hand.

"Rumors that you hide here in Zagarolo have reached the ears of the papacy," said Di Cortello. "It is too dangerous to remain in this house. You must leave—"

"That is not convenient! Where will I go?" snapped Caravaggio, scowling at the steward. "I'm in the middle of a new painting—"

"Maestro, perhaps you do not understand the risk. The papal guards will arrest you here. And the scandal for the Colonnas—"

"Ah," said Caravaggio, halting. "The marchesa."

"The Marchesa Colonna has completed arrangements for you to move to their palazzo in Paliano. And then on to Napoli."

"Napoli! Why in God's name would I move to Napoli? I must be near Roma to receive a pardon—"

"Forgive me, Maestro," said Di Cortello, his nostrils pinched. "The marchesa and her son Signor Fabrizio do not believe a pardon is . . . imminent."

Caravaggio's back stiffened. "How can I be banished from Roma? Napoli is a different universe!"

"Signore," said Di Cortello. "The coach will depart right after dark. Please let me know what assistance we can give you."

And good riddance!

Chapter 32

ROME

"It is proving very costly, sir." Fra Filippo Lupo stood at attention.

His *comandante* didn't respond, so the tall man continued.

"Two at the very beginning, sir, in Rome. Both professed knights. Then a novice at the Muslims' villa, burned. By his own foolishness, but still a loss. We were fortunate to recover what was left of him. And then two in Naples. A commander and a novice."

The man at the desk narrowed his eyes. His voice was smooth. "And let us not forget your knee. In Rome."

"That was an accident, sir. Not worth accounting." He was at ramrod attention.

"You are still limping."

"It does not impair my efficiency, sir."

"Even so." A brief silence. "So, unlike your disaster in Naples, there were no casualties in that fiasco in Malta. Is that correct?"

"Yes sir." A broken nose from that bitch's desperate kick didn't seem worth mentioning.

"So it would seem we are getting better."

The tall man flinched. "We always try to be at our best, sir."

"I suppose." Comandante Pantera looked down at some papers spread out in front of him on the desk, then snapped his eyes up again. "Why are we discussing our casualties?"

"I know you want to be informed, sir. Our ranks are already thin. Now they grow thinner."

"Are you suggesting we are defeated? That we surrender?" His voice was rising. "That we are finished? Destroyed like the Turks at Lepanto?"

"No sir. I—"

"We are *not* defeated. We will *not* surrender!"

"Sir, I—"

"We will defend our faith, our legion, and our founding inspiration." His voice dropped, suddenly quiet. "To the very end."

"Sir." Color rose in Fra Lupo's hollow cheeks, and he maintained his rigid posture as he turned and left the room. Limping ever so slightly.

∽

"And that guy—"

"Which guy?" Professor Richman interrupted from his armchair in the owner's suite in the villa at Monte Piccolo, where he seemed intent on remaining more or less forever.

"The guy who smacked me across the face." Moto worked his jaw back and forth sideways, as if he were still testing for damage from that slap in the backstreets of Naples a week before. "He said we were on our own. I thought about that, and I knew I couldn't just let Lulu wander off on her own." Lucia blew him a kiss.

"But you didn't go into the grotto to find her?"

"I don't go underground." Moto's tone was a little defensive. "So I waited in a café across the street. And I saw three of them. In those black robes—"

"With the Maltese cross." The professor had to chime in. Moto ignored him.

"—marching across the piazza. They went inside, and I kept waiting for Lulu to come running out. But she didn't. I had to do something."

"So you phoned in a bomb scare!" Lucia couldn't resist finishing the story.

"Bravo!" Professor Richman applauded softly.

"First and last call on my new cell phone," said Moto. "I bought it while Lucia was staring at the *Beheading*, and I threw it in the trash right after I made that call."

"I told you those things come in handy." Lucia couldn't resist.

Moto gave her a look. Raised his eyebrows. Then, maybe just to change the subject, he turned to Professor Richman.

"So . . . I guess you were right when you ditched us in Milan because we were certain to get in trouble."

The professor, who so far had spent the entire morning listening as Lucia and Moto recounted their adventures—and misadventures— since they'd left him at the Milano Centrale station, smiled and steepled his fingers.

"Well, that might be debatable."

And then he told them about his own adventures over the past days, starting with the fact that he had gone to Siena, not back here to Monte Piccolo as they had expected, and ending with: "It wasn't a great deal of spit, I must admit. But it was the best I could do. And I thought I was dead. I was certain he was going to kill me. Why he didn't, I don't know."

And he smiled with undeniable satisfaction at their astonishment.

"One last note. I wasn't going to tell you, but I can't resist. He pushed me down in the chair and stood there—knife in one hand, gun in the other—and looked at me like he was still making up his mind whether to kill me. Then he cleared his throat, stood up as straight and tall as a gorilla like that could, and spit very precisely on the toe of my Hotel Continental slipper. And he said, '*That's* how you spit, old man. Now go home. Read your books.'"

"Professor," said Lucia, "you continue to amaze me."

"Thank you, my dear. In any case, the advice that, um, gentleman gave me seems very much like the advice you two got in Naples. As I believe you quoted your friends—if I may use the term loosely—'Go back to your fucking books.' And that sounds like excellent advice under the circumstances—given that the circumstances include attempted abductions and heavily armed thugs."

"I agree!" Moto chimed in.

"Excellent," said the professor. "And that is exactly what I have been doing. Research. And I have come up with several interesting discoveries."

"About the painting?"

"What else? So first"—the professor ducked his head and rummaged around in a briefcase on the floor by his side—"there's . . . this!" And with a theatrical flourish, he produced a large blowup of a photo of the painting.

"And what I noticed, when I studied it carefully, was one little detail. Here."

He pointed to a dark corner of the image. In the murky shadows of the background, an arm was flung haphazardly out from the crowd, the hand falling, as if at random, on a rough stone monument in the landscape of Gethsemane. One finger pointed at a single carved letter, all that was legible on the stone. The letter *R*.

Lucia bent close over the photo, then leaned back.

"OK. The letter *R*. And what is that supposed to tell us?"

The professor shrugged. He'd been working on his Italian shrugs in the mirror every morning.

"If you're right and this is Michele's work"—the professor was again insisting that they stop using the name Caravaggio, but now it was for safety, not superstition, and Lucia was willing to go along—"and someone painted over the faces for whatever cursed reason, then the rest of it—the bodies, the background—is Michele's. And he painted a hand pointing directly to the letter *R*. So it must mean something."

"Unless it means absolutely nothing." Lucia was a determined skeptic.

"Our friend may have been a madman, but I don't think he ever did anything by accident in his paintings. The letter *R*. I don't know what it means, but it's something we have to keep in mind." He put the photograph down. "And now I have a second item to discuss with you. It may require a little explanation."

He looked down, almost a little shamefaced for a moment, then he brightened again and reached into the leather satchel next to his chair.

"This." And he proudly displayed the soft leather book with the battered cover.

"But that was in the villa. In the fire. How did you . . ."

"I borrowed it for academic purposes."

"You stole it!" Lucia almost shouted.

"I was certainly going to return it when our research was finished."

"But now you can't," she insisted.

"Indeed, now I can't."

"You stole that from a dead girl."

"She wasn't dead."

"A girl who was about to die. You stole it." Lucia didn't know why it made her so angry, but after everything that had happened, somehow this one thing was more than she could take.

"If you're going to say it that way, it's always going to sound wrong. And maybe I wasn't exactly ethical—"

"Ethical!"

"—in my methods. But now it's been saved. That poor unfortunate girl would not be any happier knowing her great discovery had been destroyed along with her."

"Nothing's going to make her happy."

"So let's be happy on her behalf that her historical document has not been lost. And I believe it can provide us with a treasure trove of clues."

Lucia took a deep breath. "All right. What are we supposed to do now?"

"We should limit ourselves to what we can actually do. I believe we have conclusively proved we are not superheroes. We should stick to our research." The professor spread his arms wide. "Back to school, kids!"

He tried to make it sound like a grand adventure.

Lucia wasn't convinced.

A chill winter rain was falling in the nighttime hills of Sicily. A scattering of small stone houses withstood the weather with patience, as they had for centuries. Though the modern age had brought electricity to even these outposts, curls of smoke fighting their way up into the sky through the rain showed that wood fires were still the main source of winter warmth.

High on the hillside, one house loomed in the dark, larger than the rest by far. Its windows were brightly lit. Three sturdy chimneys sent plumes of smoke into the dark.

In the kitchen, the air was filled with the aroma of roasting meat and the laughter of women as they cooked a meal to serve a dozen. Downstairs, in a windowless room, the air was filled with the aroma of cigar smoke and the muttering of men as they discussed business with an ingrained reticence. No names. No details. Shrugs, grunts. The Sicilian they spoke would have been nearly incomprehensible to most Italians.

"Accussi?" So?

"Taliannu." Watching.

"E . . . ?" And . . . ?

A shake of the head, a shrug.

"*Accussi . . . spittamu.*" So . . . *we wait.*

"*Ppi ssempri?*" *Forever?*

"*Sì, sempri. Idda è a famigghia.*" *Yes, forever. She is family.*

"*Arreri?*" *Still?*

"*A famigghia è ppi ssempri.*" *Family is forever.*

At the villa in Chianti, Lucia tried to dive back into the art history seminar as if nothing had happened. Moto took to cruising the piazza on his Vespa again. The professor stuck to his rooms. He went out rarely, as if concerned that the *conte* might notice he was out of the suite and reclaim his quarters, forcing Professor Richman back to the drafty dorms.

A week passed, two, then Richman summoned Lucia and Moto to his quarters.

Moto opened a bottle of wine, while Richman explained that he had been working with the *conte*'s fourteen-year-old nephew, who had taken pictures of every page in Fenelli's journal and sent them back to one of the professor's old colleagues. The nephew was quite a virtuoso. He had shot the photos on his phone and transmitted them flawlessly, even while he seemed completely absorbed in a fierce video game of some sort on another phone.

"I got some helpful responses surprisingly quickly. We old boys may be fading fast, but the old-boy network still crackles." He smiled benevolently.

"And . . . ?"

"And I think there's a lot of interesting material in there that the unfortunate young woman in the villa overlooked. I suspect that she preferred the drama of the doomed fool, the brawling poet, to the drudgery of documenting history."

He shuffled through a thick sheaf of papers and pulled out one sheet.

"There's a place in the journal where Fenelli wrote 'Back of painting' at the top of the page. My translator put in a note that the top line seemed like a label, and then below it were a few lines that looked like Fenelli had made a point of copying exactly what was written on the back of the painting and how it was written. And a suggestion we might want to look at the original journal page."

He had the leather book there, already open, and he held it for Lucia and Moto to see.

At the top was written: *"retro del dipinto."*

And below that, four short lines carefully written in a blocky script.

> *Scavare dentro,*
> *tradimento, peccato,*
> *trovare il vero*
> *Giuda Iscariota.*

And next to them, off to the side of the page, a one-word note, scrawled at an angle in Fenelli's informal writing: *"Poemetto."*

"It almost is a poem," said Lucia.

The professor nodded. "My friend added a note saying that it had required only the very slightest effort to render the lines as an appropriate little poem in English." He cleared his throat and read, "'To find the real Judas, dig within. Betrayal and sin.'

"My admirable translator also said we should note 'the eccentric capitalization.' He typed, 'trovare il vERO.'"

Again, he held out the journal. Those three letters—*ERO*—were indeed larger, darker than the others.

"Fine. *E . . . R . . . O.*" Moto spelled it out.

"Ero," said Lucia, turning to the professor. "That's 'I was' in Italian. So the message might be 'I was the real Judas.' *Il vero Giuda.*"

"No," said the professor. "Here's what I think."

Lucia bridled for a moment at the dismissal, but the professor kept going.

"We have *ERO* on the back. And that finger pointing to the letter *R* on the front. I said we had to keep that in mind. Toss in the *ERO* and you have *RERO*. Juggle that a little and you come up with 'Roero.'"

"That's nice juggling, Professor. Maybe he's spelling out 'errore.' *Error*."

"Like 'TILT' on a pinball machine."

"A man ahead of his time."

Professor Richman kept going. "*R . . . O . . . E . . . R . . . O*. Roero. Specifically Cavaliere Giovanni Rodomonte Roero."

"The one on Malta."

"Exactly."

"So why would Michele put . . ."

"He was holding a grudge. Michele lived for grudges. Remember how his grudge with Ranuccio turned out."

"Wait a minute," said Moto. "Who's Roero? I don't—"

"Roero was the knight that Michele got into a fight with on Malta," Lucia explained. "Roero was wounded. And that landed Michele in the dungeon on Malta and got him kicked out of the knights. Michele never got over it—and neither did Roero."

Moto nodded. "Another enemy. It's a long list."

"But why would Michele carry that painting with him to Porto Ercole?" Lucia kept going. "He was carrying three paintings for the pope's nephew—" She waved her hand, trying to conjure up the name.

"Borghese. Scipione Borghese."

"That one. Three paintings to bribe him for getting his uncle to pardon Michele. But why did he have this fourth one with him?"

"Insurance," Moto broke in. "He was carrying insurance. This painting was a threat. He's saying, 'Don't fuck with me. I've got this! I'll use it.'"

"What kind of a threat is that?" said the professor. "A secret message. 'Roero is Judas.' That's an insult, not a threat."

"We're missing something."

"Lucy, dear, we're missing a lot."

"Wait a minute!" Lucia held up her hand for silence. After a moment, her eyes flew open. "In the catacombs. When they were dragging me out. I told you I got a glimpse of the cross on his robe. And there was the letter *R*. Right at the top of the cross."

"An *R*. You're sure?"

"It's hard to be sure of anything from that disaster. But yes, pretty sure."

"Roero again?" asked Moto.

Professor Richman raised his eyebrows.

"Well now, that would be for us to find out. From our fucking books, as the gentlemen suggested."

Chapter 33

Napoli
1606

The Napoli awaiting Caravaggio was the serpent of dark corruption, coiled around a sapphire-blue bay. The Spanish viceroy don Juan Alfonso Pimentel de Herrera had taxed the lifeblood out of the city, slapping tariffs on foodstuffs, especially flour—while shipping grain surpluses to Spain for a tidy profit. Salt, fruit, vegetables—nothing escaped his grasp, everything was taxed beyond reach of the miserable hordes. The starving poor died alone and anonymous in the dark corners of narrow streets. The street cleaners hauled them away before dawn in rickety donkey carts, their lanterns swinging as they hunted the dead. The creaking hinges and grunting curses of men heaving the corpses into the wagon beds haunted those who still possessed life.

Compared to the wide streets and open piazzas of Roma, Napoli was a dark tangle of a city shrouded in the shadows cast by tall buildings that sprouted in the land trapped between the hills and the sea. Tripling in size in less than a hundred years of Spanish rule, Napoli was the second-largest city in Europe, after Paris.

In the hills above the city, a black-lacquered coach, emblazoned with a white column on a red background and capped with a golden crown, paused at a summit.

Inside, two weary travelers shared the stuffy air turned sour with wine, sweat, and cheese during the two-day journey from Paliano outside Roma.

"There she is! *Che bella!*" shouted the driver with a gesture that encompassed the city spread out below—beautiful, indeed, at least at this safe distance. The crescent bay embraced the clustered buildings of ochre, red, and dun. Mount Vesuvius smoked in the distance, a firebreathing dragon guarding and threatening the Napoletani.

"Wake up, Cecco!" said Caravaggio, giving the boy a kick across the coach seat. The boy shook his head vigorously, his eyes unfocused, wandering. Sleep had been almost impossible on the bone-shaking ancient Appian Way from Roma to Napoli, paved with stones laid before the birth of Christ. He groaned, rubbing his lower back.

"Look at our new home!" said Caravaggio.

The boy stared at the city, the blue sea, and the smoking volcano.

Our new home? Grazie a Dio *that we will exit this torturous rolling box and put our feet on solid ground once again.*

For most of the journey, they had lowered the canvas curtains on the coach to keep out the mosquitoes of the vast marshes along the coast. The suffocating heat in the semi-dark coach had been unbearable. In the shadowy light, Cecco had watched his master brooding hour after hour. Certain that Caravaggio was sinking into the depths of Hades, Cecco feared the explosion sure to come when the artist hit bottom.

But now, suddenly, Caravaggio was elated. Cecco knew too well the mercurial nature of his master and was cautious not to say anything that would catapult Caravaggio into yet another mood swing.

"*È bella*, Napoli," ventured Cecco, craning his neck out the window for a better perspective.

"Yes, beautiful!" said the driver, hearing his words.

"We'll be safe there, *ragazzo*," said Caravaggio. "Spanish territory—the pope has no jurisdiction here. I am a free man!"

"*Sì*, Maestro." Cecco licked his dry lips, glancing up at his master. "But they say Napoli is more dangerous than Roma. The thieves, and rough—"

"Not for a swordsman like me," said Caravaggio, touching the scars on his face. "A Milanese has nothing to fear from a Napoletano!"

The driver grunted, uttering an unintelligible curse in Napoletano. Cecco said nothing.

Hasn't my master learned anything? He flees from a murder charge. Yet he is ready to fight and spill more blood!

As the Roman coach rattled down the hill and across the ancient stones of the city streets, two ragged men jumped onto the rear luggage rack where Caravaggio's trunk was strapped. They slashed at the ropes, trying to cut it free.

"Cecco!" Caravaggio roared. "Give me my sword!"

Cecco unsheathed the sword, handing it to his master. Caravaggio shouted, balancing precariously on the running board. He swiped madly at the assailants, roaring like a wild animal. He struck one in the shoulder and the other in the shin. A thief screamed in pain, dropping to the ground, writhing. The other fell, clutching his leg. He struck the stone road hard, wailing.

"*Cazzo!* City of thieves! A fine introduction to Napoli!" said Caravaggio, waving his blade.

The driver slapped the reins hard against the two horses' backs, laughing.

"An authentic welcome, Maestro Caravaggio. *Benvenuti a Napoli!*"

Caravaggio's coach did not pull up to the grand entrance of the Palazzo Colonna but drove straight to the stables. A sweaty farrier was bent over an anvil, muscles bulging as he hammered on a horseshoe. He unfurled his great torso when he heard the coach approach, wiping his face with his forearm.

A red, puckered scar ran from his left nostril across his cheek to his ear.

"Driver! Why do we stop here?" called Caravaggio. "Take me directly to the palazzo, *subito*!"

The driver steadied the horses. "The marchesa ordered me to deliver you here, Maestro," he said.

"Get out, Maestro Merisi," ordered the blacksmith, pointing to the straw-strewn ground. "Let's see what we are dealing with."

"Who are you?" said Caravaggio, not budging. "I'm here to see the Marchesa Colonna. I am a friend and a guest of the Colonnas. I come from their estate in Paliano."

"Call me Giovanni." The blacksmith blotted the moist soot from his face with his blackened sleeve. "Giovanni Pozzo. I've been expecting you."

The blacksmith looked up and addressed the driver. "I wager it was a hot drive here from the hills of Roma." He gestured with his hammer toward Caravaggio. "This is the *teppista*, eh? Did he give you any trouble?"

"Who are you calling 'thug,' *bastardo*?" said Caravaggio.

Giovanni ignored him, speaking only to the driver. "The boy looks harmless enough."

"*Buon ragazzo*," said the driver. *A good boy.*

"Take me at once to the palazzo!" snarled Caravaggio, fingering the hilt of his dagger.

"Go ahead and unload his baggage, Francesco," said the brawny smith to the driver. "Leave them with me." He turned his back on Caravaggio, continuing his conversation with the coachman. "Put his trunk right there, next to the haystack."

"No!" said Caravaggio. "Take us to the palazzo—"

The smith turned and addressed Caravaggio directly. "You are not welcome in the palazzo, Maestro Merisi. The marchesa isn't here to receive company. She gave me instructions on how to handle you. You insult me and you are directly insulting the Marchesa Colonna. *Capisci*?"

Cecco's eyes grew wide in wonder. *Listen to this Napoletano give it to my master!*

"It is true, Maestro Merisi," said the driver as he unstrapped the trunk and bundles from the carriage. "The Marchesa Colonna holds Giovanni Pozzo in the highest esteem. She trusts him above all others."

Caravaggio's lips twisted in rage but he didn't argue. The marchesa was his salvation. He descended from the coach and supervised the unloading of his kit.

Cecco helped the coach driver, who handed him a velvet-wrapped parcel—a framed painting.

"Give me that one," snapped Caravaggio. Cecco nodded silently, gently handing the canvas to him.

That's the one he forbade me to see.

"I've got some bread and cheese for you, Maestro Merisi," said the blacksmith, wiping his sooty hands on a rag. "And some good sausage. A bottle of wine too."

Caravaggio glared.

"The marchesa sends her regrets, but she has other business in the north," said Giovanni. "She will be back within the month."

"The month? But . . . where am I to stay?"

"You'll need to find a room somewhere," said Giovanni.

"But—"

"The Marchesa Colonna left me in charge of you. 'Help the signore find a place to stay,' she said. 'So he can get to work painting.' Until we find you a place, you can sleep here in the stables."

Caravaggio's face wrinkled. "The stables?"

"You have to lie low for a while. The boy. Is he your son?"

275

"He's not my son," said Caravaggio, his lips tightening. "He's my assistant. His name is Cecco."

Giovanni nodded to the boy, his face softening. *"Benvenuto a Napoli,* Cecco."

Cecco bobbed his head. *"Grazie."*

Caravaggio shot a look at the blacksmith. "And the marchesa's son, Signor Fabrizio?" he asked. "Is he here?"

"The grand admiral?" said the blacksmith sharply. He turned away from Cecco, his face hardening once again. "No, Maestro. He is at sea fighting the Turks."

Giovanni studied the bedraggled painter.

Matted hair, a dirty beard. Black velvet tunic rent with holes and stained with wine and grease.

The blacksmith snorted. "You didn't think you were going to live here in the palazzo, did you, signore? The Spanish would certainly notice. They want no trouble with the pope. And you are a wanted man."

"Not here, I am not."

"Ha! Any hired assassin could bring your head to the pope and collect a bounty, *bandito.* And you would bring shame on the House of Colonna. Too risky."

"Do as you were ordered," snapped Caravaggio. "Find me a room."

"I leave you now, Giovanni!" called Francesco from the coach. He winked at the blacksmith. *"Buona fortuna!"*

"Arrivederci!" Giovanni called his farewell to the coach driver as the wheels spun dust into golden swirls in the late-afternoon light.

The smith turned, saying nothing to Caravaggio. He retreated into the stable and returned with a wicker basket of food. He pulled out spicy *soppressata* sausage studded with white globules of fat, ricotta cheese wrapped in damp linen, and fine white-milled bread. He laid the feast on a broad stump. His meaty fist plunged the blade of a knife into the dead wood.

"There," he said to the newcomer. "Eat. Courtesy of your benefactor, the good Marchesa Colonna. And make sure that skinny boy of yours gets some. You don't feed him enough, by the looks of him."

Caravaggio eyed the knife, determining how far the blade had sunk into the wood. He sized up the blacksmith, taking in the broad scar. After some hesitation, he moved away to sit on another stump to dine. He took a long draught of the wine from the bottle, never taking his eye off the blacksmith. Then he passed the bottle to Cecco.

"You'll help me to find a room, blacksmith. A room with light, where I can paint."

"What amount of money can you pay?"

"Three scudi a month," said Caravaggio. "Not a *quattrino* more."

"That's not much, Maestro," said the blacksmith. "*Niente!* Even here."

"It's what I can pay, *maniscalco—*"

"Call me Giovanni, not blacksmith."

"I'm not rich."

Giovanni shrugged, his palms open to the sky. "Who is but the *nobili*? You won't live in a good neighborhood—"

Caravaggio spat out a bitter laugh, almost a growl.

"—but from the looks of you, Maestro," said the blacksmith, "you will fit right in."

In the teeming neighborhood of Spaccanapoli—literally "Naples splitter"—Caravaggio found a cheap room atop a six-story building. The meager lodgings reeked of rat piss and the low-tide stench of the fishmongers below, but had a window—a single, greasy window—that looked out over the street. Feeble light found its way through the opening, particularly in the afternoon. It was enough to paint by, and the rancid smell of the burning tallow candles, olive oil lanterns, and turpentine masked the more malevolent odors.

Raucous noise filtered through the warren of tight alleyways, though Caravaggio seemed not to notice. His eyes focused on the dark gesso preparation on his canvas where life took shape with the strokes of his brush.

Napoli suited him, twisted and dark—a maze of narrow streets, cutthroats, thieves. And lost souls. But there was a vitality in the Napoletani, as spirited as their dialect, as earthy and comforting as their food.

Caravaggio and Napoli were a perfect match. Murder? A Napoletano would shrug, palms cupped to the heavens. What is spilt blood in a duel but fairly earned? Caravaggio's stain wouldn't last in this city. It would open more doors and earn begrudging respect from the gangs of ruffians and the underbelly of Napoli. And from them he would choose his subjects to be immortalized in paint.

Caravaggio's brushstrokes became more rapid, confident, and economical, as if he were racing to conclude a shady deal in a dark alley—and assured of success.

In the brawling city, in the sordid taverns and dangerous streets, he found peace.

Caravaggio ventured out often at night, walking the streets of Napoli. On one such evening, Cecco worked alone on his own canvas by oil lamp.

In the corner of the little room, the light flickered on the velvet-draped canvas, the one painting that Cecco was forbidden to see.

The boy wiped his brush clean, gazing at the folds of velvet. He stood up and walked over to the shrouded canvas. His fingers reached out, gingerly unwrapping the painting.

"Dio mio!" he gasped.

In his hands was the image of Lena as Mary Magdalene. The Magdalene in ecstasy.

His mind flashed back to what he had seen in the candlelight from his bed in Roma. The arching body of the magnificent Lena, the orgasm brought on by the hands and body of his master.

In Caravaggio's vision, he had painted Lena as the saint, the metamorphosis of erotic ecstasy to spiritual transcendence.

He remembered how Roero had grabbed her wrist, dragging her away for sex.

Lena. The boy had hated her at first sight. He had cried in jealousy, in agony. But those feelings had ebbed as he saw her as the Madonna, as mother. And now he knew beauty transcended jealousy and all the petty cares of mortals.

He wiped the tears from his eyes with his wrist. The tears of one who beholds truth.

With reverence, he carefully rewrapped the masterpiece.

He walked to the window, blinking out at the dark night and the bright stars over Napoli.

Chapter 34

Napoli
1606

Smithy Giovanni Pozzo visited frequently to check up on the painter, keeping him informed of the Colonna family's whereabouts. Pozzo had grown accustomed to Caravaggio's rough ways, not so different from those of many Napoletani.

But it was the boy, Cecco, whom he cared about.

Caravaggio learned that the blacksmith had been born into the Colonna household, his father the Colonna blacksmith before him. The family trusted him almost as much as a family member, this faithful servant.

Pozzo had a big family that lived in Spaccanapoli. There were few souls in the winding streets and alleyways who weren't his friends or relatives.

He took Caravaggio and Cecco to taverns in the neighborhood, and to brothels too. One that combined both trades was Osteria del Cerriglio—food and drink on the first floor and carnal pleasure on the second. This "den of thieves" was quite near Caravaggio's sordid studio in the tight, winding *vicoli*.

The smoky tavern was filled with the smell of cured hams, which were hung on hooks just above patrons' heads. Oil lanterns threw shadows on the soot-coated haunches.

Roasting meats on spits over the great hearth crackled and shot sparks into the laps of customers who dared to sit too close. A steady parade of waiters brought hefty jugs of wine, plunking them down on the plank tables along with wooden trenchers of sausage, bread, and pork. Terra-cotta bowls of pasta mixed with shiny-eyed sardines and pink and purple shellfish glistened in the half-light.

A sweaty waiter with a white rag tucked around his waist juggled hot dishes in his arms. He put down an array of food on the table.

"*Per i signori!*" said the waiter, clapping Giovanni on the back. "*Buon appetito!*"

"*Grazie*, Enrico," said the blacksmith, his hands still black with soot from his forge.

"*Mangia*, Cecco!" said Giovanni. "Eat! You look like a skinny worm from the north. We'll make you a Napoletano, put some brawn on your bones."

Cecco smiled and dug into pasta studded with briny clams. He twisted the linguine around his fork, shoving a great mound into his mouth. He closed his eyes in appreciation as he chewed.

Giovanni shifted his eyes to Caravaggio. "What will you paint here, Maestro Merisi?"

"I already have a commission. For the church of San Domenico Maggiore," said Caravaggio, breaking a piece of bread. "An altarpiece of a Madonna and child surrounded by a choir of angels."

The blacksmith sat back on the bench, making it creak. He looked directly into Caravaggio's eyes. "Do you really like painting angels? *Davvero?*"

"*Cazzo!*" said Caravaggio, his face flushing in rage. "Fuck! I detest fluttering angels. That's all the bastards want. A fucking choir of angels.

With Saint Dominic and Saint Francis embracing! And a smiling Saint Vitus rising from a vat of oil."

Giovanni nodded, a look of satisfaction on his face.

"I crave the stuff of life," said Caravaggio. "The dirty skin of pilgrims, the open wounds of a martyr, an old man's wrinkled face. I want to paint the world God has given us, the one we see each day and night. Not frilly lace and angel feathers!"

Giovanni laughed. "Have you been contracted for anything that inspires you?"

Caravaggio took a deep gulp of wine. "What do you know about inspiration, blacksmith?"

Giovanni fingered his ugly scar, fixing his eyes on the painter. He waited until he had Caravaggio's attention before he answered.

"Don't underestimate me, painter," he said. "I know the satisfaction of good work. I have felt swollen fetlocks in my hand, interpreted the cause, and turned out iron shoes that cure a crippled horse. I know when I have achieved my best. I suspect you do too."

Caravaggio dug at a piece of meat in his back molars. "*Davvero?* You compare my trade with yours? Your triumph is a set of horseshoes with nails in the right places?"

Giovanni raised his finger, pointing at Caravaggio. "I suppose you need to get the paint in the right places, Caravaggio. You must do that at least occasionally."

Cecco snorted a laugh through his linguine, the pasta spilling from his mouth.

"What I meant by inspiration," Giovanni continued, "was whether you have any commissions worthy of your talent. Rather than flights of angels flitting about in the clouds."

Caravaggio started to answer, then suddenly cocked his head.

Outside, dozens of voices rose in chorus. A pathetic whine of children and women made every diner stop eating.

"*Pane! Pane! Pane!*"

"Bread," said Giovanni, setting down his cup. "The poor bastards are starving in the street. Some of the richest families in Europe live here in Napoli. And the poorest of poor who die of starvation by the thousands."

Caravaggio stared out the arched doorway. "You asked me about commissions. There is one more," he said quietly. "For the Pio Monte della Misericordia."

Giovanni's eyes lit up. "Pio Monte della Misericordia!"

"They proposed I paint the seven works of mercy," said Caravaggio. "And they will pay double what the church of San Domenico Maggiore has given me for their damned flock of angels."

"What are the seven acts of mercy?" asked Cecco, glancing up from his plate.

"The good works of a Christian," said Giovanni. "They're in the Gospel of Saint Matthew. Visiting the sick, clothing the naked, feeding the hungry—I can't remember the rest. Oh, sì . . . the burial of the dead."

Caravaggio crossed his arms. "They need more burials. Dogs chew on the corpses before the street cleaners arrive."

Giovanni waved away his words. "The Pio Monte della Misericordia takes care of the destitute and incurably ill. Without their good works, there would be hundreds more. The dead bodies would lie there for the dogs to feast upon until there wasn't a bone left. Who do you think pays the street cleaners to cart away those carcasses and give them a decent burial? Who do you think feeds the starving while the Church turns its arrogant face away?"

The blacksmith crossed himself, showing his bulging forearms. Cecco noticed Giovanni's eyes glistening.

"They are independent from the Church?" said Caravaggio, tearing at a loaf of bread.

"As long as they don't crow that they got papal dispensation, they are an exception. All their money goes to the needy, not a scudo into the coffers of Roma."

Caravaggio put down his bread. He stared at the blazing hearth. A ghost of a smile played on his lips. "I was approached for the commission by the Marchese di Villa. Do you know him?"

"I know of him. He and the Colonnas entertain one another. The marchese hosts poets and radical outcasts in his salon. He is friends with Galileo Galilei."

"Galileo?" said Caravaggio, his right brow arching.

"Do you know him?"

"A most singular man," said Caravaggio. "I admire him greatly. He will face trouble with the Church one day."

"The marchese is a good man."

"I shall paint them a masterpiece," said Caravaggio, slapping his hand on the table for emphasis.

Giovanni clapped Caravaggio hard on the back. "Pio Monte are the true saviors of our wretched."

Caravaggio looked down at his hands, turning them palms up. He lifted his gaze toward the open door. The plaintive call of *"Pane, pane"* still echoed through the streets.

"We'll see," said Caravaggio.

Within the little church of Pio Monte della Misericordia, just steps from the great duomo of Napoli, Caravaggio directed the hanging of his newest painting. The light spilled from the high windows, washing the oil paints in radiance, like the crash of cymbals in a spiraling symphony.

He studied the painting with satisfaction, ignoring the cluster of well-dressed benefactors who lifted their chins in unison to survey the huge canvas that they were seeing for the first time.

One, Signor Russo, pulled nervously at his lower lip, staring at the woman baring her breast to suckle her starving father through the bars of his prison cell. Russo's eye then shifted to the limp feet of a dead body that gravediggers were carrying from the street for a proper burial.

He fingered his collar, his face tense. His eyes flicked toward his companions, trying to gauge their response.

"A perfect depiction of the mercies," gasped Signor Carafa. "Magnificent!"

"A stunning painting!" exclaimed Signor del Franchis.

"But the daughter breastfeeding her own father—will it not cause scandal?" asked Signor Russo. "Her nakedness, it's wholly inappropriate and—"

"Don't behave like a startled rabbit, Russo! The daughter is saving her father's life, a starving prisoner," said Giovanni Battista Manso, Marchese di Villa, his open palm gesturing toward the painting. "Do we not have the same suffering in our streets? Who would not sacrifice all—even honor—to save a dying loved one?"

The other nobles nodded solemnly.

"And look at the defiance on her face. A true Napoletana," said Signor Carafa. "'Dare criticize my act of mercy, and I'll cut your face!'"

"*Lo sfregio!*" Signor del Franchis chuckled. "A revenge slash to the face. Caravaggio has captured it perfectly, the pride and passion."

"Genius," pronounced the marchese. "He understands us. He has captured our blood, our soul. A whirlpool in a dark alleyway. A torrent of action as fierce as the streets of our city."

"This shall be the masterpiece of all Napoli!" proclaimed Signor Mancini in a loud voice.

The painter turned and offered a slight bow.

"We are forever in your debt," said the Marchese di Villa. All the men nodded. Di Villa was the most powerful among them. "You are welcome in Napoli, Maestro Merisi da Caravaggio."

Chapter 35

Monte Piccolo

The footsteps on the stairs were heavy. The knock at the door demanding.

Moto raised an eyebrow.

Lucia marched to the door.

"Who's there?"

"Police! Open the door."

She did.

The three men who walked in wore no uniforms, but their bearing and attitude made their status clear. They were police, they wanted answers, and they were used to getting what they wanted.

One stood by the door. One drifted toward the windows. The third took center stage. Lucia started to say something, but he froze her with a glance. The professor, in his armchair, just smiled.

The cop fixed his gaze on Moto, narrowed his eyes. "Why Roero?" he said.

"That's what we want to know." Lucia couldn't help herself.

The cop turned and pointed at her. His power was unmistakable. He turned back to Moto.

"Why Roero?" he repeated.

It had hardly been an hour since Moto had called his cousin, the Rome *poliziotto*, to ask if the name Roero had come up during their investigations. It had seemed like a long shot. Apparently it wasn't.

Unfortunately, since they hadn't really expected any response—much less the one they got—they hadn't considered an explanation for why they wanted to know about Roero. Now, under the fierce gaze of the plainclothes detective, Moto was stuck. The truth was their secret: the investigation into the missing painting. And secret or not, the truth would sound ridiculous.

Before Moto could stumble into deeper waters, Professor Richman spoke up from his armchair.

"*Scusi.*" He cleared his throat. "I . . . um . . . *no parlo mucho italiano.*"

Lucia raised an eyebrow. She enjoyed teasing the professor about his Italian, but in fact, it had improved by leaps and bounds. Now he was suddenly floundering. Worse than ever. Before she could jump in, he stumbled on.

"I am . . . no . . . *io sono professore americano.*" A broad smile. Then a frown. "*Io sono* . . . writing . . . um . . . *scrivendo? Sì. Scrivendo. Scrivendo* about *arte!*" Big smile again. Then the blank look of someone who has run out words. "Lucia, my dear, can you help me out here, please?"

Then he began to rattle on in English while Lucia tried to keep up with him, translating for the police and wondering what the hell was going on.

"I am looking into the story of Fra Giovanni Rodomonte Roero, the Conte della Vezza, a Knight of Malta who played a major role in the glorious history of Italian art, as I am sure you gentlemen know." An inclusive smile that said of course these policemen were conversant with Italian art history.

"My able assistant, Lucia, was off on an errand, so I made the mistake of trying to communicate with her young friend, whose English is, I fear, perhaps even worse than my Italian."

The professor paused, waiting for Lucia to catch up with the translation.

"I asked if he could help me find some simple facts about Cavaliere Roero—who passed out of this vale of tears almost five hundred years ago, as I am sure, again, you know well." Lucia struggled with the fake-elegant diction, but now she had an idea where he was heading. "And I am afraid our young friend misunderstood in some drastic fashion and made what seems to have been an inappropriate telephone inquiry." His broad smile again. *"Scusi. Scusi. Mille scusi!"*

Another smile. "I am sorry that this young man's confusion has forced you to come all the way here. But I think we can all rest assured that any police interest in *my* Roero ended half a millennium ago."

And now a final gracious nod and smile to all concerned.

The detectives seemed a little uneasy, but Lucia smoothed their way by explaining that the professor was in Chianti to attend the prestigious seminar here in the villa and that his paper on Fra Roero would undoubtedly prove a worthwhile addition to the history of Italian art.

And so, at last, with the professor beaming paternally, Moto looking confused, and Lucia graciously herding them toward the door, the three policemen left.

Even their footsteps going down the stairs were subdued.

"Cugino! Che diavolo era quello?" Cousin! What the hell was that?

Moto gestured so vigorously that the cell phone flew out of his hand and he had to scramble across the floor to pick it up.

"Aspetta! Che cosa? Cosa hai detto?" Wait! What? What did you say?

Now Moto was listening carefully, his eyes wide, sputtering a little as his cousin talked at length.

"Sì . . . ma . . . ma . . . Non può essere!" Yes . . . but . . . but . . . It can't be!

And then, finally, *"Gesù! Davvero? Siamo fottuti!" Jesus! Really? We're screwed!*

He stuffed the phone back in his pocket and turned to the others.

"That was my cousin." Lucia gave a shrug. *Obviously.* "The carabinieri are tracking a group of terrorists who call themselves the Roero Brigade."

No more shrugs. Lucia and the professor shared the same stunned look.

"They claim they are the true heirs of the original Knights of Malta—dedicated to protecting the Christian world against the terror of Islam. They have nothing but contempt for the current knights. They consider them imposters and cowards."

The professor, as always, had a question. "But why Roero? Aside from his involvement with Caravaggio, he was nothing much. Why not a more meaningful name? Maybe the Valette Brigade. Jean Parisot de la Valette was the grand master who fought off the Turks in the Great Siege. That would seem more like the name they would use."

"My cousin says the leader—he calls himself the grand commander—claims he's a direct descendant of Cavaliere Nobilissimo Roero. He's very proud of it."

"Still odd," said the professor, "when you consider that any offspring of a Knight of Malta would have to be illegitimate. They all took vows of chastity. Warrior monks, if you will, but still monks." He chuckled. "Amusing. Not much actual chastity, of course. But still, vows were vows. No marriage. No legitimate heirs."

"Stop it!" Lucia was almost screaming.

"Stop what?" the professor asked, puzzled.

"Stop chuckling and showing off how much you know. These bastards have murdered people all around us. Beheaded them! They tried to kill me. They're still out there. There's nothing 'amusing' about this."

Professor Richman managed to look chastened—and still a little defiant.

"Well, what do we do about it, then?" he asked.

"We still don't know what it's all about. Renegade lunatics, make-believe Knights of Malta, are slaughtering Muslims. Beheading them."

"Muslims and non-Muslims," Moto broke in. "Those two who stole the painting and killed your *zio*. I didn't get the idea that anyone thought they were Muslim."

"No," said the professor. "Just cheap crooks."

"Who got what they had coming," added Lucia, thinking of Te-Te, bitterness still in her voice. "But what does any of it have to do with us? With Michele? With the painting?"

She walked to the window and looked out over the Chianti land-scape, still bare in midwinter, no signs of spring, no touches of green.

"How did we wind up in the middle of this?"

She turned away from the window and stared at the professor, then Moto, then up to the ceiling, as if looking to the sky beyond.

"How?"

Gran Comandante Pantera allowed himself a self-satisfied smile.

"Taking into account your disaster in Malta . . . No, I will be more specific: your ill-considered plan followed by disaster—"

"But, sir, I—"

"Silence." It was barely whispered, but the effect was immediate. Fra Lupo stared ahead in rigid silence. Pantera nodded and continued.

"Taking that into account, I decided I would have to move our investigations ahead on my own. As you know, the Muslims destroyed my academic career, but I still have friends from those days who understand our mission and know full well how vital it is. Vital to the survival of our civilization." He paused for a moment. "I am reminded of the words of Sir Winston Churchill." He rose—dropping abruptly since the chair was adjusted to its greatest height to allow him to sit comfortably behind the too-big desk, which left his feet dangling several inches off the ground—and turned to the bookshelves. He pulled out a thick leather-bound volume, opened it carefully, studied one page for a moment, nodded sharply, slipped the book back onto the shelf, and, back still turned to Lupo, spoke loudly and clearly.

"From *The River War: An Historical Account of the Reconquest of the Soudan.*" He didn't mention that his copy of the book was the first edition, because of course it was. "'Besides the fanatical frenzy, which is as dangerous in a man as hydrophobia in a dog, Mohammedanism is a militant and proselytizing faith. Were it not that Christianity is sheltered in the strong arms of science, the civilization of modern Europe might fall, as fell the civilization of Ancient Rome.'" He turned back with military precision. "We must never falter, Lupo. We must learn from our mistakes—from your mistakes—and move ahead." He nodded sharply. "Always advancing."

There was silence.

Lupo spoke first.

"And your research, sir?"

"Exactly! Of course." He hoisted himself back onto his chair. "Some of my old colleagues have gone into government service. I will not judge them for their cooperation with the godless state. It has placed them in position to be helpful. Based on what little we knew—an American professor and *una ragazza italiana* in a seminar at Monte Piccolo—they have provided me with the identities of both of our key targets. The American professor, as I was certain, is relevant only because of his connection with the girl. He is retired, widowed, elderly, and, we can safely assume, he is in Italy looking only to keep himself occupied until his death. But the girl is far more interesting. She is also American, but"—he raised an instructor's finger—"she holds dual citizenship. She was born here, in Sicily, but was sent to America as a young child, where she was raised by her *nonni.*" He squinted at a sheet of paper on the desk.

"In a place called"—a raised eyebrow—"Ronkonkoma on something they refer to as Isola Lunga. Long Island."

The tall man nodded solemnly. "Brilliant work, sir."

The little man at the desk pretended not to care about the praise. "Easy enough—although it did require reaching out to contacts in America as well as here. Fortunately, I do remain well connected." He allowed himself another of what may have been smiles.

"And the third one, sir? The young man? Have you learned any more about him?"

A dismissive gesture. "The *bardassa* is irrelevant. Forget about him."

Then he thrust out a sheet of paper. "This is what we now know about the girl. She was born in Sicily and sent to . . . Ronkonkoma . . . wherever that is, to be raised. Now we need to discover why." He leaned back in the chair. "We traced the cursed painting a long way. Four hundred years. From that wretched painter to a desperate priest and his orphanage. Then we hesitated. And that girl slipped in and ruined our plans. Another fiasco." His eyes narrowed and he took a sharp breath. "We won't make that mistake again. But we need to know more. How she is connected to all of this. Who is she, Lupo? What part does she play? She is not some casual innocent who stumbled into our path. Find out. Details, Fra Lupo. Details." He took his glasses off and polished them carefully with a handkerchief. "Tread carefully. We know the Sicilians are involved somehow. They are not our enemies and we must keep it that way."

He laid his hands flat on the desk.

"Do not fail me." A curt nod. "Dismissed!"

But Fra Lupo did not turn and walk away. Instead, he remained at attention, facing the desk. The *comandante* looked up, his move surprisingly birdlike, delicate.

"You are still here, Lupo?"

"Sir. Begging your pardon, sir. I have been asked—some of our men have asked—why we care so much about this painting. Sir."

Comandante Pantera gave a thin smile. "If it were really the 'men,' Lupo, I would respond that they have no right to ask. Just as we must be obedient to God himself without trying to understand his reasons, so our soldiers must obey their orders without asking questions about matters far beyond their comprehension."

"Sir, I agree, of course, but—"

"Do not interrupt me! I said the men have no right to ask. But you were most certainly asking on your own behalf."

He leaned back in his chair and smiled again. Thinly.

"And I will indulge you, Fra Lupo. As an indication of my fondness for you, *figlio mio*." His eyes narrowed. "There is a message concealed in that painting. I cannot say exactly where or how it is concealed, but that message was put there by the unspeakable painter himself. It is filled with scurrilous, slanderous charges against our inspiration, our great leader, my ancestor, Cavaliere Giovanni Rodomonte Roero. There is no question that those charges are all lies, filthy lies from the bottomless pit of hell where that syphilitic madman of a painter most certainly burns in eternal torment. But we cannot allow his filth to stain our beloved Cavaliere Roero."

In his fierce enthusiasm, the *comandante* had risen partly out of his chair. Now he paused to catch his breath and settled back down again.

"And so we must find that painting. We must find that vile message. And we must destroy it." His glasses glinted in the light.

"Dismissed!"

Chapter 36

Alof de Wignacourt, grand master of Malta, stared up at the coffered ceiling of the ceremonial throne room. He squinted to make out the fine paintings overhead, thirteen scenes from the siege of Malta. With his open hand, he gestured toward the artwork.

"What beauty Matteo Perez d'Aleccio created over our heads," he said to his companion, Ippolito Malaspina. "I remember watching him on the scaffolding when I was a young man. Do you remember?"

"Grand Master de la Cassière brought beauty to Malta when he contracted the artist," said the knight, stroking his gray-flecked beard. "D'Aleccio does justice to the siege and the sacrifices made."

The two men craned their necks upward until stiffness set in.

"Art commemorated the virtues and victories of our order in those days," Wignacourt said, rubbing the back of his neck.

"And now? Europe forgets us. It's been forty-two years since the Great Siege. Times were harder four decades ago. Still, art found its way to these rocky shores," said Malaspina. "In the most dangerous of times."

"I'm still searching for a painter," said the grand master, casting an eye once more to the coffered ceiling.

Later that afternoon, Wignacourt stood among the rows of beds lining the long hospital room of Valletta.

The swish of tunics against leggings laced the air, giving off the brawny odor of men. The mighty Knights of Malta staffed the hospital themselves—one of eight obligations of their order: tending the sick. Even the most distinguished knight was expected to make the rounds, ministering to the afflicted.

In the years since a major engagement with the Ottomans, the majority of the sick suffered from maladies not earned in battle but accidents, diseases, and wounds from the duels that, though they were strictly forbidden, were becoming more commonplace among the knights.

This is what happens when warriors are not fighting an enemy. They war with each other.

The old knight Malaspina crouched beside a young page who had severed his finger with a kitchen knife. The doctor had tried to sew the digit back onto the bloody stump, but the sutures had ruptured with pus where an infection had set in.

"How is the boy doing?" whispered the grand master.

The knight partially turned his arthritic neck. He groaned softly as he raised himself up.

"He certainly will lose the finger," said Malaspina. "I only hope that the tincture the doctor has brewed will cure his fever. A finger—it's nothing, with nine to spare. A life?"

"And such a precious life," murmured the grand master, tears welling in his eyes.

"He is in God's hands," said Malaspina, crossing himself.

Wignacourt looked at the boy, whose eyes shone with fever. Jacques de Bonniére was a favorite page among the dozens the grand master had enrolled from the noble families across Europe. The child had been sent here to become a Knight of Malta, a champion of Christianity, fighting the infidels in glorious battles.

It wouldn't do if the boy lost his life from a slip of the knife, preparing soup for the sick.

"Come outside if you would, Cavaliere," said the grand master. "I want to discuss other matters."

"Certainly," said Malaspina, looking once more at the boy.

The brilliant sun of Malta spilled over the limestone city, accentuating the deep blue of the Mediterranean. Wignacourt cupped his hand over his brow, sheltering his eyes from the blinding light. "We must find a great painter," he said. "As we discussed this morning."

"One who will bring splendor and honor to our Maltese order," said Malaspina.

"*Sì*, Ippolito. We need a great artist. I want you to find the best. No less. I've had no luck in finding one to take up residence in Malta."

"Malta is not the most hospitable island," concurred Malaspina. "Unless one is a knight of our order."

"Even then the knights are shipwrecked on this rock," said Wignacourt. He gestured to the blinding white stone buildings of Valletta. "The least they merit is a great painter who can document our order and glorify God. Too long the cathedral has gone without adornment, without the paintings any other great church would display. We shall have an artist paint a tribute to our patron saint, John the Baptist. We will cloak the stone wall of the oratory with a scene that will inspire awe in those who kneel before it."

Wignacourt's eyes gleamed. Already, he could see the martyred saint.

"Can you do this for our order, Cavaliere Malaspina?"

The harsh Maltese sunlight bleached the wrinkled skin of the Italian knight. His rheumy eyes smiled at the grand master, his face furrowed in a myriad of wrinkles.

"*Certo,*" said Malaspina. The Tuscan knight knew about beauty, having spent time in Firenze in the Medici court.

"*Vous comprenez,*" said the grand master, resting the palm of his hand on the knight's shoulder. "Art, music. We French and Tuscans share this. We will carve civilization out of this rock . . . a court befitting the honor of our knights."

Malaspina smiled, looking over the blue harbor toward Vittoriosa. Though many nobles strove to become Knights of Malta, few were admitted. Most who did achieve knighthood found the monastic restrictions impossible. They were fighting, brawling men. Some senior knights took wives secretly, leaving their auberges for home lives in private palazzos. Others drank themselves stupid in the taverns, bedding down the local prostitutes and challenging each other to duels—despite the harsh penalty for killing a brother knight: the offender was sewn into a sack and drowned in the depths of the Mediterranean.

"Instilling more culture into court? Yes, indeed, Grand Master. A solution to many ills."

Wignacourt smiled. "I leave this matter in your hands. When do you leave again for Napoli?"

"In a fortnight."

"Find me an artist. I shall wait eagerly for his arrival."

Malaspina nodded. "I may already have the man, Grand Master. My cousin Ottavio Costa knows of one such artist, Michelangelo da Caravaggio. He is a brilliant painter but not an easy man—tough and brawling. He fled to Napoli to avoid prosecution. Murder, Grand Master."

"Murder?"

"In a duel," said Malaspina. "Some matter over a gambling debt, they say. I met him in Roma at Giustiniani's palazzo before the incident."

The grand master inhaled a deep breath, expelling it slowly.

A murderer?

"Is he really that good a painter, this Caravaggio?" asked Wignacourt.

"He is a genius, Grand Master. The best."

Wignacourt cast his eyes toward Vittoriosa, remembering the siege. "Bring him here."

Chapter 37

Napoli
1607

At last, the Marchesa Colonna returned to Napoli. She immediately brought Caravaggio to stay at her palace in Chiaia, along the shore of the Bay of Napoli.

One evening, after a sumptuous dinner, they sat together in the drawing room. Torrential rain sluiced outside the palazzo, the winds coming off the Mediterranean and rattling the crystal windowpanes.

The guttering sconces illuminated a luxurious room with a round gaming table in the center. In a corner, a fire crackled and spat behind an elaborate wrought iron screen.

A servant brought in a tulle-wrapped parcel. He murmured something to the marchesa, bowed, and then left, closing the heavy mahogany door behind him.

"I want to show you something, Michele," said the marchesa. She unwrapped the package to reveal a black-and-white garment. "What I have here is the habit of a Maltese Knight."

Caravaggio traced his finger over the eight-pointed cross, white against a wool cloth tunic. For a long time he was silent.

He remembered the knight Roero, Ranuccio's companion, who had disappeared in the midst of the brawl.

"Fabrizio wears this now?" Caravaggio said finally.

Costanza put her hand over his. "*Sì*, Michele. His salvation was to join the Order of Malta. He has prospered and has made me proud again. Think of it. Your childhood friend is now an admiral of the Maltese navy. He is an honored knight and serves on the Court of Justice!"

Caravaggio pulled back his hand from under hers. He did not look at the marchesa. "His sins were rinsed clean?" he said, arching his thick eyebrows. "All by wearing this eight-pointed cross?"

"He's made changes in his life."

Caravaggio snorted. "Fabrizio? Forgive me, Marchesa. But I know him. As well as my brother."

The marchesa stared back.

"Is it true he killed a man, just as I did?" asked Caravaggio.

"Yes. Another nobleman. In a duel," said the marchesa, looking down at her hands. "We will not discuss it further. Ever."

"*Sì*, Marchesa. I can see it pains you."

"What more can I do for you, Michele?" she said, covering her eyes with her open palm. Her golden rings sparkled in the firelight as her hand slid down her face. "You received the gift of God, this talent of yours," she cried. "You are bestowed honors, commissions. You break bread with the great families of Roma, of Genova, of Firenze! Blessings, forgiveness, magnificent opportunities are showered upon you, and how do you treat your benefactors? You hurl away your good fortune, throwing pearl after precious pearl into the sea like a madman."

Caravaggio stared at the fire.

The Marchesa Colonna shook her head. "You have a price on your head now. The pope shows no sign of forgiveness."

"You have made inquiries, Marchesa?"

"*Sì.*"

Caravaggio closed his eyes.

"And there are others who will never forgive you, Michele. They will find you here. Everyone knows now the wonder of the *Seven Acts of Mercy* you painted."

She took the artist's hand. He opened his eyes.

"Look at me, Michele. You have one more chance—the Maltese Knights."

He shook his head. "I know one knight other than Fabrizio. That knight is the devil incarnate. I spit on his soul."

"It is unfortunate you have found an enemy already in Malta," the marchesa said. "I did not say every knight is virtuous. But the order was founded on goodness, charity, and comforting the sick in Jerusalem." She pointed to the Maltese cross on the tunic. "Do you want to know what each point stands for?"

Caravaggio shrugged.

She touched the first point of the star. "To live in truth is the first. You do that every day in your art. Never have you shirked and avoided controversy."

"I am a liar," said Caravaggio. "And a clever one. You know that."

"There are different kinds of truth," said the marchesa.

Caravaggio shrugged. "Tell me the others."

"Have faith is the second."

The artist made a sound of disgust. "So trite."

"Repent your sins," continued the marchesa.

Michelangelo looked down at the floor. "I have my own communion with God. It is private. I don't trot it out for show like the sanctimonious clergy, *marchesa mia*."

"Ah! Next is: Give proof of humility. *Quindi . . .*" she said, laughing softly. "You will have to work on that one, Michele. Then: Love justice. Be merciful."

"What justice? What justice is there in this world?" said Caravaggio, his lip curling viciously. "The justice of beheading the Cenci girl, raped by her own father? Burning Giordano Bruno at the stake because he dared to think beyond the limits of the Church? Is that justice? Is it mercy? Next they will be after Galileo for studying the heavens."

The marchesa shook her head. "Listen: Be sincere and whole-hearted. Again, your work proves this. You transport us to a spiritual moment like no other. Your art seizes us and makes us bear witness, bloody and ragged, in the moment."

"My art! The best of my canvases have been rejected by the Church."

The marchesa held up her long finger in a gesture of silence. "The last vow is to endure persecution, Michele," she said. "Endure."

He looked up at her, saying nothing.

Endure. Or survive?

"I would say the eight points of the cross would serve you well," she said. "I could not prescribe a better medicine for your ills."

The attic room over the fishmonger's was lit with only a small, smoking oil lantern. The smell of low tide rose from the street level, wafting in through the open window.

Caravaggio held Cecco in an embrace.

"Malta?" said Cecco, his voice barely audible. "You are leaving me?"

"I must," said Caravaggio, releasing his hold on the boy. "The pope has heard of the *Seven Acts of Mercy*. If I remain in Napoli, I will be assassinated."

"Why can I not go with you, Master? Who will grind your pigments, prepare your canvases? Who will—"

"Stop, Cecco. *Fermati!*" said Caravaggio, holding up his hand. "I can't take you. You must return to Roma. It's time for you to make your way in the world."

"But—how?"

"Hire yourself as an apprentice. Your skills will be valuable."

"I—"

"I will give you a little money to get started. You must fend for yourself now."

Cecco looked from his master's eyes to his own hands.

I'm to fend for myself. As an artist? How can I possibly live up to anyone's expectations? I'm Caravaggio's "boy."

"It is settled. Giovanni is arranging transportation for you back to Roma. And . . . I have a favor to ask you, Cecco."

Cecco could barely raise his eyes to his master's. He was as stunned from the shock of separation as if he had been clubbed over the head.

"*Sì*, Maestro?"

"I want you to visit Lena. Find out how she is faring. Send a letter to me, addressed to Grand Admiral Fabrizio Colonna."

Cecco nodded. His eyes shot over to the velvet-shrouded painting.

Caravaggio's face colored red. "You've looked at it, haven't you?"

Cecco raised his chin in defiance. "*Sì.*"

"I told you! I told you—" said Caravaggio, his hand raised to slap him. The boy held his eyes, not flinching.

Caravaggio lowered his hand.

"What did you think of it?"

Cecco hesitated. He desperately wanted to hurt his master, to make him feel a modicum of the pain he suffered. *What do I think? I shall say it's a disaster, a sentimental, blasphemous homage to a whore!*

Cruel words swirled in his head, a rising serpent's head of rage and revenge.

Cecco met Caravaggio's eyes. "It is your greatest masterpiece," he said, the words choking him.

He had never learned to lie to Caravaggio.

"Maestro," he said. "Before you depart for Malta, I must share a secret with you. I never told you before, because Lena—"

"What about Lena?"

"When you fled Roma to Genova after clubbing Mariano Pasqualone, Lena's suitor. She—she—"

"Spit it out, Cecco!"

"She had to return to her trade to feed herself, her mother, and her son."

Caravaggio's eyes burned. "Of course. It is her trade."

"No, listen. I was speaking to her when a knight of Malta—a demon of a man—approached Lena. He spoke ugly words to her."

"What did he say?" demanded Caravaggio.

"He said he'd give it to her hard up the ass. And that . . . I should tell you what he was doing."

Caravaggio's face spasmed with anger, his nostrils flaring like a bull's.

"I didn't tell you because I didn't want to anger you. But now that you are going to Malta—"

"Stop!" said Caravaggio. "I can't stand to hear more!"

Caravaggio stumbled away, his hand over his face. These were the last words he and Cecco ever exchanged.

A donkey cart bumped over the uneven stones from Quartiere San Ferdinando toward the bustling wharf. Caravaggio winced as his canvases and paints jostled violently.

"What a bone-breaking ride!"

"Can't do nothing about them stones, signore," said the driver over his shoulder. "They're not going anywhere."

A thicket of masts rocking on the Bay of Napoli sliced the dawn into slivers. Boats of all sizes cluttered the bay, some hoisting sail, others with sailors gathering in the loosened canvas folds off the mast. The fishermen returning called insults across the water, their nets glimmering silver with their catch.

All these seafarers, so at ease . . .

The salty breeze slapped him in the face. He shivered. Never had he set foot on a boat, let alone a great seafaring galley.

"There she is, signore!" sang out the cart driver. "The *Vittoriosa*!" He pointed toward a huge vessel with three masts and its sides perforated with oar ports.

The Maltese galley measured fifty meters long. Rowers—slaves captured in battles—occupied most of the deck of the oak galley. Only the perimeters of the prow and stern were open to the crew.

Moored alongside the ancient stones of Castel dell'Ovo, *La Vittoriosa* groaned on her anchor, jerking the chain like a mare ready to bolt.

In the early light, the glint of the galley slaves' chains caught Caravaggio's eye. He heard the rattle of the metal links.

"My God," he said aloud to no one.

"Signore," said the cart driver. "Should I unload your trunk and parcels?"

"*Sì. Sì,*" he said, digging for a coin in his purse, his eyes still riveted on the galley.

Caravaggio counted the benches along the starboard side. Two men per bench, twenty-six rows. The slaves' faces were turned toward the wharf to face the cooling wind.

One with greasy, matted hair and a blind blue eye looked down at Caravaggio. With his one good eye, he looked like an old, battered eagle eyeing his prey.

The artist stared back, studying him: his barklike skin, the thick furrows in his forehead, the angry red welts and yellow pus where his skin chafed against the fetters.

The rower gathered the juices in his mouth and spat into the green water.

"*Scusi.*" A guard stopped Caravaggio. "Your papers, signore?"

"I'm sailing under the auspices of Admiral Colonna. I—"

"Michele!" called a voice from on board. A fair-haired officer dressed in the white-crossed tunic of the Order of Malta gestured with two open arms. "Welcome aboard *La Vittoriosa!*"

The artist walked up the plank gangway. His hand flew to cover his nose. The stink—a mixture of piss, shit, and rancid body sweat from the fifty-two oarsmen—overpowered him. As he boarded the vessel, he caught a glimpse of the runnel under the rowers' benches.

Brown sewage trickled, abuzz with glossy flies.

"How can you bear that fetid mess?" he asked.

"You learn to sniff around it," Colonna said, clapping his old friend on the back. "We'll be at sea soon enough, and the wind will chase away the smell."

Caravaggio stared at the weatherworn and emaciated oarsmen, their sinews sharp in their necks and arms, working under their sun-blackened skin like snakes. Most were Turks, slaves taken captive in Maltese battles with the Ottomans. Their eyes burned with hatred or merely stared vacantly, devoid of light.

The artist shook his head, his nose wrinkling in disgust.

"Even if Venti blew his cheeks wide, never could the gods chase away that stench!"

Colonna nodded, his eyebrows lifting. "It's a factor in battle. The Ottoman sailors can smell us and we can smell them. We attack from downwind, always." He shrugged and beckoned to one of the crew. "Sailor! Show Maestro Caravaggio to his bunk and where to stow his kit."

As Caravaggio followed the seaman, Colonna called, "Then come back around on deck. You'll want to breathe the sea and focus straight ahead when we are underway."

"Mind your head, signore," said the sailor as he scrambled down the ladder like a monkey. Caravaggio descended deliberately, resenting every second his hand was engaged on the rungs rather than defending his nose from the repulsive odor.

The sailor led him to a row of bunks near the hatch. "The admiral thought you'd benefit from a bunk nearest the fresh air."

Belowdecks, the stink wasn't as bad. The cook's galley smelled of olive oil and garlic.

"Tell the admiral I'll be up shortly."

The sailor eyed him. "We'll be underway soon enough. Have you ever sailed the sea before, Maestro?"

"No. Why do ask?"

The man suppressed a grin. "You'll be wanting to be on deck, then. Admiral Colonna knows best."

Caravaggio snorted and waved the sailor away.

"Leave me be. I want to rest."

Beyond the port of Napoli, the tranquil sea turned from blue to gray, hostile and rough. At first, Caravaggio could hear the rhythmic whistle of the *celeustes*, the coxswain, at the stern of the vessel. As the wind picked up, the rowing stopped and the artist heard the flap of the sails unfurling.

The white-capped waves tossed the *Vittoriosa* about, making the masts creak under the erratic gusts.

Caravaggio clambered up the hatch ladder. He lurched to the railing at the stern and vomited copiously into the slapping waves. His lungs gasped greedily in the salt spray.

"You'll feel better now," Fabrizio Colonna called to him over the whine of the wind. The Maltese admiral walked catlike across the decks to inspect the sails. He shaded his eyes, looking at the flex of the sailcloth. "Take her off the wind a bit, Marco," he called to the helmsman.

Colonna stood by Caravaggio and the landsman wiped the spittle from his mouth with his sleeve.

"Eat some salted bread, Michele," Colonna said. "It will calm—"

Caravaggio lunged again for the rail, vomiting. "Don't mention food, damn you, Fabrizio!"

"Then take a draught of grappa, you stubborn bastard. It will make the rocking seem more natural."

"All right," said Caravaggio, his eyelids half lowered like a lizard's. "Give it to me, then."

Fabrizio jerked his chin at a sailor, who went to fetch drink.

"Breathe deep. Keep your eyes focused straight ahead toward the horizon," said the admiral. The sailor returned with a bladder. Fabrizio took a pull and then handed it to the artist. Caravaggio took several long gulps, wincing at the strong bite of the liquor. He closed his eyes, drawing in deep breaths.

"What's it like?" said Caravaggio. "Malta?"

"Rocks," said Fabrizio. "And more rocks. Limestone blocks that shine in the sun like a city of the Orient, like Jerusalem itself. But still, all rock."

"You don't sound as if you like it much, Fabrizio."

Colonna laughed, taking the bladder from Caravaggio. He took a long draught. "Fortunately, I can sail away. I grow weary of rock."

"Has Malta washed away your sins?" said Caravaggio, sucking down another gulp. "I know you have a murder weighing on your soul too."

Fabrizio's eyes flashed on Caravaggio, warning him not to venture further.

"I've had at least enough splash of the sea to wash me clean of my sins. I command the fleet that battles the infidels. The pope approves," he said, dodging a wave that swept over the deck. "Damn you, Marco!" he shouted. "Take her more into the wind now, you son of a sea cook!"

"Aye, Admiral," called the voice from the helm.

"Do you think the sea will do the same for me?" said Caravaggio. "Wash clean my sins? Make me a man of honor and respect?"

Fabrizio shrugged. He looked out at the churning waves.

"You are beyond the reach of Roma, Michele. Isn't that enough? Wignacourt will determine your fate. He's a powerful man. The pope left me in the hands of the grand master, and I am now the grand admiral. Your fortunes can change under the banner of the knights. The pope and Roma need our protection."

Caravaggio looked at the gray waters and the diminishing shoreline of Calabria.

"An island of rock. After Roma—"

"You can say goodbye to that!" said Fabrizio. He fixed his eyes on his friend. "You and I are both colossal sinners, Michele. Roma has slammed its door to us. Understand that."

Caravaggio took another gulp of grappa. "What's it like?" he said. "Celibacy? Living a virtuous life?"

The Maltese admiral twisted his mouth in scorn. "How the hell would I know? We knights are no more celibate than the cardinals of Roma! There are whores in every port. You'll find them along the shore of Valletta, fattened on the scudi of the order. There is no shortage of sin. And brawls between knights hungry for battle."

Caravaggio considered. "What of the eight points of virtue of the Maltese cross?"

"How are you at serving broth and vermicelli to sick patients? Wiping their fevered brows and changing their piss pots?"

"Me?"

"It's one of the practices of the order," said Fabrizio. "You'll be required—"

"I'm going to Malta to paint!" snarled Caravaggio.

"I forgot, of course," said Fabrizio. "You aren't a knight. You can't be—" Another rogue wave splashed over the deck, drowning his words.

"Damn you, Marco! You haven't the sea sense of a blind pig, you sodding pimp!" Fabrizio charged off toward the helmsman.

Chapter 38

Caravaggio came ashore at Valletta harbor, a landing with a white stone customhouse bracketed by chains set into limestone pillars. He supervised the transfer of his rolled canvas and boxes of brushes and pigments into a cart drawn by two oxen that slowly mounted the hill toward the city gates.

Valletta was exactly as Fabrizio had described it: stone piled on stone as far as the eye could see. The roads, the towering walls, the houses—all cream-colored limestone. Colorful enclosed balconies rescued the city from the monotony of stone.

Caravaggio was taken first to the grand master's palazzo, where he was greeted by a young page who took his cloak and hat.

"Welcome, sir," said the fair-headed boy. He was dressed in a black-and-white tunic and black silk leggings that accentuated his shapely calves. He spoke Italian with a French accent. "I am Nicholas de Paris Boissy, page to Grand Master Wignacourt."

Caravaggio smiled for the first time since he'd left Napoli. "You are young to be apprenticed, aren't you?"

"I am twelve years old," said Boissy, jutting out his chin. "There are younger pages in the palazzo than me. I shall be a knight soon enough, signore."

"I see," said the artist, drinking in the boy's face and noble bearing. "Nicholas, bring me a basin of water and a towel so that I may wash the salt off my face before I meet his honor the grand master."

"*Oui, monsieur,*" said Boissy, lapsing into French. "*Tout de suite!*"

"Delightful," said Caravaggio softly, watching the boy hurry down the hall in his soft leather slippers. He thought of Cecco at that age. "Perhaps Malta has its charms after all."

∞

Grand Master Alof de Wignacourt stood at the end of a great hall, conversing with another, older knight.

As Caravaggio followed the page down the hall, he studied the grand master. A distinguished man in his early sixties with a neatly trimmed beard, Wignacourt had a supremely self-assured demeanor. His skin was bronzed and weather-beaten from countless hours in the field battling the Ottoman foes of the Christian cross. Caravaggio sensed an animallike fierceness to this man with the white Maltese cross emblazoned on his tunic.

"Michelangelo Merisi da Caravaggio," said Wignacourt, extending his hand. His perfect Italian had a light Provençal accent. "I am pleased to welcome you to Malta."

"*Un gran piacere,*" said Caravaggio, bowing. He nodded to the distinguished gentleman in a black tunic with the white eight-pointed cross who was standing beside the grand master.

"Cavaliere Martelli. I present our new artist-in-residence, Michelangelo Merisi da Caravaggio."

The elderly gentleman extended his hand. The artist noticed the gnarled joints as he clasped it.

"I am not a stranger to your work, Maestro," said Martelli. "I have admired your shield of the Medusa at the Palazzo Vecchio in Firenze."

"You are Tuscan?"

"Cavaliere Antonio Martelli is from a venerable Florentine family," said Wignacourt. "He is a hero from the Great Siege of Malta."

"Ah!" said Caravaggio, bowing. "Then I should paint you—"

The grand master laughed, exchanging a look with Martelli.

"We have plenty of other projects for you, Maestro Caravaggio," said the grand master.

"But I should paint you," insisted Caravaggio, inspecting Martelli's face, his eyes lingering on the creases in his skin. "After painting Your Grace, of course," said the artist, bowing.

Wignacourt considered the artist, his fingertips stroking his beard. "Perhaps you are correct, Maestro Caravaggio. In fact, I think you should paint Fra Martelli first. Then we will have better knowledge of your ability. I have not had the occasion to see your work. You will have to prove your talent."

"Your Excellency," mumbled Caravaggio. He ducked his chin to hide his displeasure.

"You shall be lodged with the Italian knights in their auberge, Caravaggio. I shall expect you to paint here in my palazzo."

Caravaggio looked around, inspecting the dark interior. "Is there a source of light, Grand Master? I will need lanterns, ones that throw strong illumination. It is crucial to my work—"

"You shall have whatever you need. My steward shall make sure of it. My pages may attend you as needed."

"Ah! Yes, that would be perfect. There is one who greeted me at the door—"

"Nicholas is not available, Maestro Caravaggio," said the grand master. "He is part of my personal retinue."

The artist bowed. "I see."

"There are others who will be more suited as your assistants," said the grand master. "Come, Maestro. Let us take some wine and toast to your arrival in Malta."

✺

Two of Wignacourt's pages accompanied Caravaggio to the Italian auberge, standing on the step of the carriage as the driver maneuvered his horse over the limestone roads.

The young pages spoke to one another in a torrent of French, a Provençal dialect that the artist could not work out. They bobbed their heads in lively animation, joyful at their outing. The strong sunshine glanced off their hair, one flaxen and one bright–orange red. Their livery was chocolate-colored velvet with red leggings. Now and then, a lace cuff would rise in a gesture or to point out someone they knew.

The carriage slowed at the church of Saint Catherine adjacent to South Street and Strada San Giacomo.

"The Italian auberge's church," said the redheaded page, pointing. "And that's your auberge, directly across from the Castilian one. The Italian one is much grander, Maestro."

Caravaggio saw a three-storied building with six windows on each floor.

In a second-story window he spotted a man with thick chestnut hair. The man's hand gripped the shutter as he glared down at Caravaggio's arrival.

The red-haired boy whispered in his ear. "That is Knight of Justice Fra Giovanni Rodomonte Roero, Conte della Vezza, Maestro. From the north, like you." He hesitated and then whispered, "He is a dangerous man, Maestro Caravaggio."

Caravaggio locked eyes with the man he already knew too well, not looking at the page as he spoke. "Tell me why."

"Quarrelsome, always looking for a brawl. He's despised by many of our order. We think he is not right in the head. But don't tell Grand Master Wignacourt I said anything."

"Of course not."

Caravaggio descended from the carriage, where a flight of Italian pages greeted him.

From the window above, Roero launched a gleaming gob of spit, just missing Caravaggio's head.

"You are welcome here," said a voice from the shadows within the palazzo. In the blinding sun, Caravaggio couldn't see the speaker.

A knight even older than Martelli walked out with the help of an ivory cane. "Maestro Caravaggio, may I introduce myself. I am Ippolito Malaspina," he said, extending his gnarled hand. "I'm the prior of the Knights of Malta."

"You are the man responsible for bringing me to Malta," said Caravaggio, grasping Malaspina's hand, his eyes studying the knight's sinewy forearm. "The Marchesa Colonna told me. You are related to Signor Ottavio Costa, one of my patrons."

"I have seen my cousin's treasured *Martha and Mary Magdalene* by your hand," said Malaspina. "Remarkable. Your reputation in Roma is unparalleled."

"I assume you refer to my art, Cavaliere Malaspina," said Caravaggio.

Malaspina smiled, wagging a finger. "Of course, Maestro. What other reputation could you possibly have but as the greatest artist since Michelangelo?"

The carriage driver had unknotted the ropes that held Caravaggio's baggage on the back of the carriage. The pages gathered up the belongings and panted up the stairs under the weight.

"I see you brought your own supplies."

"I wasn't sure what I could procure here."

"The grand master will see you have the best," said Malaspina. "Is it true you do not use blue in your paintings? Such a pleasant color."

"Blue? Rarely," said Caravaggio. "Blue is indeed pleasant, but I look at what lurks under the blue."

Malaspina regarded him, his eyes occluded with cataracts earned from the blazing Mediterranean sun and sparkling sea. "When you have settled, I shall introduce you to the knights of our auberge, Maestro." He turned to a servant. "Please show Maestro Caravaggio to his room and direct the pages where to store his supplies."

Caravaggio clasped the old knight's hand. He liked the warmth and firmness of the prior's handshake, the nimbleness and strength of his fingers despite his age.

"Cavaliere Malaspina," the artist said, bowing, "it is an honor to meet you."

As Caravaggio looked up, he saw, yet again, the face that had lurked in the shadows and watched his friend bleed out his life on the cobblestones of Roma. The Piemontese knight descended the staircase, glaring, his mouth twisted with hatred.

"Ah! Fra Roero!" called Malaspina, squinting at the knight, his eyes unable to discern the glower on his face. "Please come and meet Maestro Michele Merisi da Caravaggio."

Roero strode toward them. He did not extend his hand. "I know who you are," he said. "You are a filthy murderer."

"Fra Roero!" said Malaspina, aghast. "The maestro is a guest in our auberge!"

"And how would you know I killed a man, Fra Roero?" said Caravaggio. "Unless you were there yourself? Right in the middle of the fight."

Roero narrowed his eyes and darted a look at the old knight Malaspina.

"I know because evil news travels far," said Roero. "Your treachery in the streets of Roma is notorious, Merisi. You are no better than a heathen Turk."

Caravaggio's back stiffened. His right hand hunted for his dagger.

"Come along, Maestro," said Malaspina, taking Caravaggio's elbow firmly and steering him toward the great hall.

Malaspina called over his shoulder, "I'll deal with you later, Fra Roero. Your conduct toward our guest is despicable. It shall be noted to the grand master."

Chapter 39

MONTE PICCOLO

Lucia wasn't going to run. Running would mean she was afraid, and she was not going to be afraid. So she walked—strong, solid, definitely not running.

Someone was following her. That wasn't her imagination. She heard the footsteps behind her in the dark, and when she stopped—looking into a shop window—the footsteps stopped too. She turned a corner, then another one immediately. The tiny streets twisted and turned in every direction. She knew Monte Piccolo well by now, and she quickly turned yet again, making her way home, but not too directly, trying to lose whoever was following her.

It was late to be walking home alone, closer to dawn than midnight. They had talked for hours in the professor's rooms, trying to understand how they had found themselves tangled with terrorist assassins inspired by a medieval Knight of Malta.

Eventually, Moto had left to meet friends at a party, saying he desperately needed a glass—no, make that a bottle—of good red wine after so many hours arguing about murderers. And Professor Richman had retired to his bedroom with a reference to his age and his need for sleep, leaving Lucia alone in the parlor, thinking about Italy's blood-splattered past—and present.

She might have dozed off. In any case, it was hours after midnight when she stood up, stretched, listened to the professor snoring in the next room, and then slipped out the door to walk home.

And now she was alone—no, not alone, and that was the trouble. There were no streetlights, no lights in any of the buildings that lined the cobblestone streets.

She needed to get home.

And she needed to keep walking, not running.

She wasn't afraid.

And the footsteps stayed behind her. Never hurrying closer. Never fading away.

But she still was not going to run.

Her mind filled with thoughts of Aysha, the beautiful young woman, beheaded and burned, a flash of the man with blood running down his face in the street in Naples, the feel of the rough cloth of the black robes, the sour breath and the crushing grip of the man who had carried her through the catacombs in Malta.

Her apartment on the quiet piazza was impossibly far away. She might never see it again. She turned another corner, then another.

And then, suddenly, there was light and noise spilling out of an apartment on an upper floor of a building down a dark, narrow side street. Music and voices. Young voices. Maybe other students from the seminar. Maybe people she had never met. Maybe Moto. It didn't matter. She sprinted recklessly through the dark to the door of the building. She yanked the handle. The door was locked. She desperately pounded all the call buttons outside the door and waited a few terrifying seconds until someone buzzed her into the building. She slipped through the door and leaned all her weight against it until it clicked shut behind her, and then she ran up the stairs toward the party.

Inside, the apartment was exactly the crush of sweaty bodies and slightly drunken faces she had hoped for. No one she knew. No one who knew her. And no one who cared either way.

She stayed for an hour, made distracted small talk when she had to, and then, when a large group started putting on their coats, she grabbed her jacket and went out into the street with them. She hid in the anonymity of the crowd until the moment seemed right, and then she broke away and ran—definitely not walking anymore—all the way back to her apartment. She locked the door and collapsed on her bed, gasping for breath and wondering how the hell it had come to this.

∞

"We don't even know who they are."

Lucia, Moto, and the professor were back in the parlor, still trying to find an answer to the same question: What do we do now?

Lucia hadn't mentioned her experience, her terror, from the night before. After a few hours of fitful sleep, she wasn't quite certain what had been real and what had been a nightmare. But her steely determination to push ahead now had a sharper edge.

"We don't know who they are," she repeated.

"Or where they are. Or what they want," Moto added.

"Other than to kill anyone who gets in their way," said the professor. "And that seems increasingly to be us."

"We can't keep running," Lucia said, which brought back a flash from the night before, "when we don't know which way to run."

No one had an answer to that, so she went on.

"We need to take the fight to them."

"That's crazy!"

"We can't—"

The professor and Moto both spoke at once, but Lucia cut through.

"We need to lure them out into the open. Make them come and get us when we're ready for them."

"That's a terrible—" Moto tried to break in, but she wouldn't let him.

321

"I've already called a reporter at *Corriere della Sera*—"

"Reporter?" Now the professor was objecting.

"—and left a message saying I have a hot tip for him. Murder and scandal."

"You are going to get yourself killed."

"No I'm not. I'm going to be an anonymous witness who can give him inside information about the murders and the missing painting. Secret messages. He'll love it. He's a reporter."

Moto's eyes narrowed. "Lucia, you can't do this. It's crazy."

Lucia remembered running through the dark streets after she'd left the party the night before, and her lips tightened. She wasn't going to tell them about what had happened—they might doubt her, and she wasn't in any mood to be challenged. She felt brittle and she needed to feel strong. So she took the challenge to Moto.

"You have any better ideas? Because I don't."

Moto looked determined. It was that new Moto who kept emerging when he was pressured. "Give me a day."

◦◦◦

"Lo so. Sì, lo so, ma . . ." I know. Yes, I know, but . . .

Standing in a darkened doorway, Moto glanced around as he muttered into his cell phone.

"Qualcosa è successo ieri sera. Non sta parlando. Ma lei ha paura. Io la conosco. Qualcosa la spaventava." Something happened last night. She isn't talking about it. But she's afraid. I know her. Something scared her.

Moto listened for a long time.

Finally, he burst out, *"Ma dobbiamo fare qualcosa. Loro sono qui. Questo è."* But we have to do something. They're here. This is it.

He listened for a moment, started to speak, then shrugged and put the phone away. Then he stood for a long time in the darkened doorway, staring up into the night, across the tiny piazza, keeping watch on Lucia's apartment.

The last time they had spoken, they were together in a darkened room in the hills of Sicily while the women prepared a feast in the kitchen above. Now they were separated by hundreds of miles, but the conversation was still more silence than speech, as if—one still in Sicily, the other in Rome—they could see each other's shrugs and gestures over the telephone.

Plans were made. Details were checked and confirmed. Doubts expressed and set aside. And yet someone listening in would not have understood any of that. Which was as it should be—because it was assumed someone was always listening in.

Then a final question:

"*E appui, quannu timminamu?*" *And then we're done?*

"*Quannu timminamu, timminamu.*" *When we're done, we're done.*

And the call ended.

Three days had passed since Lucia had announced her plan to lure their unknown enemies into the open with a story in the newspaper. Tonight, she and Moto made their way across the piazza toward her apartment. They shared a slight unsteadiness, evidence of an evening of drinking. And the silence between them was evidence that the drinks had not dissolved the tension.

Their conversation had ended when Lucia had said, "Tomorrow I'm calling that reporter."

"But it's—"

"No! You said one day. And it's been three. I'm calling him."

On other drunken evenings, they had enjoyed clinging to one another for support, even if they hadn't really needed it. Now they could have used support, but each walked carefully alone.

Lucia was determined not to stumble. And so determined not to let herself invent unseen watchers in the shadows that she was startled when a figure suddenly emerged from a dark doorway—an unseen watcher she had been determined not to see.

But it was only Vittore, the parking enforcer.

"*Buonasera, mia signora.*"

"*Buonasera.*"

Vittore stared for a moment at Moto, then he said something about keeping watch all night, but that was more than she could deal with, so she kept heading toward home, leaving Vittore standing alone in the dark.

At the door to her building, Lucia fumbled with the key, managed to get the lock open, and started to go inside without saying good night.

Moto grabbed the door and kept it from swinging shut. "Let me come up. One more drink."

"Really? You're not drunk enough?"

"One more. To cheer you up."

"Cheer *me* up?"

She turned and wobbled toward the stairs, but she hadn't said no. Moto followed.

Inside the apartment, Lucia headed into the bathroom, gesturing vaguely toward the kitchen. "You know where it is."

When the bathroom door closed, Moto hurried to the kitchen, his gait steadier than it had been. He got down two glasses and a bottle of red wine. The toilet flushed, the bathroom door opened, and Lucia walked across the living room and collapsed on the couch. Moto was out of sight in the kitchen. A moment later, he walked into the living room with two glasses of wine.

"I didn't say I wanted a drink."

"Come on, Lulu." He handed her the glass. "A toast." He smiled. "To better ideas. May we have some very soon."

She shrugged and drained the glass.

Moto stood for a long time, looking out the window.

When he turned back to the room, Lucia was asleep on the couch, snoring lightly.

"*Tesoro,*" he said, and gently woke her just enough to help her to the bed.

In the darkened car, the driver read the text message:

"*Lei è là. Lui è andato.*" She's there. He's gone.

He started the engine, flicked on the headlights, and headed into the night, accelerating sharply. The man in the back seat, shaken awake, grumbled. The man in the passenger seat muttered, "*Sempre a correre.*" Always the racer.

The driver didn't care. He drove fast and smooth through the dark, a smile on his face. This was where he belonged: behind the wheel, foot on the accelerator, eyes on the road. Despite what some might think, not every Italian was born to drive fast cars. But he was. This was his gift.

The road unspooled ahead of him into the night. For a moment he allowed himself to think ahead—to the end of this little journey, only a few kilometers away, where the joy of driving would blend into the joy of violence. The word had been passed down: Seize the painting at all costs. "Collateral damage" was of no concern. His smile widened. Then, respecting his gift and his responsibility, he narrowed his focus to the blacktop road that twisted and turned, rose and fell, within the cone of the headlights as it cut through the hills of Chianti.

He steered through a sharp curve, his hands light but firm on the wheel, feeling the tires hold the road, and suddenly there were bright lights in the road ahead. Headlights. An instant later he could see through the glare that it was a massive American-made SUV stopped in the middle of the narrow road, blocking the way. An attack! No time to think!

He jammed on the brakes, slowing sharply. The man in the passenger seat beside him lurched forward—no seat belts, they were true Italians—and smashed his face against the dashboard. No time to worry about that. The driver turned the wheel sharply and yanked on the hand brake, just for an instant. The rear wheels locked up and the car skidded in a perfect pirouette, reversing direction in an instant, and then his foot was back on the accelerator and he let out a shout of pure joy as they raced away from the roadblock.

Beside him, his passenger cursed, blood streaming down his face. There were curses from the man in the back seat as well. But the driver didn't care. He had escaped the trap. He was skillful. He was heroic. He was born to drive.

He glanced in the mirror. The SUV was trying to catch them, but it was falling farther and farther behind. A car that big was worthless on roads this small. And whoever was foolish enough to own such a behemoth could not possibly match his driving skills. He laughed. Exultant.

The road began to rise gently, cresting a small hill, but he kept his foot firmly on the gas. To the left, a small patch of woods; to the right, a short, steep slope down into an open field. And then suddenly there was a tree, fallen across the road, blocking the way. It hadn't been there when they'd passed just a few minutes before. His foot was heavy on the brakes, but there was no room to stop. He swerved hard, but there was nowhere to go. The left front wheel hit the tree. The car lurched, tilted, started to roll, and went off the edge of the pavement onto the soft dirt of the shoulder. Then it did roll, onto its roof and then down the embankment, rolling again into the open field below, glass exploding, doors flying open, rolling one more time and then slamming down onto its wheels.

And then there was silence. One body lay motionless a short distance off the road. A second was in the middle of the field, thrown free and then crushed by the rolling car. The driver was still in his seat, his chest torn open by the shattered steering wheel, his face shredded by flying glass.

And then four men came running out of the woods, across the road, and scrambled down the embankment into the field. One stopped for a moment beside the body closest to the road, prodded it with his toe, then ran to catch up with the others. They didn't bother to stop beside the second body. When they got to the car, the driver might have been alive. If so, he wasn't for long.

Three of the men turned and started back toward the road. The fourth lingered a moment longer. He dug something out of his pocket, then leaned through the shattered driver's window and reached out carefully, poking his hand into the dead man's bloodstained clothing. The stains obscured the red Maltese cross and the embroidered *R* above it. Then he stood back, pulled a small, half-full bottle of whiskey out of his pocket, and tossed it into the wreck. The glass shattered.

"*Chi sprecu!*" he muttered. *What a waste.* Followed by a Sicilian obscenity.

Up on the road, the other three men were struggling to lift the tree. He strolled in their direction. No need to hurry if they could manage without him. The enormous SUV pulled up, its headlights illuminating the scene, and four men piled out to help with the tree. In a matter of moments, they had stood it upright and then let it topple back into the underbrush, one more fallen tree in the forest. The last man, still mourning the wasted whiskey, reached the road in time to stand with the others as the tree crashed back down.

Then they all climbed into the SUV. Big as it was, it was crowded for eight large men, and one of them complained that this had been too easy, there was no need for all of them. He could have done it by himself.

The one who had thrown the whiskey bottle looked back into the dark and laughed. *"Monici 'mbriachi."* *Drunken monks.*

"Nan veramenti 'mbriacu," said the man crowded beside him. *Not really drunk.*

"Nan veramenti monici," said another. *Not really monks.*

And they laughed as they drove off into the night. Quickly, but quietly, smoothly. No need to hurry.

And behind them, in the field, the bodies sprawled, blood still soaking into their black robes, darker than the blood-red crosses on their chests.

And a few kilometers away, even as the black SUV was slipping away from the field, a man stood in the shadows at the edge of a tiny piazza. He glanced down at his cell phone and hurried toward a car idling in an alley.

He nodded to the driver. Nothing was said.

Together they unloaded a large, awkward package from the car and carried it through the shadows.

From the far side of the piazza, a young man in a black leather jacket watched, keeping carefully out of sight.

A chill winter breeze tousled his thick black hair.

Chapter 40

Valletta, Malta
1608

"It is magnificent!" pronounced Grand Master Wignacourt. He came closer to the canvas and then took two steps back. He studied the cavaliere's likeness, the enormous cream-colored Maltese cross emblazoned across his black tunic.

"Ha! Cavaliere Martelli in the flesh! The sunburned nose . . . a tribute to his years at sea."

Caravaggio nodded.

"The furrows of his brow . . . and those folds of loose skin at his collar," said Wignacourt. "An old knight and a venerable one. This is a painting befitting the Order of Malta. It is unflinching . . . as real as he stands in real life."

"I am honored, Grand Master," said Caravaggio, bowing.

"You have not only captured Cavaliere Martelli's physical likeness to perfection, but you have captured his soul as well. Look at his eyes! The raw-edged rims, the sage determination—"

Caravaggio nodded. "He was a good subject."

"Good subject!" said the grand master. "I should say so."

"But you, Grand Master Wignacourt, will provide an even better inspiration," said Caravaggio.

Wignacourt raised his hand to his beard, stroking it like a cat. "You believe so?"

"Yes. I have some ideas already. I'd like to paint you in your armor."

"My armor?"

"As if preparing for battle, Your Excellency."

"I see," said the grand master. "Hmm . . . I like the idea of battle. The Order of Malta and its defense of Christianity and Europe."

"That defense and the stalwart bravery shall be integral to the painting," said Caravaggio.

"Ah! Perhaps along the lines of Scipione Pulzone's portrait of Marcantonio Colonna? I've admired that portrait in the Palazzo Colonna myself," said the grand master.

Caravaggio's mouth puckered with distaste. "It will be far more dramatic and better executed than Pulzone's, I assure you, Your Grace."

Wignacourt raised an eyebrow. "You are certainly confident in your skill, Maestro."

Caravaggio stared back at him. His mouth turned hard, his eyes narrowing. "If I were not, I could never attempt to pick up a brush. Your portrait will be magnificent."

"May I see some sketches?"

"No," said Caravaggio.

"No?"

"I do not sketch my work. I see it here." He tapped the side of his right eye.

"No sketches? Ever?" said the grand master, raising an eyebrow.

"Absolutely not. I would find them distracting. I paint what I see in the moment, not before . . . not after."

"Most extraordinary. But I cannot argue with the genius you have shown here with Cavaliere Martelli."

Caravaggio said nothing.

"In fact, my confidence in your genius is already so strong that I want to begin discussing a far greater undertaking."

Caravaggio lifted his chin. "That is?"

"Once you have succeeded with my portrait," said Wignacourt, "I want you to paint a commemoration of our patron saint of the Order of Malta."

"Saint John the Baptist," said Caravaggio.

"Yes. His martyrdom. Something that will stir hearts from Malta to Roma. From Roma to Paris, and Paris to London. I want an extraordinary work that will unite all of the eight languages of our knights under one banner, one heart . . . that of our holy patron saint. I want the moment of his martyrdom."

"His beheading."

"Of course, Maestro Caravaggio," said the grand master, his voice changing, somber with respect. "At the whim of the harlot Salome."

Caravaggio's immobile face quivered. Muscle by muscle, his face drew up in a smiling grimace, an expression the grand master had never seen on another human being.

"He is an artist of the highest caliber," said Cavaliere Ippolito Malaspina, admiring Wignacourt's portrait. "A stroke of genius to have the page looking out from the edge, directly into the viewer's eye."

"*Sì,*" said the grand master. "I wasn't sure I liked it at first, the boy crowding in on me. It is my portrait, after all."

"It gives the painting depth and intimacy, despite the darkness. Perhaps because of the darkness. The light on the page's face—"

"*Sì, sì.* I think Caravaggio captured strength in my pose."

"Of course," said Malaspina, a twinkle in his eye. "Grand Master, have you discussed the idea of painting John the Baptist?"

"We have discussed it," said Wignacourt.

"No contract yet?" said Malaspina. "Aren't you afraid he will bolt? Leave Malta?"

"Caravaggio?"

"*Sì!* There is nothing holding him here. Unless . . ."

"Unless what?"

"If you were able to convince the pope to instate Michelangelo Caravaggio as a member of the Cavalieri di Obbedienza—"

"The order is defunct by the pope's command," said Wignacourt. "And Caravaggio is wanted for murder."

"Anything is possible. Explain the circumstances but simply don't mention his name. If Caravaggio leaves our shores, he will never return to Malta. He is pursued not only by the law but by art collectors all over Europe."

Wignacourt looked from his friend's eyes to the painting of himself. He rubbed his finger back and forth across his mustache. "The pope is very worried about North Africa and the Muslim invaders. He does owe me some favors."

Malaspina clapped his old friend on the back. "Of course he does."

"I will write to him immediately," said the grand master.

Grand Master Wignacourt summoned Caravaggio to his study.

"Maestro Caravaggio. I want you to commence on the painting we discussed earlier. For the oratory."

"A painting of the execution of Saint John the Baptist."

"It must be striking—and large enough to encompass the entire wall behind the altar."

Caravaggio tucked in his chin like a turtle. He had studied the *oratorio* for exactly this moment. "A canvas twice the height of a man. And a full ten paces wide. Maybe wider. That will be a vast work. Difficult. Demanding."

"Can you do it, Master Caravaggio?"

"Of course I can." Caravaggio frowned. "But I have given thought to returning to Roma."

"Caravaggio!" said Wignacourt, throwing up his hands. "You are a wanted man. You are under a death sentence, a *bando capitale*. The pope will have your head."

Caravaggio looked away. Outside, he saw two knights of the order walking the limestone streets, the white crosses blazing against the black of their tunics.

"Tell me more about this commission, Your Excellency," he said.

"I will make it worth your while, I assure you."

"How?" said Caravaggio, fastening his eyes on the grand master.

Wignacourt raised his chin. "Maestro Caravaggio, perhaps we could find a way for you to join our order. A Knight of Malta. A cavaliere."

Caravaggio had played at cards too many hours to allow himself a smile. Instead, he protested. "That seems impossible. I am not of noble birth . . . I've been convicted of murder—"

"If you can paint the martyrdom of our patron saint with the same genius you have shown in my portrait, I intend to bring you into the order as a Knight of Obedience."

Caravaggio simply nodded. Any greater display would have been inappropriate to the nobility he was going to obtain.

Wignacourt nodded in return. "Get to work at once on the painting, Maestro. But it must be the equal of my magnificent portrait—"

Caravaggio threw back his head and laughed. The sound filled the room, reverberating off the coffered ceiling. Wignacourt was startled by the impertinence, his features hardening.

"Grand Master Wignacourt! Forgive me," said the artist. "You have no idea what I will create. *The Beheading of St. John the Baptist* shall be my masterpiece. I will give my lifeblood to the order, no less.

"After all, I will become a knight and have to stare at it for all eternity."

Chapter 41

Roma
1608

"Grand Admiral Fabrizio Colonna directed me to deliver this to you," said the young man dressed in a black tunic and leggings. "I will return tomorrow evening should you wish to send a response."

"Grazie," said Cecco, taking the worn letter, which was splashed with seawater and smudged by sweating hands.

"We had a rough crossing from Malta," said the boy. "And an even more difficult docking." He bowed and left Cecco Boneri standing in the doorway with the Roman sun warming his face.

Cecco withdrew into the house and opened the bruised parchment.

> *. . . I share this news only with you. Your master shall soon become a knight! No longer will the noble class disdain me! The gold-chain-wearing fumblers, the so-called artists of merit, that pezzo di merda Giovanni Baglione must recognize me as an equal. The cardinals, the landowners, the conti and contesse.*
>
> *Grand Master Wignacourt has procured permission from the pope for my induction into the Knights of Obedience. Pope Paul, of course, does not know it is*

*me. The grand master only referred to me as a man who
repents his actions having killed a man in a fight.*

> *At the moment, I am working on a canvas that will
be my greatest masterpiece:* The Beheading of St. John
the Baptist. *Such dimensions I've never attempted, but
I dream about how I shall fill that space . . . It shall lift
the gaze of every worshipper beyond the altar, beyond the
crucifix itself.*

Cecco looked out over the rooftops of Roma. He folded the letter,
his fingertips caressing the thick parchment.

*Who grinds his pigments now? Surely he must mix his own paints,
prepare his own gesso on the canvas. I have heard of the pages there of noble
families . . . they would have no training or aptitude for the task.*

Ah, but they will be young and nimble . . . eager to please.

Cecco looked down, realizing he was pinching the letter in his
hand, his sweaty hand smearing the ink.

*This is all the news I have had in four months. Damn him! I will share it
with Lena, these scraps of his life. They are a petty mouthful for the starving.*

Cecco set off to find Lena near the palazzo in Piazza Navona. She was
not there, though he found two other prostitutes sharing a handful of
roasted chestnuts. Their hands and teeth were blackened with char.

The women stopped eating as he approached them. One, a red-
haired woman, licked her fingers provocatively. Cecco noticed her swollen lip, turning slightly blue. The brunette picked the black bits of soot
from her teeth with her fingernail, studying Cecco.

"I look for Lena Antognetti."

"The girl's sick," said the brunette, her dark eyes glittering. "Has
been for weeks now."

"Sick?" said Cecco. "With what?"

The red-haired woman said, "Probably caught a chill standing in the wind, late at night—"

"*Merda!*" said the brunette. "She caught something evil from a foreigner, one of those French sailors, or worse, an Englishman. They's the ones who kill us with their diseases."

The redhead flicked her hand, dismissing her friend's words. Cecco smelled a musky odor rising from her body as she sidled close to him. "Now, you are a good-looking *ragazzo*. You want to spend some time with Lilliana?"

"Leave him alone, Lilli," said her dark-haired friend, a shawl barely concealing her olive-skinned cleavage. "He's looking for Lena. He is Caravaggio's boy."

"Doesn't hurt to have some fun, Giulia—"

"You'll find her in the Ortaccio di Ripetta, on Via dei Greci," said the brunette. "Ask there, and you'll find her. She's too sick to leave her bed."

"She's that ill? How does she feed her little boy now?"

Giulia shrugged. Cecco turned to leave.

"Wait," she said.

She dug a coin out of her bodice.

"Buy her some hot chestnuts from the vendor there," she said, pressing the warm quattrino into Cecco's hand. "Tell her Giulia and Lilli wish her well."

Lena's mother led Cecco up the narrow stairs. There was a sickly-sweet smell to the bedroom, even though the windows were flung open. Two pigeons stood on the edge of the windowsill.

"Cecco," whispered a soft voice. "You've come."

"Lena," he said, taking a moment to recognize the emaciated body. "I heard you were ill—"

Lena struggled up to her elbows, making the bed creak. She looked frantically past her visitor. "Has he come?"

It took Cecco a second to realize. "My master?" He shook his head. "No, Lena. He is far away. Now lie back."

"Far away?" she said, her voice trailing off. Her arms quivered under the exertion of sitting up. She fell back against the feather pillow.

"In Malta. He is painting the Knights of Malta."

"Malta! Is that Africa?"

"Almost."

"So far away," she said in a breathless voice.

"It is an incredible honor, Lena," Cecco said. "And he is safe from the reach of Roma."

Lena lay back, her hands crumpling together like a dying bird.

Cecco sat on the edge of her pallet.

She is so young. And dying.

"How is Antonio, your little one?"

"Antonio . . ." said Lena, a ghost of a smile racing across her face. "He is quite big and strong now. He helps his grandmother launder clothes in the Tiber." She began coughing, the spasm rocking her thin body. Cecco looked at her sunken chest where her voluptuous breasts used to strain at her bodice. "I can't look after him now."

"Of course not. I'm sure your mother adores his company."

"I'm afraid I am a burden on her."

Cecco looked away from her sunken eyes. He focused on the two pigeons at the open window.

Lena followed his focus. "Mamma says they are dirty birds, the pigeons. But they are my amusement here. I love to watch them touch beaks, coo, and strut. Sometimes they fly away together." She sought Cecco's hand, her fingers inching across the coverlet. "That's what I wish I could have done with Michele. Fly away."

Cecco squeezed her hand, feeling the sharp bones.

"I know, Lena. I know."

Chapter 42

"This beast of heat!" said Caravaggio, wiping the rivulets of sweat from his forehead and temples.

"I could open the shutters, Maestro," offered the young page Alessandro Costa. "The sea breeze would cool—"

"Leave them shut, damn you!" said Caravaggio. "It must be dark for the lanterns to cast the light—"

The heavy wooden door creaked open.

"What is this shouting?" said Grand Master Wignacourt. He glared first at Alessandro and then Caravaggio. "This is not behavior befitting a knight . . . or a knight in training."

Caravaggio glanced at his blank canvas. His lips quivered to answer, hot words bubbling on his spit.

But he remained silent.

"I have come, Maestro Caravaggio," said the grand master, "to offer you a chance to see Mdina. If you will accompany me, I think it would be good for your . . . nerves."

"What is there for me in Mdina? More rock? I'm trying to capture the spirit and breadth of this painting."

Wignacourt raised an eyebrow. "Mdina is the old capital of the Order of Malta before the construction of Valletta. It is an exquisite town of courtyards, fountains, and flowers."

"Flowers!" muttered Caravaggio under his breath.

"And I want to take you to see the grotto where the shipwrecked Saint Paul stayed under the succor extended by Publius."

"Grotto, you say?" said Caravaggio, glaring into the black gesso of his enormous canvas. "Saint Paul was housed in a grotto?"

"Along with Saint Luke, his accompanying friend and physician. You do know the Bible, do you not, Maestro Caravaggio?" said the grand master, sucking in his breath. "The Acts of the Apostles and the Gospel of Saint Luke?"

Caravaggio remained silent.

"For your education, which is sorely lacking for an apprentice knight," said Wignacourt sternly, "Apostle Paul was a prisoner being taken to Roma for trial. The ship carrying him and nearly three hundred others was shipwrecked along Malta's coast. All survived by swimming to land."

"But what of the grotto?"

Wignacourt held up his hand for silence. "'And later we learned that the island was called Malta. And the people who lived there showed us great kindness, and they made a fire and called us all to warm ourselves.' This is the Gospel of Saint Luke." The grand master bowed his head.

"Saint Paul took shelter in the grotto outside Mdina, hiding from the Romans," he continued. "The Maltese protected him. They said he had a great power—he was bitten by a viper but showed no effect."

Caravaggio tilted his head, staring at the pool of light cast by the lanterns.

"I think, Maestro," said Wignacourt, looking up at Caravaggio's vast blank canvas, "that the excursion out of this hot, dark room will do you good."

It was nearly dusk the following day when Grand Master Alof de Wignacourt and Caravaggio approached the ancient capital of Malta.

After two hours of travel in the rocking coach, the grand master pulled the curtains back from the window. He pointed to a limestone city perched atop a rocky mount, encircled by a great wall. Mdina was bathed in a soft yellow light of torches.

"There she is."

Caravaggio moved closer to the window as the coach jolted over the stone road. "It looks like paintings of Spain . . . or even Jerusalem."

"Mdina is many thousands of years old," said the grand master, swaying to the rocking carriage. "It was one of the first Roman territories to embrace Christianity."

Caravaggio looked out at the stone moat and the gate crowned with the banner of the Maltese Knights.

Two guards approached the carriage. Their flaming torches illuminated golden motes of spinning dust.

"Your Grace," said one, bowing low. "Welcome back to Mdina."

"Mdina's Palazzo Falson was built in the early thirteenth century," said Wignacourt. "There had once been a synagogue at the site."

"Jews here in Malta?" said Caravaggio.

"Malta has mixed the races for centuries," said the grand master. "Listen to the natives' language. Though it is mostly Arabic, there is a scattering of words from every European country."

Palazzo Falson's central courtyard with its graceful arches evoked Spanish influence. Tinkling fountains, bougainvillea spilling down the walls, white calla lilies and roses. The patio floor was an intricate mosaic.

"We will drink some tea," said the grand master. "Once you are refreshed, I will take you to the grottos."

As they waited for their tea, Wignacourt leaned toward the painter.

"Let me ask you, Maestro Caravaggio. Besides being beyond the reach of the pope and certain execution, why do you wish to become a knight of the Order of Malta?"

"Your Grace . . ."

"You owe me that much, Caravaggio. I risk the wrath of Pope Paul when he discovers that the man for whom I begged clemency is you. Is it only the safety you seek?"

"I want . . . I desire to be a knight. I want the right to carry a sword."

"Social class, then?"

"The honor, Grand Master. I once challenged a man—an artist!—to a duel. He refused, saying that I was beneath him. He was of noble birth and he would not lift a sword against me, as if my flesh were not good enough to meet his blade. That memory chews at my soul."

The crickets chirped in a pulsating chorus. A servant dressed in white linen brought in a tray of tea and small cakes. He poured the tea from the pot through a ceramic sieve, straining the mint leaves.

"*Grazie,*" said Wignacourt. "*Per favore*, serve my guest first."

Caravaggio accepted the cup, the steamy fragrance of mint scenting the garden air.

"You have the sin of Pride, Maestro Caravaggio. A brother of the holy order must renounce this sin."

Caravaggio set down his cup. "Has Cavaliere Roero renounced his sin, Grand Master?"

Wignacourt frowned. "What does Fra Roero have to do with this?"

"He taunts me endlessly about my humble birth. He calls me a Turk. He declares I will foul the order with my induction. That it is only the charity of the Colonnas and you, yourself, Grand Master, that allows me to be granted knighthood."

"I see," said Wignacourt. He sat quietly for a moment. He shook his head and began again. "Tell me, do you truly believe in God?"

"*Sì,*" said Caravaggio. "A cruel God who punishes."

"You are a man of the Old Testament, then?"

"Perhaps."

"I can see that trait in your paintings. All dark—but the flash of light. Perhaps the light is God?"

Caravaggio shrugged. "Forgive me, Grand Master. I do not know. It is what I see. The suffering . . ."

"The humanity too," said Wignacourt, stirring his tea with a silver spoon. "I saw what you captured in Martelli's portrait. Tell me, Caravaggio. I heard you scolding the pages in that suffocatingly hot room. I saw the great expanse of black—an empty canvas."

Caravaggio looked down at the calla lilies in the garden.

Wignacourt laid a hand on Caravaggio's sleeve. "Finish your tea, Maestro. I shall take you to the grottos of Saint Paul."

∽

Two Maltese guards with oil lamps led the grand master and Caravaggio down the millennia-old limestone steps. A single guard followed, his torch casting only a small pool of light behind the group.

Caravaggio felt the cool air meet his face, drying the sweat from his skin. He breathed deeply, his eyes scanning the cavern below him.

"This is where the Roman governor Publius sheltered Saint Paul, sixty years after the birth of Christ," said the grand master. "Paul cured the governor's father of a fatal disease. The Maltese were forever grateful."

Caravaggio reached out his hand to touch the cool rock wall.

Wignacourt nodded. "I will leave you now. Rodrigo! Stay here with the torch until the maestro is ready to retire. Then show him to his room."

The grand master climbed the steps accompanied by the men with oil lanterns. Caravaggio watched their shadows play and retreat against the stone.

He turned to the Maltese guard. The man kept his eyes focused on the grotto floor. Caravaggio retreated into the darkness.

"Look up at me, guard," said Caravaggio.

Rodrigo's jawline was taut. His eyes lifted and he looked Caravaggio in the eye.

"Have you ever killed a man?" asked Caravaggio from the shadows.

The guard moved his tongue over his front teeth, making his lips bulge. "I'm a guard working under the Order of Malta," he said, his voice hoarse. "We have Turkish prisoners. What do you think, Maestro?"

"I think you have the look of a killer. *Bene.* Look down as if you are going to behead a man."

"With what? A sword? A hatchet?"

"A sword."

"*Sì,*" said the guard. "I know how to do it."

Caravaggio's face grew animated. "*Davvero?* You have cut a man's head off?"

"More than one," the guard grunted. "But it's hard to sever the bones of the neck unless you have a proper sword. Not any sword will do—"

"How do you manage, then? If you've already swung and killed the man."

The guard narrowed his eyes. With a swift sweep of his free hand around his hip, he produced a sharp blade, its metal glinting in the torchlight.

"A *pugnale.* I always keep a sharp dagger in my sheath."

Caravaggio sat down on a rock, absorbing the words.

A dagger!

Back in Valletta, Caravaggio sealed himself in the limestone oratory of the cathedral. Rather than being soothed and rested by his excursion to

Mdina, the artist was short-tempered and edgy. He paced in the dark room, shifting his eyes from the leaping torchlight to the black gesso of the untouched canvas.

The two pages, Alessandro Costa and Nicholas de Paris Boissy, shifted nervously on their feet, their eyes fastened on the stone floor.

"Look here, Costa!" said Caravaggio, picking up a brush from the table. "Do you see the red paint still clinging to the bristles of this brush? The hairs are stiff and useless now!"

"Forgive me, I beg you," said Alessandro, his eyes wide with fright. "It is only a speck, Maestro—"

"A speck? A speck! Do you know what this 'speck' can do to my work?"

"I'm—I'm sorry, Maestro!" the boy stammered. "I can't see that well in this dim room."

"Then clean the brushes outside!" said Caravaggio, flinging his hand in disgust. "But don't let the sun scorch the hairs. It will split the ends, render them useless."

Caravaggio ran his fingers through his tangled hair in a fit of fury. He stared into the vast darkness of gesso.

The pages watched in silence, trembling. Suddenly, the maestro squinted, straining his eyes into the middle of the empty room.

"What does he see?" whispered Alessandro. "There is nothing there."

Nicholas swallowed, shaking his head. He saw the artist's mouth move silently.

Caravaggio reached for his brush, dipped it into the paint on his palette. His hand shot out, making a bold stroke on the canvas.

The boys stood riveted on the spot, paralyzed by both fear and fascination, watching Caravaggio work.

And so it began.

Each day, they saw images appear one by one against the black background. The shine of a man's forehead, the light on his finger pointing to a bronze platter. A girl stoops, holding the plate ready to receive the severed head. The muscled back of the executioner, his left hand gripping Saint John by the hair, while his right hand retrieves a dagger from his hip sheath as he prepares to sever the sinews of the saint's neck.

The pages stood in the gloom of the studio, their eyes wide as they stared at the emerging images.

"There's magic in his hand," said Alessandro.

"I'm not sure it is God's magic," said Nicholas. The boy's hand flew to his forehead, hastily making the sign of the cross.

"Be still, page!" said Caravaggio. "Your shadow is interfering with the torchlight."

The two boys moved back in unison, bumping into each other as they retreated farther into the shadows.

The Maltese servants came around the knights' table with steaming tureens of *alijotta*. The fish soup, studded liberally with garlic and seasoned tomato, breathed steam into Caravaggio's face. He drew in the aroma and smiled.

"Serve him last, you fool!" shouted Cavaliere Roero across the table. "He's no knight!"

The servant stopped in midserving, looking from Caravaggio to Roero.

Malaspina raised his hand, silencing Roero. "Serve our illustrious guest, Luca. Fra Roero, I will remind you of our knightly manners."

The servant nodded, giving Caravaggio an extra ladleful until his bowl was brimming.

"Your point about Maestro Caravaggio's standing has reminded me to make an announcement to our company," said Malaspina. He laid a supporting hand on the table and rose to his feet.

"I am honored to address our auberge," said Malaspina. "I have an important announcement to make regarding our esteemed guest, Maestro Michelangelo Merisi da Caravaggio. You know him as a talented painter—soon you shall know him as a brother."

A buzz erupted in the dining hall, then cheers.

The old knight raised his glass. He looked at Caravaggio and then to Roero.

"Our grand master has procured the special right from our Pope Paul to instate Maestro Caravaggio as a member of the Knights of Obedience!"

"Impossible," hissed Roero under his breath. "He is a murderer. And a nobody!"

The old knight at the head of the table could not hear the grumbling among the cheers and rabble. "Raise your glasses with me to our future brother in knighthood of the Order of St. John!"

"*Salute!*" shouted the knights.

Roero glared at Caravaggio. The knight gripped the edge of the table, his fingernails digging into the damask tablecloth. He leaned forward, hissing, "You struck a fatal blow to a fallen man, showing him no mercy."

Caravaggio's lip twisted. "I had no mercy to give."

"He was my friend—"

"Your friend? And yet you didn't defend him," said Caravaggio, sneering. "You hid in the shadows like a cowering dog."

Roero bared his teeth. "A Knight of Malta cannot brawl in the streets of Roma! I would have been expelled."

"I'm sure the grand master would be interested in your great friendship with a notorious Roman pimp. And your cowardice."

Roero stood up from the table, throwing his greasy, wine-stained napkin in Caravaggio's face. He stormed out of the room, cursing.

Chapter 43

The colossal height and breadth of the new painting made its evolution visible from any point of the oratory. The grand master visited daily, watching Caravaggio's progress.

One day, Grand Master Wignacourt and Malaspina entered the hall and found Caravaggio alone, cleaning his brushes.

Malaspina stared openmouthed in wonder. His whisper was barely audible, a reverent sigh. "It is a masterpiece."

"It is finished," said Caravaggio, his voice echoing in the stone chamber.

Grand Master Wignacourt walked toward the artist, his eyes still riveted on the canvas. He studied the body of Saint John, the muted colors conveying his death. A pool of blood spilled from the last pulse of his veins.

"You have surpassed all expectations," said the grand master. He pulled the artist to his breast in an embrace. "This painting shall endure when we are but dust."

The grand master felt the artist stiffen. Releasing him, Wignacourt continued.

"I've come to tell you that you are to be confirmed imminently as a Knight of Obedience. We have set the date. July fourteenth. Here in front of your miraculous creation."

Caravaggio bent down on one knee, kissing the grand master's ring.

"My son, you have done our order proud," said Wignacourt as Caravaggio rose.

"This was always my intention," said Caravaggio. "Your Excellency, excuse me."

The artist walked to the massive painting. Malaspina and Wignacourt watched as he picked up his brush, selected a paint from his palette, and made a quick movement with his hand.

He stepped back, stared at his painting, and turned back to Wignacourt.

"I shall never forget this day," said Caravaggio, bowing to the grand master.

He turned to leave, his steps echoing through the long corridors of the church.

Malaspina called to the grand master. "Alof! Come. Look what he has written in the spilled blood of Saint John."

Wignacourt approached the painting. He studied the handwriting in red. "F. Michelangelo."

"Fra Michelangelo," he said, nodding. "A knight of the Order of St. John."

Chapter 44

At the entrance to the Italian auberge, a drunken Cavaliere Roero roared at Alessandro Costa. "You wash the murderer's brushes, that heathen artist. Does he touch your private parts when you fetch his paints? Fondle you in his studio?"

Alessandro's face drew up in rage, his nostrils pinched in fury. "You are drunk, Cavaliere Roero," he said. "I suggest you take yourself to bed before you fall down and injure yourself."

"Oh, go back to your killer and the sniveling pack of pages who serve him."

"I will indeed return to the palazzo of Grand Master Wignacourt," said Alessandro. "I will not stand for anyone to insult the Costa name!"

Alessandro stepped from the dim interior of the auberge into the dazzling sun reflecting off the limestone streets. He squinted at the sniggering Castilian knights who were gathered across the road at the entrance to their auberge. They had overheard the exchange between the knight from Piemonte and the Roman apprentice, for the noonday shutters with their open slats did nothing to contain the noise and gossip of the auberge.

The grand master's carriage turned the corner, the driver having to pull up the horses to keep from running over Alessandro. Caravaggio stepped out, with Nicholas de Paris Boissy helping him tote his satchels of pigments and brushes.

"Avoid Cavaliere Roero at all costs," muttered Costa. "He is in a filthy mood and his tongue is sharp as a viper's bite."

"Ha! And my mood is all light with splendid news," said Caravaggio. He looked up and saw a green shutter push open and the sagging, drunken face of Roero looking down.

"I say my mood is light, page!" shouted Caravaggio, lifting his voice and looking squarely into the eyes of Roero. "Light as the *schiuma* atop a glass of prosecco. For soon I shall enter the Order of St. John." Caravaggio beamed up at the drunken knight. "What say you to that, Fra Roero, my brother?"

"Brother!" roared Roero. "Don't dare call me that. Ever!"

Roero slammed the shutters closed, sending a flock of pigeons flapping to the heavens.

Michelangelo Merisi da Caravaggio stood before the entire corps of the knights, his own painting of the beheading of Saint John the Baptist looming over him.

The artist knelt at Grand Master Wignacourt's feet. The banner of the Maltese Cross of Service was held on a gold staff above his head. The Sword of Commitment was held by Malaspina at Wignacourt's right.

"As you do solemnly swear to serve the tenets of the order and never to bring stain upon our fraternity," pronounced Grand Master Alof de Wignacourt. He placed the chain and gold cross around the artist's neck.

"I pronounce you Knight Merisi da Caravaggio of the Maltese Order of Obedience," the grand master said. "Go forth and serve!"

Wignacourt watched Caravaggio rise to his feet, triumph glowing in the artist's eyes. The new knight looked past the grand master, his eyes focused on the vast painting beyond.

"*Sì,*" whispered the grand master, turning to the painting. "I am eternally grateful for this magnificent gift."

Caravaggio's face quivered. Muscles that were seldom used stretched awkwardly in a rare smile.

After the long ceremony, a celebratory feast was spread in the knights' vast dining hall. The bread was passed, each knight breaking off a chunk from the long loaf. The pungent aroma of garlic from the *alijotta* wafted across the auberge table as the Italian knights were served by Maltese footmen.

"What are the next courses?" grunted Cavaliere Roero. He blew on a spoonful of soup.

"The next is *timbana,*" said the footman, his face lighting up.

"Baked macaroni pie—any farmworker can do as well in a tavern!" said Roero.

The Maltese native dipped his head. His face burned at the insult to one of the island's specialties.

"Tell us more," said Caravaggio.

"Thank you, Cavaliere," said the servant, bowing, looking away from Roero. "*Timbana* is followed by *stuffat tal-fenek,* studded with laurel leaves, capers, garlic, and tomatoes. The chef's specialty. The meat falls off the bone!"

"Rabbit stew! Peasant fare," Roero grumbled. "And more damned garlic. How I hate that stinking bulb. And the Maltese are the worst!"

The footman's face colored, his jaw muscles showing beneath his skin.

"Vile food served by a Maltese peasant whose skin is scorched dark by the heathen cultures that spawned him," muttered Roero.

"It seems you don't like much about Malta," said Caravaggio from across the table.

"Shut up, you scrawler," said Roero.

"What did you call me?"

"You scrawl like a crab drags tracks across the sand. Then you pass it off as art!"

"His painting of our holy patron John the Baptist is a miracle," said Fra Giovanni Piero de Ponte, angling the tines of his fork at Roero. "You can't deny that, Giovanni!"

"He dupes us all!" shouted Roero. "He's a filthy murderer!"

"He's a genius!" said Piero de Ponte, his fork stabbing the air. The commotion attracted the attention of the other knights at the table. The elderly Malaspina, presiding over the table, asked the church organist next to him, "What are they arguing about? I cannot hear."

"Fra Roero says Merisi is not fit to be a knight, Your Excellency."

"Fra Merisi," said Malaspina, giving the organist a withering look. "He is our brother now. What does the church deacon Fra Piero de Ponte say in response?"

The organist sneered. He hated the deacon, who declined to pay the musicians the wages they felt they deserved.

"Fra Piero urges Merisi to defend himself."

"Does he?" said Malaspina, rising from his chair. "Brothers! Stop at once!" he roared. "May I remind you, Fra Roero, that Fra Michelangelo Merisi is a knight now. He is our brother."

"I'll have no brother who murders and connives!" said Roero in a hoarse whisper only those close to him could hear. "He's below all of us, this peasant from Caravaggio! A tuppence knight who sups from the cesspools of Roma—"

Caravaggio threw down his fork and knife. "Come out to the street and say that to me, you filthy swine!"

Piero de Ponte pulled on his friend's sleeve. "Don't let him trick you, Michele," he said. "If you threaten a duel, you'll be thrown in the dungeon, the *guva*. Fra Malaspina will be bound to report you."

Caravaggio stood, his body tense with loathing. He glanced at Malaspina, who was still standing, one hand on the table supporting his weight. From the French table, he saw Grand Master Wignacourt turn his head toward the commotion.

"Cavalieri!" said Malaspina. "We will tolerate no ill will, threats, or insults in this auberge. Do you hear me? Please take your seat, Fra Merisi."

Caravaggio glared at Roero, his hand quivering near the sheath of his dagger. He ignored the voice of Malaspina, the tugs on his sleeve. His mouth filled with spit.

"Don't be a fool, Merisi! Sit down," hissed De Ponte. "You are taking the bait like a stupid fish. You give proof to Malaspina you should not be a knight if you act now. *Aspetta!* Wait, wait!"

Caravaggio eased himself back into his chair, nodding stiffly to Malaspina.

"You did right," whispered the knight at his left, Giovanni Battista Scaravello from Turin. "You aren't the only knight who despises Roero. He will pay in time."

"But not in front of Malaspina and Wignacourt," said another two places down. Caravaggio recognized Fra Giulio Accarigi, a knight from Siena who had been imprisoned several times for violent behavior. Accarigi gestured for Caravaggio to sit back to exchange words behind the torso of Scaravello, where Roero could not hear his words.

Accarigi's eyes glinted with hatred. "Bide your time, Fra Michele. Roero has made many enemies among us."

Caravaggio nodded and sat back straight. He picked up his fork again and attempted to eat.

Fra Roero lifted his lip in disgust. He whispered hoarsely, "The Tuppence Knight, a peasant from Caravaggio. Hardly a *huomo di*

Valento. You painted your way into this auberge, you miserable peasant. Everyone knows you are beneath contempt."

Caravaggio's jaw went rigid, his fingers clenching his fork. His nostrils flared, his breath hoarse and rapid.

Roero pushed his bowl of soup away, picking his teeth with his fingernail. He smirked at his foe across the table. "You have quite the temper, artist," said Roero, laughing. "You'll land in the *guva* yet."

Giovanni Pecci, a fellow novice from Siena, laid a hand on Caravaggio's shoulder, inducing the artist to turn toward him. "You did well to stand down from Roero," he whispered.

"Did I?" snarled Caravaggio. "*Miserabile porco!* Miserable pig."

"Michele, you risked imprisonment and even your knighthood with Malaspina as witness to a crime."

"No one speaks to me that way," said Caravaggio. "I will have revenge."

Pecci nodded. "You will have it. There is a gathering—"

Novice Pecci was interrupted by the angry shouts of men, several languages being spoken at once.

"Those are the musicians," Pecci said.

A motley crew of church musicians—Italian, French, and Spanish—had gathered. They spoke, gesticulating wildly with emotion.

"What are they so angry about?" Caravaggio said.

"They are threatening to strike. The elders of the order have refused their request for higher pay. The one who is stirring them up is the organist—Fra Prospero Coppini. He is a friend of Roero's."

"Then he is an enemy of mine," said Caravaggio through his teeth.

Caravaggio was ushered into the great hall, where Grand Master Wignacourt was standing looking out through the blinding light reflected off the stones of Valletta.

"Sit down, Fra Merisi," he said, pointing to a chair. "I hear you and Fra Roero were at each other's throats last night."

"Roero insulted me," said Caravaggio. "I was prepared to defend my honor."

"Fra Roero," said Wignacourt sternly. "He is your brother in the Order of St. John!"

"He called me a tuppence knight, not fit for the holy order. A murderer—"

"And you called him out. Challenged him?"

"Of course!" said Caravaggio, rising from his chair. "No one—"

"Sit down!" Wignacourt roared. "You seem to forget, Fra Michele, what an honor it is to be a knight of the Order of St. John. Under the brotherhood's banner, even the pope may not touch you. You are protected from the *bando capitale*."

The old warrior narrowed his eyes.

"But if you defy the laws of the Knights of Malta, you will be punished. You will be defrocked, humiliated, and possibly executed. The fish will feed on your bones. Do you understand?"

Caravaggio nodded.

"Do you understand?" thundered Wignacourt.

"Sì, ho capito," said Caravaggio. "I understand."

"And there will be nothing I can do to protect you," said Wignacourt, locking eyes with Caravaggio. "As grand master, I must adhere to the law of the sacred order."

Wignacourt rubbed furiously at his temples.

"Fra Michele," he said, "has there ever been anyone or anything you've held sacred? Something you would never compromise?"

Caravaggio shrugged. "Art. Art I hold sacred."

"Anything beyond that? Something you loved more than Art?"

Caravaggio took a deep breath, exhaling slowly. "No."

"No lover? No friend, no principle. Perhaps God, damn you?"

Caravaggio thought of his painting of Lena in ecstasy. His mind flashed on Cecco as the angel in *Love Conquers All*. The tenderness of both lovers, their devotion to him. For a moment he hesitated—but he knew the truth.

"No," he answered.

Wignacourt walked to the window again. Over the rooftops of Valletta he could see the deep blue of the sea. "That is the great fault of your nature. I truly regret it," he said. "And yet you have created a masterpiece here. Long after I am dead, *The Beheading of St. John the Baptist* will be the siren calling the faithful—perhaps even the infidels— to Malta to witness your miracle."

Caravaggio looked down at his hands, folding and unfolding his fingers.

"What do I do with you?" the grand master continued. "A miracle worker, yet the most selfish, destructive man I have ever met!"

Caravaggio shrugged, then lifted his chin in defiance. "And the best artist you'll ever meet."

The grand master drew in a sharp breath. "Get out!" he snapped. "Return to the auberge. I warn you, if you are charged with dueling, you will be subject to the laws of the brotherhood. Stay away from Roero."

"*Grazie,*" said Caravaggio. He stood up from the chair and made his way down the long hall coffered with paintings.

The grand master watched the stocky figure walk the length of the hall, the heels of his boots clicking an erratic beat. Even after Caravaggio had left, Wignacourt stared down the long corridor.

Fra Giovanni Pecci knocked on Caravaggio's door.

"Who is it?"

"Novice Pecci," said the young knight. "Open the door."

Caravaggio had been resting in his shuttered room, darkened against the oppressive Mediterranean sun. Pecci pinched his nose at the acrid smell of sweat.

"*Dio!*" said Pecci. "*Che puzza!* It stinks like a brothel in here, Merisi!"

"So leave," growled Caravaggio, flopping down again on his bed.

"I've come to invite you to a gathering," said Pecci. He opened the shutters to air out the room. The soft twilight colored the limestone of the Castilian auberge facing them. The blocks of stone were the color of butter.

"Who is hosting this gathering?" asked Caravaggio.

"The organist of the Conventual Church of St. John," said Pecci, grinning.

"*Cazzo!*" said Caravaggio, sitting up. "That bastard is in league with Roero."

"Exactly. And a few of us—who despise Roero and are sick of the whining demands of the musicians—are going to pay a surprise visit. Our church deacon Fra de Ponte expressly asked you to join us."

Caravaggio ran his fingers through his matted hair, which was soaked in sweat. Slowly, a smile grew, malicious and bright. "It sounds perfect, Fra Pecci," he said, rising from his bed. "Let me strap on my sword."

It was midnight by the time the six rowdy knights finished their wine in a tavern by the seaport. The three novice knights, Caravaggio, Pecci, and Francesco Benzi, were swearing revenge for Roero's verbal assaults and insults. Two senior Knights of Justice, Fra Giulio Accarigi and Fra Giovanni Battista Scaravello, certainly hated Rodomonte Roero, but they were equally enraged by the threat of striking musicians, under the leadership of the organist, Fra Prospero Coppini.

"They threaten to strike on the feast of Saint John! The treasonous swine—the day of our patron saint!"

Along with them was the hot-tempered deacon, Fra Giovanni Piero de Ponte, who carried a *sclopo ad rotas*, a pistol.

The stone streets on the summer evening were still crowded with knights who were agitated in the sweltering heat. Shouts and curses echoed and, from the dark shadows, grunts of men and moans of prostitutes. A rivulet of wine wove its meandering course along the limestone blocks of St. John's Street where a cask had been broken open and its red Gellewza poured forth.

"This way," said Fra de Ponte. "You can hear the music! They give away for free what they will not donate to our church of Saint John!"

"I hear accordions," said Fra Scaravello, frowning. "And tambourines."

The strains of a resonant male voice rose, singing incomprehensible words.

"They've included some of the islanders."

"Let's pay them a visit," said Fra de Ponte, banging his fist against the door of the organist's house.

A servant opened the door a crack. He saw the Maltese crosses on the tunics of the men and opened the door wider. *"Buonasera, Cavalieri,"* he said.

From the top of the stairs, a voice bellowed, *"Chi è?"*

Fra Coppini descended the stairs and saw the face of De Ponte. *"Chiudete la porta!"* he shouted. *Close the door!*

The startled servant pushed the door closed with all his might, pinching Fra de Ponte's fingers.

"Miserabile porco!" screamed De Ponte, jumping back. *Miserable pig!* "We'll break your door down! Brothers! Find something for a battering ram!"

The knights scattered in all directions.

Benzi and Caravaggio ran toward the nearby fort of St. Elmo. There, among other artifacts, was a small cannon that had been used in the siege of 1565.

"If it was good enough to fire the severed heads of Turks across the bay of Valletta, it's good enough to batter down the door of a pig-fucking organist! Pecci!" Caravaggio called down the street. "Come here and help."

Together, they rolled the rusted cannon down the street toward the organist's house.

"*Perfetto!*" said De Ponte. "All of you—grab behind. You, Caravaggio! Direct the blow toward the lock."

"Heave-ho!" shouted Scaravello. The six men picked up the small cannon and rammed the door.

"Again!" said De Ponte, gasping. "Again!"

After three blows, there was the splintering of wood. The knights spilled into the entryway.

Fra Giovanni Roero stood at the foot of the stairway. "You swine!" he shouted. "What is the meaning of this?"

"You didn't invite us to your gathering," said De Ponte. "An oversight, I'm sure." He brandished his gun.

"Get the hell out of here!" shouted Roero, drawing his sword. He looked at Caravaggio.

"You are behind this, you miserable beggar!" said Roero, his eyes narrowing to slits. "You bastard knight, you scrawling con artist!"

Caravaggio reached for his sword.

"You fornicator of children!" said Roero, brandishing his sword. He waved the tip at Caravaggio, urging him on. "Everyone knows . . . you and that Sicilian Minniti. And then you and your 'apprentice'—"

In a flashing instant, Caravaggio's blade sliced across Roero's face. The knight pressed his open hand against his cheek, pulling it away bloody.

"I'll kill you with the next—"

A shot rang out before Caravaggio finished his sentence. Roero clutched his shoulder, screaming in agony.

Caravaggio turned. He saw Deacon de Ponte holding the smoking gun, the mouths of the conspirators hanging open.

The sound of the gunshot brought knights running from all directions. The slap and clatter of boots rang against the limestone roads.

"Run!" shouted Fra Scaravello. "We'll all end up in the *guva* for this!"

The men ran, scattering into the dark, narrow streets of Valletta.

But Malta was a small island in the middle of the sea. There was nowhere to hide.

∾

Caravaggio—along with the other six knights—was arrested and taken to Fort Sant'Angelo. He was thrown by himself into a *guva*, a bell-shaped dungeon dug deep into the limestone. The only opening was a trapdoor in the ceiling. The steep walls made escape impossible.

Caravaggio settled down wedged against the rock wall. He lay his head in the fetid straw, smelling of the sweat and shit of men incarcerated before him. Mercifully, it was cool underground. Despite the fierce August heat above, the artist shivered and pulled his woolen tunic tighter around him.

The wooden trapdoor above creaked open, and daylight flooded down on him. Two faces stared at him, shiny with sweat.

"You the one who painted Saint John the Baptist?" said a round-faced young guard.

"*Sì.* I'm Michelangelo Merisi da Caravaggio."

"See, I told you, Rafaello!" said the man to his companion. "You are a genius, Fra Merisi! I am Pietro dei Marconi. And this is Rafaello dei Zuccharo."

"How long will I be here?" said Caravaggio.

"Years, I would think," said Pietro. "You'll know for sure after you stand trial. They say you injured a knight. The Conte della Vezza."

"I'm innocent," called Caravaggio from the pit. "I was there, but I did not fire the pistol."

"Too bad for you, Fra Merisi," said Dei Marconi, looking down with sympathy. "The justices are harsh with novices."

"Maybe you can paint down there?" Dei Zuccharo laughed. "Can you see masterpieces in the dark?"

"Leave me alone," said Caravaggio.

"Forgive him, Maestro. He has not seen your miracles," said Dei Marconi. "I have. Your Saint John the Baptist made me fall to my knees."

"Stop throwing compliments to the prisoners," said Dei Zuccharo. The trapdoor slammed shut.

Caravaggio felt the circular sloping walls with his hands, the limestone cool and dry under his fingertips.

He could hear the muffled rattle of sand blowing against the trapdoor, the scuffing of boots above, muted voices occasionally. Nothing else.

A thunderous noise echoed in the chamber—someone stomping with heavy boots on the wooden trapdoor.

"Are you enjoying yourself, Tuppence Knight?" called a mocking voice from above. "Make the most of every day you have. Soon enough, they will drag you out of there, stuff you in a sack, and throw you into the sea to drown . . . like the vermin you are."

"Roero, you bastard! I'll kill you!"

"Of course you will," said the voice from above. Then more thunderous, deafening kicks on the trapdoor.

And finally, the sound of laughter, fading as Fra Giovanni Rodomonte Roero strode away.

A shaft of light blinded him each day as food and water were lowered in a bucket on a tarred rope. The rope was encrusted with dried seaweed and smelled of salt water. Caravaggio pulled it to his nose, craving a smell other than the dirty straw, sodden with piss and shit.

Caravaggio grew pale, a greenish cast to his skin.

"You don't look much like a knight," muttered a guard, looking down at him. "More like something rotting on the beach at low tide."

"Where is Dei Marconi?" asked Caravaggio. "You are not my guard."

"Business in Valletta. He was called to the grand master's palazzo."

"Why?"

The guard shrugged. "How should I know?"

"Any news at all?"

"News? Your fellow knight Piero de Ponte, the one with the gun, is in the *guva* adjacent. The other knights are standing trial. Yours is coming up."

"When?"

"Soon enough, I think. When they finish dealing with the lesser accomplices."

"I didn't—"

"Save it for the Knights of Justice!"

The guard let the trapdoor slam closed, plunging the cell once more into coal dark.

In the black matte of absolute darkness, Caravaggio hallucinated. He saw himself decapitated like Saint John the Baptist. He thought of Lena, he thought of Cecco.

"Cecco," he murmured. He remembered how the boy would wake him from his nightmares, shaking his shoulders until he regained consciousness.

The darkness lay heavy on him, a palpable force. His eyes saw black gesso, a blank canvas yearning for his brush.

He saw the image he was to paint, the gash of red, the whites of the eyes. He saw himself holding his own bloody head, offering it up as a trophy.

"No," shouted Caravaggio. *"No!"*

Day after day, Caravaggio's mind drifted.

At unpredictable times—all time was unpredictable in the eternal darkness—the deafening stamping would fill the *guva*, pounding into his head, followed by the mocking voice from above.

"Enjoy every day, Tuppence Knight. The end is closer. The sea is calling for you."

Shapes and forms shifted in the gloom. Lines merged, colors—especially red—bled into the image of Lena, the ecstasy of Mary. In the darkness his finger reached out, tracing the outline of her neck, head thrown back.

"I abandoned you," he said aloud. "And Cecco."

A shaft of bright light pierced the mantle of darkness. Caravaggio threw a hand in front of his eyes, protecting them. Blinking rapidly, he squinted up.

"Cecco?" he mumbled.

"The *guva* is taking its toll," said a voice. "He is a ranting madman."

A rope ladder was thrown down. A man who Caravaggio vaguely recognized descended. The incense of the church clung to his clothes.

"You don't know me, do you? The *guva* has snatched your wits," said the man.

"I painted a canvas for you," muttered Caravaggio. "It was . . ."

"A sleeping cupid, *amorino dormiente*. *Sì*, Fra Merisi. I am Fra Francesco dell'Antella, secretary to Grand Master Wignacourt."

Dell'Antella looked up at the mouth of the *guva* where the guard hovered, watching. "Guard. Send down a lantern. Then seal the door for the hour. I want no disturbance."

After the lantern was lowered and the hatch closed, Dell'Antella leaned close and whispered, "I have a plan to discuss."

∽

The trapdoor opened barely enough for strong hands to pull the prisoner out into the moonless night. The hinges, smelling of the mutton grease that had been rubbed on them, pivoted silently as the hatch was closed.

A dark-skinned man dressed in black helped the prisoner steady himself. He spoke in a Maltese accent.

"Come with me."

"You are?"

"No name," he whispered. "Hurry!"

"Buona fortuna," whispered the *guva* guard, Pietro dei Marconi.

Caravaggio nodded. He was overwhelmed by the fresh sea air. The taste and scent of salt stung his nostrils. The darkness of night seemed merely a shadow to his eyes, so accustomed to pitch black. He saw no other guard in the courtyard.

"We must hurry," said the dark-skinned stranger. Stay by my side."

Side by side, they walked through the dark, weaving in and out of narrow passageways, stopping often while the Maltese guide peered around a corner and Caravaggio held his breath. Finally, they stopped by the rampart. Caravaggio could hear the waves far below, lapping against the fortress wall.

The man in black pulled a coil of rope out of the bag he carried. He swiftly knotted one end to an iron ring in the wall.

"There's enough rope here to reach the water," he whispered. "The wall is slanted—a little. Hold on to the rope, and you can almost walk down to the water."

"Walk?" Caravaggio stared into the darkness below.

"It won't be easy. But you'll be free. Just hold tight to the rope. If you fall, the guards will hear you hit the water and they'll be after you." He stopped and Caravaggio could see his white teeth gleam in the dark. "But don't worry about the guards. If you lose your grip, the fall will certainly kill you."

The artist reached out and gripped the man's shoulder, as if to show his strength. The man nodded.

"There is a boat waiting there right now. The boatman will give you a purse with some money and take you to a felucca bound for Sicily."

"Where in Sicily?"

The Maltese man shook his head. "Too many questions. May God answer all in time."

Caravaggio tugged on the rope, the jute fibers biting into his hands. "Who sent you? Who is helping me?"

"As I said, Maestro. You ask too many questions. *Va' via!* Go! Silently. Now!"

Chapter 45

Monte Piccolo

After a night of bad dreams, Lucia woke with the uneasy feeling that there was someone in her apartment. She knew there couldn't be anyone there. Her door was double-locked and—she dredged her hazy memory of the night before—Vittore had been outside in the dark and he'd told her he'd be there all night, keeping an eye on things.

So she rolled over and tried to get back to sleep. But today was the day she was going to call that newspaper reporter. Moto had told her she was crazy. That she was signing her own death warrant. She'd told him not to be dramatic, but she'd given him two extra days. Now she had to act. She remembered they'd quarreled last night. Well, he had only himself to blame. She had to do what she had to do. Now.

No more sleep.

She opened her eyes—and barely stifled a scream.

"It was here when I woke up. Right there. Staring at me."

Lucia hadn't turned her head when Moto and Professor Richman walked into her apartment. Her phone calls to them had been sufficiently urgent that the professor had ridden across town on the back of Moto's Vespa, but now that they were there, Lucia's attention stayed focused—riveted—on the painting. *The Judas Kiss*. Completely out of place. Sitting on the floor, leaning against the battered table, cloaked in its centuries of dirt. On the left side of the painting, Jesus stood, staring out, his face serene, suffused with holiness, transcendent, not the face of a mortal man. Beside him, Judas leaned in to deliver the fatal kiss, his face, too, a caricature: greedy, evil, gloating at the destruction he was causing. Behind them stood an apostle, his face a mask as well: an official saintly version of horror and despair.

For a long time, the professor and Moto stood silently, staring at the painting.

"I don't know." Lucia's voice was quiet; she might have been talking to herself. "That night, in the warehouse, in the dark. I could hardly see it. But I could feel it. It felt alive." She held her hand horizontally in front of her face, as if she were trying to block out the painted faces. "The bodies. The hands. The way Judas is leaning in, grabbing Jesus's shoulder. I could feel his hand on my shoulder."

Another long silence.

"But now, here, in the light. It's not the same. I can see everything—but I can't feel anything. Maybe it's . . . I don't know . . . not genius, not Michele. Just a painting."

Professor Richman walked over to the painting and crouched down to examine it, holding his breath, his nose almost touching the canvas.

He straightened up and took a step back, lurching as his knee almost gave way. He stretched his back with a groan.

"I'm too old for this. Never mind. We all know I'm not an expert, but the work on these faces is very different from the rest of the painting. It's all old. It's all dirty. But the faces. Not only the way they're idealized. The brushstrokes are different. Smoother, actually. More careful. I can almost see what you mean about the bodies. They're stronger."

"I don't know." Lucia's voice was still small.

Moto broke in.

"You don't have to know. We have the painting now. They can clean it. They can X-ray it. They can do whatever they do. We have the history—scraps of history, anyway. They have the science. Maybe together . . ."

"Maybe."

"How did it get here?" The professor changed the subject.

"I don't know. I told you. I woke up and it was here."

"Hard to believe you slept right through it."

"I know. That's not like me. But . . . I don't know . . ." She closed her eyes. The vertical crease appeared between her brows. Then she shook her head. "I don't remember anything special about last night. Except"—she stopped for a minute, her eyes narrowed, and she shook her head—"a lot of bad dreams."

"And then you woke up."

"To this."

The professor walked back to the painting and reached out.

"Don't touch it!" Lucia's voice had a ragged edge. "I don't want to disturb anything until we figure out what to do."

"'What to do'?"

"I can't call the carabinieri and tell them I've got the painting. All of a sudden. It just showed up. They'll never believe me. It doesn't make sense."

"*Sì. Certo,*" said Moto, walking over to the window, opening it and looking out onto the piazza. He turned back to Lucia. "But if you're going to figure out what to tell the police, you need to figure it out fast. There are two carabinieri heading this way right now."

Lucia hurried to the window and looked out. The two policemen were striding across the piazza, heading straight for her building. As they reached the sidewalk, Vittore emerged from a doorway and rushed over to them.

His voice, filled with officious enthusiasm, rose up to the apartment. "*Signori, è una bella giornata, non è vero?*"

In fact, the day was far from beautiful. It was gray and cold, and a biting wind blew through the old stone village. But Vittore was undaunted by mere reality—or the fact that the two policemen didn't seem interested in stopping to chat with him.

"To what do we owe the honor of your presence in our humble village?" he pressed on. "Surely we have no criminal activity here to merit your attention. As the local officer of the law, certainly I would know if there was anything amiss."

The two carabinieri muttered to one another for a moment and then turned their attention to the local cop, their voices still low, but audible through the open window above. "Three men were found dead, killed in a car crash a few kilometers from here. They wore monk's habits, but they had obviously been drinking. It's very strange."

"Indeed!" Vittore lowered his voice to match theirs, but his exclamation was still clear in the cold air. "But stranger still that it would bring you here."

"Yes. Well . . ." The carabiniere paused, then went on. "The driver of the car had a slip of paper in his pocket with this address on it. And an apartment number."

There was a moment of silence while he showed something to Vittore.

"Yes, of course," the local *poliziotto* said. "The American. *Una bella signorina.* But"—and now his voice rose—"I have something important to tell you. I was here last night, all night. On duty. Keeping the peace, as is my responsibility."

"Yes, yes. I'm sure it is." The carabiniere did not care.

"And I saw two men hurrying across the piazza, carrying something large. And they were carrying it to this building."

"To this building? Are you sure?" Suddenly, he was much more interested.

"Absolutely. If they were carrying something out, I would have stopped them."

"Are you certain?" There was suspicion in the carabiniere's voice.

"Please, my honored fellow officer of the law, I am sworn to keep the peace and tell the truth. That is what I saw."

"So . . . let's see what we find."

Above, in the apartment, they could hear the street door open and slam shut and then the heavy footsteps on the stairs.

Lucia turned to face the door, and Professor Richman stepped around her, grabbed the frame of the painting, and tilted it forward, away from the table, before she could stop him.

"Nothing on the back," he said, leaning the painting carefully back against the table. "No message. No *poemetto*. Nothing but dirty canvas." He paused for a moment and then couldn't help adding, because he was Professor Aristotle Rafael Richman, "Tabula rasa."

In the main room of the big stone house, looking out over the Sicilian hills, two men sat together in conversation. One was gray-haired. The other looked young enough to be his son.

The younger man shook his head. *"Non capisco."* *I don't understand.*

It was midday, the sun was bright. With just the two of them there, the older man was willing to say more.

"Era sinza valuri." *It was worthless.*

"Mah . . ." *But . . .*

"Ppi nnuautri! Sì è falsu. Sinza valuri. Sì è veru. Ancura sinza valuri." *For us! If it's fake. Worthless. If it's real. Still worthless.*

He paused to see if the younger man understood. But he still seemed puzzled. So the old man finished the lesson.

"Comu putimmu dimustrari ca è veru?" *How can we prove it's real?*

Now the younger man nodded.

"Assai attenzioni." *Too much attention.*

The older man smiled.

"*A fini. U gghiurnari.*" At last. Dawn.

He reached out and patted the younger man's cheek. Firmly. Certainly not a caress. But not quite a slap. He leaned back.

"*E ora è u problema di idda.*" And now it's her problem.

He shrugged.

The younger man started to say something, but the older one raised a finger for silence.

"*Ora timminau. Idda è ancora a famigghia. A famigghia ppi ssempri. Ma u dibbitu, u ddibitu d'onori è paiatu.*" Now it is finished. She is still family. Family forever. But the debt, the debt of honor, is paid.

And as if worn out from so many words, he leaned back and closed his eyes, and the younger man quietly left the room.

Chapter 46

Siracusa, Sicily
1608

The white line on the horizon was Sicily, the city of Siracusa. As the gulls swooped and dived, Caravaggio's eye picked out the formidable buildings of white stone.

"Siracusa looks like Valletta," he said to the Maltese captain.

"They are built of the same limestone," the captain said, keeping his eye on the flex of the sail.

"Where do we dock?"

"We will not enter Siracusa's harbor. I can't risk being stopped by the harbormaster. I'll leave you south of the city in a cove I know," said the captain. "You'll have to make your way around the harbor to the city. You forget my face, this boat, everything. *Capito?*"

Caravaggio shrugged.

"Do you know anyone in Siracusa?" asked the captain.

The artist nodded. "An old artist friend. One who likes his artichokes cooked in oil."

The captain squinted at Caravaggio. "Doesn't everyone?"

Still dressed in his sweat-crusted Maltese tunic—stitched with a filthy once-white cross—Caravaggio limped into Siracusa. The purse the boatman had given him held only a few coins. Little enough to survive on for a few days at most. Caravaggio suspected the boatman had added most of the contents of the purse to his fee for the dangerous rescue.

Siracusa pulsed with life. Carts piled with fruits—bright-yellow lemons and brilliant oranges—rolled down the stone streets, edging between creaking wagons packed with Oriental silks and Far Eastern spices. Wild and domestic fowl squawked in wicker cages. The wheels of merchant wagons churned through the waste deposited by herds of cattle, pigs, and sheep. Portuguese traders cried out their wares in barely intelligible Italian while the natives exchanged news and gossip in their Sicilian dialect.

Caravaggio stared at the bustling scene, trying to understand what the people were saying.

"Are you a knight?" asked a little boy stroking a flea-bitten kitten in his doorway.

"I am."

"You look more like a beggar," observed the child.

"What do you know of knights, you little bugger?"

"My uncle is one," said the boy. "He's a Maltese knight and wears a cross on his tunic just like you. Only he's clean and the cross is bright."

"Your uncle."

"There are many knights who visit Siracusa."

Caravaggio raised his eyebrows and dodged two men carrying a stout pole between them, with a bloodied wild boar swinging side to side, skewered through the snout and hind end.

"Where is a good place to eat? Cheap."

The boy eyed Caravaggio from head to toe. "Rafaello's," he said. "They serve anybody. Sardines and the leftover catch nobody else buys."

"Where is it?"

"Behind the cathedral about twenty paces to the right." The boy pointed. "You'll smell the fish frying. And the stink of the sewer!"

Caravaggio nodded, eager to get away from the boy whose uncle was a knight. He turned toward the cathedral, dodging the parade of merchants, farmers, and peasants. He crossed the Piazza Duomo, clogged with stands covered with makeshift awnings and peddlers calling out their wares.

The boy was right. The smell of fish frying in garlic and olive oil scented the street. A carved wooden sign of a fish hung over a doorway.

Caravaggio's stomach lurched. He was starving, but the heavy smell of oil and sardines was almost more than he could stand.

He stepped into the dim doorway hung with long strands of rawhide to keep out the buzzing flies. A young boy was mopping up a puddle of dirty water.

"*Buongiorno, signore!* Sit there," said a stout man with a rag tied around his waist. "Wine? Fish? Fish stew?"

"Wine and fish," said the artist. "And bread. Lots of it."

The fat man gave him a look, taking in his northern accent. Staring at Caravaggio's ragged tunic, he plunked a terra-cotta pitcher of wine in front of his customer. Then he crossed his thick forearms, resting them on his ample *pancia*.

"*Il pesce sta friggendo,*" he said, giving Caravaggio a hard look. "My wife is preparing the fish now. You are a cavaliere? The Order of Malta?"

"*Sì.*"

"What happened to you? Shipwrecked?"

"Bring the fish when it's ready," said Caravaggio, staring hard at the proprietor.

The man grunted. "I don't care about your history, signore. A coin is a coin no matter whose palm it's from."

Caravaggio stuck his nose in his wine cup. "This wine is rancid."

"That wine is cheap."

"Bene," said Caravaggio, knocking back a gulp and wincing. "My kind of wine."

The stout man grinned, exposing his rotten teeth. "You need a place to stay?" he said. "As cheap as the wine?"

"Forse," said Caravaggio. *Maybe.*

"I have a room off the kitchen. Where I store the fish—"

Caravaggio scratched his chin, his beard matted with dirt and salt from the sea journey. "I don't keep company with fish," he said. "Do you know an artist by the name of Mario Minniti?"

The man hesitated, wiping his hands on the soiled rag at his waist. "Everyone knows Maestro Minniti!" he said, taking another look at his customer. "He has his studio on the other side of Piazza Duomo."

Caravaggio dug in his purse for his coins.

"Send the boy to fetch him here," he said. "Tell him an old friend who likes his artichokes prepared in butter wants to join him for an early supper."

Mario Minniti parted the rawhide strands with the backs of his hands and stepped into the tavern. He stared at Caravaggio and his face erupted into a smile.

"It *is* you, Michele!" he said, moving forward to embrace his old friend.

The owner came bustling out of the kitchen with a plate of artichokes, shiny with oil. Upon seeing Minniti, he bowed, nearly dropping the platter. "Maestro Minniti! It is an honor to have you here," he said. "I—"

"Give us the food before you spill it," said Caravaggio.

The owner placed the artichokes on the table. Caravaggio poured his friend a cup of wine.

"Wait!" said the owner, holding up his hand to stop him. "I have better wine—much better wine—for Maestro Minniti. Let me get it."

As the man bustled out, Mario leaned over, speaking in a low voice. "What trouble are you in, Michele?"

"A lot."

"Another man dead?"

"Not as bad as that, but the knights will come looking for me."

"Just as bad, then. The Knights of Malta have a long arm, especially here in Sicily."

"You've got to hide me."

"They'll know to question me. I'm working on a pardon from the pope, so I can return to Roma."

"Hide me, Mario! And get me work."

Mario pressed his lips tight together. He nodded. "I'll talk to the Capuchin friars. They hid me when I first arrived under the *bando capitale*. I think I could convince them to take you in."

"What?" scoffed Caravaggio. "Me? In a monastery?"

"Why not? Who is going to come searching for you among a pack of monks?"

"No monastery! I can't stomach that—a brothel, now that would work."

"You'd end up in a brawl," said Mario, sighing. "You always do." Then he smiled, clapping his hand over Caravaggio's. "You can come and live with me and my wife as soon as we think it's safe. We'll shelter you. But first, the monastery."

"Can you find me a patron?"

Mario snorted. He had never known Caravaggio to ever thank anyone. "I'm sure I can. Everyone knows your work, Michele. I have patrons who would give you their teeth on a platter in exchange for one of your brushstrokes. Leave it to me. I have some influence here. I think I could arrange for some sort of protection in exchange for your paint—"

"Here it is, signori!" said the stout owner, returning with a large pitcher. "Now this is the good vino," he said, splashing the ruby-red liquid into their cups. "*Nerello*. Here's to your good health, signori."

Mario lifted his cup. "*Salute!*" he said, smiling at their host.

Caravaggio watched Minniti as if he were preparing to paint, studying the composition. "Capuchin monks?" he said, snorting. "Mario, for such a genius, you really are a shitty artist."

"*Salute,*" said Mario. "You son of a whore! May you paint your way out of trouble once again."

This time Caravaggio raised his cup.

∞

Mario met with a few members of the senate of Siracusa in a room off his busy studio.

Closing the door on the dozen young apprentices hard at work completing his canvases, Minniti told the senators about Caravaggio's presence in the city and the special circumstances.

Would they be interested in protecting the artist and in exchange have the opportunity to procure his work?

"*Sì! Sì!* I'd shelter the devil if he could paint half as well as Maestro Caravaggio!" said Senator Russo. "I know his paintings well. I've seen them in Roma myself—*The Calling of St. Matthew, The Madonna of Loreto*. And of you, Mario . . . Bacchus!" He gave Mario a sly grin. "You were a handsome youth, Minniti. How did you become so ugly as an adult?"

"It must be the company I keep," said Mario.

"We must have Caravaggio paint our Santa Lucia!" said Senator Moretti, gesticulating wildly. "Do you think your friend would consent?"

Mario nodded. "*Sì, certo.* If you senators would agree to keep him alive and speak nothing of his residence here. The Maltese Knights will be searching everywhere for him."

"Of course we can agree to that," said Senator Caruso. "I can't stand those swaggering knights. They have no jurisdiction in our city."

"Tell him to come to my home this evening," said Senator Moretti. "We shall talk in secrecy and arrange his commission."

∽

The Burial of Santa Lucia depicted the final moments of Siracusa's patron saint in the year 304 AD.

Caravaggio painted the immense canvas in the medieval Basilica di Santa Lucia al Sepolcro, above the Christian catacombs where Saint Lucia was originally interred. Sometimes Caravaggio would descend into the catacombs, his eyes scanning the rock and shadows, the niches that cradled the dead.

The painting of Saint Lucia emerged in muted colors—the young martyr lying on the bare ground, enormous stone walls dwarfing her figure and the others gathered in the scene. Her body was diminutive, vulnerable, with her right hand cast out on the ground, the left crossed over her belly. Her upper body shone in muted light, though it was the gravediggers who commanded the viewer's eye: two men in filthy white loincloths, leaning over their shovels. One looked up, watching Saint Lucia's mother weep over her daughter's lifeless body. The other plunged his shovel into the stony earth, light spilling on his muscular buttocks.

Mario entered the basilica, watching his old friend dab more white paint onto the gravedigger's rump.

"You can never resist poking your public in the eye," he said.

"You don't like it?"

"It is magnificent," said Mario, his breath exploding in a whistle. "The Siracusans will love it as well. As will all Sicily. But . . ."

"But what?"

"It's . . . rude. So like you. A laborer's ass leaping out of the canvas. And you have Santa Lucia already stone dead rather than at the moment of martyrdom while she still breathes. I've always marveled at your choice of timing."

"She can't be a martyr unless she is dead."

"Well . . . she looks dead, all right. *Basta!*"

"*Bene.* I've succeeded, then," said Caravaggio.

"I bring you news from the senate, Michele," said Mario. "The knights sail the coasts of Sicily looking for you. Inquiries have been made in Messina. The members of the senate have pledged your safety but suggest you stay hidden in the monastery for a while yet."

Caravaggio shrugged. "All right."

Mario cocked his head. "I thought you'd find the monastery dull."

"It is. But it is quiet. The monks do not bother me with questions. I'm content to eat in my cell and focus on my work."

"Perhaps they will take you into the order, Michele! What a monk you would be."

"I doubt that. The whores here are tasty."

"*Sì, hai ragione.*" Mario laughed, shaking his head. "You are right. Perhaps the brothers would not accept you as one of their own."

"I think not," said Caravaggio. He went back to dabbing paint on the gravedigger's buttocks.

"Michele. What will you do in the future?"

"I have another commission in Messina," Caravaggio said without looking away from his work.

"Did you not hear?" Mario gaped. "The knights have a presence there! Malaspina is the prior of Messina—"

"I am to paint the *Resurrection of Lazarus.* The subject appeals to me and the patron will pay well. Then I would like to see Palermo."

"You are mad, Michele. Palermo?"

"Then I am returning home. Napoli first to wait for my pardon. Then Roma."

"The pope will have your head if the knights don't find you first."

"I cannot stay in hiding. I must return to Roma, Mario. Nothing else matters. Roma is where I belong."

Caravaggio remembered Galileo saying, "Roma is your sun, Caravaggio."

He needed that sunshine.

Caravaggio stood on the terrace of the Colonna palace in the wealthy Chiaia neighborhood of Napoli, watching the waves lap against the rocks. Palm fronds grazed the balcony of the palazzo, the chatter of birds filling the air.

The artist gazed across the bay. After two months in Palermo, rumors had reached his ear that a Maltese knight had been looking for him in the city. Sicily had become too dangerous.

Napoli suited Caravaggio. Though he vastly preferred Roma, he felt at home here in the rough streets and back alleys where only the cutthroats and wary survived. Yet this time, the artist was living at the Colonnas' castle at the invitation of Costanza Colonna.

"Fabrizio has negotiated on your behalf," said the marchesa. "Alof de Wignacourt is amenable to unofficially ending the search and the demand for your return."

The marchesa studied Caravaggio's face. "Your art bewitched the grand master, didn't it? I cannot see how else you would have escaped Malta."

Caravaggio shrugged. "I am good at keeping secrets, Marchesa. Even from you."

"You will, of course, be required to paint for him in exchange for his cooperation."

"I shall send him a painting—John the Baptist's head on a platter. In the hands of Salome herself. But what of Roma? When may I return to Roma?"

The marchesa widened her eyes at the artist's reckless intentions. "You don't understand the danger you are in, do you, Michele?"

"I'm always in danger."

"Alof de Wignacourt has considered pardoning you, but the pope, the Tomassonis, and the wounded knight—what was his name, the Conte della Vezza?"

"Fra Giovanni Rodomonte Roero."

"*He* is still out for your blood, says Fabrizio. You are not out of danger."

"None of this matters, my marchesa. I must return to Roma."

The marchesa shook her head adamantly, loosening a tendril of hair from her immaculately coiffed upsweep. "You cannot return to Roma, nor should you venture into the streets of Napoli. Michele—you are a wanted man and a despised one! Your enemies will track you down, mark my words."

Notwithstanding the marchesa's determined warning, Caravaggio pursued negotiations with the Borghese pope. Through the young cardinal Gonzaga, son of Duca di Gonzaga who had acquired *The Death of the Virgin*, Caravaggio was in contact with Cardinal Scipione Borghese. The pope's nephew desperately wanted Caravaggio back in Roma, beholden to the Borghese and once again producing masterpieces. The cardinal's keen lust for Caravaggio's art motivated progress toward a papal pardon.

One night, after taking pleasure with the whores in the upstairs rooms of Locanda del Cerriglio, Caravaggio stumbled out the door into the black alleyway. The flickering oil lamp placed at the entrance was the only illumination in the narrow passage.

Before he had taken five paces, three men surged out of the dark and grabbed him. They stunk of sweat and unwashed clothes.

Caravaggio jerked back, his tunic tearing in an assailant's hand. He ran down the narrow street, his leather shoes slapping the cobblestones.

The men pursued him. One swifter than the others, a dagger in his right hand, lunged wildly. His dagger sliced into Caravaggio's left arm. Caravaggio turned, slashing with his sword. The blade struck the young man's knife hand, cutting deep into his wrist.

Blood spurted and the assailant crumpled to the ground, writhing.

Caravaggio faced the other two men, who advanced, swords gleaming in the torchlight. One thrust forward, engaging Caravaggio. As the artist parried the attack, the other man moved quickly around him. With both hands grasping his weapon like an axe, he struck downward, knocking the sword out of Caravaggio's hands.

"Enough of that, you bastard!" he growled, grabbing Caravaggio by his hair. He yanked the artist backward. The man dropped his sword, his hand now holding a dagger.

"I do this," the man panted, "in the name of one you have wronged."

Caravaggio saw the glint of the dagger like the flash of a silver fish.

The blade sliced Caravaggio's face deep across the cheek, nicking his eye. The last thing he saw was the three men disappearing into the shadowy warren of Napoli's streets.

After that, there was only black.

Chapter 47

Monte Piccolo

Sometimes, Lucia wished she had an old office typewriter. Solid. Heavy. A clattering, bell-ringing thirty-pound chunk of iron. Just so she could have the pleasure of ripping a sheet of paper out of the roller, wadding it into a ball, and hurling it into the trash.

She was trying to write an academic paper about her work tracing the troubled provenance of *The Judas Kiss*—*Il bacio di Giuda*—alleged to be by Michelangelo Merisi da Caravaggio. The painting Te-Te had died for.

She had thought it would be easy. After all, it was her story. But it was turning out to be a tangled, endless frustration—which was why she wanted a solid machine. You can't take out your frustrations on a computer. Silently deleting text doesn't come near the exhilaration of crumpling paper in your fist and throwing it across the room.

Still, she kept at it because she suddenly, astonishingly, didn't have anything else to do. Everything was normal again. She had been returned to her ordinary life. Which was, for better and for worse, very different from the excitement and fear and challenge of the past few months.

The police said the Roero Brigade had been wiped out in *l'incidente dei monaci ubriachi*—the incident of the drunken monks—which the detective had called it with a bit of a smirk. He wasn't as charming as he seemed to think, but his report was reassuring all the same. The carabinieri had ruled the three deaths accidental—drunk-driving, high-speed crash—and were more than glad to leave it at that. Happy that someone had taken care of their problem.

And so it was over. The case was closed. The police insisted it was finished. The painting, recovered—perhaps "seized" was a better word—from Lucia's apartment, had disappeared into official custody, safely buried beneath multiple layers of security, as evidence in the murder of Father Antonio.

So Lucia had headed back to Monte Piccolo—where she was still enrolled in an art history seminar.

When she got back to her apartment on the tiny piazza, spring was making itself felt at last. The cluster of small trees had bludgeoned themselves into bloom—grudging but still blooming. The cobblestones, some historic, some patched with asphalt, glistened with dew every morning, without a hint of ice anywhere. She opened her windows to the sounds of children shouting, Vespas buzzing, nuns murmuring. Life moving along as it always had.

And Vittore, the *poliziotto di parcheggio*, still tipped his hat and called her *"mia signora,"* and he still wasn't giving her tickets.

So all was well—if a little lonely.

Moto wasn't there. He'd left two or three days after the police came to Lucia's apartment and took the painting away. They'd had a big dinner—Lucia, Moto, and Professor Richman—to mark the official end of their pursuit of the painting, and Moto had raced away the day after that, off to somewhere down south where yet another cousin was having—he shrugged—romantic problems and needed cheering up.

Professor Richman had left as well, heading north, saying, "I'm off to Piemonte. Research." Details were not offered. But when he left, he seemed invigorated by the events of the past months. He managed to cut something of a dashing figure, his step jaunty as he headed for the train.

So Lucia was alone. She focused on her dissertation, on the painting. She had thought of it as her painting, their painting, for so long. But now it was just "the" painting, a painting, something to parse and study, passion restrained by scholarship. Preserving the academic tone meant leaving out a lot of the story. This year's deaths, this year's terrors, meant nothing. All that mattered were events of the distant past, lives and deaths that were centuries old. And untangling past from present, documenting a purely academic effort to trace the painting, was not only difficult, frustrating work, but it seemed pointless.

Still, she might as well get the semester credit she'd paid for. And she had nothing else to do. Except be alone.

She was working from her memory and a few sketchy notes she'd scrawled along the way. She picked her way through the story, skipping over the parts that didn't fit in academia, separating out strands of reasoning from moments of panic, so she could weave a consistent fabric as she pursued the painting back through time into the dark corners of one of art's great mysteries: the final days of Caravaggio. She had a pad next to her computer, and she jotted notes on the parts she had to slice out of the story to preserve the paper's proper academic focus. From time to time, she'd stop and look at that lengthening list and consider the very different shapes of the very different stories outlined there. On the computer screen, calm logic and reason. On the pad, blood and death and dark nights. And two good friends who had suddenly disappeared from her life.

She was unraveling one particular tangle, juggling events and ideas, holding them in her mind and sorting them—even while she was staring out the window at the blossoms blowing in the breeze and wondering how winter could have ever been here or could ever return.

That was when Moto burst through the door.

"Great news!"

His explosive entry scattered her thoughts, and the tangle escaped her grasp, tied itself even tighter, and rolled away under some heavy furniture in a far corner of her mind. For a moment she was annoyed, but her pleasure at seeing him again and his enthusiasm overrode any objections.

"We got it!"

"Got what?"

"Approval."

"For what?"

"For everything!"

"Moto! What are you talking about?" She was glad to see him again, but something felt wrong, something in the back of her mind nagged at her. Something hiding in those notes on her yellow pad was keeping her from leaping all the way back into their old friendship.

Moto didn't notice.

"The painting. A real investigation. Science." The words tumbled out in his excitement. "Not yet," he went on, "but they'll start soon. In a week or two at most. X-rays. Thread samples. Paint analysis. Computer interpolations. Everything! All of it!"

She narrowed her eyes. "How?"

"The police are going to let us—"

"Us?"

"OK. Not us. But top scientists and art restorers and historians. Everyone. They're going to prove we're right!"

She should have smiled, joined him in celebrating, but that something was still gnawing. "I can't believe the police are letting anyone even near it. How did that happen?"

Moto gave his smile, his shrug. "You know. A little money. A little leverage."

She didn't say anything, but her face demanded answers.

Moto stopped. He looked down. Maybe his enthusiasm had carried him too far. He shrugged—more to himself than her.

"My fath—" He stopped. Tried again. "My fam—" A shake of the head. Again. "Friends. Friends of the . . . friends"—a quick correction—"friends of the family. They offered to—"

But Lucia wasn't listening. The words "friends of the friends" had shot her back decades, back to Long Island, back to her life alone with her widowed *nonna*—Nonna with her hawk nose and her hawk's pitiless eyes. Bitter, savage, and endlessly dedicated to the memories of Sicilia, her Sicilia, a land of *omertà*—the code of silence. And "the friends of the friends."

That phrase meant one thing. Always and only. The Mafia. The families whose endless battles for territory, influence, and profit affected all of Sicily and spilled across the ocean to poison Lucia's life in the United States.

And suddenly, all the stories, the threads, the missing pieces she'd been juggling, fell into place with a snap, and she was catapulted out of the chair by the twin shocks of rage and shame. Rage at Moto for not telling her. Shame for herself for not seeing it before. She exploded upward and grabbed Moto by his unzipped motorcycle jacket. Caught by surprise, he stumbled backward and her momentum carried them a few steps across the room until his back slammed into the wall. She pinned him there.

He instinctively struggled, but they were evenly matched. He was a little taller, but she had surprise and rage on her side.

She spat his own words back at him. "Friends of the friends!"

American, Italian, Sicilian warred within her. And the American won. She wasn't going to be afraid to say the word.

"Mafia."

Still breathing hard.

"Your father is . . . You are . . . one of *them*."

Moto tried to laugh. He spread his arms wide. "Does this look like someone 'they' would embrace?"

"Stop it!" She was almost screaming.

It wasn't the idea of the Mafia that enraged her. It was the lying. Her best friend, and it was all a lie. She didn't know anything about him. She shook him.

"Who are you?"

He didn't say anything and she let him go.

"Lulu . . ."

"Mi chiamo Lucia." She spat it out. *My name is Lucia.*

There was a long silence. They both caught their breath.

"I was just watching out for you." His voice was reasonable. Slightly pained, slightly bewildered, wounded puppy, pure Moto. The old Moto. But he didn't need that charm to get her to say what came next. She would have said it anyway.

"You saved my life. I will always love you for that." Then she said the rest—what his charm couldn't stop. "But you were lying to me the whole time. Lying about who you are. Friends don't do that. Real friends don't do that." She stopped.

He stared at her. She studied his face. He was still Moto.

"You're my best friend," he said. "Ever." He was almost pleading. She almost believed him. "And I never would have met you if those . . . friends . . . if my father . . . hadn't suggested I come up here and make sure you were all right. That's not a bad way to meet a new friend, is it?"

Her eyes narrowed. There was a tightness in her jaw. Now everything he said just made her angrier. "I wasn't a friend," she growled. "I was an assignment."

The Sicilian in her was taking over, and she could feel herself ready to lunge at him.

He saw it, but he didn't move any farther away from her. He stared into her eyes, and she could see he was almost crying.

"It was the first time my father ever asked me to do anything for him. The first time he ever acted as if he could trust me. He was always ashamed of"—a long pause, and then all he could say was—"who I am." He said it again. "My father was ashamed of who I am. And I thought I could make him proud of me. One time. Just one time."

Lucia watched him get control of his emotions and leave that confession behind. She couldn't forgive his lies, but she also couldn't deny the painful truth of what he had just told her.

And Moto went on. His voice tighter, under control.

"And my father is a businessman. Very successful and very respectable. And when those friends suggested I come up here, he thought his arty son might enjoy hanging out with the intellectuals in Chianti. And I did. I found my best friend."

"Stop it," she said.

"Lucia, back before that damn painting, everything was simple. I thought you would finish the seminar and go home. And then you would always be my wonderful American friend and I'd come visit you. It was perfect. I love happy endings."

He stopped. Straightened his jacket.

"And once everything . . . started, I was only trying to look out for you. Keep you safe. And I did, didn't I?" His expression changed again. No more puppy dog. "*They* did. They kept you safe. And with the murdering bastards that were after us, we were very lucky to have those friends."

He took a breath.

"They were looking out for you. I was looking out for you. Even Vittore was looking out for you while he was writing his parking tickets. It was all family. Here. Rome. Naples. Sicily. Maybe I didn't tell you everything—but maybe you ought to thank me."

Angry as he suddenly sounded, she matched him and spat it right back at him.

"Why, Moto? Why were you looking out for me?"

"Because you needed it."

"That's not an answer. Why did they care about me?"

His face stayed hard, lips tight. "I don't know." His lower lip tucked in and he bit down on it for an instant. "Family. That's all I know. It's always family. *Cosca.*"

She knew that word. *Cosca.* Sicilian for "artichoke"—densely packed, spiny leaves, clinging together to protect the core. And the way he said it, she heard the echo of a lifetime of knowing he could never really be part of the family, the clan, the *cosca.*

She wanted to hug him, but she shook it off. He'd been lying to her from the moment they'd met. She thought his secret was that he was gay—and that wasn't a secret. But his real secret was his Mafia family. And he hadn't trusted her with that. She couldn't feel sorry for him now. But she didn't want things to get any worse.

"Moto, let's stop all of this right now. Let's just say I'm already gone. OK? The seminar is over and I'm flying home. The happy ending you expected. I'm gone. You can move back to wherever you were when whoever he was suggested you might enjoy a little time in Chianti." Her voice softened a little. "And maybe someday you *will* come visit me in the United States. Just not anytime soon."

There was an awkward pause.

She managed a smile. "It'll be all right. It's not as if I'm carrying your baby."

They almost laughed—almost—and he left.

If the blossoming trees and birdsong in the mornings were the signs of spring in Chianti, drunken singing late at night and taxi horns in the morning were the signs of the changing seasons in Rome.

Moto's departure from Monte Piccolo had been followed the next day by a postcard from Professor Richman saying he was ensconced in a "more than merely deluxe" hotel in the Castello di Guarene, a former summer residence of the counts of Roero with "glorious views and magnificent cuisine" and assuring her that his research was "proceeding brilliantly."

Lucia couldn't stay in Chianti one more day. She packed a suitcase and took a bus to Siena and then the train to Rome.

The tiny apartment she found—three long flights up from the street, tucked under the eaves of an aging building in the Campo Marzio, Caravaggio's old neighborhood—undoubtedly fell far short of the professor's suite at the *castello*, but it would do. There was a table and a hard wooden chair where she could sit and work on her dissertation. There was one almost comfortable armchair. And a window large enough for light by day and noise at night, when she would consider whether to throw something breakable and shout for silence, or get dressed and go downstairs to join the party. She never actually threw anything, but sometimes she shouted. And sometimes she went down to join the nightly celebrations.

She had been spending time every day with the handful of Caravaggios scattered right there within a few blocks of the apartment. After a week or so, the paintings began to feel like friends from around the neighborhood. So far, they were the only friends she had in Rome. Which was about as many as she needed.

She'd start every morning early, with the *Madonna di Loreto*, at the Basilica di Sant'Agostino, tucked away a tight dark squeeze off Piazza Navona. The painting was famous—scandalous when Caravaggio painted it—for the dirty feet of the two pilgrims kneeling in front of the Madonna, but from the first moment she saw it, Lucia could only think of it as "the Woman with the Giant Baby." Genius and realist though Caravaggio had been, he'd painted the infant Jesus several times larger than any real baby could have been. Filled with religious fervor and Holy Glory though it most certainly was, Lucia thought the image had a tang of the sideshow, a woman displaying her freakishly large infant to the adoring multitudes—though apparently only two at a time. Lucia wondered if her feet hurt, having to constantly rush to the door to meet the next wave of adoration. And the kid must have been heavy.

Sometimes, if she got there at the right time, there would be only the three of them—Lucia and the two kneeling, dirty-footed pilgrims—staring up together in astonishment. And when that happened, Lucia forgot her little jokes about the enormous baby and surrendered to a sadness, deep inside, a lance of loneliness at the vision of a loving mother cradling her child.

From Sant'Agostino, she'd take a brisk walk to the grander landscape of the Piazza del Popolo, to visit Peter and Paul. As she got to know them, they seemed an odd pairing, mismatched roommates facing each other across an altar for more than four centuries. She was always moved by the pain and fevered concern of Peter's martyrdom—and then, turning her head, she'd be struck by the sheer violence of God's Ecstasy that had knocked Paul sprawling. But the two saints were actually part of a trinity: Peter and Paul and Paul's Horse's Butt, which was at least as prominent as his owner's holy seizure.

And then she would walk back through the neighborhood, past the military guards with assault rifles, to San Luigi dei Francesi, to visit what she thought of as "the Three Matteos." The *Calling*, with its majestic grace, the *Martyrdom*, with its violent energy, and between them the *Inspiration*, with the holy man at his writing desk, deep in conversation with an angel, perhaps debating which of the other two paintings was the best of the three.

Lucia felt she ought to prefer the *Calling*. But it was the *Martyrdom* that still caught and held her full attention, as it had on that first visit, that night in the dark. With Moto.

And every day she thought about that night, standing alone with the *Martyrdom*, feeling a rush of life from the flashes of faces and bodies, arms and legs, that showed in the near total dark of the church. And then she'd remember sprinting through the street, lost in the dark, with Moto running in a blind panic ahead of her—his version of looking out for her, keeping her safe. Certainly not a young prince in his family. She had to smile. He was telling the truth about that. But he'd hidden the truth from her too much and she wasn't ready to forgive him.

She spent the most time at the Francesi every day, working to see those paintings—to see the *Martyrdom* as it really was. Right there. She had to get rid of the memories of that earlier visit that were splattered all over the painting, bad varnish that she couldn't see through. She wanted to get back to what she'd felt at first, alone with the painting, before everyone started running and everything spun out of control.

And she needed that because, after all she'd seen, especially after the time in Malta standing in front of the *Beheading*, she was hammered by doubts that their painting—Te-Te's *Judas Kiss*—could really join these works of dangerous genius.

Now, suddenly alone, the chase ended, the deaths permanent, her two companions gone, she wondered how she had found the nerve to declare that, yes, she absolutely knew the painting—"their" painting— was by Michelangelo Merisi da Caravaggio.

She needed to rally her convictions, to recapture what she'd felt alone in the long, terrifying night in the warehouse with *The Judas Kiss*. The feeling had been strong enough to make her certain the painting was a Caravaggio. Strong enough to keep her going through everything that had happened since then.

She needed to test that feeling again if she was going to move on.

So she needed to find her way back to Caravaggio's painting. This painting, here in the chapel. She had to find her way past all the varnish: the awe of Caravaggio, the centuries of history, the gold leaf and grandeur of the churches. Thick varnish. And she had to see past all the great tales of Michele the Maniac, the *tipo tosto* of the art world. And see past her own experience. Thicker varnish yet.

Clear away the varnish, clear away the gossip, and maybe she could get back to how she felt when she saw the *Martyrdom* that night. The frenzied power she had felt flooding off that painting. The whites of the arms and the robes, the muscular body, the screaming face that emerged as her eyes adjusted to the dark. Those strokes of light in the shadows were less a painting and more a lightning storm.

And then, if she got there, back to that powerful moment, could the feeling she had from *The Judas Kiss* stand up to the torrent?

CO

Lucia started every day with those three visits. She got to know the guards and the beggars at each church, the days when she would be jostled and days when she might be alone.

And as spring in the ancient city deepened into the sweetest days of the year, she felt as if her life was becoming a prolonged sigh of relief. She spent her mornings with Michele and her afternoons working on her dissertation. The frustration with the paper was fading; she'd reached a point where the tangles were dissolving and the heart of the matter, the true pursuit of the painting, was becoming clear.

She was slipping into the rhythm of life in the neighborhood. She began to recognize faces in the shops, in the street, in the restaurants. The man who made her *caffè doppio* every morning. The woman at the cash register in the grocery store. Her daily rounds were filled with smiles and nods. And when the neighborhood got noisy late at night, more often than not she'd head down and join the throng.

One day in late April, to her great surprise, she found that she had finished the dissertation. It was all there: it had been read, reread, and proofread half a dozen times. She had accepted that there was no grand conclusion. No final proof. She—they—had traced a reasonable connection from the painting in Te-Te's orphanage chapel to a man who had perhaps sailed in the same felucca with Caravaggio from Naples to Palo—and then onward, without Caravaggio, but perhaps still with his paintings, to Porto Ercole. That's what she had found, and that was enough. Enough for this dissertation, anyway.

She waited two more days before she had it printed. She had to be sure—sure of what, she didn't know, but she knew she had to wait. Then, with a hollow feeling, as if she was saying goodbye to a friend for the last time, she mailed it to the professor who had run the Monte Piccolo seminar and who had now returned to his position at UniMi, the Università degli studi di Milano.

And that night—and the nights that followed—she didn't wait for the crowds in the street to get raucous before she joined them. She headed down as the day drew to a close and fell in with new friends from the neighborhood *per il vino e la cena, musica e risate. For wine and dinner, music and laughter.*

But no matter how late she stayed at the party, she was out early every morning, visiting Peter and Paul, the Matteos, and the Lady with the patient smile and the aching back. Lucia knew the model for that Madonna was Lena. Caravaggio had painted her so many times. Though history portrayed him as a man incapable of love, Lucia wondered if maybe he had found it in himself to love Lena.

Then she found herself more and more often home at night. She sat in her almost comfortable chair, stared out across the rooftops, and thought about *The Beheading of St. John the Baptist, Decollazione di San Giovanni Battista.*

Flooded with darkness, churning with violence, it was Michele's best, she was certain. The prison courtyard embraced by darkness, the handful of figures flickering in the light. The saint at the edge of death. The executioner reaching for his knife to finish the beheading. The jailer. The girl. The old woman, there because someone had to show horror. And off to one side, almost lost in the shadows—but persistent in Lucia's memory of the painting—the two prisoners peering out the barred window at a fate that might soon enough be theirs.

The genius of that masterpiece was the genius she claimed she had seen in the *Kiss.*

She knew that what she thought about the *Kiss* didn't matter. It was in the hands of the experts, and they would declare who was the fool. She was hoping it wasn't her.

∞

After too many long nights threaded by nightmares of that dark scene, Lucia needed to clear her mind. Right now, the *Beheading* obsessed her, it swept all the other paintings away. She needed something new. Something strong. So after a *doppio* at the café on the corner, she headed off across town through the morning bustle, working her way through the crowds, dodging taxis and Vespas, and thinking how pleasant the city was in the morning sun—though that might have been by contrast with the dark painting that haunted her nights.

She was on her way to the Palazzo Barberini to see *Giuditta e Oloferne—Judith Beheading Holofernes*—a Caravaggio painting of a very different beheading, a bloody slaughter: Judith, the heroine, sword in hand, saving her people by severing the head of Holofernes, general of the invading Babylonian army. Lucia hadn't seen the painting before. She had limited her Caravaggio visits in Rome to that small circle of friends in her neighborhood. And that meant that now she could have a fresh experience to clear her mind.

She crossed the wide-open courtyard into the Barberini Palace, bought her ticket, stuffed her coat and backpack into a locker—all the things that have to be done—and then marched up the stairs and through the galleries until she was standing in front of *Judith Beheading Holofernes*. This was a museum, not a church. No shadows. No ornate gilding. No flickering candles. Clean, well-lit spaces. For the moment, she was almost alone in the room: just her, a guard slumped, dozing, in a chair—and the bloody horror on the wall.

Still a little bleary-eyed, despite the *doppio* and the brisk walk across town, she felt the painting slap her across the face. The spurt of blood on the canvas popped her eyes wide open. Michele had watched executions. He had seen how blood spurted. He had studied his art.

But painting the blood was mechanics. The mechanics of a genius, to be sure, but the faces that filled the canvas above the bloody gash of Holofernes's ruined throat were genius beyond mechanics. The terror and pain on the face of Holofernes as he hurtled into death. The intense, strange calm of Judith, concentrating on the task, sword in hand. And the deadly glare, the lizard eyes of Judith's servant, holding a sack, ready to catch the head.

The painting didn't have the majestic power of *The Beheading of St. John the Baptist* in the Malta cathedral, but it had an edge as deadly as the blade in Judith's hand. And Lucia could feel that sharp edge slashing through her mind as she locked eyes with the terrifying stare of the servant. She knew that lizard stare. Those eyes sliced into her heart. Her balance fled. The planet spun beneath her. In a panic, she looked away from the servant, back to the doomed Holofernes. But his face had changed somehow. It was the same, but different. Entirely different. Two faces in one image. Her heart was pounding. Her eyes darted to Judith, but she had changed too. Her white arms stretched out—a woman reaching for her lover, but no, she was an executioner, reaching only for death, one hand grasping her victim's hair, the other wielding the sword.

Lucia's eyes jolted sideways again, fleeing back to the servant. That face was unchanged, but there was no relief there—it was already somehow the worst of them all as the crone hovered at the edge of the violence and watched eagerly, a vulture waiting to snatch the carrion.

Lucia's eyes went back to Holofernes. Then Judith. The servant. The faces whirled, tangled. Terror, concentration, the pitiless stare.

A scream surged inside her, but before she could make a sound, she was knocked sideways, staggered by a massive explosion, the sound of shattering glass. Surrounded by a wave of flame, she was engulfed in darkness. She could feel herself screaming at last, but she was lost in silence.

Chapter 48

Roma
1609

News reached Roma that Caravaggio had been murdered. Then fresh reports came to Scipione Borghese's ears that the artist was not dead but lay on the brink of death.

"He is unrecognizable," said a messenger reporting back from Palazzo Colonna. "His sight is severely compromised—"

"Can he paint?" demanded Borghese.

The messenger made a futile gesture, his palms turned upward. "I do not know. He lives."

"He is useless to me if he cannot paint," said the cardinal with a sweep of his arm. "Send a reply to him—and to Cardinal Gonzaga—that any further steps toward clemency will be suspended until I know my investment is worthwhile."

"*Sì*, Your Excellency."

"What the devil was he doing at midnight in the heart of Napoli? He is a wanted man! Not only under *bando capitale* in Roma but by the Order of Malta."

The messenger shook his head. "Forgive me, Your Excellency. I do not know."

"He is a madman, chasing his own death. Go! Send my message to Napoli."

∽

The Marchesa Costanza Colonna saw that Caravaggio received the best care and nursing. For eight months, the artist convalesced in the palazzo overlooking the Bay of Napoli.

She insisted her guest take tea with her in the afternoons on the terrace.

"I despise the light," said Caravaggio, blinking at the Mediterranean sun. "It hurts my eyes."

"You need light to heal," said the marchesa. "As long as you are my guest, Michele, you will indulge me this."

"*Sì*, Marchesa," he muttered.

The marchesa regarded the artist's face. "The butchers!" she said. "You know it is a miracle you survived."

"I have only survived if I can paint. Scipione Borghese has made that clear."

"Well, I have good news, Michele," said the marchesa. "Marcantonio Doria in Genova wants to commission a portrait of Saint Ursula. Here will be your test."

Caravaggio was silent.

"Come, come! It would be a perfect subject for you, Michele."

"I will consider it," he said slowly. He sipped his tea, gazing over the bay. "My eyesight . . . is not what it should be."

"I see you staring off at night across the sea. Here on the terrace, pacing. You truly are a haunted soul. Take on the commission, I beg you, Michele. I know you better than any mother. Your art will cure you."

Caravaggio touched the wounds on his face with his fingertips. "If I cannot paint, I would rather die."

404

The Marchesa Colonna was right.

Caravaggio's healing began as he started his work on *The Martyrdom of Santa Ursula*, depicting the noblewoman who led eleven thousand virgins on a disastrous pilgrimage through Germany. All her companions were slaughtered by the Huns, whose leader then killed Ursula when she refused his offer of marriage.

Caravaggio painted an intimate tableau, with the Hun killing Saint Ursula, sending an arrow into her breast from within arm's reach. The image of the murder—the rejected bridegroom, the arrow sunk deep into the chest of the virgin—conveyed a feeling of sexual violation. The martyr—colored ashen gray as her spirit fades—inclines her head over the protruding arrow. She looks mildly surprised to see it there.

There is a small crowd behind her. At her right shoulder is a man's face that looks up blindly toward the murder as if the commotion has caught his attention, but he cannot see the act. He appears frightened and panicked.

It is Caravaggio's likeness.

"You painted yourself into such a tragic scene," said the marchesa, regarding the canvas. "Why, Michele?"

"I am a witness to the ugly nature of men," said Caravaggio, staring at his image. "Now I am nearly blind, but I know the nature of death, even if I can't quite make out his face. I know he's there, standing close."

The marchesa noticed the imprecise brushstrokes, the unfinished quality of the work. She had begged the maestro to paint, but she could see the flailing effort.

He can barely see! Blindness—even partial blindness—is the death of an artist.

Still, despite the marred execution, the image was haunting. The marchesa knew her niece's husband would be pleased—especially when he saw Caravaggio's upturned face, pale and sightless behind the saint.

A cold shiver seized her spine. She turned away and walked from the room.

∞

"Michele! You can't be serious. You are in no condition to travel—" said Fabrizio Colonna.

"I board a felucca tomorrow," said Caravaggio. "It is settled. Scipione is arranging it. I will be released from the *bando capitale!*"

"Do you have the reversal in writing?" asked Fabrizio. He was still dressed in his salt-stiffened tunic and sailing clothes, having only just arrived home to visit his mother.

"No, not in writing. But I do have word from Cardinal Borghese that we have struck a deal. I am to deliver three canvases to him and he will see that I am a free man. I have already painted them. Two of Saint John the Baptist . . . and one of Mary Magdalene I painted in the Alban Hills at your estate. For my own reasons, I have never parted with it," Caravaggio said, looking away in the distance. "But if it can buy my freedom, I will give it to Cardinal Borghese."

"That devil," muttered Fabrizio.

"He may be," said Caravaggio. "But only his uncle the pope can grant me my freedom to walk the streets of Roma again."

"I don't like this idea," said the marchesa. "You are still not well. Your eye is not healed and your wounds still ooze pus. You aren't steady on your feet yet."

Fabrizio and his mother exchanged looks. Their brows were furrowed with concern.

"Michele," said Fabrizio. "You haven't received the pardon yet. *Aspetta.* Wait a few more days."

"*Scusi,*" said Caravaggio abruptly. "I must see to packing the paintings and preparing my trunks. If you will excuse me."

The marchesa nodded. As Caravaggio left the room, she looked up at her son.

"Fabrizio!" she said.

Salt crystals from the sea still clung to Fabrizio's beard. He rubbed his sea-weary eyes.

"I, too, feel a dark foreboding. Caravaggio will be seen by every sailor and cutthroat on the wharfs. And though Grand Master Wignacourt may have forgiven him, I know Fra Roero never will. He is a proud—and dangerous—*bastardo*. When he learns that the pope has granted a pardon, he will be rabid with fury."

Chapter 49

Rome

Lucia whirled around, reeling from the explosion. The museum guard was still dozing in his chair. A flock of chattering high school students surged into the room, milling, gossiping, flirting, glancing at the painting, giggling at the mayhem.

Her back turned to the painting, Lucia fought to regain her equilibrium, fought for calm, fought to clear away the rubble in her mind.

She waited until the students were gone and the room was silent again, keeping her back to Judith and Holofernes. She wasn't going to look again. Steady on her feet at last, she walked straight out of the gallery, through half a dozen rooms, down the stairs, and out into the sunshine. She kept walking with no sense of direction. At one point, balancing on the edge of madness, she almost laughed: She was Lot's wife, fleeing fire and brimstone, facing damnation if she looked back. She wondered how Caravaggio would have painted Lot's wife, which of his whores he would have turned into a pillar of salt. But she lost that thought in an instant, still battered by her own vision of blood and darkness, explosion and shattering glass, a vision more real than even Michele could have painted.

And she saw those faces again. The faces in the painting. The faces they had become in the instant before the explosion.

Faces she'd never seen before. Faces she somehow knew as well as her own. Faces she couldn't bear to see again. She banished the images, filling her mind with darkness, wandering blindly through the streets of Rome.

The glories of the past. The flash and squalor of the present. The streams of people and cars and buses and Vespas. She walked for hours, through the day and into the evening. Seeing none of it. Never looking back.

Sunlight was what Lucia needed. She spent her days outside, walking endlessly through the city, staying on the broad avenues where she could enjoy the increasing warmth of the sun as it strutted into full spring-time. She stayed clear of the old twisting byways that she used to prowl, the narrow *vicoli*, shrouded in shadows. For now they were too close to the darkness that had sent her reeling in the Palazzo Barberini. She didn't even let herself think of the name of the painting she had been standing in front of. The name might recall the image, and the image the darkness, and . . .

Rome was a wonderful way to fill her mind.

She walked for hours. Tired by sunset, she'd have an early dinner with a bottle of wine and sleep until it was light.

After a week on the Sunlight Cure, she was feeling solid again. Not ready to return to the Barberini, but ready for the comfort of her friends at San Luigi dei Francesi, Santa Maria del Popolo, and Sant'Agostino. One evening, after a long afternoon visit with the Matteos, she stopped back at the apartment to wash her face and hands before going out to dinner.

She was putting on her jacket to leave when there was a knock at the door.

In the time she had lived there, no one had ever knocked on that door. She had friends she smiled to in the street, friends she drank with in the bars, but no one who would ever stop by to visit.

For a moment she hesitated. She thought of men in long black robes. She remembered the foul stench of the one who had crushed her face to his chest as he dragged her through the catacombs. And with a conscious act of will, she cast her vote—and not for the first time—with the carabiniere who had assured her that the Roero Brigade was gone. Scattered. Destroyed.

She shrugged, tossed her keys back on the table, and shouted, "Coming!"

"How did you find me?"

"Really, my dear Lucy, I have been tracking down the intimate details of the life of a family of Italian aristocrats four centuries ago. Do you really think that finding you would pose an insurmountable obstacle?"

"I haven't seen you for months, and I already want to smack you."

Professor Richman smiled. "One very helpful clue was the return address on the dissertation you mailed to our professor."

"You've seen the paper?"

"A bit of a logical jump there, but, yes, I have. He asked me if it shouldn't have my name on it too. It did start out as our joint project, as you may recall."

"And you told him . . . ?"

"I told him it was an excellent piece of scholarly work and that you deserved exclusive credit."

"Thank you."

"Though maybe you might find room for me in a footnote? Perhaps dealing with the recovery of the journals of the common thief and shockingly bad poet Signor Mario Fenelli."

"I think we might arrange that," she said and laughed for what felt like the first time in months.

"Now why don't you put on your jacket and let me buy you a nice dinner."

"And just like that, I go from wanting to smack you to being really glad I opened the door when you knocked."

The restaurant was tucked in a dark corner of a small piazza, up a narrow winding street, in the old Jewish ghetto. As Professor Richman paid for the taxi, Lucia took a step away from the car and spun around, letting the force of her spin pull her arms away from her body. Suddenly, the dark didn't bother her. The professor was glowing with energy and good cheer that kept the blackness at bay.

As they walked inside, the manager rushed up.

"*Buonasera, Professore. Che piacere rivederla.*" *What a pleasure to see you again.*

Beaming with apparent pleasure, he escorted them past a waiting crowd to a perfect table in as quiet a corner as there could be in the bustling restaurant.

"I'm seeing a new side of you," Lucia said once they were settled into their chairs and the manager had presented the menus with a flourish.

"Well, my research has required a few quick trips to Rome—and a man must eat, after all."

"And eat well." Lucia smiled at him over the top of the menu.

He leaned closer. "You must try the *carciofi alla Giuda* and the agnolotti. After that, *pesce* or *carne*, you're on your own."

And then—over the next two hours, four courses, and two excellent bottles of wine—the professor told her everything that had been happening with the *Kiss, il bacio. Il nostro bacio. Our kiss.*

"Your Italian has certainly improved."

"Yes, well. Practice."

"Research?"

"Of course."

But he didn't talk about his research. He talked about the now-official project to evaluate the painting.

Everything was looking good. The X-rays revealed different faces hidden below the too-perfect faces that clearly hadn't been painted by Michele. A thread plucked from the canvas checked out: the right age, the right material, the right weave. The pigments had been traced to formulas and processes appropriate to the time and place—and Caravaggio. There were some tests that were waiting for the relining.

"Relining?"

"They believe that Fenelli—that's Fenelli the monk, the painter—was concerned about the well-being of the painting. So he stuck it to a heavier canvas—a damask tablecloth, if you can believe that. I don't know where a monk would get a damask tablecloth."

"Your usual cognac, Professore?" The waiter took advantage of a moment of silence.

"Certainly."

"Signora?"

"Lo stesso." The same.

The waiter glided away and the professor continued.

"There are some anomalies in the texture that they can't figure out without taking the painting off that tablecloth."

Two snifters of cognac appeared on the table.

"And the X-rays show what appears to be something written on the back of the original canvas."

They raised their glasses to science and art and drank—well, sipped, it was very good cognac.

"Why do you think Fenelli was so concerned about preserving the painting?"

"He knew what his drunken poet brother had stolen. He was an artist of some skill. Michele was the most famous painter in all of Italy. The monk knew what he had. So he lined it with sturdy backing and disguised it by painting over the faces. I like to think he did his very best work on those faces—and knew that no one would ever mistake them for Michele's. And then he sent it away."

Lucia raised a questioning eyebrow and took another sip of cognac.

"In my younger days, I would have considered a look like that to be flirting," the professor said.

Lucia gave him a thoroughly happy smile. "Forget it."

"Forgotten." A smile back. "He knew the painting couldn't stay there. That's the heart of Roero country."

"Professor?"

"Yes, I'm sorry. I am showing off a little."

"I'm impressed."

"The monastery was right on the edge of the original home estates of the Roero family. That region was dominated by the Roeros for several centuries. And after what happened in Malta, the whole family was determined to kill Michele. He had, after all, badly wounded their Cavaliere Giovanni, the Conte della Vezza. And even then, there were rumors that Michele had some kind of secret, something that would seriously damage the family's reputation. A blot on the old escutcheon." The professor held up a finger, a lecturer's gesture. "They were deadly serious. Remember, our romantic poet Fenelli barely made it out alive. He didn't live very long after he got to Siena."

"Is this all from your research, Professor?"

"And a certain amount of intuition."

He caught the waiter's eye. "The wine bottle?" Apparently, they had already discussed this, because the waiter had the empty bottle ready and showed it to Lucia, as if presenting a full bottle to the table.

"This is what we've been drinking," said the professor.

The label said, in big letters: "Roero."

And below that:

Azienda Agricola

Parussa Giuseppe

"One of the best," said the professor.

"More of your extensive research?"

"Exactly."

"Did you learn anything about the Roero Brigade?"

"Indeed I did. But it wasn't easy. It took a while to get anyone to talk about it. There's a certain amount of fear—they all know what's been happening. But once they trusted me, they made their feelings very clear. I believe 'loathing' would be the proper word. They say it all started with a lunatic who claimed to be part of the Roero family. No one seems to know where he came from, but he made quite a spectacle. Ranting about the family and its sacred mission. The known descendants of the Roeros—the 'official' family—rejected him completely. Scornfully. But some others think his claims of Roero descent were pretty solid. In any case, rejected by the family, he declared his own holy war on Islam to prove he was worthy of the name. And attracted followers, the way people like that always seem to. And he expanded his personal jihad to include anyone who threatened the glorious name of Roero. He was fixated on Caravaggio—maybe trying to bolster his position by stirring up the old feud. And then we came along."

"You have become quite the expert."

"Thank you, my dear. In fact, I am going to give a little talk on what I have learned as part of a small symposium next month."

"A symposium?"

He nodded gravely. "On the painting—which I cannot help but consider 'our' painting." He leaned closer and lowered his voice. "They are close to declaring it a fully authenticated"—he couldn't help glancing around—"Caravaggio. We experts will discuss what we have learned."

Lucia felt a mix of glee and bitter disappointment. The disappointment won out.

"I wish they had taken the trouble to invite me too. It's not as if I—"

The professor cut her off, producing a thick envelope from his jacket pocket with a flourish. "I wanted to deliver this myself."

Lucia's face lit up. Before he handed over the envelope, the professor added, "But bear in mind, your presentation is scheduled right before mine. So make certain you are prepared to stay within the time limits outlined in the cover letter."

"My pre—"

"—sentation. Of course. Certainly you don't think they could have a symposium without you."

It was a gift that for a moment almost made up for all the bitterly unhappy Christmases on Long Island with her *nonna*. Lucia resisted the Christmas impulse to tear the envelope open on the spot. Instead, she smiled and tucked it away.

The professor grinned as if he had something else in store.

"You haven't asked me where the symposium is being held," he said.

"Should I?"

"Please do."

"All right. Professor Richman, could you tell me where this symposium is being held?"

"Indeed I can." Pause. "La Posta Vecchia Hotel." Another pause. Lucia looked puzzled. "In Palo."

Now Lucia did indeed have the smile of a child at Christmas.

"Palo! That's perfect."

Palo was the last place that anyone had almost certainly seen Caravaggio alive. After that, it was all conjecture, mystery, dispute. And Palo was the place where Mario Fenelli had snatched up one of the four paintings Michele had left on the felucca and tucked it in among his own belongings in preparation for racing north once he disembarked in Porto Ercole.

"Palo." She said it again.

"Perfect," Professor Richman agreed.

They walked through the narrow streets of the old ghetto in search of a taxi.

"You've kept yourself well informed on the scientific investigation."

For a moment, the professor stopped scanning the traffic for a taxi. "Our friend Moto has been in touch on a regular basis. He's kept me informed."

Lucia had expected that, but she wasn't quite sure what to say in response. The professor filled the silence.

"I understand the two of you had a . . . falling out."

"He lied to us!" She started to fill in the details, but Professor Richman stopped her.

"Lucy, I realized who he was a long time ago."

"When? How did—?"

"When that, um, gentleman at the hotel in Siena refrained from killing me, I started thinking. With everything that had happened, it suddenly became obvious."

"Why didn't you tell me?"

"It didn't seem like something that one would talk about. For all I knew, you were part of it too. And as long as he was keeping thugs from slitting my throat, I saw no need to complain."

With that, the professor lurched out into the street and flung his arm in the air. As a taxi pulled to a halt, Professor Richman added, "Moto wasn't lying, Lucy. He was keeping a secret that wasn't his to tell. And he was trying to protect us. Protect you, really. You're the one he cares about. I was just along for the ride."

He opened the door and waved for Lucia to get in, but she paused and said, "No, thanks. I think I'll walk. It's a beautiful night."

Chapter 50

ROME

Fra Filippo Lupo struggled to control his emotions. He knew he had done well in his investigations. Still, he was careful to erase any trace of pride from his face before he entered the office. He knew he could not betray any emotion—most particularly pleasure. He would not give his commander any reason to question his presentation. He could almost hear the snarl in that deep voice: "Pleased with yourself, Fra Lupo?" No, he would not chance that reception. Particularly today. His presentation was going to be two-edged and more than merely difficult. The good news of his own work, followed by much more painful information. It almost scared him to think of it.

His commander was demanding, harsh—and still beloved. It had been that way for decades since Lupo (though he hadn't yet adopted that nom de guerre) had been a college student in a class led by Gran Comandante Militare Pantera (then calling himself Gustavo de Roero) during the single academic year before the uproar over the *comandante*'s thesis had resulted in his banishment from academia.

The years since then had been challenging, often enough painful, but certainly thrilling, as the *comandante*'s curious charisma had drawn followers to his cause. Some had become fanatically dedicated. Others had fallen along the way. But their ranks had grown steadily—and Fra

Lupo had been by the *comandante*'s side through it all. He had accepted discipline when it was merited and he had refrained from any self-congratulatory excesses—most certainly in the *comandante*'s presence.

And so he banished all emotion—pleasure or regret—as he entered the office and snapped to attention in front of the enormous desk and the tiny man behind it.

"Pleased with yourself, Fra Lupo?"

Damn.

"No sir. Pleasure or regret rests entirely on your decision, sir."

"Fra Filippo Lupo! Report!"

"Comandante! Following up on your own excellent work, sir, I was able to determine that the *ragazza* was born in a tiny village called Cuoremontagna. As far as I could discover, it no longer exists. It was abandoned almost twenty years ago after most of the inhabitants were killed in several years of combat—more a series of vicious assaults than real warfare—between two Mafia families seeking control of the worthless territory."

"Sicilians," hissed the *comandante*. "Sometimes I wonder if they aren't really all Turks."

Lupo paused to be certain his commander was finished. Then he continued.

"The girl's entire family was killed in one such assault. She alone survived, although there is no record of how she escaped. There are only reports of those who once lived there and those who were found dead. But with assistance from my own contacts in America—you have indeed taught me well, sir—I was able to determine that the elderly couple who raised her were her *nonni* and were from that same village of Cuoremontagna, and they were driven out following an earlier outbreak of similar violence."

"Interesting."

"Sir. And although firm answers are elusive, it seems clear that her family—grandparents, parents, and several uncles—played an important part in one family's victory in that war. If any result of such petty violence could be called a victory. And she is the only survivor of her immediate family line."

"Is that your entire report?"

"No sir. I have also learned that Father Antonio—"

"Ah! The meddlesome priest."

"Yes sir. Father Antonio was from that same village. He had been part of the violence, but he left to join the priesthood at about the same time the girl was sent to America."

"Ha!" Comandante Pantera's hand slammed down on the desk, but this time—for the first time in a long time—he was definitely smiling. "Brilliant work, Lupo. Brilliant. We've got it."

Lupo's brow was furrowed. "Thank you, sir. But I'm not sure how it all fits together."

"That's the brilliant part, Lupo. It doesn't matter exactly how the pieces fit—we just know that they do fit somehow. It's all connected, and that's all we need to know."

His smile was actually warm.

"Fra Lupo. Filippo. *Figlio mio.* You have justified the faith I have put in you. You have made me proud."

Then he stopped, closed his eyes, and raised his fingertips to his temples. He sat that way for a long minute, and then the blue eyes flashed open again.

"Yes! It will be perfect. Not easy, but easy enough. And perfect."

Fra Lupo shifted uneasily. "Sir, I . . ."

The *gran comandante* didn't even bother to reprimand him. He just kept talking, his excitement rising.

"The carabinieri have turned the painting over to the academics. That will make it almost too easy. They are having a symposium in Palo. The painting will be there. Certainly the girl will be there. We will grab them both. Both! And . . . yes! We will be disguised as Muslim terrorists. We will issue threats in the name of Allah, declaring we will kill the girl and destroy the painting unless they grant us . . . whatever. And then, then we will announce as ourselves, as the Roero Brigade, that we have rescued the girl and we will set her free. We'll be heroes."

Fra Lupo was looking increasingly unhappy, but the *comandante* didn't notice.

"By rescuing the girl, we will have the mafiosi on our side. They apparently feel some sort of obligation to her and they will appreciate her rescue. Then we can destroy that cursed note. Cavaliere Roero's reputation will be safe and we can let the mafiosi sell the painting. They will certainly be pleased with that arrangement—and we will only ask for half the proceeds. That's enough to fund our mission for years to come."

He leaned back in the chair. "All thanks to the meddlesome priest." He smiled, and as if welcoming Lupo into his club of scholars, added, "You know, of course, that Henry the Second didn't actually say 'Will no one rid me of this meddlesome priest.' The best history we have tells us that—"

"Sir! Stop!"

There was a moment of silence, as if neither man could believe that Lupo had actually dared to interrupt so recklessly.

And then, before the *gran comandante* could speak, Lupo rushed ahead.

"It will not happen. It cannot happen."

"What!" Puzzlement and outrage mixed.

For an instant, the man sitting behind the desk seemed about to explode out of his chair and launch himself at the throat of the much larger man, who still stood straight and tall, nothing in his expression expressing fear or regret. But that explosion never occurred. The smaller man's supreme self-control kept him sitting. He leaned back in his chair, seeming almost relaxed.

"I do not understand what you are trying to tell me," he continued.

The other man's posture relaxed just perceptibly. He was going to be allowed to explain.

"Comandante, it pains me deeply to have spoken as I have. But out of my deep loyalty to you and to our cause, I had no choice."

"No choice?"

"Sir, we do not have the men for this mission."

"Really?" His tone was relaxed, simple curiosity.

"After the latest . . . incident—the car crash, sir—there are very few of us left."

"The mission I have described does not require more than a handful of men."

"Sir, we do not have a handful. Not even that." A brief pause. A breath. Out with it. "They have all abandoned us. They have deserted. There is no one left. Except myself. And you. Just we two. And we cannot do this alone. It is madness to think otherwise, sir."

There was a long silence.

Then Comandante Pantera spoke.

"So, after all we have done, all we have sacrificed, all we have achieved, now with victory in reach, we are forced to turn back, to betray our cause, to betray the man whose glorious memory has inspired us, just because a pack of cowardly dogs have turned tail and run!"

Fra Lupo said nothing. The other man, still seated, nodded slowly.

"It would seem I have no choice. I must accept this new state of affairs." He closed his eyes for a moment. Shook his head slightly. "I have loved you like a son. I have favored you above all others. I have trusted you."

The other man still said nothing.

Fra Pantera's eyes snapped open, white showing all around the icy blue. His fighting-dog's ears somehow tucking even more tightly against his skull.

"I thank you for your service. You are dismissed."

"Sir." With military precision, he turned on his heel and walked slowly to the door, limping slightly, knowing that once through that door, he would breathe easily for the first time in longer than he could remember.

As Fra Lupo reached for the doorknob, the man at the desk drew open a drawer and without hesitation raised a pistol and fired a single shot into the back of Fra Lupo's head.

Then he set the pistol gently on the desk and sat for an endless moment looking down at it.

"*Figlio mio?*" There was contempt in his voice. "Cowardly fool! I will take care of it myself."

Chapter 51

Napoli
1610

Caravaggio carried his rolled canvases under his arm. As he stepped down from the Colonna carriage, he called to the coachman.

"Drop my trunk off over there—that brown-and-blue boat, the *Gabbiano*. See that no one meddles with it and don't leave until I return to see it loaded. I want to stretch my legs before the sail."

The coachman muttered something and drove on to the hitching posts, looking for a strong-backed workman to wrestle with the heavy trunk.

Caravaggio took a sip of salt air into his lungs. Soon enough, he would be at the seaport of Civitavecchia and then on to Roma. His eyesight was still compromised, but he saw busy hands weaving something a few paces ahead on the rocky pier.

"Are you leaving us, Maestro?" said a burly fisherman, his skin wrinkled as an elephant's hide. He stopped mending his nets. "I thought Napoli suited you."

Caravaggio stopped to look at the fisherman's gnarled hands, crisscrossed with scars and lacerations from hauling nets over the years.

The fisherman jabbed his finger at the artist's face. Caravaggio noticed the tip of his finger was missing.

"Don't hold it against us what some foreign cutthroats did to you," said the man.

"How do you know they were foreign, fisherman?" asked Caravaggio.

The man spat into dirty foam ebbing against the dock. "You think a Napoletano would cut you? *Ecco!* You, Maestro, you who gave Napoli the *Seven Acts of Mercy*? Next to Faccia Gialla, you are Napoli's favorite son! For a foreigner . . ."

"Faccia Gialla . . . ah, the yellow face," said Caravaggio.

"Our patron saint, Gennaro, Maestro," said the fisherman, bowing his head in reverence.

"Whose blood liquefies each year as a blessing?" said Caravaggio. "*Pescatore*, I cannot claim such miracles."

"Your paints are liquid. They dry into miracles. Your gift to Napoli is the *Seven Acts of Mercy*," said the fisherman. "The most magnificent painting!"

"He's right," said another fisherman next to him, sorting his catch. Beside him were piles of shellfish, sea urchins, small silverfish, and a good-size branzino. "They are foreign *bravi* who attacked you, not one of us, no matter how desperate. No Napoletano would lay a hand on you."

Caravaggio nodded. The morning light glinted bright off the water. The artist squinted at the fishermen crouched over their nets.

"A foreigner. I'll consider that," he said. He turned back and walked toward the bobbing felucca moored to a massive stone pylon.

The captain, slit-eyed with sun-bleached hair, nodded to his passenger as he approached. "You are the last," he said. "This carriage driver wouldn't let my crew load your trunk. What do you have in there, Maestro? Gold?"

"None of your business," said Caravaggio. "Put that trunk next to my bunk."

"I'll put her down in the hold," said the captain. "No water will seep in there."

"Do as I say," said Caravaggio. "Next to my bunk."

"All right. Don't blame me if it flies loose in a storm and knocks you senseless," said the captain. "Emilio! Get some help and carry that trunk down to Signor Merisi's bunk." The captain looked at the heavy lock on the chest and snorted. "Won't have anybody trying to pry her open either. She'll be good and safe. You can ride sitting on her if you want to." The captain winked at one of the sailors.

"Don't act the arse with me, Captain," said Caravaggio. "Nothing but sickness in the hold. I'll stand my ground up on deck."

"Not your first sail, then, Maestro?"

Caravaggio said nothing. He made an agitated gesture with his hand for the crew to load the chest.

The felucca was loaded with cargo and a few passengers. Among those already on board was a scruffy, long-haired man with a carelessly groomed beard. He wore a crimson scarf around his neck in a loose knot. He stared at Caravaggio.

"You're the artist—Caravaggio," he said.

"What business is it of yours?" said Caravaggio, turning to watch his locked chest carried down into the hold. "Be careful how you handle that trunk!" he shouted.

"*Sì, signore,*" grunted the two sailors struggling to move the coffer down the hatch.

"Put it by his bunk," said the captain. "He can watch over it there."

"Aye, Captain," said the sailors.

"Why are you leaving Napoli?" said the stranger with the red scarf.

"Again, what business is it of yours?" said Caravaggio.

"Allow me to introduce myself. I am Mario Fenelli, by profession a poet. Perhaps you have heard of me in Spaccanapoli?"

"Why should I have heard of you?"

"I've recited poetry at the Cerriglio. You are a frequent visitor."

"I keep company with real poets, signore," said Caravaggio. "Giambattista Marino—"

"You know him?" said Mario, his eyes widening.

"He is an intimate friend. I painted his portrait."

Fenelli fingered his dirty scarf. "You don't by chance have it in that chest, do you?"

"You are a colossal fool, 'poet'!" snarled Caravaggio, walking away.

Hour after hour, the sailboat bobbed along the coast of western Italy, heading north to Civitavecchia. Caravaggio shaded his eyes with his hand, scanning the rocky cliffs and sunlit villages clinging to land's end.

"We'll make Palo by Tuesday, midnight," said the captain. "You've got your papers in order? We'll shove off as soon as we pass customs."

"Palo?" said Caravaggio.

"The papal guard keeps the fortress there. We must show our papers before sailing to dock in Roman territories."

Caravaggio pressed his lips together, making his mustache buckle.

"You have your papers in order, do you not, Maestro?" said the captain.

"Certo," said the artist, looking out to sea. *Of course.*

The small bunk room was empty except for the two passengers occupying two lower beds. Mario Fenelli sat on his bunk, pulling items out of a carpetbag.

"You might be interested in the art supplies I'm bringing my brother, a monk in Piemonte," said Fenelli.

"I'm sure I wouldn't be," said Caravaggio, unfolding the linen sheet to make a bed.

"Look. Horsehair paintbrushes. This one is made from ferret hair. And I have pigments. Madder root and the finest lapis lazuli."

Caravaggio looked over his shoulder at the nugget of lapis lazuli.

"See! This cost me dear," said the poet. "I—"

"I can see you are a fool with your money," said Caravaggio, taking the nugget in his hand. "Too much ash and not enough pigment."

Fenelli frowned. "And this," he said, pulling out a steel hammer and chisel. "My brother is interested in sculpture."

"A sculpting monk," muttered Caravaggio. "Where did you say your brother's monastery is?"

"Roero."

Caravaggio grunted. *Roero!*

"That's where?" he asked.

"In Piemonte. Way up north."

"I know where Piemonte is. Put away your toys, poet, and blow out your candle. I want to sleep."

"*Sì, signore,*" said Fenelli.

With the candle extinguished, the bunk room was dark except for the guttering light of the single sconce bolted to a timber. Mario Fenelli stared from his bunk at the tar-sealed trunk strapped in leather.

Giambattista Marino. Europe's most acclaimed living poet! For Mario, who spouted poetry to anyone who would listen—more often those who wished not to listen at all—Giambattista Marino was a god. *This artist, this Caravaggio—he paints masterpieces, worth hundreds of scudi! If I could only glimpse—*

"Close your eyes, 'poet,'" growled a voice in the darkness.

When the erratic light shifted with a drafty gust, Mario saw the brutal sheen in Caravaggio's eyes, and the bright gleam of a dagger cradled in his hands.

Mario rolled over, shivering under his blanket.

The following morning, Mario Fenelli woke to see the rumpled blanket of an empty bunk. Caravaggio had already risen to watch the sunrise.

Fenelli crept quietly out of his bunk and walked barefooted to the black-tarred chest. He stooped and held the iron lock in his hand—it was the breadth of his palm, heavy, and solid.

He licked his lips. *What the artist has locked inside this sea chest must be worth a fortune.*

"What are you doing?" growled a voice. Fenelli saw Caravaggio drop off the rope ladder onto the floor and pounce at him.

Fenelli stumbled to his feet, dropping the lock. *"N-n-niente!"* he stuttered. *Nothing.*

Caravaggio grabbed Fenelli by his shirt, twisting the material in his hand so it choked him. "If I see you within an arm's length of that chest again, I'll cut your face."

Mario Fenelli stared at the puckered scars crisscrossing Caravaggio's cheeks and eye. *"Sì, signore,"* he squeaked.

Caravaggio let go of Fenelli's shirt and pushed him. Fenelli stumbled backward, hitting his head on the bunk. The artist climbed back up the hatch, leaving the poet moaning.

The sea turned gray green as the wind came up, frothing whitecaps curling as far as the eye could see.

"Rough weather ahead," said the captain. "Let's hope it clears before we reach Palo."

Caravaggio eyed the purple-black clouds. In the distance he could see squalls ripping across the sea, churning the waves white.

"How long do we dock in Palo?"

"Only long enough to show the Roman officials your papers. They mark your entry in their ledger. Then you are back on board."

Caravaggio looked back at the squalls. A gray shroud of rain descended and the wind began to howl.

"Take down the mainsail. Tighten the jib," shouted the captain.

Sharp, stinging rain pelted Caravaggio's skin. The boat lurched up and smacked down hard, knocking him off his feet.

"Get below, signore!" shouted the captain.

Caravaggio went down through the hatch, his fists clinging to the rope ladder. The hatch slammed shut above him in a shower of seawater. He swung left and right, smacking against the wood. He jumped down from the ladder, sprawling across the floor, next to a retching Mario Fenelli.

The stench, acrid and foul, assaulted Caravaggio's nostrils. The timbers of the boat squeaked and groaned above them.

"I hate the sea!" cried the poet, wiping the vomit from his mouth.

"Poets can't hate the sea," said Caravaggio. "They write odes and sonnets to it."

He climbed into his bunk. "At least you won't be tampering with my possessions, the state you are in," he muttered, pulling the blanket over his nose and closing his eyes.

Dawn was still hours off when the anchor splashed into the sea and the first mate called down the hatch.

"The captain says get your papers in order. We'll anchor here. In the morning, they'll send a small boat to ferry us in."

Caravaggio rolled out of his bunk and climbed up through the hatch.

The sea was still rough. The *Gabbiano* pulled on the anchor line, fighting left and right to free herself, like a hooked shark.

The sea air filled his lungs, salty and clean. Across the water, not far off, stood a castle, the waves beating against the seawall.

"You have pretty good sea legs for a Milanese," said the captain, a ghostly presence in the moonlight.

"I've had some experience in recent years."

The captain regarded him in the darkness. A tattered cloud sped past the moon. Both men stood silent, watching the changing light and shadow.

"They say you were a knight," said the captain. "A Maltese knight, the Order of St. John."

Caravaggio said nothing. Waves lapped against the boat and the rigging creaked above them.

"Beyond the castle is the customhouse," said the captain. "There won't be anyone there until morning, but their sentinels will have already spotted us."

Still, Caravaggio remained silent.

"*Guardi*, Signòr Merisi," said the captain. "You don't know me, but everyone in Napoli knows you. You say you have your papers in order. *Bene.* You'll need them."

"I'm traveling with special permission from the pope's nephew, Cardinal Scipione Borghese."

"And he's given you approval for entry?" asked the captain. "Because, from what I know, there is a bounty on your head."

"That's none of your business, Capitano," said Caravaggio.

"It will be my business if you don't return to my ship. And that chest of yours—"

"The chest stays on board."

"They may inspect it."

"They may not."

The captain snorted. "Signor Merisi, I don't care about you. You are a difficult man to like. But I am indebted to the Colonna family—as many Napoletani are," he said, tapping his pipe against the mast. "I know you have many enemies. I cannot protect you from them."

"I didn't ask you for protection."

The captain held up his hand to silence the artist. He trained his eyes toward the coast.

"What is it?" said Caravaggio.

"What the devil are they doing?"

"What?" said Caravaggio. "I can't see—"

"You can't see that torch in the stern of the boat?"

"Boat?"

"The guards are rowing toward us. In the middle of the night!"

Chapter 52

LADISPOLI

Lucia spent three days in a small room on the shore west of Rome. Spring on the Mediterranean Sea was not as mild as in the city. It was raining and chilly, and the man at the hotel desk smiled— *"Ciao, bella"*—and charged her the off-season rate.

As soon as she got to her room, she pulled out her cell phone and checked her e-mail. There was the usual swamp of unwanted messages and one, astoundingly, from Professor Richman, a man who generally refused to have anything to do with such nonsense as e-mail.

"Great news!" he exulted. The painting had been removed from the damask lining. The *poemetto* was there, exactly as Fenelli had transcribed it. But—better yet!—the "anomalies in the texture" turned out to be a single thin sheet of parchment, a document of some kind. There was going to be a presentation on it at the symposium.

In a gesture of celebration, Lucia turned off her cell phone and stuffed it deep into her suitcase. She didn't need any more messages.

She felt as if she had escaped. Escaped from being the only one insisting Te-Te's painting had to be real, whatever the cost. In a few days, she would speak at the symposium, and whatever she said would be overwhelmed by the brilliantly credentialed voices of the experts who would agree with her—and drown her out in the process.

It was a perfect ending, as far as she was concerned. A perfect time to get on with something else, because this wasn't going any further. Not for her anyway. The experts would take it from here. Eventually, the painting would be auctioned and the proceeds would go to Te-Te's orphanage.

Maybe it was time for her to move on with Moto's happy ending and head back to the States, where eventually she could be his great American friend. Maybe. The uncertainty of what might come next gnawed at her.

Here on the coast, the weather was gray and the beaches were gritty, but the sound of the waves helped calm her down.

The first night, staring out to sea, she thought about disappearing. It was a good time for her to slip out. And everything here would go on perfectly well without her.

She could even go right now. Forget the symposium. What did she care? Just get on a plane and it was done.

But she didn't. She spent the next two days walking on the beach, dressed warmly against the sea-chilled wind, seeking out sheltered places to sit and listen to the waves.

Sit and listen and consider that, no, she hadn't escaped. She might step out of the story now, but people had died. People who would still be alive if she had simply let it go. If she hadn't insisted on finding Te-Te. Hadn't gotten in touch with him. Hadn't felt so strongly when she did meet him.

She had done all that.

And she still didn't know why.

She was barely five when she was sent away to live with her *nonna*. And Te-Te was much older. One of the *adulti*, the adults. He must have only been in his twenties, but when you're five, they're all just huge and old and Te-Te was one of them.

That was all she remembered. The only scraps she'd been able to fish out of that fog. Not much. No reason to care about Te-Te. Except, years later, Nonna had spoken his name in the last hours before she died. There was something in her voice that sounded like unfinished business, a family story to track down. A mission for Lucia to focus on during her time in Italy. If she found him, he might be the only person still alive that she remembered from the days in the village when she was young. That was something.

It was part of the reason she enrolled in the seminar in Monte Piccolo—she knew Te-Te lived just a few hours' drive away.

And if she hadn't done that, if she'd gone to school in Rome, Te-Te would still be alive. No visiting American "experts" from the art seminar to stir up the orphans and the thieves.

That's where it all started. With her. So, no, she wasn't off the hook for any of it.

But the crashing surf did help.

After two long days and restless nights, Lucia packed her suitcase and took a taxi a few kilometers down the coast to Palo. The Posta Vecchia was an elegant manor house hotel, originally a simple inn on the coastal road north from Rome. It had been built centuries ago by a prince, conveniently close to his castle. In the twentieth century, it had passed on to a modern-day prince, an American oil billionaire who converted it to his own private villa. Now it was a small, nearly perfect hotel, beyond deluxe in a slightly informal way, a grand old house looking out over the water. Way out of Lucia's league, of course, but as a presenter at the symposium, this was where she stayed. It was a short drive from where she'd spent the past days, but it was a different world.

She unpacked her bags in a room with a beautiful view over the sea and then went out to find her way along the shore toward the castle. The castle was centuries older than the hotel and had certainly loomed—grim and forbidding then as now—over Caravaggio's ship as it approached land.

She made her way along a narrow strip of beach and then up onto the rocks piled along the shore beneath the walls of the castle.

This was the spot, the last place where anyone had almost certainly seen Caravaggio alive, the point in time and space where the mystery of his death really began.

It was the beginning of the trail she had been following back in time, back from Te-Te's chapel through counts and countesses, knights and fools and scoundrels, a monk and a poet-thief. Here is where it started, and now here is where it would end. For her, in any case.

She turned her back to the castle and looked out to sea.

The surf broke on the rocks and the wind blew a chill spray into her face.

When Lucia woke the next morning, the hotel was full and cheerfully bustling. She went down to the elegant breakfast room and sipped a cappuccino. The tables were filled with chattering groups of what seemed to be old friends and acquaintances who'd all spent years traveling the symposium circuit.

A flutter of action caught her eye, and she glanced up to see Professor Richman sweep into the room, in an elegant blazer with a deep-red scarf at his throat. He looked to fit in perfectly with the rest of the crowd, and Lucia wondered for a moment if he would strike up conversations, find new friends, and abandon her to get by on her own. She knew she could, although she wasn't certain she wanted to.

The professor stopped, looked around, broke into a smile, and headed straight for Lucia. As he crossed the room, she saw that he had an ebony silver-headed cane in his hand, though he certainly wasn't leaning on it for support. He bent over, kissed her on the cheek, and settled into a chair.

"My dear young lady . . ."

"Ralphie . . ."

They laughed and settled in to sip cappuccinos and talk with the freedom of old friends who had nothing to do but relax and enjoy themselves in this perfect seaside retreat.

When she asked about the cane, he cocked his head and said, "Looks distinguished, don't you think?"

A raised eyebrow was her only response, and Professor Richman shrugged. "And that knee of mine does act up from time to time. I'm getting too old to stumble and fall."

"You getting old, Ralphie? Never!"

He gave a self-deprecating smile and they moved on to other subjects.

After half an hour, Lucia was getting ready to excuse herself and go up to her room when she looked toward the door.

And there was Moto.

His expression was uncertain. His eyes darted, scanning the room.

Lucia jumped to her feet and rushed over. Before he could say a word, she embraced him, gave him a solid kiss, and stepped back to look him in the eye.

"Amico mio." My friend.

Then she hugged him hard, which she hoped settled all of that. For now, at least.

Moto's discomfort dissolved in a smile. He threw his arms around her and—still and always Moto—almost knocked a tray full of elegant breakfasts out of the hands of a passing waiter.

Lucia led him back to the breakfast table. The professor rose to his feet, and the two men reached out for a handshake—then Moto pulled the professor closer, or perhaps it was the professor who pulled Moto closer, and the handshake turned into a gently awkward embrace. Lucia smiled and threw her arms around their shoulders, joining all three of them in what became a thoroughly awkward embrace. For a long moment, they stood in warm silence.

Then Moto stepped back abruptly and sat—almost collapsed—into a chair. He took a deep breath and leaned forward, his face grim, as the others sat down. All the joy of a few moments ago was gone.

"They found a body." His voice was thin and tight.

No one reacted.

"No clothes. No identification. But tattoos. The Maltese cross with an *R* above it. Two of them. One on his hip and the other below that, on his thigh." His eyes darted back and forth from Lucia to the professor. "And between them—"

"Wait!" Professor Richman broke in. "Don't say it."

"What?" Lucia had no idea what he was talking about.

The professor looked at Moto. "Between the crosses there was a tattoo reading something like '*J* fifteen eight.' Right, Moto?"

Moto nodded. His lips pressed thin.

"Judges 15:8," said the professor, sounding almost annoyed. "Samson and the Philistines. 'He smote them hip and thigh.' Hip and thigh. This Roero gang was in a fever of biblical megalomania."

"Not 'was,' 'is,'" said Moto. "They found the body three days ago. Dead a day at most. Shot in the back of the head."

The sky out over the sea was improbably beautiful. Rose and delicate pink, a canopy of glorious light. But dark clouds were blossoming, drowning the colors as Lucia stood at her window.

Lucia didn't notice.

She was holding a single sheet of paper in her hand. It had been sitting on her bed—on her pillow—when she returned to the room after an early dinner. Its presence was unsettling. Its contents worse. She had read it once, twice, and then, obsessively, a third and fourth time. The handwriting was precise, careful, the message less so.

I know who you are. I know your family. I know their secrets. I can tell you what you need to know. Tonight at midnight, below the castle, at the edge of the Mare Tyrrhenum.

That much of the note was at least comprehensible. Then it continued, the handwriting still perfect, even as the message ran wild.

You must choose whether you will be Queen Tamar the Great who inspired her troops to victory over the Sultan of Rûm and his vile Muslim hordes at Basian. Or the Whore of Babylon, clutching her golden cup full of abominations and the filth of her fornication, running with the dogs and sorcerers and whoremongers and murderers and idolaters! The truth awaits in the dark at the edge of the waters! The decision is yours.

It was signed with a single initial: *R.*

She stood motionless as the sky turned black over the Tyrrhenian Sea, *Mar Tirreno* in Italian. And for some reason, the note's lapse into Latin—*Mare Tyrrhenum*—tore at her mind almost more than the ravings from the Book of Revelation. Or the reference to the unknown Tamar the Great.

A speedboat cut across the dark water, moving fast, carving a wake, searchlight dicing the black. If Lucia had been outside in the night, she would have heard the slap of its hull against the waves, like gunshots above the roar of the surf.

The night deepened as, one by one, the lights inside the hotel went dark. The gibbous moon had disappeared, swallowed by black clouds. As the darkness became nearly complete, she threw open the window. The roar of the surf was deafening. The wind rose, as if to match the sea. Flags of foam were torn from the crests of the waves, and the air was wet and heavy with the tang of salt.

She knew he was out there in the dark.

Roero.

Whoever he was.

She wasn't crazy. He was real. Very real. And the people he murdered were very dead.

She thought of those people who would still be alive if she hadn't been compelled to find the tough-guy priest she'd never really known. And then compelled to prove to the world that he wasn't a fool.

Right now she was the fool. Because only a fool would answer this call from an obvious madman. But she knew she had to.

No, she didn't have to. Even in her turmoil, she knew she didn't have to.

But she knew she would.

She would put herself in harm's way, just as she had put others there.

She would stand, teetering at the very edge of the world.

And he would be there.

He had always been there, everywhere, one step ahead of her.

He always knew where she was. He always knew when she was weak.

And Roero would know that tonight she stood in the dark.

Alone.

She was ready to accept whatever the night brought her way. She wasn't frightened. She wasn't brave. She was just sick of it. All of it. It wasn't clear how it would end. But she didn't care. As long as it ended.

An enormous wave crashed, the foam somehow catching light even in the darkness. The spray slapped her face.

She stood on the rocks, tall against the wind and waves, and shouted, "I am not Michelangelo Merisi da Caravaggio, and I am not going to spend my life running away from assassins from the House of Roero!"

And no one heard her.

Not the young man tucked in the lee of an enormous rock, as near to her as he dared get, one hand clutching the cold steel of a pistol in his pocket, the other pulling the collar of his leather jacket tighter against the biting wind.

Nor did the sound of her voice reach a second man, in a gray tunic, concealed higher up in the rocks, almost at the foot of the castle walls. But now, seeing her standing at the edge of the water, he rose and moved down toward her, slowly. He had a gun. He had a knife. But all he expected to need right now were the handcuffs and the length of chain in a bag at his side. He would capture her and punish her tonight—slowly, painfully, the punishment she deserved—before returning tomorrow to deal with the painting.

Time passed, burrowing into the deepest part of the night.

Lucia leaned against a boulder, shivering, her mind raging like the Tyrrhenian Sea, the *Mare Tyrrhenum*, stretching out before her into the dark. She thought again about what a fool she was, to be here alone. Unarmed. Before she had left the hotel to head into the night, she had considered finding some kind of weapon—perhaps a knife from the restaurant kitchen. But then, fool that she was, she had decided she had to remain true to her motto, Caravaggio's motto: Without hope. Without fear.

And arming herself would somehow be cheating.

A faint glimmer of moonlight found its way through the clouds, and the young man in the leather jacket thought he might get closer. He leaned slowly, silently, out of the shelter of the rocks, just as the moon broke free for an instant, lighting a ragged circle of clouds.

And a scream tore like lightning through the black of the night.

The young man leapt into action. Already moving, he tried to move faster and his foot slipped on a wet rock. He skidded down to the beach but landed on his feet and ran, pistol in hand, to find another path up through the rocks.

But then he stopped.

Through a break in the rocks, he could see her, standing alone, standing strong, arms reaching up as if she would embrace a fading shaft of moonlight. And then in an instant, she crouched down, hugging her knees, staring into the dark.

So he stopped and waited where he was. Watching.

And still above them both, the man in the gray tunic also stopped and stared down into the night. In that brief moment of moonlight, he had seen the younger man and seen the glint of the pistol in his hand.

His shoulders sagged, his gray tunic blending into the rocks. "Siciliano," he hissed under his breath.

He knew he could go no further tonight if they were still guarding her. But his military mind had another plan. Always. And unlike the cowards who had deserted him, he was not going to turn away.

The vision that had wrenched the scream from her was a single image: an enormous face, floating above her, peering down at her, with great bloody gouges running from beside the eyes down across the cheeks. It was a dark, brutal face, and the wounds made it more terrifying, more dangerous.

That was when she had screamed.

But the scream didn't shatter the vision, it drove her deeper under its spell.

The face disappeared. There was a fleeting moment when she saw herself, as if from a distance, one of the two prisoners, peering out through the barred window at the beheading of Saint John, at the fate that might soon be theirs.

And then she was seeing as they saw, seeing a scene that played out in the dark: blood and death. And like those prisoners, she was powerless to do anything but watch.

But what she was watching wasn't the martyrdom of Saint John. It was the scene seared into her mind by the explosion that had rocked her as she looked at *Judith Beheading Holofernes*. She felt the world tilt and spin, as it had then, but now there was so much more to see.

She saw the man lying bloody and torn, Holofernes's look of horror and surprise on his face. But it wasn't Holofernes. Now she knew. It was Lucia's father.

And the woman racing to him, arms outstretched, face an incomprehensible blend of puzzled horror and concentration, wasn't Judith reaching out to kill. It was Lucia's mother, reaching in desperation to save what was already hopelessly lost.

And now Lucia was there too, lying on the floor amid the swirling dust and debris, knocked sprawling by the blast. Voiceless, helpless. She was only five, what could she do?

She could see her baby sister's crib, crushed under the rubble from the explosion. One tiny hand lay uncovered. Motionless.

There was a moment of silence. Untouched by the explosion, a clock in the next room began to chime the useless hour.

With a sudden crash—almost a second explosion—the door was kicked in, and an enormous man leapt into the room, a shotgun held ready, sweeping from one figure to another: mother, father, Lucia.

He paused for a moment at Lucia. The shotgun wavered. Then he looked down at the tiny hand under the rubble.

"No!"

He threw the shotgun violently, as far from himself as he could, and ran back toward the door, waving his arms and shouting.

"No! Stop! It's wrong!"

A volley of shots from men outside, men who had been his companions up until that moment, sent him reeling back into the room, and as he caught his balance, Lucia's mother was at him like a cat. Her face hideous. Her fingernails clawing at his eyes, gouging his cheeks. Her arms, her blouse, her face—everything smeared with her husband's blood.

"*Assassino!*"

He threw her off and she fell to the ground sobbing. There was shouting outside.

The man, blood running down his face from the woman's attack, looked wildly around the room and then ran toward Lucia. She knew she was going to die, even though she was too young to know what that meant. But he swept her up and cradled her in his enormous, soot-covered, surprisingly gentle arms.

And through the darkness and the years, she distinctly heard him say, "What bastards we are."

And she looked up, and there it was again, the enormous face floating in midair, the bloody gouges running down his cheeks.

And now it wasn't terrifying. It was Te-Te.

She tried to say his name, but she couldn't.

There were shouts outside. More shots.

She felt herself spinning as Te-Te turned one way, then the other, with her in his arms. A moment of hesitation—the world stopping, hanging in the balance—and then Te-Te ran into the darkness, breathing hard, holding her tight, sheltered against his chest.

There was a shattering explosion behind them.

Te-Te stumbled, but he didn't fall.

The sea threw a bucket of cold water in her face. She blinked hard to clear her eyes and worked her way back across the rocks in the half dark—stiff and sore, half-frozen and limping. She had no idea how long she'd been lying there or whether she'd been awake, asleep, or unconscious.

She'd gone out to face Roero, ready to die, half expecting to. Thinking she didn't care. Prepared to die, she had been battered instead by a vision of death, a bolt that seared her.

How was she still alive?

After last night. After that other night, so long ago, that she had now faced for the first time.

Te-Te had saved her. She didn't know how he had smuggled a five-year-old out of the village, out of the endless Mafia war for territory, pitting neighbor against neighbor, out of the country and far beyond, to her *nonna* and *nonno* in the United States.

She didn't know and there was no one to tell her. There was no one alive who knew. But he had saved her.

And she was saving him.

Too late, but still.

"Lulu!"

Moto came running toward her, careful of his balance on the rocks. He hugged her fiercely and wrapped her in a blanket. In a moment, she realized he was as wet and cold as she was, so she pulled him closer and they shared the blanket.

By the walls of the castle, the man in the gray tunic was still watching. He saw the slim, graceful figure of the young man in the black leather jacket, and although he hadn't seen him before, he knew who he was. *"Checca,"* he spat. *"Fottuto bardassa e puttana di Babilonia."* Faggot! *Fucking faggot and the Whore of Babylon.*

Down below, on the rocks, Moto caught his breath. "Standing out there all night alone. Were you trying to get yourself killed?"

Lucia turned to face him. The blanket wrapped tighter and pulled them closer together, face-to-face. And she answered him with the same words she had shouted into the wind hours—a lifetime—before. But this time she whispered them, fervently.

"I am not Michelangelo Merisi da Caravaggio, and I am not going to spend my life running away from assassins from the House of Roero!"

Chapter 53

Palo
1610

The men in the rowboat emerged from the midnight darkness and mist just as the moon rose in the east, spilling light across the water.

They rowed up to the *Gabbiano* and rapped sharply on the hull.

The captain looked down at them. In the shadow of the hull, he couldn't make out their features.

"What are you doing out in the middle of the night?"

"Special orders," said a hoarse voice. "Send down your passengers. The customs officer expects them."

The captain said nothing. He disappeared from sight.

"Don't keep us waiting!" shouted the hoarse voice again. "We are under orders to deliver the passengers immediately to the customhouse."

When the captain appeared again, he leaned over the deck, a big oil lantern swinging from his fist.

"Show yourselves. Come under the light."

Murmurs and curses were whispered, but the oarsman rowed the boat into the pool of light.

The captain studied the man standing at the bow. He wore a dark tunic under a maroon cloak, but the hood of the cloak was pulled up and his face was still in shadow.

"Hand over the passengers," growled the hoarse voice from the shadowed face. "If you don't comply, we'll impound your boat."

If you can catch me. I don't like the looks of this.

"You show me your documents first," said the captain. "Or we will wait until morning."

"You are tempting fate," answered the man. He jerked his head to his assistant, who fumbled through a leather satchel and drew out a paper. The man in the bow handed the paper up to the captain, and in that moment, the hood of his cloak fell back. A broad scar ran across his cheek.

The captain knew this face. A cold shiver ran through him. He had faced without fear the worst the seas could throw at him, but this man was not someone he would willingly battle. He pictured the man as he had seen him before, in a black tunic with a white eight-pointed Maltese cross on his chest, a sword by his side, radiating the power of the knights of the Order of St. John.

And now he saw, in the brief looks they exchanged, that this man recognized him as well.

The captain gave the paper in his hand a brief glance. It no longer mattered. He handed it back with a nod, as if the paper's authenticity had convinced him, though they both knew better.

"All right," he said. "I'll rouse them. They'll be sleeping at this hour."

"Get them!" snarled the scar-faced man.

Caravaggio and Fenelli stood in the shadows. When the captain walked back, he whispered to them.

"I have no choice, Maestro," said the captain.

Fenelli shivered. Caravaggio looked up, studying the rising moon. For a long time, he was silent. The captain watched, saying nothing more.

This is a death sentence, thought the captain. *Why?*

Finally, Caravaggio drew a deep breath and nodded. "I'll go," he said. "But you see that my chest is protected. Promise me that."

The captain shook Caravaggio's hand. "I will. I am a man of my word."

Caravaggio walked to the sea ladder. The captain watched from the rail.

See how he walks without fear, accepting his fate. Has some angel whispered in his ear? Caravaggio will look upon God's face this morning.

Below, the scar-faced man's nostrils flared, and an ugly smile of triumph stretched his lips.

As Caravaggio descended into the boat, he said, "We meet again, brother Roero."

The man yanked at Caravaggio's shoulder, sending him sprawling into the gullet of the boat.

Then he held up a hand, signaling to the captain. "We approve the entry of your second passenger."

"What do you mean?" said the captain. "He needs a stamp of entry."

The assistant threw a jute sack over Caravaggio's head, and the scar-faced man lashed out with the butt of his gun. The form in the bag sagged in silence.

The captain watched the rowboat disappear into the luminous mist. There were four figures in the boat: The oarsman, bent hard to his work. The two knights, standing tall. The shrouded form in the jute sack.

Chapter 54

PALO

The room was filled with the happy buzz of scholars and experts meeting and greeting friends, cronies, allies, and enemies, all filled with breakfast and ready for the start of a daylong program that might be educational, entertaining, profitable, or simply boring.

Moto leaned closer to Lucia. "I'm sure the carabinieri are here. Somewhere." His voice trailed off into a shrug.

Professor Richman strode into the room and, with a cordial wave to Lucia and Moto, joined a cheerful chatting circle of experts. Dressed in a finely tailored blue pinstripe suit, his silver-headed cane lending exactly the distinguished air he had hoped for, the professor was clearly in his element.

The room lights dimmed slightly, and there was the scratch of a fingernail on a microphone, followed by an instant of feedback, instantly squelched.

"If I may have your attention, please."

The room quieted, if not completely. People turned toward a man standing behind a podium at the front of the room.

"Ladies and gentlemen," he began, "I am honored to present the scholar who organized this symposium, the distinguished professor emeritus of art history at the Sapienza University of Rome, Massimiliano Antonelli."

There was a polite scattering of applause as a tall, cadaverous man, his bald pate balanced by an impressive mustache, spent endless moments fiddling with the microphone, blowing into it, trying to raise it, and finally shrugging.

"Welcome, distinguished guests. I do have a few words of introduction and orientation to begin our time together. However, before we formally open today's session, I would like to note that we have a very special guest with us today. A surprise guest. And I would like to introduce that guest to you right now. So if I could please have your full attention for a moment."

The last chatterers quieted.

"Ladies and gentlemen, *signore e signori*, may I present . . ." He gestured and an assistant drew back a curtain that had covered a space next to the podium.

And there it was.

The painting. Their painting. Te-Te's painting.

". . . *Il bacio di Giuda*. Attributed to Michelangelo Merisi da Caravaggio."

Two uniformed guards emerged from the shadows to stand by the painting.

The room was filled with a hum, at first eager, then trailing off somewhat into puzzlement. The man at the podium continued, "As you may have noticed, our 'guest' is not quite ready to receive the general public. But we knew that this distinguished group of scholars would understand."

The painting had been mostly cleaned. The rich shadows now had hidden depths and mysteries, shafts of light picked out hands, arms, swords—gestures, embraces, threats.

But the faces still weren't clear. The capable, bland images painted by Fra Federico Fenelli had been cleared away, but beneath each one, the restoration team had encountered a thick layer of tenacious opaque white.

One presenter on the day's schedule was advancing the theory that when Fra Fenelli had painted over the faces, he had used that thick, opaque layer in an effort to protect the work of the criminal genius, Caravaggio. A holy man rescuing the work of a lost soul.

Whether or not that white paint had been intended as protection, it was certainly a challenge to the restorers, who had struggled to remove it without damaging the priceless brushwork beneath. For now, the faces were barely visible, emerging slowly, strangers in a fog.

Lucia left Moto behind and slipped through the crowd, working her way as close to the front as she could. A velvet rope held her back. The guards stood at a careful distance to avoid interfering with the scholars' eager inspection of the painting. Very civilized.

Lucia had watched that painting carried past the dead body of the man who had saved her life. She had been alone with it through one very long and dangerous night, locked in a warehouse. She had woken up to it one very difficult morning in her apartment. It had been the focus of her life for months.

Now, just to see it, she had to fight to hold her place as an overweight, overeager expert tried to elbow her aside.

And from as close as she could get, the faces in the painting in front of her were no more certain than the blurred images in the X-ray photos of the painting that were in the folders laid out neatly on every chair in the room.

It was a room filled with evidence and experts. But no answers.

None of that mattered to Lucia. Strangely, now that it was about to be declared a true Caravaggio, the painting itself had faded in importance. Te-Te's reputation was safe. And Lucia had the answers that mattered to her.

She had two images that would stay with her and challenge her for the rest of her life.

One was the image of Te-Te's face, enormous and ravaged, streaked with blood, looking down at her as he swept her into his arms and carried her into the darkness.

And the other was the image of her mother, Lucia's beautiful young mother, her face a savage mask of rage as she launched herself at Te-Te, her nails clawing for his eyes, leaving the scars that would mark him for the rest of his life. It was Lucia's final image of motherly love. Bitterness and revenge were her blessing, a mother's gift of infinite savage love.

Lucia was shoved and she stumbled. The expert beside her, using the leverage of his weight and the righteousness of his résumé, elbowed past her to the front of the pack.

She looked around for Moto, but he had disappeared. She saw Professor Richman fading back into the crowd, refusing to join the pushing and shoving.

Meanwhile, Professor Massimiliano Antonelli was still talking.

"I also call your attention to the small companion next to our honored 'guest.'"

Lucia peered through the mob and saw that there was a frame standing on a small easel next to the painting. The frame enclosed a single sheet of parchment covered with faded script.

"That companion," continued the professor, the lights gleaming off his bald scalp, "is a message, a secret message, if you will, that was concealed beneath the—"

His next words were lost as the room was rocked by a violent explosion.

For an instant, Lucia thought she was back in Palazzo Barberini in front of *Judith Beheading Holofernes* and that when she looked around, everyone would still be chatting and working their way closer to the painting. But—and Lucia actually felt a moment of relief that she was not losing her mind—the room was instantly plunged into panic.

The ringing in her ears was replaced by the screams and shrieks from the crowd. She was knocked forward, then back, then tossed sideways by people surging in all directions, no one knowing which way to flee.

It took a moment for her to realize that the explosion had not been in the room. It was outside the building. But very close.

The two guards were heading toward the door to the outside.

In the swirling panic, a clear path to the painting opened up, and without a thought, Lucia sprinted toward it. She was almost there when the crowd surged and her path was blocked. She kept fighting, but the fleeing mob pulled her even farther away.

Then the room was shaken by a second explosion outside, followed by a rattle of gunfire. Everything was frozen. No one seemed certain which way to run.

And in that instant, a short, thin figure, dressed in a loose gray tunic, burst out of the crowd and grabbed Lucia, pinning her arms to her sides and dragging her toward the painting. She fought to get free of his grip, and as she thrashed and tried to batter him with her fists, she felt something bulky and hard strapped around his waist, protecting his midsection. And in a moment of inexplicable clarity, she knew that what she felt strapped to this maniac wasn't protection. It was an explosive belt. The weapon of a suicide bomber.

She fought back wildly. He was smaller than she was, but he seemed filled with a superhuman strength, his scrawny arms carved from hickory. He pulled her inexorably closer to the painting.

The death she had waited for last night was here now.

For an instant his grip loosened and she thought she could break free, and then she was yanked back toward him by something cold and metallic around her wrist. Somehow, in that moment, he had managed to handcuff her to him.

She started to scream and felt a sharp knifepoint dig into her throat.

"I'll kill you." His voice was a growl in her ear.

Then he shouted, "Stand back!" His voice was surprisingly deep and powerful for a man so slight.

"He's got a knife!" someone shouted, and a space opened around them. Now everyone knew what they were fleeing. The maniac with the knife. They didn't know about the bomb under his tunic.

The arm with the handcuff wrapped around her waist, the knife still pressed against her throat, he dragged her toward the painting. She tried to resist his pull and felt the fierce point of the knife puncture her skin. A trickle of blood ran down her neck.

"I'll kill you," he growled again.

But if it was a bomb strapped to his waist, why should she worry that he might cut her throat first?

She lunged away from him, and in a blinding flash of pain, the edge of the knife slashed across her throat. Now the blood came in a rush, not a trickle.

The handcuff stopped her short at arm's length—there was no escape—but for a moment, he was caught off-balance. As he staggered, a figure lunged out of the crowd, swinging a black silver-tipped cane. The cane smashed savagely against the extended arm that was hand-cuffed to Lucia. The cane shattered, and perhaps the arm did too. Even in her haze of pain and the gush of blood down the front of her dress, Lucia could feel a sudden slack in his urgent pull.

But there was no cry of pain from the gray-clad figure. He lunged toward the man who now held only the shattered stub of the cane in his hand, and like the trained *comandante militare* he had declared himself to be, the little man plunged the long knife through the finely tailored pinstripe suit, between two ribs and deep into Professor A. R. Richman's side.

The professor staggered back and fell, the knife still lodged in his side.

Lucia tried to fight, but her hands were slippery with blood and she could feel darkness closing in around her. The little man was dragging her by the chain and handcuffs that linked them, she could see the effort in his body, but she felt she was floating. She wasn't really there. The only thing real was the pain and the overwhelming darkness.

Standing at the painting, the man stopped, dug something out of his pocket, and held it high overhead, wires trailing down to the bulky package strapped around his waist.

"In the name of Fra Giovanni Rodomonte Roero!" he boomed.

And in that same instant, a slim figure in a black leather jacket burst out of the crowd and dived headlong between Lucia and the man in gray, wrapping her in a fierce embrace, shielding her with his body from whatever was to come. And with a final desperate surge—one arm reaching out, hand still clutching the detonator, the other stretched to its limit, dragging Lucia and Moto behind him—the man in gray went sprawling against the stand that held the painting.

Lucia saw Jesus and Judas toppling toward her.

And then the darkness embraced her.

She never heard the explosion.

She never felt the flames.

Chapter 55

Palo
1610

"Hoist anchor!" shouted the captain.

Fenelli grasped his arm. "But what of Caravaggio?"

"There's nothing I can do!" shouted the captain above the flapping of the mainsail. "But I'll see that the chest returns to the Colonnas."

The first mate turned the boat into the wind as the captain watched the white mainsail. He gave a nod, and the *Gabbiano* turned off wind, her sails filling.

Fenelli looked back toward the castle shrouded in mist.

As the *Gabbiano* plunged into the rough seas, the captain could see the rowboat emerging from the mist. He strained his eyes and looked again. And again.

There were only three figures in the boat now, not four.

Chapter 56

ROME

Finding Professor Richman's hospital room was a struggle. There was no one to help her. She wasn't supposed to be out of her room. The heavy bandages on her neck made it impossible to turn her head. The concussion from the bomb blast had left her balance uncertain. The cast on her right arm kept her from opening doors. And the burns left her in a haze of constant pain.

But Lucia was determined to say some sort of goodbye before the limousine (courtesy of a deeply embarrassed officer of the carabinieri who had failed so terribly to protect her or the painting) took her to the airport.

No one had prepared her for what she would find when she finally got to the professor's room—because no one had imagined she would be foolish enough to fight her way through the labyrinth of the hospital on her medically unauthorized mission to say goodbye.

The professor was in no shape to exchange farewells—or even to hear them.

Almost two weeks after the self-styled *comandante militare* had plunged a knife between his ribs, Professor Richman was still unconscious. The doctors were keeping him heavily sedated while he recovered from the extensive surgery to repair his kidney, liver, and colon.

A doctor followed Lucia into the room and hovered next to her, as if trying to find a safe spot on which to touch her and lead her away.

"*Sembra morto,*" she said. *He looks dead.*

"*Lo era quasi.*" *He almost was.* And then reassurance. "*Si riprenderà.*" *He'll be OK.*

Slowly, painfully, Lucia turned her entire body so she could look the doctor in the eye. Tears were running down her cheeks. She wanted to tell him that, no, nothing was ever going to be OK again. They had lost too much. But she found she couldn't say a word.

After a long silence, the doctor looked away, shrugged uncomfortably, and left her alone with the professor.

She'd been told that sometimes people can hear what you say when they're unconscious, so she wanted to be cheerful. Hopeful, at least. But she was in no mood to call him "Ralphie." This was serious business. Too serious.

"Professor . . ." What came next? "I have to leave. I'm going home." Where was that? "Back to New York." So what? "I hate leaving you here. Leaving you like this." So much for cheerful. "But I have to go." Now she was crying openly. "I have to." Deep breath. "I'll miss you." Another. "I'll miss you both."

And now she had to tell him. In case he could hear. He needed to hear it from her.

"He's dead." No. She needed to say it straight out. "Moto's dead." She couldn't go on. Her voice failed. But she had to say the rest. So she waited in silence until she found her voice again.

"He saved my life. And yours too. He saved us. He . . ."

And now, no matter how long she waited, she couldn't go on.

Moto was dead and she would never see him again.

So she turned and made her way painfully back through the labyrinth to her room.

Chapter 57

Porto Ercole
1610

The sea was rough, though, by now, Fenelli had nothing left in his stomach. As the boat rocked, the oil lantern swayed, casting an erratic pool of light.

Fenelli stared at the black iron padlock. Without taking his eyes off it, he dug his right hand into his carpetbag.

He withdrew the hammer, feeling its weight in his hand.

The swaying light illuminated the figure of the poet, his arms wielding the heavy tool over his head. The padlock shattered into black bits.

Fenelli opened the chest, watching over his shoulder for anyone to descend the ladder from the deck.

Inside, he saw four rolled canvases. One had some inked writing on the back. He chose that one, slamming the chest closed. Then he dragged the chest, turning the side with the smashed lock away from the hatch.

He opened his carpetbag and buried Caravaggio's painting in among his belongings.

The captain's experienced hand guided the ship safely into Porto Ercole.

Mario Fenelli was already on deck, carpetbag in hand.

"I am reporting I have no passengers," said the captain. "You are going to have to enter the Roman state as a crew member of the *Gabbiano*. Get in line with the other three sailors."

He called to the crew, "We sail at noon. If you are not here, I'll leave without you."

"We're not overnighting, Captain?" called a sailor.

"You heard me. Noon sail. As soon as they unload the hold, we're off."

There was a low grumble and then: "Aye, Capitano!"

Mario shifted his feet, his eyes glancing from the dock to the captain.

"If I were you, Fenelli," said the captain, "I would forget I ever saw Michele Merisi."

The whites of the poet's eyes shone in the early-dawn light.

"And get out of the Roman state as fast as you can," added the captain. "All right, go on."

The sailors and first mate jumped nimbly onto the dock. Fenelli eyed the gap between the gunwale and the dock.

"Throw us your bag," said the first mate. "It'll make it easier."

Fenelli shook his head adamantly, clinging tightly to the bag.

He looks like a scared rabbit, thought the captain.

Fenelli took a deep breath and jumped, carpetbag flying forward first. He landed stumbling, the bag landing at a sailor's feet. The first mate helped him to his feet, but Fenelli slapped away his hands and grabbed his bag from the sailor.

"Are you all right, signore?" asked the first mate.

"*Certo!* Of course I'm all right," said the poet, straightening his posture. After a few days on the water, now the solid ground seemed to pitch and roll, and he swayed clumsily.

"*Arrivederci*, then," said the first mate, walking down the dock. "And may our paths never cross again," he added under his breath.

The captain stared at Fenelli as he weaved down the dock, trailing the sailors.

He rubbed his salty beard with his thumbnail.

That poet is a shifty son of a bitch.

The captain set sail at noon, heading directly back to Napoli. The sea was rough again. At midnight, the first mate took over watch and the captain descended into the passenger cabin, lantern in hand.

As he walked closer, he saw the broken padlock.

"*Bastardo!*" he cursed.

The captain opened the chest. Nestled within the cedarwood and linen lining were three rolled canvases.

He closed the chest without inspecting further.

Three paintings. What else had been in the chest before Fenelli broke the lock?

I will see that these canvases are returned to the Colonna family. They may be the only friends Caravaggio had.

He fell asleep in the passenger's bunk, his lantern swinging erratically, spilling light over the tarred sea chest of the dead artist.

Facing the rage of Cardinal Scipione Borghese, the messenger ran his fingers nervously over the rim of his cap.

"What do you mean Caravaggio is dead?" roared Borghese. "I arranged his pardon with the pope!"

"The news just reached us from Porto Ercole," said the man. "They say he died on the beach between Palo and Porto Ercole."

"On the beach?"

"He was detained in Palo. His papers were not in order. He was imprisoned for a day, then released."

"Released? He was released?"

"The guards at Palo say he was weak and disoriented. The boat he sailed on set off without him. He went raving mad. The word from Porto Ercole was that he chased after it."

"Chased after a boat? That's madness. As if he could catch it!"

"We're not sure if he leased a horse or ran."

"This is all lunacy! Only a fool would believe this tale. The beaches between Palo and Porto Ercole are infested with malaria. In July? A man running after a ship?"

"The speculation is that he died of fever—"

"Bah! Lies! The guards were bribed."

"The rumor is Caravaggio was buried by a fisherman on the beach in an unmarked grave."

"*Basta!* Where are the paintings?" roared the cardinal.

"They were delivered by the sea captain to the Marchesa Colonna in Napoli."

"Seize them at once! They are my personal property—recover them before the Maltese Knights get there!"

The Marchesa Colonna stared at the three paintings, now unrolled and simply framed.

One canvas was of Saint John the Baptist as a young man. The second was Caravaggio's boy, Cecco, posing as David, the head of Goliath in his hand. The severed head was a self-portrait of Caravaggio, his eyes open, mouth agape.

The third was a beautiful woman with dark hair, her head thrown back, throat bared. Mary Magdalene in ecstasy.

The marchesa stared at the woman.

I recognize her. She is the model for his last paintings in Roma.

She was the one he loved. He painted her from memory in the moment of ecstasy.

The marchesa's pale mouth twisted in a rueful smile.

There was a rap on the door.

"Avanti," said the marchesa, startled out of her reverie.

Her footman rushed in the door, his face a mask of terror.

"There is a band of Maltese Knights at the door. They insist they see you at once, my marchesa!"

The marchesa looked once more at the paintings, the images searing into her memory.

"I know what they have come for," she said.

Chapter 58

New York City

She sat in a coffee shop at the edge of East Harlem, two blocks from her apartment. The city surged past the window, vivid and unstoppable. A turquoise silk scarf hid the almost-faded scar on her neck. Her wild black hair was only slightly tamed in deference to a job interview earlier that day, a promising opportunity almost certain to lead to something better. Her life was back on track.

But for now her mind was far away from the city. She was focused on the letter in her hand.

> *My Dear Lucy,*
> *If I may start in media res, as the immortal Horace advised, I am currently continuing my recuperation in a villa looking out over the magnificent Piemontese estates belonging to the delightful Contessa dei Marsi—I am sure you remember her well. She and I have become quite good friends at this point. Quite. I expect I will be staying here awhile longer. What, after all, remains to draw me back to the hurly-burly of life in the Stati Uniti? (You can see I am practicing my* italiano *every chance I get—and I get a lot of chances.)*

*I must assume you have read the newspaper accounts
that related the full story of that villain "Roero," whose
departure from this world will apparently have to count
as the best happy ending we can manage for our story.*

The letter trembled in her hand. "Happy ending." Moto loved
happy endings. She could feel the tears gathering, but she was not going
to cry. She had already cried too much. Besides, Moto's happy ending
was that she was going to be his very special American friend. And she
was. She always would be. And now she was crying. She forced herself
to stop and looked back to the letter.

*But I expect that you have not heard anything relat-
ing to the report I recently received from a scholar who
was scheduled to make a presentation at the Palo symposium about the document that had been retrieved from
its hiding place on the back of our painting after nearly
half a millennium of concealment, only to be destroyed
in the Posta Vecchia cataclysm.*

*Sadly for him, an unpublished paper on a now-
destroyed document involving a destroyed painting of still
slightly questionable provenance (though we know better,
you and I, don't we?) has a very limited audience. In this
case, that audience consisted, in its entirety, of Aristotle
Rafael Richman, which is to say, me.*

*Still, as far as I was concerned, he did reveal some
fascinating information about the document.*

*Having studied it in detail, he had no doubt that
it was authentic—after a fashion. That is to say, it
was contemporary with the painting itself; however, he
was equally certain that it had not been actually written by our relatively unlettered friend, Michele. The*

handwriting in the document was far too educated to have been inscribed by our friend. The tone and vocabulary, however, seem likely to have been entirely Michele's. (And we all know that he was quite capable of getting others to wield a pen on his behalf.)

The document consisted almost entirely of a savage attack on an unnamed "cavaliere," accusing him of blasphemy, sodomy, devil worship, and other "unspeakable practices." (Although one wonders what practices Michele would have considered "unspeakable.")

The key passages, our frustrated scholar said, referred back to the painting itself. They declared that the face of Judas was a portrayal of pure evil and that no one could fail to recognize the sodomite he portrayed.

With the painting destroyed, of course, that portrait will never be certainly known, but I would think you and I can agree there is very little doubt that it was Cavaliere Giovanni Rodomonte Roero.

I refrained from discussing this with the presenter—it was late, I was tired, and I feel that you and I should do our little bit to cleanse the world of the final traces of the nasty feud between Roero and Caravaggio.

May Michele's troubled soul finally rest in peace.

And if you will forgive a moment of sentiment from an old man, I will close by saying, Mi manchi. *I miss you.* E mi manca anche Moto. *And I miss Moto too.*

May his heroic soul rest in peace as well.

She put the letter down.

And she sat for a long time, looking out the window at that endless stream of life surging past, vivid and unstoppable.

Chapter 59

Cecco laid the calla lilies at the head of Lena's grave.

Lena.

"He's dead now too," he whispered. "Though no one knows how or where he is buried. All we hear are lies and rumors. I don't believe any of the tales they tell."

The wind rustled in the ancient poplars standing sentinel over the Roman cemetery. Cecco lifted his eyes to the quivering leaves, the sunset coloring the tombstones in a golden light, sifting through the shadow of the trees.

Cecco stifled a sob.

He told me that a true artist has no need for friends, only inspiration.

Perhaps I am becoming an artist. For I have never been as lonely as I am tonight.

Cecco rearranged the lilies on Lena's grave and said a silent prayer. Then he rose from his knees, brushed the dirt from his trousers, and walked back into the raucous streets of Roma.

Epilogue

COMUNE DI PRIZZI, SICILY

The weathered trees still stand guard over the hillside. The cemetery in their care has a fresh grave, but it makes no difference to the trees. There have always been fresh graves. Though many fewer now than in decades past. The old keep dying, as they always have, but fewer die young, and still fewer stay to grow old and die in their turn, as the old ways fade and the hill towns empty.

Today, just one man stands, on a rise beyond the spears of the iron fence, looking down at the graves. At the new grave. He is dressed in the somber suit of a businessman, a successful businessman. He has cried. But not today.

His lips tighten. Is there a hint of pride? Now he speaks, almost silently. One would have to stand very close to hear what he says. Perhaps it is only this: *"Figghiu meu."* *My son.*

He closes his eyes for a moment, then turns and walks back down the hill to the village.

It is not his home.

But he is family.

Historical Note

In telling the story of Caravaggio's life, we have compressed the timeline of his paintings and life events to give a flow to the story. Similarly, we made the decision to house Caravaggio at 19 Vicolo dei Santi Cecilia e Biagio, even though we were aware that he lived in several other residences in Campo Marzio after leaving Palazzo Madama. Some dates are slightly modified for the flow of the narrative, e.g., the date of Pope Paul's accession.

For the reader's information, Rome during the seventeenth century was a notoriously dangerous city, particularly at night. Language in the streets and taverns was particularly lewd, as evidenced in the slanderous poem penned by Caravaggio and friends. The population was predominantly male, with a great number of prostitutes among the city's women, especially on the Via di Ripetta and in the Campo Marzio neighborhood in general.

Life for a prostitute was hard, and many died young. Anna (Annunccia) Bianchini died in 1604, long before Caravaggio left for Malta. One historical record claims that she drowned (and was possibly murdered) in the Tiber River. Some sources conjecture that Caravaggio visited the mortuary, using Anna's corpse as a study for *The Death of the Virgin*.

Fillide Melandroni, on the other hand, was a shrewd courtesan who lived to the ripe old age of thirty-seven, dying in 1618.

Lena Antognetti, as portrayed in the book, died before Caravaggio.

Cecco (Francesco Boneri) became an artist of note, in both Rome and Tuscany. At least one of his paintings, a self-portrait, hangs in the Uffizi in Florence. Also, his painting *The Resurrection* is located in the Art Institute of Chicago, while his *Christ Chasing the Money Changers from the Temple* is in Gemäldegalerie, Berlin. Cecco's style imitated Caravaggio's chiaroscuro, but his vision was his own.

Caravaggio was a genius, though his conduct in Rome—and possibly before his arrival there—qualified him as a notorious thug. According to records, he was arrested fourteen times and imprisoned six.

Artemisia Gentileschi, daughter of Orazio Gentileschi, Caravaggio's friend and coauthor of the libelous poem, became perhaps the best-known woman painter in Italian history. Her style was greatly inspired by Caravaggio's . . . and she is the protagonist of Linda's next novel.

The last record of Caravaggio was at Palo—beyond that, no one knows what became of him, though there are many speculations. Scipione Borghese recovered at least one of the paintings, *St. John the Baptist*, from the Knights of Malta after the knights confiscated them from the home of Marchesa Colonna in Naples in 1610.

Acknowledgments

In writing this novel, we relied heavily on research contained in these brilliant books: *M: The Man Who Became Caravaggio* by Peter Robb and *Caravaggio: A Life Sacred and Profane* by Andrew Graham-Dixon. We also appreciated the insights of the following books: *Caravaggio: A Life* by Helen Langdon; *Caravaggio: The Artist and His Work* by Sybille Ebert-Schifferer; *Caravaggio: The Complete Works* by Sebastian Schütze; *Caravaggio: The Art of Realism* by John Varriano; *Caravaggio: Art, Knighthood, and Malta* by Keith Sciberras and David M. Stone; and *The Monks of War: The Military Religious Orders* by Desmond Seward.

We also read many documents and websites both in Italian and in English to give us insight into seventeenth-century Rome, Naples, and Malta. Thank you to Lucia Caretto, who helped us translate the Italian documents and understand their contents.

Also our thanks to:

In Rome: Dottora Isabella Botti and Francesco Apice of Rome Walking Tours.

In Naples: Vincenzo Pauciullo of Mondo Guide and especially our guide Vincenzo Russo.

In Malta: Joan and Chris Sheridan and our incredible guide Mario Falzon. We are grateful for your insight into the Knights of Malta and especially Caravaggio. Also thanks to Marius Zerafa for sharing his tremendous knowledge of Caravaggio both in articles and through social media. Father Marius Zerafa, a Maltese priest, risked his life to rescue a Caravaggio painting from the Mafia.

Our special gratitude is reserved for our editor, Danielle Marshall, who championed our manuscript and shepherded it from first draft through production. Thank you, Danielle. So much.

David Downing led us around our own self-inflicted land mines and safely out the other side. Thank you, David, for your guidance—and deft demolition—in escaping that treacherous field. It was a pleasure working with you.

Michelle Hope Anderson rigorously researched every character and event of our novel for continuity, consistency, and historical accuracy, even though this is a work of fiction. Any errors—or fictions—are entirely our doing. (We are novelists, after all.)

Nick Allison, thank you for guiding us through the proofreading stage.

To Nicole Pomeroy and the entire production team—our gratitude for overseeing every step of the manuscript's development. (What a staggering amount of work.)

A special note of gratitude to our agents, Deborah Schneider of Gelfman Schneider/ICM Partners and Victoria Skurnick of Levine, Greenberg, Rostan Literary Agency. We'd be lost without you.

And on a very personal level, our thanks to the following people for their support (moral, physical, and emotional) in the writing of this book: Sarah Kennedy Flug, a great friend who cheered us on and provided special shelter, places to hide away and write; Lucia Caretto, a source of knowledge and inspiration on the Italian language and the

Italian spirit; Bridget Strang and the Strang Ranch; Maree McAteer; Emily Longfellow; Natasha Riviera; Sandy MacKay; and Dave Mortell, who saved Linda's life one evening, for which we will always be deeply grateful.

And first and last, special thanks to Linda's sister Nancy Elisha, who is always a first reader and enthusiastic supporter of our writing.

About the Authors

Photo © 2015 Roger Adams

Linda Lafferty is the author of *The Bloodletter's Daughter*, *House of Bathory*, *The Girl Who Fought Napoleon*, and the Colorado Book Award winners *The Drowning Guard* and *The Shepherdess of Siena*. She holds a doctorate in bilingual special education and taught in Spain for three years. She is an avid equestrian and horse lover.

Andy Stone worked for thirty-five years for the *Aspen Times* as a reporter, editor, award-winning columnist, and eventually, the publisher of the newspaper. He is the author of the novels *Song of the Kingdom* and *Aspen Drift*.

Linda Lafferty and Andy Stone had their first date on the ski slopes of Aspen, Colorado. They were married in 1986 and still live in the Roaring Fork Valley.